FOUR DADDIES & I

D. E. BARTLEY

BOOKS

By D.E. Bartley

O'Reilly Fight Club

To all who need to hear it. You are loved, you are wanted and you matter. xx

Vinci Books

vinci-books.com

Published by Vinci Books Ltd in 2025

1

The publisher and the author have made every effort to obtain permissions for any third party material used in this book and to comply with copyright law. Any queries in this respect should be brought to the attention of the publisher and any omissions will be corrected in future editions.

A CIP catalogue record for this book is available from the British Library.

Paperback ISBN: 9781036709662

Trigger Warnings

This book is darker than book one and some contents may cause upset, including kidnapping, murder and sexual/physical assault. If you are a survivor of sexual assault please know there is help out there.
You and your mental health matter.

Sexual assault
Kidnapping
Strangulation (non con)
Choking kink
The murder of a loved one

Chapter One

JASMINE

"Jazzy, there is a perfectly good desk over there," Jason sighs stepping over me as he heads to the bar.

"I know, but I prefer it here," I reply, sticking my tongue out for good measure.

"How the fuck can you sit like that?"

I look up from the floor where I'm working on my laptop and see Maximus looking over the back of the sofa he is sitting on.

"What? It's how I always sit when I work," I protest looking at my legs on either side of me in a perfect box split.

"I guess it explains how you're so flexible," Sean adds with a wink, from beside his twin. I smile before going back to my essay.

Being a ballerina certainly helps with my flexibility, and having four hot daddies who love to bend me to their will helps too.

Three months ago, my life was a mess. I'd escaped my abusive drug addict of a mother by living in a run-down shithole of an apartment and working in a dive of a pub. I couldn't even afford to eat properly because I needed any cash I made to pay rent and tuition fees for my dance school. I'm training to be a ballerina and studying for a degree in dance. I hid the extent of my issues from everyone, including my four hot and very rich stepbrothers.

Christian, Jason, Sean and Maximus O'Reilly were the best stepbrothers a girl could ask for; there was nothing they wouldn't do for me. But because people abandoned me throughout my life, the thought of losing the O'Reilly brothers was too much, so I hid everything from them. Until Jason found out, and I finally confessed to how bad things had become.

Instead of running off and leaving me to deal with my life on my own, he bundled me into his car and brought me to the house he shares with his brothers. That was the night my whole life changed for the better. The O'Reillys are no longer my stepbrothers; they've become so much more.

You see, I'm in a relationship with not one, but all four of the O'Reilly brothers. With our parents now divorced, they have lost the title of stepbrothers; they are now my daddies. I no longer need to worry about where my next meal is coming from or if I can make payments for my dance school. They pay for everything and look after me in a way no one has since I lost my grandparents.

I know how that sounds, and no, I'm not with them for their money, although they have a lot of it and make thousands of pounds an hour. I'm with them because they make me happier than I have ever been; they show me nothing but love, and I love them all just as much. But having been alone for so long, it's been hard for me to accept they aren't going anywhere. However, every single day, they go out of their way to show me they are here to stay.

"You never said how the meeting went this morning. Is

2

the fight on for a week Saturday?" I hear Sean ask. I look up to watch his interaction with his twin, Maximus.

"Yeah, all set. We finalised everything with the other fighters and their managers. Word got out, so it should be a good turnout."

I look at Maximus as he sips his whiskey.

"You have a fight coming up?"

He looks down at me and nods.

"Can I come and watch?"

"No."

I look to Christian, who's sitting opposite the twins. His eyes not leaving the tablet in his hand as he sits back relaxed.

"Why not?" I demand moving so I can see him better, making it easier for me to argue with him.

"Because it's an underground fight. You can go to the next competitive one," he replies, not looking up from the screen. "Plus, you have an essay due three days after."

Out of all my daddies, Christian is the strictest and least likely to back down. He is also the most likely to dish out punishments, too.

"But what if the essay is done early? Can I go then? I want to watch Daddy Max fight," I argue. Christian looks at me then and gives me the 'Daddy' look I've learnt there's no point arguing with.

"I said no. These fights are not like competitive ones. They're loud, full of drugs, with highly dangerous men and women present who aren't always on their best behaviour. The fights are dirty with no rules; it's no place for someone like you."

If I missed the warning to stop arguing in his tone, I certainly don't miss it in his cocked brow. When he gives me that look, I know it's his way of warning me to behave, or there will be consequences.

"I can't see it being a problem, Christian."

I turn and look at Jason, who's filling up his glass. "If it was both the twins fighting, then yeah, there's no way she could go. But Sean and I can stay with her the whole time, and there's already going to be plenty of security. It's on our turf as well, so we can get her to safety quickly if there's a problem," Jason continues as he turns around and looks at Christian whilst leaning against the table behind him.

"Jason's right. If we stay with her, no one will try anything. They know we are always armed at these things. You can concentrate on Maximus and the business side, and we'll watch Jasmine," Sean adds. I watch Christian looking at his two brothers before turning his attention to Maximus.

"You've met the other guys; what do you think?"

Maximus shrugs as he looks at me. "I get where you're coming from. My first instinct is to keep her as far away as possible. But if Shorty's going to be in our lives, she needs to see what we do. She never needs to go again if she doesn't like what happens. At least this way, she's protected by Jason and Sean. You could also ask Terry to have Layton guard her. I don't think anyone is stupid enough to try something on our turf anyway," Maximus says as he looks between me and his big brother.

"Plus, it will help get the word out that she is ours and what will happen if anyone hurts her." I chance a look at Jason, who gives me a little wink, obviously realising that he's winning this argument. I look back at Christian and chew on my bottom lip nervously. Christian lets out a sigh.

"Fine, you can go."

I jump up and rush to him, squealing excitedly. "However!" he announces as I jump onto his lap. "There are rules."

I put my arms around his neck.

"I will stick to them!" I promise quickly. Christian rolls his eyes before looking at his brothers.

"You two don't let her out of your sight. If she needs to pee, you go with her. If she wants to leave, you go with her."

"You aren't the only one who gives a shit, Christian," Jason warns as he walks away from the bar to sit on the third sofa.

"No, but I know she can wrap you around her little finger when she wants to," Christian says as he looks at me. I give him my best puppy dog eyes.

"I'll be good, I promise," I declare, making a cross over my heart.

"Jason, you'll need to sort her outfit, and I'll speak to Terry about having extra eyes on her."

"Christian, she'll be fine; stop worrying," Sean says from his spot on the other sofa. I watch as Christian's blue eyes frown at his younger brother. "I dare anyone to try anything; I will kill them myself," Sean adds. Christian nods, and I hug him tightly.

"You are going to see a side of us that might scare you, but I promise we will *never* be like that with you," Christian says firmly as he looks into my eyes and tucks a section of hair behind my ear. "Why do I feel like I'm going to regret letting you come?"

"It'll be fine, I promise, Daddy."

"It better be because I will kill anyone who hurts you."

5

Chapter Two

JASMINE

I open the messaging app on my phone and stare at it for a moment before closing it. I stare at the locked screen and unlock it again before growling and shoving the phone into my pocket.

Get a grip, for fuck's sake, Jasmine.

It's been three months since I last had any contact with my mother, and I know I should reach out.

The last time I saw her, she was dirty, skinny and addicted to all kinds of drugs as well as alcohol. She stood in front of Christian, Jason and me, shouting all kinds of vile shit. Although I like to think it was mainly the substances talking, I know it wasn't.

My mother and I haven't been close since my father left us when I was eight. Mum always blamed me for him leaving, even though it was mainly due to her substance abuse and shopping addiction. I missed him for the first few years and would often dream about him coming back for me and saving me from the abuse Mum would dish out when high or drunk. But he never came. By the time I was a teenager, I had given up on those dreams and threw myself into my dancing as a way of escaping the shitshow that was my life.

That all changed three years ago when Mum got sober and met Tommy O'Reilly. She fell head over heels in love with him, and they married shortly after. Even though her marriage didn't last, and they divorced less than three years later, their marriage led me to my four guys, and I will always be eternally grateful for that.

The problem is that although I'm the happiest I've ever been, I know Mum is struggling with her addiction again, and I want to help her. Yes, she said some horrible things to me the last time we spoke, but she is still my mum and the only blood family I have left. I want to reach out and message her to check that she's okay and at least alive, but I can't seem to do it.

I look down at the phone in my hand and come up with an idea. I might not have the guts to message her, but I can at least check that she has everything she needs and see for myself that she is still breathing. I throw my phone into my bag and head out with a plan of action.

"I don't care what you say; I'm coming into that house with you, Jasmine. The O'Reillys would kill me if anything happened in there."

I turn to face my personal bodyguard, Layton and smile.

"They wouldn't *actually* kill you."

Layton looks at me with arched brows, and I hiss through my teeth.

"Okay, yeah, they might," I admit before smiling.

The O'Reillys are successful businessmen who own hundreds of fight clubs, gyms, and other sporting venues, but they are also very powerful and dangerous men. Their father, Tommy, dragged them into the darker world from a young age, and they built up quite an empire. I don't know much about what they do, but I know they have all killed people to get to where they are. But I also know I am safer with them than I have ever been with anyone else.

"Fine, you can come in, but keep your mouth shut. My mother doesn't do well with new people."

We climb out of his car and head around to the trunk. Layton collects the bags of food I brought for Mum, knowing there won't be much in the house. When I go to grab a bag, Layton gives me a look, which promises an argument if I even attempt to take one.

"You are worse than my daddies at times," I sigh as I reach up and close the trunk for him.

"That's because I have seen what your daddies are capable of. I don't plan on being the receiving end of one of their moods," Layton says as he walks next to me.

"Are they that scary?" I ask. Layton nods and turns to look at me.

"I've seen them at their scariest, and I have seen the way they are with you. They really would burn the world to ashes to protect you."

"Do you ever regret working for them?"

They employed Layton after seeing the way he looked after me one night about nine months ago when I was so drunk I couldn't stand. He had been a bouncer in the club I'd been in. Maximus and Sean found me and took me home after giving Layton their business card; the rest is history. He now works for them full-time, watching my back. It's a role he takes seriously, but sometimes, it's easy to forget he is paid to be with me. We have developed a good friendship during all the time we spend together.

"No, not only is the money good, but I enjoy my job, even when you are being difficult," he adds with a smirk. I slap his arm as we reach the front door. Coming to a stop, I feel my chest tighten. Now I'm here, but I'm not sure this is a good idea.

"You don't have to do this, you know. You could just leave the food on the doorstep and go."

I shake my head and take a deep breath before opening the door.

"Be careful. It was a mess last time I was here," I warn him before stepping through the door.

Inside the house is quiet. I can't hear or see anything. I head straight to the lounge and look around.

The place seems a little tidier than it did the last time I was here. It's still far from how it was when I lived here alone, but there are no obvious signs of drugs and empty cans and bottles. It smells a damn sight better too.

"Mum? Are you here?" I call out, only to be greeted by silence. "I guess not," I sigh as I continue to walk through the house and into the kitchen. I find the kitchen much better than it was three months ago. The bin is no longer overflowing, and the sides are cleaner than they were.

"Let's just leave this stuff on the table, and she can put it where she wants it," I sigh as Layton places the bags down. We quickly arrange the bags, and I put the milk and cheese in the fridge before leaving a note.

Mum,
I popped by to see you and see if you needed anything. I
hope you are okay.
Happy birthday.
Jasmine x

I place the note on top of the cake box, which contains a rich chocolate cake, her favourite, and look at Layton.

"Let's get out of here."

He offers me a sad smile, and we head out of the door and back to the car.

I take one last look at the house before we drive off. I hope she is happy and safe, whatever she's doing.

Chapter Three

JASMINE

I wave goodbye to Layton before walking through the back door, where I find Mrs Brown, the housekeeper, in the kitchen cutting up some veg.

"Afternoon, Mrs Brown. Can I help at all?" I love it when I get to help in the kitchen. We've started baking together now and again when all the O'Reillys are busy, and I'm left home alone for a few hours. I like those times when we put the radio on and just have a fun time making cookies and cakes. Mrs Brown makes the best pastries and has promised to teach me one day.

"No, thank you, Jasmine, love. The two older O'Reillys are waiting for you in the sitting room."

"Why?" I ask, stopping in my tracks nervously. Mrs Brown looks up at me and smiles.

"Don't look so nervous; I'm sure you have nothing to worry about."

"That's easy for you to say; it's not your ass on the line," I point out, walking through the kitchen and heading to the sitting room. I can hear Mrs Brown chuckling as I leave. I have to stop myself from rushing to my room and refusing to see the guys until they tell me what they want.

I know Layton would have told Christian that I went to Mum's, and I'm sure he will have something to say on the matter. He was there the last time I saw her and witnessed first-hand how badly she treated me. But I had to go today, even if I just left a note.

I come to a stop outside of the sitting room door and take a deep breath to calm my nerves before walking inside.

Opening the door, I'm greeted by the sight of the two older O'Reilly brothers. Both are standing over the desk in their suit trousers and black shirts. Their broad and muscular shoulders are emphasised by the way their shirts tighten around them. Both have had their hair cut today as the sides are almost shaved bare, and the dark brown hair on the top of their heads has been tidied. Considering these two aren't the twins in the family, they both look almost identical from behind. The only difference is the way Christian's tattoos flow up his neck and the back of his head.

"You going to stand there staring all day, Jazzy? Or do we get a hello kiss?" Jason calls, not taking his eyes off the screen on the desk that they are both looking at.

"How did you know I was here?" I ask as I approach them. Jason turns around smiling, which lightens his grey eyes. Wrapping his arm around my waist, he pulls me against him and my heart races as I place my hands against his chest. I will never get enough of this man or being held by him.

"Angel, I always know when you're around; I can feel it deep inside me," he says with a smirk before his lips find mine. The O'Reillys may be dangerous men and do unspeakable things to others. But for me, nowhere is as safe as in their arms.

12

"You know, for a big scary man who always carries at least one weapon wherever he goes, you say the sweetest things," I smile before turning to Christian, who is now facing me.

"That's because you bring out the soft side in us, baby girl," Christian adds as he cups my cheek and kisses me sweetly, putting a warm feeling in my stomach, which spreads through my whole body. As he pulls away from me, I look into his eyes and smile.

I'm rarely seen without a smile on my face when I'm home. I've never had much to smile about until I had these men in my life. But they all changed that, and I can honestly say I have never been happier. No matter how bad my day has gone, I know that everything will be okay once I get back home.

"Want to tell us about this afternoon?" Christian asks, quickly chasing the warm feeling away.

"Layton told you then," I sigh as I step out of Jason's arms and head to the makeshift bar they have in here.

I used to try and have an alcoholic drink whenever we were in here, but I soon learnt my daddies won't let me unless they've seen me eat a full meal and all my schoolwork is done. Yes, they treat me like a small child at times, but in their defence, for a while, I wasn't looking after myself or keeping on top of my schoolwork.

Other than my grandparents, who died seven years after my dad left, I never had someone to teach me how to take care of myself, as my mother was too caught up in herself to care about what I was doing.

I pick up a bottle of water from the small fridge and open it up.

"Jazzy, stop stalling."

I look at Jason and roll my eyes, quickly regretting it

when I see him flash his 'Daddy' look, and I know I'm treading on thin ice.

"It's Mum's birthday. It felt wrong to ignore it," I answer as I face the two of them.

"How did it go?" Christian asks, crossing his arms over his chest. The guys don't hide their dislike of my mother. They have each told me they cannot forgive her for the years of abuse she has inflicted on me. My mother may not have always physically abused me, but emotionally, there was a lot of damage done. The guys are all helping me to recover and grow and proving to myself I'm not the person she made me out to be.

I sigh as I put the lid on my bottle and walk over to one of the three leather sofas we have in here. I slump down and lean my head against the back.

"She wasn't there, so I left a few bits and a note." I close my eyes, yet I can still feel them approaching. Jason sits next to me as Christian perches on the coffee table in front. I realise I understand what Jason meant before. I can tell if one of the guys is close by. I don't need to see them. I can tell them all apart even with my eyes closed.

Christian takes my hand, and I look at him.

"You are too pure and kind for this world," he sighs softly. I can't help smirking.

"I think my mother would argue that."

"Your mother is an idiot whose judgement is clouded by the substances she pumps into her body," Jason sighs next to me as he places an arm around my shoulders. I lean against him, keeping hold of Christian's hand.

"I think she's having a few good days. The house looked and smelt a lot cleaner than when we were last there," I point out.

"That's because we send in a cleaner twice a week. We told her it was that or she moved out."

I look at Christian, shocked. "Why did you do that?"

"Because it's our house, sweetheart, and I don't want the health board coming down on us for letting her live in squalor. Also, we are hoping it will help her to clean up her act."

"Why haven't you just kicked her out?" I ask, but Christian shakes his head.

"We don't care for Carol, especially after the way she has treated you, but we would never make her homeless. That would punish you as much as her."

I look at him for a moment before leaning away from Jason and wrapping my arms around Christian's neck.

"Thank you," I whisper as I blink back the tears. He's right; I would never relax knowing that my mum didn't have a roof over her head. At least if she is in the house, I know she is reasonably safe.

"You don't need to thank me, but you can tell us when you want to go and see her. I would prefer if one of us were with you rather than Layton."

I pull away from him and nod. I had expected that, but as much as I want to argue that the O'Reillys' presence makes Mum worse, I don't want to get into that argument either.

"Now that conversation is over with, we need to tell you something," I hear Jason say beside me. I turn to look at him, frowning.

"Why don't I like the sound of that?" I ask, my heart starting to race with panic.

"The four of us are all away tonight. The twins, as you know, have already left to head up to Scotland. I'm leaving for Wales in a minute, and Christian will be the closest in London."

"Why are you all away at the same time?" I ask, looking between the two of them.

"It's just the way it's come about. The twins' trip has been planned for a while. I need to go and check out a new venue for a club. Christian has a meeting with some of our contacts to discuss some issues that have arisen overnight."

"Can't I come with one of you?" I ask, slightly annoyed. I knew the twins were going to be away; it's a friend's bachelor party. But I thought I had the weekend just the three of us and was looking forward to it.

"No, Jazzy, we need to have our wits about us. Neither of us knows how our trips are going to go. I would rather know you are safe here," Jason adds as his hand runs up and down my back.

I nod as I look down at my hands in my lap.

"It's the first time you've all been away overnight at the same time," I point out quietly.

There have been many times one or two of the guys have been away, but there has always been someone here with me. I know they spend a lot more time at home since I moved in, as before they would often stay away to deal with various premises or meetings and so on.

"I know, sweetheart, but you will be fine here on your own. Layton and Calvin are staying on-site and will take you anywhere you need to go. If you have any problems, you can shout for them, and they will come running," Christian adds. I nod as I look at him.

"Okay," I reply, trying to hide how gutted I am.

Christian stands, pulling me to my feet. He wraps his arms around me and kisses the top of my head.

"Good girl, it's only for two nights at the most. I'm sure you can keep yourself occupied in that time."

I nod into his chest and look into his blue eyes.

"We need to get going. Come here, Jazzy."

I let go of Christian and walk straight into Jason's arms.

"Behave yourself, and I'll think about bringing you home a surprise," he whispers into my hair. I lift onto my tiptoes and press a kiss to his lips.

"I'm always good," I point out, smiling innocently. Jason grins down at me as he kisses me again.

"That's debatable."

I roll my eyes as I give Christian a quick kiss before they both pick up the bags I hadn't spotted before and head out of the sitting room. I follow them until we get to the garage door at the back of the kitchen.

"Be careful, both of you," I call as they climb into their cars. I notice Terry in Christian's and another security guy in Jason's. I feel a little calmer knowing they're not going on their own.

"We will, baby. Behave!" Christian calls out as he drives out of the garage.

"See you later, angel," Jason shouts as he follows closely behind. I sigh as I close the door and look into the kitchen where even Mrs Brown isn't to be seen.

This weekend is going to suck.

I feel my phone vibrate in my pocket and pull it out. I quickly read a message from one of my friends and smile. Or maybe it won't.

Chapter Four

JASMINE

I climb out of the car and salute playfully at Layton, who points to the house angrily.

"Get in there, now!"

"Oh, lighten up!" I laugh, heading to the back door. My good mood quickly shifts when my mobile rings in my hand. I look down at the caller's display and curse.

Uh oh.

"Hey, Daddy," I answer in my sweetest voice, in the hope of keeping the peace.

"Don't 'hey Daddy' me! You're drunk!"

I guess it won't.

"No, I'm not!" I argue before Maximus growls down the phone.

"Don't fucking lie to me, I can see you."

"How?" I demand, looking around. Shit, have they come home early?

"Look up, Shorty."

I slowly look up and see the camera looking straight at me.

Ah, shit.

"If you can see the camera, that means…"

"Yep, your other daddies can as well. You're lucky I'm not close enough to drive home and tan your ass! What were you thinking?" Maximus growls angrily. I roll my eyes and enter the house.

I walk through the kitchen and head for my bedroom, almost tripping over my own feet as I attempt to take my shoes off as I go.

Everything is dark, and the house feels so big and empty when you are on your own here. This was why I jumped at the chance to go out tonight when my friends messaged me yesterday evening. At first, I had turned them down, but when Christian and Jason both told me they would be away for a second night, I decided to go.

"I'm twenty years old. Why can't I go out and get drunk?" I demand. "Daddy Jason said it was fine," I point out. I tried to call Christian first, but he didn't answer, so I called Jason. He laid down some rules but was happy for me to go out for a few hours.

"Well, he shouldn't have! You obviously can't be trusted to know your own limits!" I hear Maximus mutter something, followed by the phone changing hands.

"Princess," I hear the warning in Sean's voice and let out a deep sigh.

"Daddy," I reply sarcastically.

"Get a glass of water and go to bed. We will talk about this tomorrow."

I frown at the phone in my hand. I thought Sean would go harder on me than Maximus, who usually likes my rebellious side.

"Aren't you going to give me hell, too?" I ask nervously.

"What's the point? You are too drunk to listen and

remember what I say. I will save it for when I'm in front of you tomorrow."

"Are you going to punish me?" I ask, racked with equal measures of nerves and excitement.

"I haven't decided. Go to sleep; we will talk tomorrow," he adds before hanging up. I only manage two steps before it rings again. I look up at the camera as I answer.

"Yes, Daddy, I've had a drink, and yes, I'm a little drunk."

"Watch your tone, baby girl," Christian warns. I sigh as I head to my room.

"Daddy, I'm fine. I didn't go to the club with everyone else. I stopped drinking when I realised it was hitting me a little quicker than usual, and Layton was outside each bar I went to. I did nothing wrong," I protest.

"Then why is Layton annoyed with you?" Christian asks.

"Because he thinks you will have a go at him for me being drunk," I moan, throwing my bag onto the chair by the window and walking into my walk-in wardrobe. I hear Christian hum deep in his throat.

"See, I wasn't reckless, and I stuck to the rules Daddy Jason set out as I promised him. I'm twenty years old, and I deserve the odd night of acting like a normal person," I sulk.

"We will discuss it tomorrow," Christian says, a little calmer. I place my phone on hands-free and start to undress to get into my pyjamas.

"Daddy Sean said that too; I don't think it's fair if you all shout and discipline me," I point out. Christian hums again, and I watch the phone, waiting to see what he'll say.

"Fine, I will speak to the others, and we will decide on your punishment together."

I huff and roll my eyes as I throw my clothes into the laundry basket in a temper, causing it to topple over. "Lose the attitude and pick up the basket. You are skating on thin ice as it is."

I scream and hold a blanket I grab from a shelf over my bare chest before looking up at the camera.

"That's meant to be off if I'm undressing!" I yell.

"Security has turned it off from their screens, but your daddies can still access it," Christian points out. I throw my blanket back onto the shelf and reach for my night clothes.

"I'm going to bed. What time will you be home tomorrow?" I ask, pulling on my top.

"Lunch time, we will talk then."

"Fine," I reply through gritted teeth.

"Get some sleep."

"Night, Daddy," I reply as I end the call. I finish getting my night clothes on. I'm just walking back into my room when the phone rings again.

"If you are phoning to shout at me too, I'm tired and don't want to hear it," I snap as I climb into bed.

"So you are drunk then?" Jason chuckles.

"I'm not even that drunk, and if I was before, I'm not now everyone keeps shouting at me," I sulk. I pull the covers over me and sigh. "I know I can be irresponsible at times, but I'm twenty years old and should have the chance to act it occasionally. I'm sure you and the twins all got drunk once or twice at my age," I point out as I look at the camera, and I know the others are all looking at it, too.

"I agree with you, Jazzy. I'm only now looking at the cameras. I set out rules and trust that you followed them."

"I did. I even came home early," I pout, wishing the others had been as calm as Jason.

"I know. I wasn't calling to have a go at you. I wanted to know if you had a good night?"

"I did, thank you," I sigh, looking up at the ceiling. "I hate you all being away at the same time," I moan, placing my hand on my stomach.

"Why's that?"

"Because I'm horny, and no one's here to help me out," I whine as I let my hand drift a little further down.

"Where is that hand heading, angel? I hope you aren't attempting to touch yourself. You know the rules."

"But none of you are here to help me, so the rules shouldn't count. I'm really horny."

"Go to sleep, Jazzy. I will be home in the morning before everyone else, and I promise to take care of all your needs," Jason growls down the phone, but I need something right now. "Show me your hands, Jazzy."

I sigh, pulling my hand out from under the covers and waving it at the camera.

"I'll be watching, angel." I hear the call end and sigh as I place my phone on the bedside cabinet to charge.

It's not fair; they all have a go at me for being a normal girl my age, and then they are all away the same night, and I can't even touch myself to relieve the pent-up sexual frustration in my stomach and aching core.

I look back to where I know the camera is and turn my back to it. With the lights off, they shouldn't be able to see what I'm doing anyway. I pull the bed covers up to my neck and try to appear like I'm curling up to go to sleep. If I leave it for a few minutes, they should all have turned their attention to something else and no longer be watching the camera. Would security be checking them? Who cares if they are? They should know better than to watch me.

I count off five minutes in my head and then let my

hand wander down until my fingers come in contact with my aching clit. I close my eyes and imagine the guys watching me as I rub myself, starting slowly at first and then getting faster as the pleasure builds. I move so I can slide my fingers into myself and find that spot the guys rub against each and every time. The problem is I've never been one to masturbate. Before the guys, it was very rare I even thought about sex. On the rare occasions I would, it would be the O'Reilly brothers I pictured touching me, licking me, and doing unthinkable things to me. That's why it was so easy for me to give them my virginity; I never wanted anyone else to take it but them.

I think back to the first time the five of us came together in this bed. How their hands and lips were everywhere, how Christian felt as he slid into me for the first time. I'm a ballet dancer; my hymen probably broke years ago just from all the stretching I do, but there was still that distinct feeling of pain as he entered me. That may be because I was so tight or maybe because of the sheer size of him, but soon, he felt so good sliding in and out of me.

The more I think about that first time, the more pleasure I manage to give myself. My fingers are moving faster in and out of me as a moan slips past my lips. If I hold my hand just right, my palm presses against my clit, quickly causing me to moan again a little louder as I cum all over my own hand.

I keep it moving, trying to release as much frustration as possible, but as good as it is, it's nothing compared to how any of the guys make me feel.

I sigh as I climb out of bed and head to the bathroom to clean myself. The guys tend to do this part for me. After sex, they always clean me with a damp flannel or shower with me, making me feel even more cared for than anyone ever has.

As soon as I finish cleaning myself up, I head to the bedroom and fall into bed, feeling relaxed enough to sleep. But just before I do, I see my phone flashing, signalling a message. I quickly open it and curse to myself.

Daddy Jason: Don't say I didn't warn you.

Chapter Five

JASON

I sit in the chair by the side of Jasmine's bed and watch her sleep. A whiskey in one hand and my loose tie in the other. It's three in the morning, and she has no idea I'm here.

It was late by the time I finished my business there, and I decided to stay over for one last night and head back after a few hours of sleep. That all changed once I hung up the phone. I planned on coming home and helping Jasmine to relieve some of that pent-up frustration before the others came home. I was already in the car when I watched my Jazzy pleasuring herself even though I told her not to. We have set rules for her to follow, one of the main ones being that she can't touch herself without our say-so, but our little brat ignored that rule tonight, and now I have to decide how I want to teach her a lesson.

Jasmine moans in her sleep as she rolls onto her back and puts her hands above her head.

Bingo.

I stand and place my glass gently on the bedside cabinet before walking around to her side of the bed. Whilst her hands are still raised, I make short work of tying them to the headboard. It isn't until I test the strength of the binding that she wakes up.

"Daddy?"

I look down at her and watch as her face goes from a look of shock to confusion as she realises she can't move her arms.

"What are you doing?" she asks, fighting against the restraints. I place my fingertips against her hands and slowly run them down her arm, making her shudder at my touch. As I reach the bedcovers, I slowly fold them down until they are bunched at the bottom of the bed, revealing her in nothing but some hot pants and a vest top she likes to wear as pyjamas. Shame these need to get ruined; they look cute on her.

"What was the last thing I said to you, Jazzy?" I ask, letting my fingers run up her leg slowly. I look at her face to find her with her eyes closed, savouring my touch. I come to a stop at her hip and pull back up the top of her shorts before letting them snap back into place. She hisses with shock, and I look at her again.

"Answer me."

"To not touch myself. That you would be watching." I nod as I walk away from her to the other side of the bed and slowly refill my glass from the decanter I brought up with me. I take a sip before picking up my phone and opening my group chat with my brothers. I snap a picture of Jasmine tied to the bed and send it with a short message.

Jason: She broke the no touching rule; I've come home early to discipline her. Feel free to watch if you are still awake.

I lock my phone and turn it over so as not to get

distracted by any replies. I pick up my glass before walking back over to her side of the bed.

"Why did you touch yourself, knowing it was against the rules?" I watch as Jasmine chews on her bottom lip nervously. I take a sip from my glass and place it on the bedside cabinet before using my thumb to pull her lip from between her teeth. "I asked you a question."

"Because I was horny and wanted a release," she answers quietly. I nod to myself as I look down her body again and see her shorts. I reach for the elastic waist and slowly pull them downwards, revealing her black lace thong.

Fuck I love this set on her.

I continue to pull her shorts down until I discard them in a pile on the floor. I undo the buttons of my shirt, taking my time with each fastening, knowing it will be driving her wild. Even from here, I can see how aroused she is; her eyes are burning into my skin as she anticipates my next move, but I know she will never see it coming.

"Did I not tell you I would be back early to help with your frustration?" I ask as I let my shirt fall to the floor and start undoing my belt and trousers.

"Yes." The word is barely a whisper on her breath as she stares at me. I cock a brow at her.

"Yes?"

"Yes, Daddy," Jasmine corrects quickly. I nod before retrieving something from my pocket and stepping out of my discarded trousers and boxers. Leaving me completely naked.

I slowly climb onto the foot of the bed and crawl up until I'm straddling her hips. I can feel the heat coming from her no doubt aching pussy. I kneel over her hips and take her top in my hand. I open my other hand and reveal my knife. Jasmine spots it and gasps, which brings a smile to my lips. I flip it open in one move and start to cut away her top. The whole time, Jasmine has been as stiff as a board underneath me.

"Do you not trust me not to cut you?" I look at Jasmine, who looks me in the eye as she answers.

"You would never hurt me."

"So, you trust me with a knife this close to your body," I whisper as I allow the blade to rest against her stomach as I discard the now ruined top, leaving nothing but the black matching lace bra in place. "But you don't trust me to keep my word when I say I will come home early to relieve your pent-up frustration?"

"I do trust you," Jasmine protests loudly. I look at her with raised brows.

"But you relieved yourself, so you mustn't have believed me," I point out. I run my finger over the edge of the black lace, which rests against her small but firm breasts. Jasmine's eyes roll back as she savours my touch.

"I've always liked this set," I whisper before taking my knife and cutting the small section of fabric between the two cups, freeing her breasts as Jasmine gasps.

"Daddy, what are you doing?" she protests as I take myself in my hand and stroke my hard cock whilst moving up the bed.

"Do you want to know your punishment for disobeying me, angel?" I come to a stop over her breasts so my cock is close to her mouth. Jasmine looks at it and licks her lips before nodding. I slap her cheek with my cock, surprising a small yelp out of her. "Use your words, Jazzy," I remind her.

"Yes, I want to know my punishment, Daddy," she blurts out quickly. I nod, letting go of my cock and running a finger over her soft lips.

"I'm going to fuck that mouth of yours, then your tits.

I'm then going to move down to that sweet wet pussy and fuck you with my tongue, fingers and cock, before fucking your ass with all three. But I'm not going to let you cum. This will be for my pleasure and my pleasure only."

"But that's not fair!"

I look at her wide-eyed. "But you have achieved your own pleasure, angel. You don't need me to do that." I have to stop myself from smirking as Jasmine protests under me.

"But, I want you, Daddy! I need you!"

"Well, how about this: you be a good girl and relent from coming, and when I'm finished, I will reward you with the most intense orgasm you have ever had. How does that sound?"

"Okay, Daddy."

I can hear the disappointment in her voice, and again, I need to stop myself from smirking at her. Instead, I lean down and press my lips to hers.

"That's my good little angel. Continue doing as you are told, and I will make sure you get your reward. Don't forget to use your words if it becomes too much. When you can't, lift your hips three times." I sit back up and start stroking myself in her face again as she agrees.

"Open wide, angel."

Jasmine immediately does as I ask, and I start rubbing my cock over her lips before letting it go a little further into her mouth.

I start slow but then pick up the pace as I allow myself to go deeper into her mouth and throat. Fuck I love the way her mouth feels around my cock. Considering Jasmine had never sucked a cock before she became ours, she is so fucking good at it.

I continue to use her mouth for a few minutes; I love the way the tears stream down her face as she gags on my hard length. Jasmine knows that even when we are disciplining her, she can stop it at any time. After five minutes of fucking her face, I have to pull out of her warm mouth before I shoot my cum down her throat. There is no way I want to finish yet; I want to fulfil my promise of fucking every hole she has before I find my release.

I slid down the bed a little, just until I'm in a position to hold her tits together as I fuck them. But first, I wipe the tears from her face and press a kiss to her lips.

"You are so good at that, angel. I fucking love how your mouth feels around my cock." I start kneading her breast and watch as she moans before biting her bottom lip.

"Remember, Jazzy, don't cum," I warn.

"I won't, Daddy," she replies, looking at me as I slide between her breasts and start rocking my hips back and forth, using her body as a way of finding my release. Everything about her is perfect, from her looks to the way her small flower-shaped birthmark on her right shoulder seems to dance whenever she moves. I will never get tired of watching this amazing woman, especially when she is lying beneath me.

As much as I'm loving the feel of her tits around my cock, I need to taste her and feel her around my fingers. I have to keep reminding myself that I'm teaching her a lesson, that no one can touch her other than me and my brothers, that includes herself.

I move further down the bed before leaning down and pressing my lips to hers. She wipes her tongue over my lips, begging for access, but I pull away, smiling. I kiss her jaw before making my way down between her breasts, over her stomach, until I reach the apex of her thighs.

Before I even touch her, I can tell how wet she is. I can smell her arousal, and it's making my job of holding out even harder. I slowly allow my tongue to slip between her thick lips and run it from her hole to her clit and back again. Instantly, Jasmine starts to lift her hips from the bed as she moans out with pleasure. I place an arm over her lower stomach to keep her in place before doing it again. Fuck she tastes so good, and I know she is building towards an orgasm.

"Do not cum, angel."

"It feels too good," she moans as I lick her again before sliding one finger into her. I can feel her starting to tighten around my digit and look up at her as she looks back at me. A pleading in her eyes for me to carry on and let her cum, but I just smile back. I lift a little and just slide my finger in and out of her, knowing that if I keep changing up what I'm doing, she won't be able to find that release she is so desperate for.

"Does this feel as good as your hand?" I ask, removing my finger, earning me a frustrated cry from her. I smile as I scoop some of her juices onto my finger and start rubbing them about her back passage. She groans as the pleasure starts to build up again, and I change to rubbing her clit slowly. Every time she gets close to reaching an orgasm, I change where I'm touching her, and she cries out in frustration.

"Answer me, angel. Does your hand feel better than mine right now? I ask as I push a digit into her ass. She pushes against me, desperate to feel it deeper inside her; as her breathing picks up again, I withdraw my touch completely.

"NO! Nothing feels as good as you four!" she cries out as I run my finger up the inside of her thigh.

"Nothing?" I ask, "Not even your fingers as they were pushing into yourself?" I tease as I slide my tongue up the inside of her thigh and across to her back passage, rimming her just how she likes it.

"Nothing! I had to imagine you all to get off! But it wasn't enough. Nothing is ever enough without you!" she cries out as I remove my tongue and blow against her core. "I'm sorry, Daddy! I will never touch myself again without permission. I'm sorry!" she cries out. I slide my aching cock into her soaking wet pussy as I bury myself balls deep inside her. I pull at the tie and loosen her arms, which she wraps around me. She holds me so tight I'm scared I've pushed her too far.

"Cum, angel, cum for me," I whisper as I kiss her jaw and reach between us to rub her clit. In seconds, I feel her clamping around my cock as she screams with pleasure. I keep working her clit, knowing she will need more than one orgasm. I milk her of one, two, and then three before her whole body shakes underneath me. The whole time, I smother her jaw, cheeks, and lips with light pecks, whispering to her the whole time.

"You are such a good girl."

"Good girl, angel, give Daddy one more."

"That's it, little angel, good girl."

As Jasmine screams with her fourth orgasm, I climax alongside her and fill her with hot ropes of my release. I cum so hard I swear my vision blurs. I collapse next to her and pull her into my arms, holding her tightly as she shakes and cries into my shoulder.

"I'm sorry," she gasps as I run a hand over her head and hold her against me.

"I know, angel, I know you are," I whisper as I rub my hands all over her body, hoping to warm her up. Even though we're both covered in sweat, we are both starting to feel cold, and I need to take care of her before she catches a chill.

"Stay there, angel. I'll be right back." I roll out of bed and rush into the bathroom, grabbing a warm facecloth and a towel. I quickly wash my hands and then go back to Jasmine.

"Roll onto your back, Jazzy."

She does as I ask, even though she's already half asleep. I use the facecloth to wash in between her legs and quickly dry her off. I then pick up my discarded shirt and get her to sit up. I remove what is left of her top and bra before helping her to put my shirt on and fasten the buttons. Jasmine told me once she loves wearing our shirts, especially when they smell of us.

As soon as she's clothed, I grab the covers off the floor where I must have kicked them off and put them back on the bed. I cover her before walking to the other side of the bed and climbing in next to her. Jasmine instantly rolls into my arms and places her head against my chest as I hold her.

"Are you okay, angel?" I ask, running my hand over her head. She nods into my chest as I feel her body relaxing into me. She is physically and mentally exhausted, and I know I'll let her have a lie-in in the morning.

"I love you, angel," I whisper as her breathing starts to even out. "I always have and always will," I add as I close my eyes and hold her tightly to me. Only just hearing her as she replies,

"I love you too, Daddy."

Chapter Six

JASMINE

When I wake up at midday, I find myself alone. I listen out for Jason, but the room is silent. I get out of bed and pull on my shorts that are discarded on the floor, making a mental note to replace the underwear set Jason had cut off me last night.

After taking care of some personal business, I make my way onto the landing to see if Jason is in his room, but when I open his door, it's empty. I decide to head into the kitchen to make myself a coffee before trying to find him. I will need something to wake me up a bit before the others get home. Hopefully, Jason will help them realise I wasn't in the wrong last night. But there again, the brothers never disagree, and I don't want to be the reason that they start.

Just as I reach the kitchen door, I hear raised voices coming from inside, and I freeze when I hear Jason.

"I don't give a fuck, you are not giving her shit for being a typical twenty-year-old. She didn't do anything wrong."

"She was so drunk she staggered when she got out of

34

the car. She should know better than to get into that kind of state," Maximus growls.

"So what?" Jason exclaims. "I've had to carry your ass to bed more times than I can fucking count! She walked into the house unaided; she was home before midnight, she was able to hold a conversation with all four of us, and she made sure her security was close by the whole night. She did nothing wrong!"

"Yet you felt the need to come back in the middle of the night and discipline her," Sean adds.

I feel my stomach erupt with a million butterflies as I remember how Jason tied me up when I was asleep and stimulated every part of my body before allowing me to orgasm. It was horrible and amazing all at the same time. Fuck I'm getting wet just thinking about it.

"That was for a different reason. She hinted she was going to touch herself; I told her to wait until I got home. I was already on my way home to wake her up and surprise her, but she did it anyway."

"So, the fact that we all go away for a night, and she takes the opportunity to get smashed doesn't mean anything?" Maximus asks.

"She was far from smashed, and you know it! She didn't go out of her way to get drunk. She realised she'd had one too many and made the sensible decision to come home rather than stay out with her friends," Jason argues before letting out a sigh.

"Look, I get it, okay. You two saw her that night when she was so drunk she couldn't stand. I know it scared you. Christian, I know all you want to do is protect her, but if you all keep stopping her from living her life, she's going to resent us. Before she moved in here, she didn't have to answer to anyone. It's been a long time since someone told her no, like we do. But we didn't agree to be her daddies to stop her from living; we did it to guide her in the right direction. Last night showed that it's working. I, for one, am proud of the fact she listened to the rules and did as she was told. She could have easily thought fuck it, and stayed out and carried on drinking, but she didn't."

I hear Jason sigh again and can almost see him rubbing his face like he does when he's had enough.

"Before you have a go at her, just do me one favour and ask if she had a good night. Because I can guarantee none of you did last night. I've watched the CCTV footage, and when she got out of that car, she was smiling from ear to ear and looked so carefree. The moment she answered the phone to whichever one of you it was, that light went out. By the time she was in her room, she looked deflated. Is that what you want for her? Because it sure as hell isn't what I want. If you do, then I suggest changing or walking away. We all fell in love with the light Jasmine brought into our lives. I never want her to lose that side of her, and I sure as hell don't want to be the reason it gets stubbed out."

I take a deep breath and walk into the kitchen, where all four guys are standing around the breakfast bar; they all turn to look at me as I enter.

"Morning," I say quietly as I play with the bottom of Jason's shirt, which I'm still wearing, and let out a sigh. "I heard you arguing, and I hate that I caused that," I admit as I look at them.

"We weren't arguing," Maximus sighs.

"Yes, you were, and it's because I went out last night. I know you want me to say I'm sorry, but I'm not." I stand a little taller as I look at them all. "I had fun, I laughed, and I enjoyed myself knowing all my coursework was up to date.

It wouldn't have been so easy to relax if you guys hadn't pushed me to get on top of it all, so thank you.

"I stuck to the rules, and I kept Layton informed of every bar I went to. I didn't leave until I knew he was in a position to follow me. I asked Mrs Brown to make me dinner before I went out, and I made sure to eat it all. As soon as I realised I was a little drunk, I came home. Old me would have kept drinking and not cared how smashed I was. But I did because I didn't want to disappoint you guys." I look down at the floor to hide that my eyes are filling with tears.

"I hate it when I disappoint you; I always have. I never cared what anyone thought of me before you four, and knowing that I caused you guys to argue and feel disappointed in me sucks."

I stay looking down, unable to face the four men who mean the absolute world to me. I hear footsteps getting closer and can smell Christian's aftershave as he comes to a stop in front of me.

"Look at me, baby girl."

I slowly lift my head and look him in the eye as mine fills with tears.

"I'm sorry. You and Jason are right; I was too hard on you last night. My fear of anything happening to you makes me overprotective, which makes life difficult for you, and that's the last thing I want. I know I'm strict, and I will try and work on that."

"I don't want you to change, not one bit," I admit. Christian frowns at me, and I smile at him a little. "I like the new, slightly more sensible me. I liked waking up and not feeling like death this morning or worrying about the time I lost, which should have been spent studying. My grades are up, and that's all thanks to you guys, not me." I look over at the twins and offer them a small smile.

"You have taught me to know my limits in the bedroom, which has taught me to know them outside of it. I knew I had hit my limit last night and came home." I step closer to Christian and wrap my arms around his waist. I feel him letting out a deep breath as he holds me and kisses the top of my head.

"I'm proud of you, Shorty. I'm sorry for killing your buzz. I guess I was a little drunk and panicked when I knew you were, too, and no one was here to look after you. I promise not to be such a killjoy again."

I walk up to Maximus and hug him.

"Thank you," I whisper before looking up at him. "I hope there weren't any strippers at this bachelor party?" I ask, not missing the look Maximus and Sean share. I step out of his arms and place my hands on my hips. "Were there strippers?" I demand.

"We didn't have a say in it, princess. It was organised by the best man," Sean explains nervously.

"So, if I went to a bachelorette party and there were strippers, that would be okay?"

"Hell no!" the twins protest together.

"But it's fine for you? Like it was fine for you to get drunk and not me!" I yell dramatically as I turn my back to them, throwing a smirk at Jason as the twins splutter excuses behind me.

"Bet they had a wank when they got back, too," I add with a raised brow. I turn to head for the kitchen door. "So many double standards, and you all say I'm hard work," I declare as I hold the door open and look over my shoulder, throwing them all a wink, knowing they will see. Christian stares at me for a moment before a face-splitting grin appears, and he charges towards me. I squeal as I rush forward, hearing the others laughing behind him. I turn around and jog backwards to find all four grinning at me as they stalk forward.

"You can run, baby girl, but when we catch you, you are ours to do with as we please," Christian growls.

"And if I manage to get away? Then what?" I ask, smiling back at them.

"Then we are at your mercy and will do anything you ask," Sean answers behind him. I look to my right and grin.

"Deal," I declare as I rush into the downstairs toilet and lock the door as Christian grabs the handle.

"You sneaky little brat," I hear Maximus laugh as Christian gives up trying to get in. I'm smiling so hard my face hurts as I laugh at the sound of them cursing me outside.

"I think this means I win!" I yell through the door.

"You know what, for your quick thinking, I think we should let you win this one," Jason laughs.

"So if I come out, you are all at my mercy? I can make you do anything I want?" I clarify as the others all agree. I unlock the door and poke my head around to see all four smiling at me.

"I want you all to take today off and spend it with me. Comfy clothes only, pizza for lunch and Indian for dinner, sweets, popcorn, and film day in the movie room." I watch as the four men look at each other and then at me, nodding.

"Sounds like the perfect day, sweetheart," Christian answers with a smile before pressing his lips to mine. "Just one thing missing," he points out.

"Oh, did I forget to mention sex whenever I say?" I add with a wink. I hear Jason chuckle and turn in time to see him smirk.

"Now that sounds fucking perfect."

Chapter Seven

JASMINE

"Do you remember the rules tonight?"

I roll my eyes as I tighten the towel around my chest and walk out of the bathroom.

"Yes, Daddy," I sigh, sitting in front of the vanity table. I Place my phone on the desk and hit the hands-free button.

"This is serious, baby girl; there will be a lot of highly powerful and dangerous people there tonight. I'm sure a few of them would love the opportunity to get one over on anyone with the O'Reilly name," Christian warns.

"I know, and I promise to be on my best behaviour," I answer as I check the hair and makeup that I spent the last two hours doing.

"Is Daddy Max there?" I ask, standing up and heading into my walk-on wardrobe where the long dress bag is hanging.

"He's with his ring team, going over a few last-minute things," I hear Christian say before someone calls his name in the background. It sounds like he places his phone against his top as he addresses them, so I wait patiently, checking my necklace and earrings to make sure they are all okay. When he comes back on the line, he sounds irate, to say the least.

"I have to go."

"Okay, tell him good luck from me," I reply, knowing it's best to let him end the call quickly. I walk out of the wardrobe and see Mrs Brown walking into the room.

"I will. See you later, sweetheart."

"Bye, Daddy." I hang up and look at Mrs Brown.

"Jason said you would need some assistance getting your dress on," she says with a smile. I look at the bag hanging up and chew on my bottom lip before remembering my lipstick and quickly letting it go.

"Have you seen it?"

She shakes her head, smiling, "I have no doubt it's beautiful. The O'Reillys have impeccable style and will want to show you off tonight," she says with a wink. I nod and let out a deep breath as we walk into the wardrobe.

I look in the mirror and can't believe how beautiful the dress is. It's a navy full-length gown with a low back that stops just above my curved backside. Even with the low back, it hugs my figure and leaves very little to the imagination. I'm so glad Mrs Brown suggested putting my stiletto strap sandals on before the dress because I don't think I could bend over without my breasts or ass falling out.

My long hazel hair is curled and fastened to the right side of my head with a couple of diamond-studded hair combs.

"The O'Reilly men aren't going to know what's hit them

tonight," Mrs Brown says, smiling at me over my shoulder in the mirror.

"I can't believe Daddy Jason picked this dress out. It's so revealing," I exclaim as I look at myself in the mirror. I move my right leg forward, revealing the slit that starts at the top of my thigh. Part of me wonders if Christian has seen the dress, as I'm sure he would never let me leave the house with so much on show.

"I did warn you they would want to show you off, and honey, there won't be a single person there tonight who won't wish you were on their arm," she says, smiling as she places her hands on my upper arms.

"Mrs Brown, can I ask you something?" I ask, turning to look at her properly.

"Of course, what's on your mind?"

"What do you think others will think of me being with all four of the guys? And me calling them Daddy?" I ask nervously.

"Do you care what others think?" she asks. I shrug as I look at the floor.

"I know I shouldn't. But there's still a part of me that worries people will think I'm childish or a slut," I admit to someone for the first time.

"Can I tell you something, honey? And I want you to listen as I think it might help."

I nod as she takes my hands.

"I've worked for the O'Reillys for a very long time. I was here before their mother died, and I have stuck by them ever since. I've seen many sides of the four brothers, but one side I never thought I would see was the side of them that appeared after their father's wedding to your mother." Mrs Brown cups my face and smiles at me as a mother would smile at a daughter.

"They were besotted with you from the moment they laid eyes on you. All they've talked about for three years is you and your dancing and what you've achieved all on your own. I have been to a few of your performances with them, and they never take their eyes off you when you are on the stage. They are so proud; they really would do anything to protect you and would give you the world if you asked for it," she says as I feel tears fill my eyes.

"Did it cause arguments with them?" I ask; Mrs Brown shakes her head.

"I waited for the day it would, but it never came. I dreaded what would happen if you chose one over the others. But they knew you wanted them all; they knew there was no way they could all love you and you not love them all in return. The more they talked about you, the more I could tell that you really cared about them, too.

"As for what others think, I believe you'll be surprised how many women will also have daddies. If people have an issue with you and the O'Reillys, they will know to keep their mouths shut and play nice, as those four men will kill in your honour, and people will see that when they witness how much they love you."

I look at Mrs Brown for a moment before throwing my arms around her. She chuckles, hugging me back.

"Thank you, Mrs Brown. You have no idea how much better I feel now."

"I'm glad I could help," she says before stepping back from me with a big smile on her face. "Now off you go, I'll tidy up here. You have two very handsome men waiting for you downstairs and two more waiting for you in the arena. Go out there with your head held high."

I smile before picking up my clutch bag from the bed, taking a deep breath, and heading out of the room.

As I reach the top of the stairs, I look down to see Jason and Sean talking together at the bottom. Both look so handsome in their black three-piece suits. They turn at the same time and look up at me as I place my hand on the railing and slowly make my way down the stairs, praying I don't trip and make a fool of myself.

They don't take their eyes off me, and I feel like a princess in the movies where the handsome prince is standing at the bottom of the grand staircase at the ball, waiting for her to descend. Except I have two gorgeous princes who look like they want to devour me rather than dance. The intensity of their eyes makes my skin burn.

As I reach the bottom three steps, Sean holds up his hand. I place my hand in his and let him help me down the last couple of steps.

"You look breathtaking, even more like a princess than usual," he says as he leans in and kisses my cheek.

"Absolutely gorgeous," Jason adds as he kisses my other warm cheek as Sean steps back. Jason takes my hand and holds it up. "Give us a twirl, angel."

I do as I'm told with a big smile on my face.

"I love my new dress. Thank you, Daddy."

"Angel, you are more than welcome. I knew it would look good on you but never dreamt you would look this amazing. I'm not sure whether to show you off or take you back upstairs and fuck you all night whilst you wear it," Jason growls as he leans in and kisses my neck.

"Stop!" I giggle, stepping away from him.

"As much as I love that idea, we need to get a move on before Christian messages again!" Sean sighs as he walks up to me and holds out an arm. I link mine through his and then Jason's when he stands on the other side of me, and they lead me to the entrance hall.

"Are we not taking one of the cars?" I ask. Jason shakes his head as he lets go of my arm and opens the door. Parked at the bottom of the front steps is a limousine.

"Tonight, we are being driven," Jason grins. I smile back as Sean leads me down the steps, and we come to a stop beside the car. The driver opens the door and dips his hat.

"Ma'am."

I smile as I get into the car and place my bag on my lap. Sean sits beside me, and Jason climbs into the seats at the side of the car. The door closes, and the driver returns to his seat behind the wheel.

"When you are ready, Stephen," Jason says as he reaches out and picks up a champagne bottle from an ice bucket in front of us.

"Of course, sir. We will be there in forty minutes." The window between us and the driver closes, and the car pulls away from the house. Jason pours a flute of champagne for each of us. I hold my glass out in front of me as the others clink theirs against it.

"Here's to a great night, introducing you to our world, angel," Jason says with a wink before taking a sip of his drink. I sip mine as my stomach tightens with nerves. I look at the two men with me and know that as long as I'm with them, nothing and no one will harm me.

Chapter Eight

JASMINE

The Gentlemen's Club we pull up outside of looks no different from any others I've seen. The guys gave me a tour of another venue a year ago before they opened it to the members.

The car door opens, and Jason gets out first before holding his hand out for me. I climb out and stand next to him as Sean appears to my left.

"Remember, angel, no matter what, you don't leave Sean's side. I might get called away, but you stay with him. The only security that will take you from Sean is Layton. If he grabs you, go with him, and don't try to find any of us. We will meet you at home."

I look at Jason and nod nervously.

"If Layton grabs me, I take it all hell's breaking loose."

"Angel, Hell doesn't even cover it. If shit starts to go down, you run and don't look back," Jason enforces before cupping my face. "I'm sure tonight will be fine, but we need a plan for every situation. Just remember, no matter how we are with others in there, we would never hurt you," Jason reassures me for the tenth time tonight.

"I know, Daddy," I reassure him. Jason kisses me gently before looking to the left of me at Sean.

"Everything ready?"

Sean looks up from his phone and nods. "Christian's in the front bar greeting people. He said to meet him there." Sean holds out his arm, and I wrap mine around it. "Come on, princess. Let's show them what a real knockout looks like."

I roll my eyes as Jason laughs and places a hand on the bottom of my back, guiding me forward.

The bouncers open the door, both giving a nod to Jason and Sean. Just inside, I spot Layton, who gives me a wink before he falls into step behind us, as we head into what appears to be a large bar.

Inside, there are dozens of tables with people sitting around as waiters and waitresses carry trays of drinks to them all. Maximus explained to me this morning that this area is just as it seems: a normal bar where people with a lot of money come to meet, discuss business and have a few drinks. It is a legitimate gentlemen's club that the guys opened a couple of years ago. Women are welcome here, and looking around, I can see a lot of them sitting next to the men. You can't mistake the ones who are the trophy wives, as they look around boredly as the men talk. Others pay attention to what's being discussed and seem to participate in the conversation.

When I first heard of the underground fight, I assumed there wouldn't be much of a dress code. Even after the guys had told me otherwise and I'd put on the beautiful dress, I was worried the guys had dressed me like this to make me stand out. However, looking around now, I can see how wrong I was. Every person here is dressed in designer suits and dresses and looks as immaculate as the guys next to me.

As we walk into the room, a few people turn and look at us. A few nod to the guys and stare at me, and I feel the nerves rising again. I quickly put my "show face" on, the one I use when I'm on the stage and trying to forget about all the eyes on me. That becomes easy when I spot Christian in the crowd, and my stomach gives a jolt.

There he is, sitting at a table surrounded by other men, a whiskey in one hand as he sits back in his chair. He looks so at ease, yet his body language screams respect and dominance. There's no mistaking how powerful and dangerous he is, yet all I see is my Daddy, who holds me when I'm sad and does all he can to make me smile. He says he loves me and would fight the world for me.

Before we've even reached him, Christian's head turns and looks straight at us. For a second, that powerful persona slips as his eyes widen and his jaw drops. I hear Sean laugh quietly next to me.

"Not seen his composure slip in years," he mutters under his breath as Jason chuckles. I think that is the biggest compliment anyone could give me. Christian is a businessman through and through, but knowing I have that effect on him makes my heart swell and my body heat. I watch as Christian blinks twice before his mask slips back into place with the addition of a slight smile.

As we reach the table, Christian stands quickly, followed by those around him. Sean lets go of my arm but stays close as Christian takes my hand to place a kiss on my knuckles.

"Sweetheart, you are a vision," he whispers as he leans in and kisses my cheek. I smile at him as he stands tall.

"Thank you."

Christian places a hand on the bottom of my back as he turns back to the people around us.

"Gentlemen, may I introduce our Jasmine. This is her first experience of a fight," Christian announces proudly as I feel his thumb rub against my bare back, sending shockwaves through my whole body.

"It's a pleasure to meet you," an older man a little shorter than Christian says as he holds out his hand. I place mine in his and give it a quick shake. Christian sits first before everyone else, pulls me onto his lap and places a hand on the bottom of my back before picking up his glass with the other. I steal a quick questioning glance, but Christian gives me that look that tells me there is no point arguing.

"Sweetheart, this is Geralt Young. He's the manager of one of the five warm-up fighters tonight and an old friend of the family," Christian explains as he nods to the gentleman whose hand I have just shaken.

"I see; well, I hope the fight goes in your favour, Mr Young," I answer with a smile. Sean spent some time with me this week going over the other fighters whom we support and whom we are a little less inclined to show support for.

"Thank you, and so do I," he answers before leaning back. I see Sean out of the corner of my eye, taking two drinks from a waitress. He turns and hands me a champagne flute, which I take with a quiet thank you.

Christian and Jason introduce me to a few more people, all of whom they do business with in one way or another, whilst Sean sits beside us deep in conversation with Mr Young about fighting techniques and how his training is going.

Even though I'm sitting on Christian's knee, the three men don't hide that I belong to all of them. Every touch or compliment sends a warm feeling to my heart as well as between my legs.

"If you will excuse us, gentlemen. We'll see you in the arena later," Christian says as he stands and tightens his arm around my waist. I say a quick goodbye to everyone before Christian turns with me and stalks towards a door at the back of the club where a bouncer is standing guard. As soon as they spot us, they use a keypad to unlock the door and hold it open as we walk through.

"Layton, we're going to the office; stand guard outside of it, please," Christian orders as we walk down a corridor. I hadn't realised Layton was so close.

"Of course, sir."

Jason reaches forward and presses his hand over a sensor, which beeps, and I hear the door unlock. The four of us walk into the office.

"Is everything okay?" I ask, looking around and wondering why we're here. My question is answered the moment Christian grabs me and forces me against the wall as his lips find mine. I instantly wrap my arms around his neck and kiss him back as his hands slide down until he cups my ass. He runs his hand further down and then lifts my leg so he can grind his hard restrained cock against me, causing me to gasp against his mouth. Christian growls as he pulls away from me, leaving me breathless.

"I knew you coming here tonight was a bad idea. How am I meant to concentrate when you look and smell that fucking divine?"

"I don't know whether to be flattered or sorry," I admit, worrying my bottom lip between my teeth.

"Flattered, baby girl, never be sorry for the effect you have on me," Christian replies as he uses his thumb to pull my bottom lip from between my teeth before forcing his lips against mine again.

"Christian, as fuckable as Jazzy is right now, you need to go and check on things with Maximus."

Christian pulls away from me and stands straight whilst checking his tie. I look ahead to see Jason and Sean looking at a computer monitor. Christian runs his fingers through his hair, straightening it before turning back to his brothers.

"Everything looking okay?" he asks, taking my hand and leading me to the desk. Jason nods, still looking at the screen.

"Yeah, the only one that may be an issue is that dick-head, Harriot. I'll give the guys a heads up that he's here and get them to keep an eye on him at all times."

"He usually gets high and fucks off with an escort before the main fight anyway," Sean states as he walks over to the bar and grabs a bottle of water. He holds it up to me, and I nod before accepting it. Christian smiles approvingly as I take a sip.

"Good girl, don't drink too much tonight," he warns as his hand finds my bare skin again. I shake my head, smiling sweetly.

"I won't, Daddy," I reply as his eyes darken. He reaches out and threads his fingers into the hair and the base of my head, pulling me closer to him.

"Carry on being a good girl, and I think all four of your daddies will help reward you tonight," he whispers in my ear as he kisses my neck. I can't stop myself from moaning aloud.

"Jazzy, come here before someone forgets why we're here," Jason chuckles from his seat. I look into Christian's eyes, smiling, and shrug before walking away. I lean against Jason as he wraps an arm around my waist from where he's sitting. I don't miss the smug look Jason gives his older brother, who moans as he repositions himself and turns towards the door. He stops before he opens it, turns with his phone in his hand and the light flashes as he snaps a photo.

"Making sure Maximus knows how amazing you look before seeing you so he isn't distracted later." He turns his back to us again. "Give it twenty minutes, then all three of you head to the arena; I will meet you there," he demands as he opens the door. "Remember the rules, baby girl," he calls as he exits the room.

"I will, Daddy," I call back before the door closes. I look down at Jason and then at Sean, who's stalking over from the bar, and both of them are staring at me. "Where can I patch up my makeup?"

"Wait, I've been wanting to do this all night," Jason declares as he stands up, sending his chair flying from behind him. He presses his lips to mine, holding me against the desk. "I want to know you are full of our cum as everyone looks at you in that arena tonight." He pulls away from me too quickly and smiles at Sean. "How many times do you think we can make her scream in twenty minutes?"

Sean looks back at him as he shrugs off his jacket quickly, followed by his waistcoat and tie.

"I reckon at least twice. But I'm willing to try for three," Sean groans as he drops to his knees and slides my dress up my legs. "Fuck you're going commando," he growls, looking up at me. I shrug before looking at Jason innocently.

"I thought it would look better than having a panty line."

"Oh angel, you have just upped the game," he growls as his lips find my mouth and Sean's land on my pussy.

Chapter Nine

Twenty minutes and three orgasms later, the three of us join Christian in the arena underneath the club. This is an entirely different scene from upstairs. Some of that professionalism and control I witnessed before has gone as many openly sniff drugs, smoke cigars and drink enough alcohol to drown their livers. I haven't touched a drop since coming out of the office as I'm feeling light-headed from all the smoke that's floating around the room.

Another thing present here that wasn't upstairs is the number of male and female sex workers. All in revealing outfits and some openly performing sex acts on anyone who requests it.

"I thought you guys were against things like this?" I ask Sean quietly as we walk past one guy getting a blow job against the wall at the back of the room.

"We are against people being sold for sex or forced into the sex trade. Believe it or not, some people are happy to be paid for it," he explains as he nods towards the wall. "All the men and women we provide here do so willingly, and we let them keep one hundred percent of the money they make. If anyone tries not to pay or disrespects them, they are removed and taught a lesson, and the victim is highly compensated. People know how we feel about sex workers being mistreated and tend to stick to the rules."

As the night progresses, people become more open about the sex acts, and everywhere I look, there are people at it or receiving oral. At one point, I felt someone touch my shoulder from behind and turned just in time to see Sean grab the guy's hand and twist it until he cried out in pain.

"Touch her again, arsehole, and I'll fucking break it before cutting off your tiny dick!" Sean snarls before letting go of the guy's hand and placing an arm around me as the guy stammers a sorry and hurries off.

"Was that really necessary? He might have just wanted to ask a question."

"He's been watching you since we walked in, princess. Trust me, the only question he wants to ask is if you want to join him back there, and not for a friendly chat," Sean replies before glaring over his shoulder to see where the guy is now sheepishly sitting with others.

"A few people are watching you, Jazzy, and some are working up the courage to come over to approach you," Jason adds as he looks over to a couple of young men on the other side of the arena; they don't look much older than me. When I follow his line of sight, I see they are indeed staring at me whilst deep in conversation.

"Come here," Jason says as he pulls me onto his lap. I'm more than happy to oblige as I feel protected and safer in his arms. I want to learn and experience as much of their lives as possible, but this is a little too much for my liking.

"Do you usually partake in this kind of behaviour?" I ask Christian, who shakes his head.

"All you need to know is none of us ever had to pay for it. We won't hide there were women before you, but there's been no one since we decided you would be ours."

"I don't believe you weren't sexually active at all," I laugh as Jason squeezes my ass cheek whilst grinning.

"I know I certainly wasn't, but when I jerked off in bed or the shower, I was always thinking of you, angel," he growls in my ear before nipping it playfully, making me giggle out loud.

Throughout the night, a few people would come over to talk to the guys, usually Christian, and I felt the tension radiating off Jason, his hold on me becoming more protective, and he wouldn't take his eyes off whoever was in front of us.

One guy in particular came over to speak to Christian, but Jason wouldn't allow him to even look at me.

"Keep your fucking eyes to yourself, Michelson. You look at her again, and I'll make sure my face is the last thing you ever fucking see."

The guy apologises quickly and runs off with his tail between his legs.

"Take it he is an arrrr -arrogant guy?" I frown at myself for the pathetic attempt to cover up the fact I was about to call him an arsehole. I look at Christian, who's frowning at me, and shrug, "At least I didn't *actually* swear."

Jason and Sean both burst out laughing as Christian shakes his head, pinching the bridge of his nose.

"You're learning at least," he sighs, but I see a slight smile behind his hand, and I relax into Jason, glad my ass is saved from a spanking, for now anyway.

"To answer your question," Christian continues as he sips his drink and looks in front of us. "Michelson comes across as quiet and timid, but in fact, he has a history of sexual abuse as long as his arm and if he so much as touches you, I will remove that arm from his body."

I lean back into Jason, who wraps his arm around me protectively.

"I don't know why he's even here," Sean sighs next to us.

"Because you keep your friends close and your enemies closer," I answer without thinking. Both Jason and Christian stare at me for a moment before I notice the pride in their eyes.

"This is why you are perfect for us," Jason declares, kissing my cheek.

Ten to Midnight, Christian disappears to spend the next twenty minutes with Maximus to ensure he's ready for the fight. Leaving me to stare at the large ring in the middle of the arena.

It's just like the boxing rings I've seen in their gyms and at home. Sean informed me earlier that tonight isn't a normal boxing match; it's an illegal one. There are no rules, and all forms of fighting and martial arts are allowed. People have even died when their ring team haven't thrown in the towel quickly enough.

The guys have assured me that Maximus has the best ring team, and there's no danger of him dying. They are all sure Maximus can take his opponent and will win tonight.

With all five warm-up fights over, three ended with guys being stretchered off. My heart starts racing as I worry about what state Maximus will be in by the time his fight is finished. Jason and Sean are so calm as they sit in their seats, drinking their whiskey and sharing the odd comment about the fights so far. Now Christian is busy with Maximus and will be purely focused on the fight when it starts. I have moved from Jason's lap to Sean's in case Jason has to leave for any reason. Luckily, I did, as not long after Christian left, one of the two guys from across the ring approached us as Jason was talking to someone a few feet away.

"Hey, darling. Fancy joining us over there when these guys are finished with you?"

Before I even get a chance to open my mouth, Jason grabs him, throws him to the floor and has a gun to his head in seconds.

"What the fuck did you say to our woman?" he growls in his face. I've never seen his angry side before. Not like this anyway.

"I didn't realise she belonged to you; we thought she was a hooker," the guy stammers before Jason hits him with the handle of his gun. Sean's arms tighten around me, I want to curl up into him, but I also don't want to appear weak.

"Does she look like a fucking hooker?" Jason demands. The guy shakes his head as his nose and lip bleed. "That's not what you just said, arsehole," Jason growls before lifting him to his feet. "Get this bastard and his mate out of here!" he yells as two security guards take the guy, and I see two others grab his friend, who's standing by his seat looking very pale.

"The next fucker that approaches our woman will leave here in a fucking body bag!" Jason yells as he looks around. Everyone starts looking anywhere but at me, but I'm focused purely on Jason as he stalks over to me and kisses me roughly.

"My big protective, Daddy," I grin, staring into his eyes as my toes curl in my strappy shoes. Jason reaches up and grips my chin as his eyes darken.

"I told you, no one disrespects you. That's the only warning they get," Jason growls as he kisses me again before heading back to the group he had been speaking to, tucking his gun back into the top of his trousers.

You can feel the buzz in the air as we get closer to the starting time of the main fight. The sex acts have all ceased around us, and people are deep in discussion about the upcoming fight.

"I take it there is a lot of betting going on?" I ask as I see people walking around gathering up cash and taking down people's names.

"Of course, there is. That's the main reason for these fights," Sean answers.

"How many have you done?" I ask; Sean shrugs.

"Three, same as Maximus."

"We don't allow them to do more than one illegal and two competitive a year," Jason adds, not looking at me but at a guy further along our row.

"Who's that?" I ask. Jason shakes his head and looks back at the ring.

"No one for you to worry about," he mutters. I look at Sean who shakes his head, signalling for me to drop it.

I'm just leaning back into Sean when the lights all drop down again, and the spotlights flood the ring. My heart starts racing as the room becomes silent.

"Ladies and Gentlemen, it's time for the fight you've all been waiting for!" the MC announces, and I feel my hands starting to shake.

"Let's get this party started!" he adds before the lights turn to green. "Tonight, in the red corner weighing in at sixteen stone ten ounces, at six foot one, with six matches and five wins under his belt, Tim 'The Machine' Hades."

The lights fly to the entrance on the other side of the arena, and the red lights land on a man who looks like he could eat Maximus for breakfast.

"He's huge!" I yell at Sean over the sound of his entrance music. "Eye Of the Tiger" fills the air, and Jason and Sean both groan.

"He's cocky and heavy. Anyone who picks this song as their entrance thinks highly of themselves," Sean states as he takes a sip of his drink. I take it from his hand and down what's left of it.

"Jazzy, calm down. Maximus will be fine. He will win this one," Jason says as he takes my hand. I look at him as I feel myself starting to shake.

"You really think so?"

Jason cups my face, looking into my eyes.

"The only people I love as much as you are my brothers. Would I put any of you in danger?"

I shake my head.

"Yes, Maximus will get hurt, but that's what we do. He *will* beat this guy."

I don't get a chance to reply before the MC's voice fills the room again.

"And in the blue corner, weighing in at fifteen stone twelve ounces, fighting on his home turf, with twelve matches, winning every single one, is Maximus O'Reilly!"

Nickelback's "This Means War" blasts as the room erupts, cheering far louder than when the other fighter walked into the arena.

I jump onto my feet with Jason and Sean clapping and cheering as I see Maximus walking down with his arms in the air as Christian walks behind him with the rest of the ringside team.

Maximus looks hyped and ready for the fight, and my nerves calm a little when I see how big he looks in his shorts.

Maximus spots us as he nears the ring and claps hands with his brothers before kissing me quickly on the lips.

"Be my lucky charm, Shorty?" he asks with a wink.

"Always, Daddy," I reply before he walks to the ring. Christian holds the ropes for him as he climbs in.

Christian and his team climb in after him. Maximus starts hopping from one foot to the other, and the MC starts talking again.

"You all know the rules; there are none. All forms of martial arts and fighting are allowed. You fight until one of you can't fight anymore. Each round is two minutes. It's down to your ring teams to end the fight," he announces as Maximus and his rival stand in the middle of the ring facing each other. "Bump fists!" the MC calls, and they do so before turning around and heading to their corners.

I watch as Christian grasps Maximus around the back of his head, and they rest their foreheads against each other. I can see Christian talking and Maximus occasionally nodding. Christian stands up and faces his brother before nodding and walking away from him.

Maximus watches him until he is out of the ring and standing next to Sean and Jason. He places his wrapped hand over his heart, and his brothers automatically do the same.

I can see the love shared between them more at that moment than I have ever seen before. Maximus looks from them to me and blows me a kiss. I quickly blow one back before his team surrounds him, and his trainer gets in his face and makes him focus.

"Is he going to be okay?" I ask Christian, who takes my hand and pulls me to him.

"He'll be fine. He wants to end the fight quickly so he can get you home and out of that dress," he whispers in my ear. I smile as I stand against Christian and watch Maximus prepare mentally for the fight. Christian must feel me shaking as he wraps his arm around me from behind and lowers his head to my ear.

"Breathe, sweetheart. I wouldn't let him fight if I thought there was any chance he wouldn't win."

"I know, I'm just nervous," I reply.

"Don't be," Christian whispers before kissing my cheek. "Go back to Sean, baby girl and stay calm."

I nod as I kiss him quickly on the cheek and walk past Jason, who gives my hand a quick squeeze before Sean pulls me to him, standing behind me with his arms around my waist.

"He's got this in the bag, princess. You're his lucky charm. Why do you think he has Nickelback as his entrance music?" Sean whispers in my ear. I smile, thinking of all the times I thought I was forcing the twins to listen to my favourite band.

"What's your entrance music?" I ask, smiling over my shoulder.

"*Burn It to the Ground,*" Jason answers, grinning at his brother. "You have them both listening to that shit even when you aren't around," he laughs as Sean shakes his head.

"I always thought you only listened to it because of me?" I ask, turning to look at Sean, who grins.

"We do, but having them as our entrance music made it feel like you were with us," he replies, leaning down and kissing me. Before I can reply, we hear the bell, and we both look up at the ring as the first round starts.

Chapter Ten

JASMINE

I've been looking forward to tonight, but now I wish I was at home and not watching Maximus getting hit, kicked and thrown around.

The others promise me he isn't losing, but it looks that way to me, and it's hard to watch.

For the first two rounds, I couldn't move as I watched the fight.

In the third round when I saw Maximus spitting out blood, I thought I was going to be sick, now they are breaking after the sixth round, and I feel faint.

I watch Christian walk over to the ring and stand beside Maximus, who is sitting on a stall and being patched up by his team. He is spitting out a lot of blood; his eyebrow is swollen and split, as is his cheek.

"What's Christian saying?" I ask Sean, as I see Christian shouting something at Maximus, who's nodding and listening to his big brother.

"Giving him instructions. He will spend more time over

there the longer the fight goes on," Jason explains as he waves over a waitress and asks for three whiskeys and a bottle of water. I quickly add a glass of champagne to the order earning me a raised brow from Jason.

I look at the opponent and find him staring at me with a grin on his face. Sean follows my line of sight and curses under his breath. The guy blows me a kiss, and I turn my nose up at him.

"Daddy Max needs to kick his ass before I do," I growl as I take the champagne from the waitress as Jason and Sean chuckle next to me.

"Just wait, he's getting tired. His swings and kicks are getting sluggish," Sean whispers as Jason nods.

"And Maximus?" I ask. Jason turns and grins.

"He's fine, he's trained for long matches, this kid hasn't, and it's starting to show."

I look back at Christian, who looks like he is giving Maximus hell.

"It's part of the act; we let them think Christian isn't impressed, but he's the complete opposite," Jason whispers in my ear. "The thing with fighting is it's as much to do with acting as it is physical strength. You let your component think you're getting tired or angry, and you wait for the opening and then you let all hell break loose. Maximus is far from tired; he's just letting him think he is."

I swallow and nod as I look back to the ring. Maximus is staring at the opponent, who's watching everything I do. I can feel his eyes drifting down my body, and as much as I want to hide from him, I lift my glass to my lips and flip him off with the same hand. Sean and Jason laugh out loud, as does Maximus. I glance at Christian, who's shaking his head at me. However, the guy in red looks furious.

"So worth being spanked for," I shrug as Sean continues to chuckle behind me.

"Princess, if he insists on spanking you, I will ensure I have my face between your legs at the same time," he growls in my ear. I instantly start wishing I had underwear on to absorb how wet I suddenly am.

Christian storms over to his usual position before beckoning me with his finger.

"Uh-oh," I whisper under my breath before walking over to him. "I'm not sorry," I declare, holding my head high.

"Good, I might not approve of your swearing, but I'm glad you didn't back down either," Christian says as he threads his fingers into my hair and kisses me.

"He's trying to get at Maximus by using our relationship. Teasing him about it taking four of us to satisfy you, expecting it to annoy him," Christian whispers into my ear.

"It isn't, is it?"

Christian stands up and shakes his head. "Not in the slightest. Maximus is comfortable with all of us being in a relationship with you, and it doesn't bother him what anyone else says."

I smile as I look up at Maximus's corner as the bell rings for the next round. He stands up and winks at me before heading back into the ring.

Two more rounds pass with just as much blood, but even I'm seeing his opponent is getting tired. But to me, Maximus is looking just as tired, too.

The guys assure me he's okay, but I'm starting to see it

in their eyes and hear it as they shout at him; they are worried for their brother.

Christian stays with the ring team after the eighth round, and by the end of the tenth, he's screaming at the team. I have no idea what he's saying, but he isn't happy.

He climbs into the ring himself and holds Maximus's face as he speaks to him. Maximus keeps shaking his head, but Christian won't let go as he forces Maximus to look at him.

By now, Sean has his arm around my shoulders, and I'm curled up against his side. None of us is even attempting to sit between rounds. We're too on edge.

Jason watches the exchange between Christian and Maximus and looks at Sean.

"Stay with her. If the worst happens, give her to Layton," he orders before walking to the ring. I spot Layton walking closer and giving Jason a nod as he stops beside us.

"What does he mean by 'if the worst happens'?"

Sean looks from his brothers to me, and I can see the answer in his eyes.

"Stop the fight," I demand, but Sean shakes his head as he pulls me against him.

"Maximus won't let them," he says into my hair. I hear the bell ring for the next round and look to see Maximus heading into the centre as his brothers watch from the side.

As soon as the fight starts, the guy in red kicks Maximus's chest, and he goes down. The guy wastes no time jumping on to him, and they start wrestling. I can't watch anymore.

I bury my head in Sean's chest as a sob bursts from my throat. Sean runs a hand over my head and holds me as he yells at his brother to get off the floor. A few times, I try to look, but Sean holds me tighter, stopping me from moving, and I start to shake violently.

The noise around us has become more and more sombre as the fight has progressed. Now, less than half are cheering or shouting as they watch the two getting tired and weaker. I'm about to ask Sean what's happening when he curses loudly seconds before the room erupts.

I peek from Sean's chest to the ring and spin around to see Maximus on top of the other guy, punching him as if his life depended on it. He growls and screams as he pummels the guy who has his arms up but isn't fighting back.

Maximus stands up and pulls the guy to his feet before attacking him again. He has him up against the ropes, but they are all that's holding the guy up. I start screaming for Maximus to finish him with Sean, I don't look anywhere but the ring.

Suddenly, a white towel flies into the ring, and the ref tries to separate Maximus from the guy, but he's in attack mode.

Christian and Jason jump into the ring and grab their brother, dragging him away as he tries to get back to his opponent.

"I'm going to fucking kill him!" Maximus screams as he fights against Christian and Jason. Another member of the ring team takes Christian's place, and Christian stands in front of him with his hand over his chest. He says something, and Maximus's eyes snap to me.

My knees nearly buckle under the intensity of his stare. Everything from the ring and arena fades, and all I can see is Maximus's face.

He stops fighting against the guys and shrugs them off before climbing out of the ring and heading straight for me.

I step out of Sean's arms and rush to Maximus as tears

stream down my face. I throw my arms around his neck as he picks me up in a bear hug.

"I fucking love you, Shorty," Maximus says into my ear. I look into his swollen eyes as I chuckle through the tears.

"I love you too, Daddy."

Maximus's lips find mine, and he kisses me, split lip and all.

Chapter Eleven

CHRISTIAN

Jasmine's lying down at the back of the limo with her head on Sean's lap and Jason's jacket over her. We are all exhausted and just want to get home. The fight ended two hours ago, and it's just gone three in the morning.

Maximus has been checked out by doctors; he has a broken nose, two black eyes from it, a split lip, cheek and brow, as well as a bruised and possibly fractured rib. Maximus is refusing to get x-rayed and insists he's fine. The doctor knows better than to argue with him, as he gave him a ton of painkillers and told me to call him if Maximus becomes unwell or shows signs of concussion.

"Is she asleep?" I ask quietly.

"Seems to be," Sean replies, nodding.

"She handled tonight far better than I thought she would," Jason says from the other side of me.

"When she flipped that prick off, I thought he was going to lose his shit," Maximus chuckles before hissing in pain.

"I was always worried she was too pure for our world,

but she certainly managed just fine tonight," I admit as I watch her sleep for a few seconds longer.

"You going to tell us what he said to trigger you to go into kill mode before?" I ask, turning to face Maximus, whose whole face shifts with the anger that consumed him before. "I need to know, he's on life support," I point out.

"Good, turn the fucking thing off," Max growls.

"What the hell? I thought he wasn't getting to you?" Sean curses from his seat.

"He wasn't, he kept going on about how shit we must be if it took four to keep Shorty satisfied. That didn't bother me at all."

"So, what happened?" Jason asks. Maximus sips his water and sighs.

"He upped his game. I kept to the plan, letting him think he was beating me physically to wear him out, and it was working, especially as Shorty couldn't even watch. When he saw you get in the ring, Christian, he was gloating, saying he was going to kill me in front of you all. I was just waiting for the next round to bring him down as planned, but then he'd been saying all the ways he was going to satisfy her, how she would be screaming his name by the end of the night, and when that didn't bother me, he went further."

"He threatened to hurt her," Sean whispers as he looks at his twin, who nods.

"He told me he was going to take her and went into detail about how he was going to break her, so I broke him first."

"Did you really think he would have been able to take her?" I ask, shaking my head, but Maximus glares at me.

"I knew he would never get to her, but you didn't hear

70

what he was saying, I snapped and would do it again to anyone who threatens her."

"If you had done that in a normal fight -" I start, but Maximus stares at me.

"Everything is different in a normal fight, and you know it. He would have never pulled that shit for one thing! I won't apologise for protecting her any more than you would for killing that prick landlord!"

I shake my head and look back at Jasmine, who's surprisingly still asleep.

The thought of people using her to get to us is exactly why I didn't want her there tonight, why I wanted to keep her our secret, to protect her. But I know that's not the life she deserves or wants. Jasmine proved tonight that she can handle the people around us. Not once did she cower away when people were coming to talk to us. She looked them all in the eye and when that prick annoyed Maximus through her, she just flipped him off and didn't back down for a moment. That is what the others can see when they look at her. They can see the woman who has had to fight for everything in her life to have the peace that she has now, and it's who I need to focus on seeing myself.

"Where did you disappear off to after the fight?" I ask Jason in the hope of distracting my overactive mind.

"Trying to find Hudson."

I turn and stare at him, "You didn't think to tell me that arsehole was there?" I ask in disbelief. Jason looks at me with an arched brow.

"I was planning on telling you when we got home. He was gone by the time I left you all in the changing rooms."

"Hudson doesn't do anything without Taylor's say-so. Taylor wasn't there tonight; he turned down the invitation,"

Sean says as he runs a hand over Jasmine's head absent-mindedly.

"I know. I spoke to Terry, and they know to keep an eye out for them both elsewhere. There's a reason Taylor would have wanted Hudson there tonight, and I'm sure we're going to find out why soon," Jason says, and I have to agree with him.

"Has he been in touch with anyone since we cut all business ties with him?" I ask, looking at my brothers, they all shake their heads. "That will be it then. He will be looking for a way back in."

I look back at Jasmine, needing to think of something other than the worry the latest development has just caused.

She looked amazing when she walked into that club this evening. It has taken all my strength and self-control to not drag her into the office and fuck her senseless. A huge part of me is considering waking her up when we get home so I can lose myself between her legs. Fuck, I want all four of us to enjoy that sweet fucking pussy.

"Daddy, I can feel you watching me."

"Which Daddy are you talking to, princess?" Sean chuckles as he runs a hand down her body seductively. She opens her eyes, and they instantly find mine.

"I could feel you all watching me," she replies as she looks around at us all before sitting up.

"What do you expect when you are that gorgeous," Jason says with a smile. Jasmine shakes her head and looks at me as I beckon her with my finger.

Jasmine moves so she is in front of me. She reaches up and presses her hands to the roof of the car to steady herself as I place my hands on her ankles and slowly slide her dress up, revealing her perfect sex.

I always hated this limo; the twins wanted one they

could stand up in and party with as they travelled. But now I realise I'm in the perfect position to lick my baby girl's pussy as we drive home; I love it.

"Did Jason and Sean get to enjoy this in the office?" I ask as I look up at her.

"Yes, Daddy."

"Do Maximus and I get to when we get home? Or do you want all four of us?" I ask as I run a finger between her legs.

"I need all four of my Daddies," she gasps as I run my finger through her again, this time scooping some of her juices and trailing them back against her back passage.

"Do you remember what I said, I wanted to see that time in the bath?" I ask as I rub against her puckered entrance, and she gasps, closing her eyes.

"Yes," she gasps loudly as I apply a little pressure and enter her slightly.

"Say it so your other daddies know," I answer as I slip a little more of my finger into her, and she gasps louder.

"You want to watch me take the other three of my daddies at the same time. One in my mouth, one in my pussy and one in my ass."

I hear all three of my brothers groan and curse as I grin at our girl and tease her with my finger and thumb, which is now entering her front passage.

"Would you like that baby girl? Will you let us try it when we get home?" I ask as I lean forward and lick her in just the right place.

"Yes!" she calls as she starts to sway with excitement and need. I grin up at her as I feel the car come to a stop. She moans as I withdraw my digits and tongue.

"Good, because we are home, and we are heading straight to your room."

Chapter Twelve

JASMINE

I've never seen this side of the guys before. As soon as the car stops, we are rushing out, all laughing like children. By the time Terry, who had been in the car's passenger seat, opened the front door, I'm already pulling my shoes off, giggling as the guys chase me into the house. All desperate to get to my room as quickly as possible. I have only just gotten to the bottom of the stairs when Sean sweeps me off my feet and carries me up the stairs as the others pull off their jackets, waistcoats and ties, leaving a trail of destruction behind us.

"Look at the mess!" I laugh as Jason takes my shoes from my hands and drops them on the stairs.

"That's nothing compared to the mess I plan on making of you," he replies, pulling his shirt off over his head and leaving it on the landing. I look at Christian and see the biggest grin on his face. He looks happier than I have ever seen him, and my heart races.

Sean carries me into the room, and we all make short work of getting out of our clothes. Jason gives me a hand by pulling the dress over my head. When I come face to face with Maximus, I see him staring at me, his jaw hanging open.

"Were you completely naked under that dress?"

I nod whilst grinning at him.

"Shorty, if I had known that, I'd have ended the fight in seconds." Maximus steps forward, threads his fingers into the hair at the back of my head, and kisses me, his tongue finding mine in seconds. I lose myself in his touch and his kiss. He backs me up to the side of the bed until I feel it knock against my legs, and I have to stop myself from falling backwards. Maximus hisses as I jolt against him.

"Oh god, did I hurt you!" I panic, but Maximus shakes his head.

"I'm fine." I can tell he's lying to me as his face is swollen, and the bruising is coming out fast and heavy now.

"There's no way we can do this tonight without hurting you," I insist as I look behind him at his naked and smiling brothers.

"Think you will find there is, Shorty," Maximus grins as he steps back. Sean steps forward and lifts me with ease before throwing me onto the bed. I squeal, bouncing as I land. Sean crawls over me and kisses me on the lips.

"Are you going to be a good girl and lie there whilst we do unthinkable things to you, princess?"

I smile as I look into Sean's eyes. Two loud pops sound, causing me to jump. I squeal, looking to the left where Jason and Christian are holding a bottle of champagne each.

"Looks like Mrs Brown knew we would all end up in here tonight," Jason announces as he pours some into a glass and holds it out for me. I reach for it, only for Sean to get it first.

"Hey, that's mine," I protest, but Sean grins before taking a sip.

"If you want some, you will have to come and get it."

I push myself up into a sitting position, but Sean leans back and takes another sip from the glass before grabbing the back of my head with his free hand and pressing a kiss to my lips. As soon as his lips are against mine, I open them slightly, and he allows the ice-cold champagne to pour into my mouth. The bubbles pop against my tongue before sliding down my throat.

I swallow the last of what he offers and pull back, smiling. I reach up and take the glass from his hand as I put my legs underneath me. Lifting the glass to my lips, I don't lose eye contact with him as I kneel up. Keeping the cold drink in my mouth, I thread my fingers into the hair at the back of his head and tug slightly, tipping his head back. With my mouth hovering just above his, I allow the cold drink to pour from my lips into his open mouth. As soon as both our mouths are empty, he takes the glass from my hand and holds it out. I don't know who takes it as my eyes don't leave Sean's.

"I love champagne, but fuck you make everything taste like heaven."

I get no warning before he pounces and knocks me onto my back as his lips find mine. He grabs hold of my wrists and holds them over my head as I move my legs and wrap them around his waist. My heart races as I realise I'm powerless against whatever they have planned for me, and fuck, I'm dripping wet and ready for them.

Christian moves into view and stays near my head as he sips a glass of champagne.

"Here's what's going to happen, baby," he starts as he looks down at me. "You will sit on Sean's face while you suck my dick. I've just given Jason a little something to help your back end prepare for what will happen then. Because once you cum, you are going to sit on Sean's cock, whilst you suck Jason's, and Maximus takes your ass."

I pull out all the stops, fluttering my eyelashes at Christian, and try to look as sexy as possible.

"But what about you, Daddy?"

Christian leans in, allowing his lips to brush across mine as he replies.

"I, baby girl, get to watch the most beautiful woman in the world get fucked by three men. I have the best seat in the house." His lips crash into mine again, his tongue forcing its way into my mouth. I can taste the whiskey and champagne he's been drinking.

I turn my head away from Christian to see Maximus standing beside the bed. Sean, still straddling my hips leans down and takes my nipple between his teeth. I gasp as Maximus's mouth finds mine. Even as I kiss him, I know I shouldn't, not with how injured he is, but even as that metallic taste lands on my tongue where his lip splits open again, I find myself moaning, and it's not due to the way Sean is playing with my nipples.

"Come here, Shorty."

Sean releases my nipple with a pop before climbing off my hips so I can kneel in front of Maximus.

"I don't want to hurt you," I whisper, pressing my lips to him gently.

"You could never hurt me, Shorty; not physically anyway. You ever leave me, and you would destroy me, more than any man could in the ring." Maximus threads his big hands into my hair and holds my head in place as he looks into my eyes. I run my knuckle over his swollen cheek before pressing a light kiss to it.

"I'm never going anywhere," I whisper. Slowly, I kiss each bruise and cut he has on his face. "I'm your Shorty," I whisper as I kiss his lips again. I watch as Maximus's eyes darken.

"Too fucking right you are," he growls as his lips press mine hard again. "Now sit on my brother's face, gorgeous. He needs to taste that pussy, now." Maximus grins as I turn to see Sean lying on the bed. I eagerly move, and as soon as I'm over his face. He runs his tongue over me, and I moan loudly.

"Open your mouth, baby girl." I open my eyes to see Christian kneeling beside me. I spot the glass in his hand as he lifts it to my mouth and pours a little in as soon as my lips part.

"You are so fucking beautiful," he whispers as he takes a sip of champagne and kisses me, allowing a little drink to run into my mouth. It's still ice cold, and I purposely keep it there for a moment before allowing the bubbling liquid to flow down my throat.

"I need you, Daddy," I moan as Sean's magical tongue works wonders against my clit as he pushes a finger into me.

"Daddy needs you too, baby girl," Christian growls as he moves into position. I kneel over, placing my hands on the mattress, ensuring I don't smother Sean and reach out to take Christian in my hand and stroke him.

"One more sip, Daddy?" I whisper, nodding to the glass in his hand. He lifts it, and I let the cold liquid flow into my mouth. I hold it for a second before swallowing half. I look up at my hot daddy and smirk before taking him into my mouth along with the rest of the bubbling cold champagne. The noise that leaves Christian is like nothing I've heard before. I swirl my tongue around him with the champagne before I swallow. I know I've dribbled a bit on the bed covers, and I don't care.

"Fuck!" he curses aloud as I suck the last of the champagne from his rock-hard cock. His fingers thread into my hair as he tightens his hold, tilting my head back before kissing me hard. "That mouth of yours is getting fucking naughty," he growls as I stare deep into his blue eyes.

"Should I stop?" I ask innocently.

"Never, baby girl. Never, fucking stop," he growls before pressing his cock to my mouth, and I take him hungrily.

Before long I'm gasping around Christian's cock as Sean licks and sucks on my clit. Suddenly, something cold presses against my back passage making me gasp aloud. I don't even have to look and know it's Jason behind me. He runs his tongue around my back entrance as I moan again before he pushes a finger in. My eyes roll back, and I have to stop myself from letting Christian's cock fall from my mouth.

"Fuck, I love the way your body responds to our touch," Jason growls behind me as he moves his finger in and out of my ass.

"Jason, you better get her ready because I don't think I will be able to last much longer before getting inside her," I hear Maximus groan behind me, pushing me closer to climaxing. I hear Jason chuckling before something bigger presses against my back passage, and I can no longer hold Christian in my mouth.

"What is that?" I gasp as it pops past my entrance. It feels hard and wet at the same time.

"It's a butt plug with lube."

My bulging eyes snap to a grinning Christian before they roll back from the pleasure. It's stretching me in just the right way. Christian used this on me once before, and I know in a moment it will be in place, and I know how good it will feel as I fuck Sean with it in.

"Oh my god, Daddy," I cry out as Sean inserts a second finger and pushes me closer and closer to that first orgasm. I grind against his face as his magical tongue does its thing.

"You are so close, princess."

"Daddy Sean, please!" I beg as I feel the butt plug pop into place. Christian hooks a finger under my chin and grins at me.

"Cum, baby girl. Fall apart like I know you want to."

A scream leaves my throat as the orgasm takes over my whole body. I can feel my ass tightening around the butt plug as my pussy clamps around Sean's fingers.

"Fuck, princess," Sean gasps as he licks me again, and my body quivers over him.

"Daddy, stop please," I beg as my body becomes over-stimulated, and the slightest touch of his tongue is enough to make me shake. I hear Sean chuckle as I lift off him. I move slightly and groan as the feel of the butt plug just stimulates me further.

"Shorty, we are far from finished with you yet," Maximus gloats as he stands behind me. I can see his hard cock behind me, and I realise how much I want and need it.

I look at Christian, who is grinning at me, his cock hard in his hand. He moves and climbs off the bed before leaning in to kiss me.

"Baby girl, you were the most beautiful woman I have ever laid eyes on tonight. How I managed to stop myself from fucking you in front of everyone there in that arena, I will never know. But it was worth the wait to see what my brothers are about to do to you." Christian kisses me again as I feel the last of the effects of the orgasm leave my body wanting more. He stands up and looks at me as he cups my face. His blue eyes not leaving mine as he grins.

"Sean, you know what to do."

Sean's grip on my hips tightens as he pulls me down hard on his cock, which slams straight into me.

"Fuck!" we curse together as he fills me.

"Maximus, you heard our girl swear, give her five as you fuck her ass," Christian calls as he winks at me. I'm gasping for breath as Sean grows even bigger inside of me. Pressing against my walls and the butt plug, which is still situated deep in my back passage.

"Daddy, that's not fair." I don't know why I'm protesting; I want Maximus to spank me.

"Princess, I can feel your pussy contracting around me. You love being spanked, you brat," Sean gasps as I grind against him. He's not wrong; the thought of Maximus spanking me as his dick thrusts into my ass is -

"Yes!" I cry out as I orgasm again whilst riding Sean's dick.

"Fuck!" he curses underneath me as he grips my hips and holds me in place for a moment. "Guys, you need to get in on this. Our girl's going wild!" he calls through gritted teeth as he holds me still whilst I gasp for breath.

I can feel people moving around me, but my eyes are shut fast as I try to ride through my orgasm without moving again. Every time I move even the smallest amount, the butt plug and Sean rub those spots in me, and I quickly head towards another. I don't know how the hell I'm going to take all three of my daddies and not fall apart in moments.

I feel a hand cup my face and know instantly it's Jason.

"Open your eyes, Jazzy." I do and find him grinning at me. "Are you up to this? Is it too much?"

I go to shake my head but quickly stop myself.

"I'm okay. I need you all," I gasp as the smile on Jason's face widens and his eyes turn a darker shade of grey.

"Thank fuck, because I need your pretty mouth around my cock, now!" he growls. I grin as I lean forward until my hands are on the mattress on either side of Sean's head. I look down at him for a moment and smile.

"Fuck you are killing me here, princess," he groans as I press my lips to his.

"Are you okay?" I ask playfully. Sean winks at me with a grin.

"Never been fucking better."

I find myself giggling as I kiss him a little harder before looking behind me, where I know Maximus is already between my legs.

"Shorty, I'm so ready to bury myself in you," he growls. I look back to Jason, who is kneeling with his cock in his hand. He reaches up and threads his fingers into my hair, tightening his grip before pushing his cock into my mouth.

"Fuck!" Jason curses as I use my tongue around the tip before taking him further into my mouth. "Christian's right. That mouth of yours is getting naughtier," he growls as I start bobbing on his thick cock. I love giving head; it turns me on as much as receiving it.

As I start grinding myself against Sean when I feel Maximus kneading my ass cheeks.

"You don't need to count," is all the warning I get before his hand lands on my skin. I groan as my eyes roll back.

"Fuck," Jason and Sean both curse together, and I know I tightened around them both. I can feel Maximus toying with the outside of the butt plug and I push slightly to help him to discard it. I'm so sensitive I almost come from him removing it alone. As soon as it's removed, Maximus spanks me for a second time.

"Stay still, Shorty," Maximus warns behind me, and I feel Sean's hold on my hips tighten as he holds me in place. Jason pulls his cock out of my mouth as he tips my head up to look at him.

"Use your words, angel," he whispers as Maximus pushes into me. I gasp as he fills my behind as Sean fills my pussy.

"Fuck, I can feel that, Maximus!" Sean growls through gritted teeth as I hiss from the slight pain; it's no more than when any of us participate in anal play.

"You, okay?" Jason asks as I nod slightly.

"It's okay," I gasp as I feel another orgasm building.

"Fuck princess, you're insatiable," Sean growls underneath me.

"Please let me move," I beg as Maximus fills me further.

"Slowly, Shorty, don't move too fast," Maximus groans behind me. It sounds like he's struggling to hold it together, which turns me on even more.

It takes a few moments, but soon Sean, Maximus and I get into the perfect rhythm, which means we all get the right amount of movement, and it doesn't hurt. I'm just taking Jason back in my mouth when Maximus spanks me again.

"Ahhh," I cry out as I nearly cum again.

"Fuck you are so tight, Shorty," Maximus growls through gritted teeth as Jason starts fucking my face a little harder.

"Two more, Maximus."

I look at the sound of Christian's voice and see he has moved the chair away from the window. He is sitting in it, still naked and stroking his hard cock. His eyes burn into mine as Maximus's hand lands against my ass again, and my eyes close as I moan.

"Eyes on me, baby girl."

My eyes shoot open at his command.

"Keep those eyes on me." I can't miss the warning in his voice and do as I'm told as Jason, Maximus, and Sean fuck me in perfect sync.

The whole time, Christian's eyes burn into mine, and he looks to where his brothers are pounding into me. The sight of him sitting there stroking his hard cock is more of a turn-on than I thought it would be.

I can feel myself quickly heading towards another orgasm, and I don't know if I will be able to handle another after this one. My body is close to being spent. I've lost count of how many times my daddies have made me cum tonight, and the thought of more than one more is enough to bring tears to my eyes.

"One more, Maximus," Christian orders, and I know when his hand lands against my ass, I will cum harder than I ever have.

"Last one, Shorty." I can hear the promise in his voice before his hand comes down on my ass. I scream around Jason's cock as my whole body comes alive with the orgasm that rocks through me.

I hear both the twins call out at the same time as I feel my pussy and ass clamp around them. I know they both instantly cum within me, and I can feel their warmth inside of me as I spasm around them.

"Fuck, get ready, angel." I manage to just register what Jason means before I feel him swelling in my mouth and exploding down my throat. I quickly swallow his load down, and again as he fills my mouth a second, then a third time. He is just pulling out of my mouth as Christian approaches the bed, and I know exactly what he's going to do. I turn my head and take him in my mouth. I only just take him in time for him to explode down my throat.

"Fuck!" he growls as he squirts ropes of warm cum straight down my throat. I have no idea how I manage to swallow it all, but I do.

As he pulls his dick out of my mouth, I feel my eyes closing from exhaustion. Maximus removes himself from my back end, and I hiss slightly from the discomfort.

Christian moves so he is beside me. My arms and legs are starting to shake from holding myself up over Sean. Christian places a hand on my shoulder and hip.

"Roll onto my arms, baby girl. I've got you."

I ignore him and move to the bottom of the bed. But as I climb off, my legs go from underneath me.

"Fuck," Jason curses as he only just catches me before I hit the floor.

"I'm okay; I tripped," I say as I lean against him, as he lifts me. I feel another set of arms take me from him, and curl up into Christian's arms.

"Maximus's getting the washcloth and towel. Then Sean, help him to bed," he orders as he sits in the chair and holds me against him.

"I want you all with me," I whisper, but I feel Christian shake his head as he kisses my hair.

"Maximus needs more space with his injuries. He will go to his room, take some painkillers, and probably pass out."

I look up from Christian's chest as Maximus comes up beside us.

"I love you, Shorty, and will see you in the morning," he whispers as Christian sits up slightly so Maximus can kiss the top of my head without leaning down too far.

"I love you, Daddy. Sorry if I hurt you more," I reply, looking at his face, which looks more bruised than before. Maximus smiles at me.

"That was worth every ounce of pain, Shorty."

I watch as Sean steps forward and presses a kiss to my forehead.

"Get some sleep. I'm going to sleep in my room so I can hear Maximus if he needs anything. Love you, princess."

I whisper a 'love you' before watching the twins walk out of the room as Jason turns the covers back on the bed and lays down a towel.

"Put her down here."

Christian lifts me with ease and moves me to the bed, where he places me on the towel and holds me as Jason cleans between my legs and sensitive back passage.

Whilst he dries me off and removes the towel from underneath me, Christian helps me to take some painkillers and drink some water.

"You are amazing, do you know that sweetheart?" he whispers into my hair as I lean against his chest. I feel Jason climb into the bed behind me as the lights go off.

"I will second that. You were so brave tonight in the arena and out of this world when we got home. You have no idea how loved you are, angel," Jason says as he kisses my shoulder and puts an arm around my waist.

"Everything I am, is because of my four amazing Daddies," I reply as my eyes close. "I love you all," I whisper as exhaustion takes me.

I wake a few hours later to Christian and Jason, both snoring softly beside me. I look at them both in the early morning light and smile, remembering the way the night ended.

I slowly lift my head as I hear a soft moaning coming from outside my room. I climb off the bed, trying not to wake the guys and head out onto the landing. It's there, and I realise the moaning is coming from Maximus's room. I head straight down to him to find him groaning in his sleep. I look at the time and know he won't be able to take more painkillers yet. Instead, I climb into bed with him and run my hand over his head as I place my other hand in his. Maximus instantly starts to settle. He lets out one slow moan, and my heart breaks knowing he's in pain.

"Shorty?" Maximus turns his head and looks at me. "What's the matter? Are you okay?" he asks as he lifts my hand and kisses the knuckles.

"You were moaning in your sleep, Daddy," I whisper, pressing a soft kiss to his cheek. "I hate not being able to help you when you are in pain. Is there anything I can do?" I ask. I see the corner of Maximus's mouth lift slightly.

"You being here is more than enough," he replies before pressing a kiss to my forehead. "Go to sleep, Shorty."

"Night, Daddy," I whisper as I relax, my head resting on his shoulder. He leans his head against mine, and we both quickly fall back to sleep.

Chapter Thirteen

JASON

I walk into the sitting room and see Christian on one of the sofas.

"Penny for your thoughts?"

Christian ignores me and continues to stare into space, spinning his phone in his hand, a million miles away. I know this look; he's fighting with his demons.

As much as he likes to pretend the choices he's made in his life don't affect him, they do. There are days he disappears into his own head and all we can do is give him space when he asks for it. The fact that he isn't hiding in his own office tells me that today, space isn't what he wants.

I don't say anything else to him. I head to the bar and pour two glasses of whiskey before placing one in front of him, and then I take a seat. Christian looks at me like I was the last person he expected to see.

"When did you get home?"

I watch as he picks up his glass and examines it for a moment before taking a sip.

"Just now. Where is everyone?" It's quiet which tells me they are either out or Jasmine is keeping them busy.

"Jasmine's in her studio, and Maximus and Sean are training. I'm sure they will all be up soon enough." With it only being two weeks since Maximus's fight, he shouldn't be training for more than an hour every couple of days. Christian looks at his phone and turns it upside down as if hiding from whatever is on it.

"Everything okay?" I ask sitting back and taking a sip of my drink. Christian nods, but there is no conviction in it. "Try that again, but this time don't lie to me."

Christian looks up and sighs.

"It's nothing. Someone is trying to get to me, and right now they are succeeding."

"Do I need to keep an eye out for trouble?" I ask, but Christian shakes his head.

"No, it's all past shit they are throwing at me, dating right back to that Grant guy."

"Your first kill?" I ask, frowning. "How would anyone know about that? Tommy and I never mentioned it again, and Hardy, who made you do it, is dead," I continue, but looking at Christian's face I'm just saying shit he already knows.

"I don't know, they just keep asking what Jasmine would say if she knew the truth about me. How do I sleep at night knowing I destroyed a family? Why should I get to move on when his family is still struggling? I would think they were trying to blackmail me, but they aren't doing anything but taunting me with old shit." I watch as he downs his drink and lets out a deep sigh.

"Did you ever find out anything about them?" I ask. This is why Christian never kills someone with a family; that first time he had no choice, but he knew he was making a child fatherless. He swore he would never do that again unless that child were better off without the parent, and he hasn't.

"I just sent a couple of letters and then a large check, pretending to be him, as you know. I sent a second check, but it never got cashed. When I checked, they had moved as I had suggested."

I know it took Christian a long time to get over that kill. It's like a part of him died with the guy. He was given no choice but to kill him, it was him or me. The guy even told Christian to do it to protect me and his child, which made it harder on Christian.

"Do you think they will use Jasmine to get to you?" I know he would never allow any harm to come to that woman; he would die before someone hurt her to get to him.

"I don't know, so I have given her security a heads up. They will be keeping a closer eye on her when she isn't with us."

Christian stands up and heads to the bar. I hold out my glass for him to give me a top-up when a deep yell sounds through the house.

"What the fuck?" I jump to my feet as a laughing Jasmine rushes into the room and runs to Christian.

"Hide me!"

Seconds later, Maximus storms into the room, dripping with water and with a wicked smirk on his face. Jasmine and I burst out laughing as he points at our girl.

"Come here now, brat."

Jasmine hides behind Christian, shaking her head.

"Daddy, save me," she begs as Maximus takes a step

forward. I see Sean standing behind him, smiling as he watches the two of them.

"What did you do?" Christian sighs as he looks at Jasmine, who stares up at him like butter wouldn't melt.

"Daddy Max said he was hot, so I cooled him down," she answers innocently.

"By spraying a bottle of water in my face!" Maximus adds.

"But it cooled you down!" Jasmine points out as I burst out laughing. Christian turns and looks at her, shaking his head.

"You really expect me to save you when you bring it on yourself?" he asks her with arched brows.

"Yes! You always save me!" she protests.

"Not this time. Maximus, she's all yours," he announces, smiling as he moves out of the way. Jasmine screams as she tries to run, but Maximus manages to grab her and throw her over his shoulder before marching out of the room.

"Daddy, you traitor!" Jasmine shouts, pointing at Christian, who is smiling at her. I laugh, and her focus snaps at me.

"You are just as bad!" she yells, now pointing at me.

"Don't do the crime if you can't do the time, Jazzy!" I yell as Maximus carries her away. The rest of us stay in the room laughing as we hear Jasmine's protests getting quieter as he carries her through the house, probably to his room.

"Well, I don't expect to see them for the rest of the night," Sean laughs as he walks out, shaking his head. "I'm going for a shower, then to bed. Shout if I'm needed for anything," he calls disappearing.

I look back to Christian, who's still grinning, looking at the open door.

"No matter what we've done in the past, just think that

we now have that woman in our lives making the darkest days brighter."

Christian looks at me and nods before looking to the door again.

"You aren't wrong there. I will kill anyone who ever tries to put out the light in her."

Chapter Fourteen

JASMINE

"Okay, dancers, back to starting positions, please."

I rush to the side of the stage and get ready.

"I want a flawless performance this time. No heavy feet, slack arms. Hold those heads high," I hear Mrs Florence call from where she's standing, watching us all.

"Easy for her to say. She hasn't been practising non-stop for two hours," someone mutters behind me, and I have to stop myself from chuckling aloud. They aren't wrong. Every bone and muscle in my body aches.

"Ready! And go!" I hear the music begin and make my way onto the stage following my fellow dancers; my head held high, my arms perfect in front of me as we start to move and dance as practised over and over again.

I put everything into the dance; I perform as if in front of an audience. My jumps are perfect, as are my landings. I'm confident this is my best performance today. That is until a large bang comes over the music, and we hear Mrs Florence shout.

"Stop! Stop! Stop!"

We all turn to look at her, wondering what's happening when I see Layton charging towards the stage from the back of the hall.

"Jasmine, you need to come with me now!" he orders. I can see his hand on his hip where his gun is hidden.

"Excuse me! We are in the middle of a rehearsal!" Mrs Florence calls out as she stares at Layton. Layton stops in front of her and points to me.

"I don't give a shit. If I say Miss Connors needs to come with me, she is. The principal knows the score, so take it up with him!" Layton snaps before turning to look at me.

"Move it now!" he growls as I rush towards him. Once at the front of the stage, he takes my hand to help me jump down. "Where's your bag?" he demands. I point to the back of the hall where all our coats and bags are hanging up. "Get it and let's go!" he places a hand on my back, rushing me along.

I rush towards my bag, knowing that something must be seriously wrong. I can hear people talking on the stage and know that this gossip is going to spread like wildfire.

"What's going on?" I ask as I find my bag and jumper. Layton doesn't give me time to put either of them on; he grabs them and then rushes me towards the door. He is on edge, looking around, and his hand hasn't left his gun.

"No idea, I was just told to get you now!" he growls under his breath as he looks out of the door before rushing me out. He rushes me through the school to the back entrance, where I can see the car is parked right by the door.

"When we get outside, keep your head down and head straight for the car; it's unlocked. Get in and lie down in the back," he commands. I turn and look at him wide-eyed.

"What the fuck is going on?" I demand again.

"I told you I don't know; just do as you are told," he snaps as he opens the door, looks around and grabs me. Layton drags me outside, and I keep my head down until we get to the car. Layton throws open the door, and I jump in before he slams it shut. I stay down as he asked until I hear the driver's door open, and Layton jumps in, slamming the door behind him. He doesn't even put his seatbelt on before speeding away from the school.

"Sit up and put your seatbelt on, Jasmine," Layton orders. I quickly do as I'm told.

My whole body shakes as I try desperately not to cry. Has something happened to one of the guys? Is someone hurt or worse? So many different things running through my head that I can't catch my breath as the panic starts to take hold. I see Layton connecting his phone to the car before calling Terry.

"I've got her. We are heading back to the house."

"You have her? It's definitely, Jasmine?" Terry demands. I can see Layton frowning at the dashboard before looking at me in the rearview mirror.

"Yes, it's her! Unless she has a twin I'm not aware of."

I hear a short commotion on the other end of the phone before Maximus's voice rings out.

"Shorty? Are you hurt?"

"I'm fine! What's going on?" I ask as my voice trembles. I hear Maximus let out a deep breath before yelling.

"If she's there, then who the fuck is in this picture being held hostage?"

We pull up outside the house where Terry and Jason are

standing, waiting for us. Jason opens my door and helps me out before pulling me into his arms.

"What's going on?" I ask as he walks me into the house with his arm wrapped around my shoulders.

"We don't know, Jazzy. But we are going to find out."

Jason leads me into the house and to the sitting room, where Maximus and Sean are both pacing around. As soon as we enter, both turn towards me, and the look on their face is one of pure relief.

"Is she there?" I hear Christian's voice and realise he is looking through the computer screen.

Maximus rushes and sweeps me up in a bear hug, burying his face into my neck as I wrap my arms around him.

"Thank fuck you are okay," he growls against me. I can hear Jason somewhere in the room talking to Christian, reassuring him that I'm there, but I can't move from Maximus, who is still clinging to me like a lifebuoy. It's as if he's scared to let me go.

"Maximus, let the poor girl breathe," Sean sighs as he stands beside us and places a hand on his twin's arm. Maximus lets me go, and Sean pulls me straight to him.

"You okay, princess?" he asks, kissing my cheek before stepping back. I nod as I feel Maximus's hand on my back leading me towards the sofas. I go to sit down, but Maximus pulls me to him and forces me to sit on his lap. I instantly curl into him as he wraps his arms around me.

"Baby girl, are you okay?" I turn and look at the laptop screen and see Christian looking pale.

"What happened?" I ask as I look around at my four daddies. Maximus's hold tightens on me as he places a kiss on the top of my head.

"I received a message with a picture attached to it. It

was a girl with long brown hair tied up; it looked just like you, sweetheart. I could even see your birthmark."

I pull away from Maximus and frown at the computer screen.

"But why? What would be the point in sending a fake picture like that?"

"We don't know anything other than the person wanted to get Christian worked up," Sean says as he sits on the other sofa.

"How is it even possible for someone to look like me and have the same birthmark?"

"That's what we would like to know," Christian says through the screen. He has been away from home for three days, seeing to some business. Something about damage to one of their clubs, but they haven't told me the ins and outs, so I haven't asked.

"Are you coming home tonight?" I ask as I look at the screen. Christian shakes his head before sitting back in his seat.

"No, sorry, baby girl. I need to stay here another night. I would do anything to come home, though." I look at his face and know he's telling the truth. He will hate being away whilst something is going on. "How many people know about your birthmark?" he asks as he takes a sip of his bottled water.

I shake my head as I shrug.

"It's not like I've hidden it. You can see it whenever I wear strap tops," I point out. Christian nods as he runs a hand over his face.

"The fact that they made sure to pick someone with similar features and a birthmark on the right shoulder tells me the person who sent it knows you well, or they have been watching you."

My body starts to shake again at the thought of being watched.

"Is the girl in danger? Have they taken her thinking it was me? Or is it staged?" I ask, praying it's not a case of mistaken identity. The thought of someone else being harmed just because they look like me makes me feel sick to my stomach.

"There's no way to tell, angel. Terry is going over the photo now, but it's not of great quality. It's like it's taken on an old phone," Jason answers.

"What if it's someone they think is me? You can't leave her to get hurt!" I curl back up into Maximus's arms and rest against his chest.

"We won't; if we can get to her, we will. The chances are they know it's not you, and it's staged to try and scare us," Christian says before letting out a deep breath. I bury my face into Maximus's top as a sob leaves my chest.

"Oh, Shorty, don't cry," Maximus sighs as he holds me to him.

"Is she crying?" I hear Christian asks. There is a hint of anger in his voice. Maximus nods his head before kissing my hair.

"Fuck this shit, I'm coming home!" Christian declares. I can hear the others telling him he needs to stay there, but he starts shouting.

"If the fire officers need me, they have my number, or they can email me. I'm not staying here when she is so scared she's fucking crying! I'm coming home, and we are going to find out what the fuck is going on!"

I sit up, move out of Maximus's arms and kneel on the floor, turning the laptop so Christian can see me.

"I'm okay, Daddy, stay there. I'm just being silly." As

much as I want him home, I know he would only be away if he were really needed.

"Baby, say the word, and I will get in the car now and be home in four hours. I don't give a shit about the crap here; I only care about you."

I look into his eyes and force a small smile.

"I have three Daddies here to keep me safe. I'm okay, do what you need to do and come home tomorrow if you can. But don't come home just because I'm being stupid."

"You are not being stupid, baby girl. You have every right to be scared and upset. I swear to you, when I find out who it is that sent that picture, they will pay," he promises, and I nod, as I don't doubt in my mind that he will always defend me.

"I know, Daddy. Go and do what you need to do and call me when you are free next. I miss you."

Christian smiles at me as his eyes lighten a little.

"I miss you too, baby girl. I'll phone you all in a bit. If anything comes to light, message me, and I will call you all back."

Jason turns the laptop around and starts talking to him. I climb back onto Maximus's lap and curl up against him.

"That was kind of you, Shorty. But I know you wish he were coming home," Maximus points out as he runs a hand over my head and whispers into my ear.

"If he rushes the trip, he will have to go back there later. He should have everything sorted before coming home," I answer before looking up at him. "Can you show me the picture, please?" Maximus nods and goes to get his phone out of his pocket when there is a knock at the door. We all turn to look at it as Jason calls out for them to enter.

Terry walks in with Layton behind him.

"I have done all I can on the picture, and as far as I am

aware, it is genuine. The girl in it could be Jasmine. The features are a perfect match, and the birthmark too." He looks at me and offers me a small smile. "I'm sorry, Jasmine, but unless Layton's right and you have a twin we are not aware of, or you have been tied to a chair before, I am stumped to find a reasonable explanation." I feel Maximus's arms tighten around me again as I sit up.

"Tied to a chair?"

Terry nods at me, and a distant memory resurfaces.

"Show me the picture."

Terry hands me a tablet, and I look at the photo on it. I find myself relaxing as I let out a deep sigh. "It's me. It was taken for a drama project two years ago."

"What?" I hear numerous people ask at the same time.

"Who had access to this picture, Jazzy?" Jason asks as he leans forward. I look at him and shrug.

"Anyone who knew what college I went to. It was on their website the last time I looked. Jason takes the tablet from me and starts tapping on the screen. He lets out a sigh as he turns it around and shows us the picture on the website.

"I'm sorry. If you had said to start with that they were tied to a chair, I would have realised sooner."

"Don't apologise, baby girl. This isn't your fault. At least we know no one has been mistaken as you. Whoever sent it to me wanted me to feel what I did," Christian says from the computer. He lets out a deep breath and rubs his face again. "I need to go; keep me posted if you find out who sent it. At least we can relax whilst Jasmine's at home." We all agree and start to relax a little until Christian points out something we may be missing.

"I want her security doubled until we know more. This could be a warning of what's to come."

Chapter Fifteen

JASMINE

I walk out of my classroom and head straight for the coffee shop. My phone to my ear as Layton falls into step beside me. I manage a quick smile before my call connects.

"Hey, Jazzy. Are you okay?" Jason answers after only two rings.

"Not really, I'm exhausted," I sigh, pouting as I reposition my bag.

"I'm sorry, angel. You've been working so hard I'm not surprised you're feeling burnt out."

I haven't stopped in the three weeks since Christian received that photo. Between exams, essays and rehearsals for the next production, I just don't seem to get a minute to stop and breathe.

Last night, Sean found me sitting against the wall of my studio, fast asleep. I vaguely remember him carrying me to my room. When I woke up this morning, I was curled up in bed, still in my dance clothes and alone.

"I know. I just want to go home and sleep until next week." I sigh, my eyes burning as I blink back the tears.

What is wrong with me today? I feel like I could burst into tears at any moment.

"Don't forget you have that extra lesson in the morning. But after that, I will personally wait on you hand and foot until you feel refreshed."

I feel myself deflating further as I walk into the café. The last thing I want to do tomorrow is dance.

"Can I not cancel it this one time?" I ask, hopeful he will take pity on me. But I hear Jason laugh, and I know what he's going to say.

"You need to go to the daddy who booked it to do that. He's more likely to let you if *you* ask him."

I know he's right, but it still doesn't stop me from wanting to throw a tantrum. The likelihood of Christian letting me cancel is as slim as him letting me move back into my old flat. It isn't going to happen. I spot my friend Verity and wave to her.

"I have to go; I'll speak to him when I get home later after rehearsals. Hopefully, he'll take pity on me," I sigh. I say a quick goodbye to Jason and head over to where Verity is sitting, waving at the two cups in front of her.

"I'll get a coffee and do a quick walk around whilst you are here," Layton mutters under his breath before walking away. It's been weird having him with me all the time whilst in school, but after the other week, I'm just glad Christian isn't insisting that Layton is by my side every second of the day.

As soon as I reach Verity, the smile on her face drops.

"Jaz, are you okay? You're looking a little pale." Great, I look how I feel.

"I'm fine. I think *you know what* is around the corner, and it's leaving me feeling drained," I sigh as I rub my aching back. It would probably explain why I'm feeling emotional as well.

"Oh no! If you can't make class let me know, and I will send all the notes to you," she offers as she gives me a reassuring smile.

"Thanks, I appreciate it. Hopefully, it won't be too bad though, and I'll be able to handle it with pain relief," I reply as I take a sip of my drink. I find myself looking around the café.

I haven't been able to relax properly since Christian was sent that picture. I know I'm probably being paranoid, but I constantly feel like I'm being watched and not by Layton or whoever else is on duty. I pull out my phone and check for any messages. Other than one from Maximus telling me he's home if I need anything, there is nothing.

Most nights this week, only one or two of the guys have been home by the time I have gone to bed. There have been several venues targeted by vandals or competition, and the guys aren't happy. I know they have found some of the people responsible for the damage, and I'm pretty sure none of them are still breathing.

Jason assures me this happens now and again. He explained that occasionally, people like to test to see if they can overpower the brothers and take what they have built as their own. I pity anyone who gets on the wrong side of the O'Reillys. It's not a place even I would want to find myself. I know there is probably more going on than I'm aware of, but the guys all assure me I couldn't be safer, and I believe them.

"I'm just going to pop to the toilet, and then we can head to the rehearsal studio."

I look up to Verity and nod, smiling.

"No worries, it gives me time to finish my coffee," I

reply as she gets up and walks out of the café. I quickly pick up my phone and let Layton know we are leaving in a minute and which studio we have booked for the next two hours. Layton replies instantly that he will be here in a minute and to wait for him.

I take another sip of my drink and freeze when out of the corner of my eye, I spot someone staring at me. I put my coffee cup back down and look at them as I see them walking into the coffee shop and heading to the sofas at the other end of the café. As they pass, they smile at me and carry on walking.

"Jaz, are you ready?"

I snap back to look at Verity, who has returned and is picking up her bag. I turn back to where the guy has gone, but I can't see him anywhere. I turn around to ask her to wait for Layton when I spot him standing by the door. He gives me a nod and I know it's safe for me to leave.

"Yeah, come on, let's get out of here," I reply as I look around again for the guy, but he seems to have disappeared.

"I may have to shoot a little early as my boyfriend wants to hang out for a bit. You don't mind, do you?" Verity asks as I look at her and smile. Feeling a little unsettled, we head towards Layton, who smiles at Verity as he joins us.

As soon as he is beside me, I see the frown on his face.

"What's the matter? You look on edge. Did something happen whilst I was gone?"

I consider telling him for a moment about the guy but decide against it. It could have just been another teacher I don't recognise. I think Christian's paranoia is rubbing off on me. I'm perfectly safe here after all.

"No, I'm fine. Just tired," I tell him before forcing a smile. I can tell from his face he isn't buying it, but I also know he won't fight me until he has a good reason to.

Layton, Verity and I all head to the studio and Layton heads in to do a quick search of the room before we enter.

"It must be so weird having someone watching every little thing you do," Verity says as we hang our bags up at the back of the room.

"Keep the door closed and locked. I will be back in an hour to check on you. If anything happens-"

"Press my panic alarm," I interrupt him, having heard the lecture three times a day, at least, for three weeks. He gives me a look, and I smile. "I know the drill and I know that I need to be careful." Layton looks at me for a moment and nods before leaving the room, and I quickly lock it behind him.

"To answer your question," I say, turning around and looking at my friend. "It is annoying as hell. I wish I could spend just half a day without feeling like I'm being watched or having to wait whilst he checks every single room I walk into once I leave the house," I sigh, dropping to the floor and starting to put on my pointe shoes. "I'm tired of it all."

I realise that's the first time I have ever admitted that out loud. I get why the guys are worried. Christ, I am a little, too, after that picture was sent. What if it was a warning that someone plans to take me? The best way to hurt the O'Reillys is to hurt one of them or me. Let's face it: it will be easier to get to me than it would be to any of them.

I take a deep breath and look up at Verity before forcing a smile. I refuse to be scared, and I refuse to think the worst. I want to just forget about it all, and I can achieve that while I dance.

"Come on. Let's get this routine choreographed."

We've only been practising for an hour and a half. Layton returned, saw we were okay and promised to return in an hour.

"I'm done, I don't think I can do anything else. Mind if I leave and go to see my boyfriend?" Verity asks as we lean against the wall, taking a drink break.

"Not at all. I think I might head off a little early. My back and stomach are starting to hurt." We have also been using Verity's phone for the music as the music player is broken. "I might just go through it one more time using my ear pods before leaving," I add as I pull my headphones out of my bag and connect them to my phone.

I walk back into the middle of the room and test out the range for my headphones whilst Verity changes her shoes and chucks everything in her bag.

"I'm going. Don't forget to lock the door," she calls as she walks out. I give her a thumbs up and continue to play about with the music until I find the track I want. Placing my phone back in my bag, I head to my starting position. Closing my eyes, I take a deep breath, trying to ignore the way my stomach and backache and start to dance. I quickly realise I haven't locked the door but decide I will do it when I have finished this routine.

I regret that decision when, halfway through, I catch movement out of the corner of my eye. I stop to turn around, but an arm wraps around my waist, and I feel something sharp press against my throat.

"Move, and I'll slit you ear to ear," A deep cockney voice growls. I freeze with fear. "Glad to see you can follow instructions," he adds as his hold on me tightens.

"What do you want? I don't have anything on me." Every word causes the knife to scrape against my throat, and it stings.

"The boss wants you to pass on a message to the O'Reillys," he says as his breath flows over my ear, and I want to pull away from the smell of cigarettes and coffee.

"What message?"

I feel the sharp side of the blade glide across my throat before I feel it slide down my side a little harder as it grazes against the material of my leotard and cuts through it effortlessly. My mind is in overdrive; it wants to run and hide and get help, but I'm frozen to the spot, knowing that if I fight, I'm more likely to get seriously hurt or killed. Why the fuck didn't I lock the fucking door?

"Tell those four losers that they need to stop hiding their father. If they know what's good for them, they'll pay my boss what he's owed. It's time for them to watch their whole empire crumble." I feel the knife dig further into my side and have to stop myself from crying out in pain.

"They have three days to pay up, or next time you and I meet, I won't be so gentle." I feel his hand slide down my stomach and grope between my legs. "The boss's guys and I will take great pleasure using this over and over again. We will fuck you so hard that by the time we send you back to them, they won't know what end to fuck and what end to feed!" he growls as a sob escapes my chest as his grip on my pussy tightens to the point it hurts.

"Please, they don't know where Tommy is! They've cut him off!" I plead as he spins me around and grabs my face before pushing me backwards and slamming me into the wall with such force; I swear I see stars for a moment as I hear my head or the mirror crack.

"Bullshit! If they want to find him, they can!" he growls before tightening his grip on my face and grinning at me. "You know, part of me wants them to fail just so I can hear what noise you make as I fuck you!" He forces my head back against the wall once more before letting me go and standing in front of me, grinning. His hair is shaved short, and his eyes are so dark they look black. The way he grins at me is like something from a stalker movie. I don't doubt that if he wanted to hurt me, he could.

"You know they will kill you. Do you really think they will care who you work for? You hurt me, and they will kill you, slowly," I declare as I stand tall, refusing to let him see how scared I am. But his grin just widens.

"Better make sure they see you aren't untouchable then."

I don't see it coming, he moves so fast. The back of his hand connects with my face harder than I have ever been hit, and I fly to the floor, hitting my head again as I land. My ankle is screaming as it twists. I don't have time to register what's happened before he wraps my ponytail around his hand and lifts me by it. I cry out as I feel the hair being torn from my head.

"Three days bitch. Make sure they follow through; otherwise, it's your life on the line." He throws me to the floor and storms towards the door.

"You never said who they need to pay!" I cry out, cursing myself for stopping him from leaving. He turns around and smiles. "Just tell them Hudson sends his regards; they will know." With that, he walks out of the door, pocketing his now-closed knife.

I feel my throat burning as I lift myself. I can't cry. I refuse to.

Pushing myself away from the wall I'm leaning against, I try to walk but my ankle screams underneath my weight, and I have to lean against the wall again. I look over to the other side of the room where my bag's hanging on the peg. My phone and panic alarm tucked in the side pocket. I try to walk but my ankle goes from underneath me again and I nearly fall back to the floor.

I cry out a mixture of pain and frustration. But as I try to move again, I fall to the floor, and a sob leaves my burning throat.

"Have you finished yet?"

I turn to look at Danielle as she storms into the room. She stares at me for a moment before cursing. "What the fuck happened?"

"My bag. Please." I beg as my eyes fill with tears; she looks around the room and rushes to my bag before bringing it to me. I want to cry, knowing that I can get help as soon as I have my bag. I look down at my ruined leotard; it's sliced open down one side. I quickly pull the fabric together to cover the exposed bleeding skin.

"What do you need?" Danielle asks as she drops to the floor next to me. I open my side pocket, pull out my panic alarm, and quickly activate it before falling to the side. Danielle catches me and holds me up in a seated position, and for the first time ever, I'm so grateful that she's there.

Chapter Sixteen

CHRISTIAN

It's been nearly half an hour since I received the notification that Jasmine had activated her panic alarm.

The protocol we have in place is we don't contact her security; we wait for them to contact us so they can concentrate on the situation. They are to get her to the house as quickly as possible. When they know she is safe, they make contact.

I'd been on the way to a meeting when the alarm was activated, and I instantly dropped everything to rush home. I'm now pacing by the front door as Maximus attempts to keep me calm.

"I'm sure she is fine, Christian."

I spin around and stare at him.

"Then why the fuck would she activate her alarm!"

"Fuck. I don't know! I'm trying to keep myself from going mad as well as you!" he yells back. I open my mouth to tell him to shut up when I hear a car screeching to a stop outside. We both jump and head for the front door.

Before I get to the passenger side door, where I can see Jasmine sitting, Layton jumps out of the driver's side.

"What the hell happened?" I yell as I throw open the door to find a dazed and pale Jasmine. There is dried blood down the side of her face and I can see she's holding back the tears. I reach around her to unbuckle the seatbelt and pull her into my arms.

"Hold on to me, baby girl," I whisper as I lift her out of the car.

"Keep the compress against her head; it is still bleeding," Layton calls as he reaches us.

"I want to know what the fuck happened, now!" I growl at him as I turn and head back to the house.

Jasmine is shaking in my arms, and I make an instant decision to take her to my room. That way, we are close to a bathroom to get her cleaned up.

"She was attacked whilst in a studio on her own," Layton says, falling into step beside us.

"Who the fuck was it, and how did they get anywhere near her?" Maximus yells next to me.

"It was Hudson, he knows how we work and managed to keep out of sight, striking when he knew she'd be distracted and away from her bag, and her alarm," Layton explains as we walk into my room. The whole time Jasmine leans her head against my shoulder.

As I go to place her on my bed, she shakes her head and looks up at me with pleading eyes.

"What do you need, baby girl?" I ask softly as she buries herself into my neck.

"You," is all she says, and my heart breaks. I place a kiss on the top of her head before sitting on the edge of the bed and holding her to me.

"Where was Terry?" Maximus asks as I gently pull the

compress Jasmine is holding to her head away. Underneath is an open wound that starts bleeding as soon as the pressure is removed. My anger starts to rise like a red mist. I will kill Hudson for causing her to bleed. I will count every single one of her injuries and inflict them on him, so he feels her pain before ending his life.

"He's been with Jason since ten. Neither of them has been reachable for the last hour," Layton sighs. "I had no idea anything was wrong. I had left Jasmine half an hour beforehand in a practice studio. She was locked in with Verity. Turns out Verity just left, Jasmine hadn't locked the door or let me know she was alone. I was doing the usual walk around and checking for anyone who shouldn't be there. I never saw Hudson, not until a millisecond before Jasmine activated her alarm. I couldn't follow him as she was my priority.

"When I got to the room, Jasmine was with that girl Danielle, who was helping to get her cardigan on. I saw the state of Jasmine's face and head, so I followed protocol; grab her and bring her back here and wait for further instructions."

I feel a growl escape my throat before leaning back a little, trying to get a look at Jasmine's injuries.

"Where are you hurt, sweetheart?"

She looks up at me through her lashes, but I get my first real look at her face and my anger rises further.

"Did he hit you?"

She nods and leans back against my chest, but Maximus grips her chin and stops her.

"Show me your neck."

"I'm fine," Jasmine protests, but Maximus forces her head up, and I see what he did. I stand and place her on her feet, but her leg buckles underneath her, and I have to hold her up. I look at her throat, and the red mist descends.

"Did he threaten you with a fucking knife?" I growl through gritted teeth, reminding myself repeatedly that Jasmine does not need to see me lose my shit right now.

"Yes," she answers with the smallest squeak before bursting into tears. I pull her back into my arms and hold her before placing her on the bed. As much as I want to stay there and hold her, to help her feel safe, I need to be doing something to try and get the situation under control somehow.

Where the fuck is Jason when I need him?

Jasmine

"I'm getting the doctor here now; I want this and the head injury looked at!" Christian growls as he runs his knuckles over my bruised cheek and marches to the other side of the room.

"Why didn't you show me this before?" Layton demands as I watch Christian with his phone to his ear.

"I just wanted to come home," I answer quietly. Layton opens his mouth to answer but his phone rings out to stop him. "It's Terry," he says as he answers his phone.

"Jasmine has been attacked; we're at the house," I hear him say as he walks out of the door. Maximus is standing at the side of the bed, and I can see the anger on his face. He goes to storm away from me, but I reach up and almost fall from the bed, trying to stop him. He manages to grab me before I hit the floor.

"Please don't leave me; I need you to stay," I beg as the tears continue to stream down my cheeks.

Maximus climbs onto the bed next to me and pulls me into his arms, holding me as I cry quietly. I hear his phone ring, which he answers without looking at the screen.

"What's happening? I've just seen a notification that Jaz activated her alarm," I hear Sean call frantically.

"Layton just brought her home. Hudson attacked her."

"What the fuck?" Sean roars. "Is she okay? Put her on," Maximus holds out the phone, and I take it.

"Hey, Daddy." I instantly hear the change in his voice.

"Princess, what happened? Are you hurt?" he asks.

"I'm okay," I instantly lie, not wanting to panic him. Maximus looks at me and takes the phone back.

"She's lying. He has taken a sharp knife to her throat. She also has a split lip and head wound and can't bare weight on one foot," Maximus growls through gritted teeth as Sean yells on the other end of the line about how he's going to kill him.

"Tell Sean to get back home. I want everyone here before any retaliation is dished out," Christian orders as he looks at Maximus. "Stay with her, and I'll be back. The doctor will get here in ten minutes. I want you to tell him exactly where you are injured, and when he's gone, I want to know what was said!" Christian leans over and kisses me on the forehead. "No one hurts you and lives to see another day," he growls before storming out of the room.

Chapter Seventeen

JASMINE

I hiss as water touches the thin cut across my throat.

"Sorry, Shorty," Maximus whispers as he moves the sponge away from my neck and starts washing my shoulders.

The doctor arrived ten minutes after Christian left. He checked over my injuries and confirmed the worst was the head injury from hitting the mirror. He cleaned and glued it and gave me strict instructions to keep it dry for five days.

When the doctor left, Maximus brought me to my bathroom, where Mrs Brown had run me a deep bath, as I couldn't have a shower with my glued head. I lean back in the bath as Maximus washes my side and catches the thin cut from where Hudson had slid a knife down over my ribs, causing me to hiss again.

"If I wasn't terrified of letting you out of my sight, I'd go and help Christian plan how to kill the bastard," Maximus growls as he throws the sponge into the sink across the bathroom.

115

"I have a feeling he won't need help," I admit as I open my eyes and look into Maximus's.

"It would make me feel like I was doing something useful," he sighs.

"You are being useful. I don't want to be alone right now," I admit. Maximus reaches up and brushes a stray section of hair off my face.

"How you feeling?" he asks for the hundredth time.

"Like if you ask me that once more, I may drown you in this bath," I sigh with my eyes closed. When I open them, I smirk at him, "I have three other Daddies who I'm sure know how to hide your body."

Maximus laughs as he stands up and heads to the side where my towels are placed. He picks one up and walks over to sit back on the stool next to the bath.

"Can I get out now? The water stings."

He nods before helping me get out and to balance on my good leg. He wraps the towel around my chest and carefully dries my neck and shoulders with another.

"You'll get blood on the white towels!" I protest, stepping away from him, but he just follows me, shaking his head.

"Mrs Brown can get blood out of anything. Trust me, she has the experience," he says, offering a small smile. He kneels in front of me and pat dries my legs. "How's your ankle feeling?"

"It hurts, but I'm sure it will be fine after some ice."

"When you couldn't stand, I thought he had broken it," Maximus says as he stands up.

"I knew it wasn't broken, just badly sprained. I may need to rest it for a couple of days, but it'll be fine."

Maximus carries me out of the bathroom and into the wardrobe, where he helps me to put on some shorts and a vest top I like to wear to bed. Christian and Sean walk in as I stand up on my good leg.

"How are you feeling, baby girl?" Christian asks as he walks over and places a hand on my bruised cheek.

"I'm okay. It's possibly a mild concussion, nothing serious," I reply, forcing a smile. Christian shakes his head and steps out of the way for Sean. As soon as he's in front of me, he pulls me into his arms, causing me to hiss in pain.

"Watch her side, you idiot," Maximus hisses as he goes to push his twin away from me, but I shake my head as I lean against Sean.

"I'm okay, I promise."

Maximus sighs, walking over to the bed and pulling back the covers.

"Why does your side hurt?" Christian asks as he lifts up the left side of my top and sees the thin cut going from my breast down to my hip. "Is that from his fucking knife?" he growls. I nod and pull down the top to hide the cut; I look up at Sean and force a smile.

"Can you help me to the bed, please?"

"What hurts, princess?" He asks as he takes my right arm.

"My ankle, it's only sprained, but hurts like a *fucking bitch*!" I curse as I put too much weight on it by mistake. I quickly look at Christian with my hand over my mouth. "Sorry, Daddy! Please let me off this one time," I beg, giving him my best puppy dog eyes. Christian shakes his head before stepping forward, scooping me up into his arms, and carrying me around the bed before placing me on it.

"I'm just going to get changed whilst these two are here with you. Try to behave for the next ten minutes, will you?" Maximus says, grinning at me.

"I'll try," I reply, sticking my tongue out. The three of them roll their eyes as Maximus walks out of the room.

Sean climbs on the bed and pulls me into his arms so we are both sat up, leaning against the headboard. I lean back into him, resting my head against his shoulder.

"What did the doctor say?" Christian asks as he starts rubbing some pain relief gel into my ankle. I moan as he presses a little too hard. I wait for Christian to tell me to stop making a fuss, but instead, he looks at me with sad eyes and whispers a sorry.

"He's glued my head, and I have to keep it dry for five days at least. Other than cuts and grazes, I'm fine.

"My ankle's going to hurt for a few days, but if I rest and ice it, it'll heal quickly," I explain before looking at Christian and biting my bottom lip. "Can I cancel my extra lesson in the morning, please?" I ask quietly. Christian leans over and presses a kiss to my head gently.

"Already done it, and you aren't going to class until at least Wednesday. I have sent an email explaining what happened," he says as I relax further into Sean's arms.

"Thank you, Daddy." I look up into his eyes as I feel mine filling with tears.

Suddenly, the door flies open, and Jason rushes in. I don't even see Christian move. One moment, he is holding my hand; the next, he has Jason pinned up against the wall.

"Where the fuck have you been?"

"I had my phone off, and I was busy!" Jason yells at him. "You knew what I was doing; you know I would never have my phone on in that location; I couldn't risk it!"

"He targeted her because of you!" Christian yells at Jason, whose face drops.

"Let go of him, please!" I beg as I start to climb off the bed, but Sean stops me. "It wasn't his fault!" I yell. They both turn to look at me; Jason's eyes widen as his eyes fall on my face. Christian lets go of him, and he stands for a second, watching me before closing the gap between us and sitting on the bed.

"Where are you hurt, Jazzy?" Jason asks as he gently brushes some hair from my face, revealing the bruise on my cheek; he then looks down at my swollen ankle. "Anywhere else?"

"Show him your neck," Christian demands behind him. I shake my head but hiss from the movement.

"Jasmine, show him," Christian commands, and I look at Jason before lifting my head to expose the cut.

"We all know how much he likes to slit throats!" Christian growls as Jason just stares at my throat. I can see the pain in his eyes and that he blames himself.

"Angel, I'm so sorry," Jason starts, but I stop him and cup his cheek.

"None of this was your fault. This was about Tommy, not you," I start but quickly realise it was the wrong thing to say.

"What the hell has Tommy got to do with this?" Sean demands as Maximus walks into the room. Jason wipes his thumb against my cheek to dry my tears.

"That guy, Hudson, said that I was to tell you to stop hiding your father and that his boss wanted the money owed to him," I reply. "This wasn't any of your faults; it was your father's. He's the one they are after," I explain as I look at Maximus and Christian, who are both looking at each other.

"Maximus, go to my office and call the guys. I want everyone here in two hours," Christian demands.

Maximus nods and goes to walk out of the room but stops and turns back.

"The doctor said to give her these if she needs pain relief, but they will make her drowsy," Maximus says, taking a packet of tablets out of his pocket and handing them to Christian before leaving the room.

Jason looks at me before speaking.

"Where else did Hudson hurt you?" I lift my top and see his face tense as he takes in the long cut that runs down my side.

"I want Tommy found and handed over, and I will be the one to deal with Hudson," Jason replies as he slowly lowers my top.

"We will discuss this downstairs whilst Jasmine rests," Christian replies. Jason looks up at me, and for a moment, I honestly think he has tears in his grey eyes. I look deep into them before smiling at him.

"I can sleep in tomorrow now. Daddy cancelled my extra lesson," I exclaim, beaming as Jason and Sean all start laughing. Christian gives me his best 'Daddy' look.

"Baby girl, I'm sure I can find another reason for you to get up early if you want me to," Christian warns. I turn my head and look at Sean through my lashes.

"Daddy Sean, can I sleep in tomorrow, please?"

Sean leans down and presses a kiss to my lips. "Yes, you can. If he tries to wake you up, I'll lock him in his office," he replies, smiling.

"Thank you, Daddy," I turn and look at Christian before sticking out my tongue. "Daddy Sean loves me."

"Be careful, little girl, or your bottom will also become sore," Christian warns.

"You can't put me over your knee; it would hurt my side," I protest quickly.

"There are other positions I could put you in before spanking you."

I quickly swallow as I start to tingle between my legs.

"Sorry, Daddy, I'll be good," I whisper as I lean into Sean more, who chuckles as he kisses the top of my head.

"That's better, now get some rest after you take these tablets." Christian hands the packet to Jason. "I'll get you some water, then you are going to sleep," he commands before walking into the bathroom.

"I don't need to sleep. I'm okay," I call out.

"You need to rest, princess. You've been through a lot," Sean says as he holds me.

"Can't I do that downstairs? I don't want to stay up here alone," I reply, looking at Christian as he walks in.

"Angel, we are going to be busy anyway. We need to organise a big meeting with some of the guys we know and sort out security; you don't want to be involved in all of that," Jason says as he takes my hand in his. I look up at Christian and find him looking at me.

"I'll stay wherever you are until everyone gets here, and then I'll leave. I don't want to be up here alone. Please, Daddy?"

Jason and Christian share a look. Christian nods and looks back at me.

"Fine, you can come downstairs, but you will lie on the sofa in my office and rest," Christian orders. I smile and nod.

"I'll be good, I promise." I sit up out of Sean's arms and move to the edge of the bed as Jason stands up.

"Can you give me a hand to walk, please?" I ask, but Jason lifts me into his arms with ease. "I need my Kindle!" I call as he starts walking to the bedroom door.

"Already got it," Sean calls, walking around from the other side of the bed. I call a thank you as Jason carries me out of the room and down the stairs to Christian's office.

Chapter Eighteen

JASMINE

I wake up in an empty office, the guys are nowhere to be seen. I must have dozed off after taking my pain relief. I slowly sit up and feel my whole body protest as all the aches and pains of my injuries remind me of their presence. I slowly stand up to test my ankle. It hurts when I put weight on it, but I know I'll at least be able to hobble on it now.

I walk to the office door and listen but hear nothing outside of it. I leave the room, planning to make my way to the kitchen, when I hear voices coming from the dining room next door. I hear Jason's voice first.

"She's asleep, but I don't know how long for."

"I don't want her left alone for long, especially with her concussion," Christian replies. I reach out for the door handle to let them know I'm awake when Sean's voice stops me.

"What are we doing here?"

"What do you mean?" Maximus's voice rings out.

"I know we all love her, but is it right to put her in

122

danger like this? Should we maybe just let her go? Let her move on and have a chance of a life away from this and us."

"You think I haven't thought about that a hundred times over the last few weeks? Even more so since I saw the state of her today. I've seriously considered buying her a house, giving her everything she needs, and promising none of us would ever darken her doorstep again.

"I'll never forget how broken she looked when the car pulled up. I must have died a thousand deaths between getting the notification she had activated her alarm and her getting home," Christian says as I hear the pain in his voice.

"Are you really suggesting we let her go?" Maximus asks.

"I don't know," Christian sighs.

"You said you would never leave me! You promised!" I yell as I storm into the room. All four guys turn to face me. None of them expected me to have been outside the door.

"Baby girl, we just …"

"Don't you 'Baby girl' me, Christian O'Reilly. You will shut up and let me speak for once," I snap as my anger gets the better of me.

Christian stands there for a second, just staring at me. I know if I give him the chance to interrupt to argue, I will lose my battle and won't say what needs to be said.

"Today fucking sucked," I quickly hold up a finger to Christian, "Don't 'watch your language' me right now, either. You can have your say after I've had mine!" I add quickly before looking at the others. I can't miss the smirks on Jason's and Maximus's faces, but I'm too pissed off to smile back.

"Today sucked, But I survived, and if you think for one moment that it scared me away from you, from us, you are fucking mistaken! I'm not going anywhere. You can kick me out and force me to move on, but I won't. You might all be able to walk away from *me*, but I know I won't be able to walk away from *you*. None of you. So, buy me a house! Kick me out! I don't give a fuck because I'll just move my shit back in and stalk your asses until you admit you were wrong. "You promised you would never leave, and I'm holding you to that promise whether you like it or not!"

I look around as they stare at me, none of them saying a word.

Christian's the first one to move, and he strides towards me. I expect him to take me over his knee for swearing. Instead, he thrusts his fingers into the hair at the back of my head and brings his mouth crashing down to mine. His tongue's in my mouth in seconds as he devours me, and I meet him with every ounce of passion before he pulls away from me sharply.

"You are so fucking hot when you're angry," he growls, smiling down at me. "But you're still getting spanked twenty-five times for your language," he winks before walking away from me as Jason laughs.

"Why twenty-five? I only swore four times!" I protest as I cross my arms over my chest.

"You called him Christian," Sean laughs as he steps behind me and wraps his arms around my waist. I turn around and push against his chest before pointing at him.

"Don't think I don't know who started that conversation, mister. '*What are we doing here?*' Do you really believe I'll let one guy scare me away from you all?" I ask as Sean holds up his hands.

"No, princess, but I'm worried."

"We all are," Maximus says as he steps forward. "But do you really think we could all walk away from you?"

"You all said as much," I whisper as he cups my cheek and looks into my eyes.

"I know I, for one, am not going anywhere. I'm too in love with you to walk away now. There's no going back for me, for any of us."

"You're stuck with us, Jazzy," Jason says behind me. I turn and look at him as I lean against Maximus.

"I want to be stuck with you," I reply, looking at him before looking around. "All of you."

"You have us, Shorty," Maximus whispers as he kisses me on the lips.

I lean into him as he wraps his arms around me and look at my four daddies. I always knew I loved them and have feared for so long that they would leave me, but now I truly feel like this is the place I'm meant to be. Here with the guys, the five of us, together. If being with them is a risk, then there is only one thing to do.

"I want to learn to fight."

All four of them stare at me like that was the last thing they expected me to say.

"No, you don't need to," Christian declares as he shakes his head.

"I think today proves otherwise," I point out, but Christian continues to shake his head.

"I'm upping the security for you and making sure someone is with you at all times," he says, but I cross my arms over my chest angrily.

"You guys don't have security with you twenty-four-seven."

"Jazzy, we're trained fighters and always armed. But even on days like today, I have security with me, and there's always someone on duty in the house," Jason explains. However, I'm determined, and I won't back down over this. I look at Jason and know that if I can win him around, he'll help with Christian.

"Today, when he held a knife to my throat, I had no idea what to do, how to protect myself or fight back. I don't want to feel that helpless again." I look deep into Jason's eyes and let the tears come to the front. "Please, Daddy, just teach me to defend myself." I watch Jason's face soften and know I've won. He looks up at Christian.

"No!"

"She has a point, Christian," Jason starts, but Christian shakes his head.

"No. She'll have extra security," he starts, but I hear Sean sigh loudly.

"For crying out loud," Sean exclaims as he looks at me. "If you want to learn to defend yourself, I will teach you myself," he starts and looks at Christian. "She has a right to learn self-defence, and I, for one, would feel better knowing she could do something to protect herself."

I look back at Christian and try to hide the smile that is threatening to burst onto my face. I quickly pull my lips between my teeth and wait.

I watch as his shoulders slump, and he rubs his face.

"Fine."

I jump out of Maximus's arms and go to rush to Christian, only for my twisted ankle to go out from underneath me. Jason and Christian both catch me as I curse loudly. Christian takes some of my weight and looks at me with that 'Daddy' look he has perfected.

"Oops," I whisper as I smile at him sweetly.

"Thirty. I want you in my room at the time I tell you, waiting. You are spending tonight with me," he warns. I feel my shoulders slump in defeat as I let out a deep breath.

"Okay, Daddy."

"Good girl," he smiles, and I instantly feel my stomach

tighten with excitement, damn it. He looks down at me, and I can see he knows exactly what he does to me.

"Are you going to come into the office with me so I can keep an eye on you? Or are you going to your room?" he asks.

"Your office," I reply as he nods before scooping me up into his arms.

"Come on, then. You can rest whilst I make a few phone calls," he says before looking at his brothers.

"You all know where and what you got to do?" They nod and take turns kissing me before disappearing to do things I don't think I want to know about.

I lean into Christian as he carries me into the office.

"Have I caused problems?" I ask as Christian places me on the sofa and pulls a throw from the back to place over me.

"Not at all. This is all on Tommy, Hudson, and his boss," Christian says as he sits on the coffee table in front of the sofa. I turn on my side so I can look at him.

"He hasn't scared me off from our relationship," I say as I look up at Christian, who is leaning on his knees.

"He should have, but I'm glad you're seeing that you are stronger than you've believed for a long time."

"I've got four amazing Daddies who are making me see it," I reply smugly. Christian drops down to his knees and presses a kiss to my lips.

"I'm glad to hear it. We love you so much, baby girl, and you gave us a real fright today. Hudson will pay for what he did to you," Christian whispers.

"Why did you blame, Daddy Jason?"

Christian looks down for a moment before letting out a sigh and standing up.

"Lift your head a minute."

I do as I'm told, and he sits down before telling me to place my head on his lap. I feel him instantly place a hand on my head and start running a hand over it, avoiding the injury.

"Hudson was the first fighter Jason ever trained. Jason put everything into his development. He paid for his accommodation, his bills, everything. He was sure he would be the next big fighter, and for a while, he was heading in the right direction.

"Jason had Terry train him in security to keep him off the streets and on the straight and narrow. Hudson wanted the darker side of life, though. He liked the power and the respect Jason and I get when we walk into a room.

"Then, one fight, after he won, he was offered a chance to fight for more money in another fight just a month later. Hudson wanted to take it, but Jason said no. He said it was too soon, and he wasn't as strong as the other fighter. Hudson argued and argued, but Jason wouldn't back down. That was when Taylor approached him and told Hudson that Jason was holding him back, that he had no faith in him and that if he went to work for Taylor, he would get bigger fights and more money. Taylor also gave him the chance to do what he wanted and to walk with the big boys, so Hudson took it.

"One day, he stopped turning up to training, and Jason couldn't get ahold of him. Eventually, he learnt what had happened, and he tried to give Hudson a way out. Hudson refused all help and went with Taylor."

"That doesn't sound like it was Daddy's fault, though. Why did you blame him?" I ask as I lie on my back to look up at Christian.

"Because things went downhill for Hudson after that, he lost the fight and was stuck in a contract with Taylor. He asked Jason for help, but his pride was bruised, and he told him that he had made his bed, and he would have to lie in it. Hudson fought back by killing two of Jason's other fighters. He slit their throats."

"Why is he still alive?" I ask. "If you will kill someone for threatening me, why not someone like that?"

"Because we swore to Jason we wouldn't, and that's come round to bite us in the ass. If we had retaliated the first time he stepped out of line, you wouldn't have been hurt after what he did today; Jason has put a price on his head. He's to be brought to him alive. Jason wants to handle him like he should have done from day one.

"Hudson isn't as good as he thinks he is. The only reason he got as far with you is that you are unprepared," Christian sighs as he runs a knuckle over my cheek. "You're right; you need to learn to fight, to protect yourself. I'll put the others in charge of that. I want to believe that you'll never be harmed or threatened, but I need to face reality. You are in danger just by being with us, and you need to know what to do if you are ever in danger again."

I roll onto my side, facing him.

"I thought I could be with you all and not be involved in that side of your lives, that we could keep them separate, but today proved we can't." I look up into Christian's eyes before continuing. "I want you to include me in things. I want to know what's going on. I don't want to be kept in the dark all the time. I know you have been hiding stuff from me, like the fact two clubs have been set alight and gyms vandalised. I'm not stupid, Daddy. I still find out stuff."

"You realise, baby girl, that once you're part of this life, there's no way out? Even if you left us, you would still be dragged back into it if things went wrong." He tucks some hair behind my ear and looks deep into my eyes. "This wasn't a life we chose; we always said you would have a choice, that we wouldn't make you do anything you don't want to do. You are so pure, so kind. We hate the idea of this changing you."

"I won't change who I am, but I'll be in the know and have a better understanding of what it all means. I know the four of you will always protect me, and I also know that you will teach me to protect myself should I ever be in a situation like today."

"Okay, I'll speak to the others. We'll work out the safest route from here onwards," Christian says as he leans down and presses a sweet kiss to my cheek.

"I thought you were the boss, Daddy," I tease. Christian's face shifts and I see his playful side, he only ever shows when it's just him and me.

"I am the boss of many things, baby girl. Which I will show you later when you receive your thirty spankings," he says with a raised eyebrow.

"I've been thinking about that," I say quickly, trying to think of a way out of it.

"Oh, yes?"

"Well, you see-" I get cut off as a ringing fills the room, and Christian's head snaps up. He quickly jumps out from underneath me and looks at the door as he rushes to the desk.

"What's that?" I ask, sitting on the edge of the seat. Christian grabs his desk phone and presses a button.

"What's happening?" he yells. "Fuck! Secure my office windows; get someone here now!" He slams the phone down and pulls a gun out of his desk drawer. I watch as shutters slide down the window, and someone bangs on the office door.

"Daddy?" I ask as I hear my voice wobble as I see

Christian checking his gun. He holds out a finger, and I watch as he approaches the door before throwing it open and pointing the gun at Layton, who's on the other side with his hands up.

"Get in!" Christian snaps as he pulls Layton in and slams the door closed.

"Two black cars outside. All security is armed and ready. Jason's with Sean by the front door waiting for you," Layton says as he listens to the earpiece in his ear. "Terry's with Jason and Sean . Maximus is out, but on his way back," Layton adds before looking at Christian, whom I can see is thinking through everything quickly.

"Stay with Jasmine. You know the knock?"

Layton nods and looks at me.

"Daddy?" I say again, trying to get his attention. Christian marches up to me and presses a hard kiss to my lips.

"Stay here, Layton will protect you. Do as you are told," he says before marching towards the door.

"Be careful," I call, not knowing what else to say to him. He looks back at me and smiles before disappearing out the door.

Layton quickly closes it behind him and opens a hidden panel where he punches in a code. I hear the locks click into place.

"What's going on?" I demand as I look at Layton, who stands in front of me facing the door, his gun in his hand.

"No one knows. Two blacked-out cars arrived unannounced. The protocol is that we lock down and expect the worst."

"What's the worst?" I ask nervously.

"War."

Chapter Nineteen

CHRISTIAN

"Layton's with Jasmine secured in my office. What do we know?" I demand as I walk up to my brothers, both standing in the entrance hall, guns in hand.

"Two cars, no one exited yet, no idea who they belong to," Terry replies, pressing his finger to his earpiece.

"How many guards are in place?"

"Six are in various areas of the property, excluding Layton with Jasmine. Lucky for us, they picked now as I had called a meeting following this morning's incident, so more people were on site," Terry says as he taps on his tablet and shows me the view outside, where the two cars are parked, and the guards are all in place guns pointing at the vehicles.

"How do you want to play this?" Jason asks.

I look from him to Sean. I *want* to tell them both to hide with Jasmine. I want my brothers safe, but I know neither of them would ever listen to me. We are in this together; we have been since our father dragged us into this lifestyle.

I turn to Sean and place a hand on his shoulder.

"Jason and I are going out there. If there is any sign of

trouble, you grab Jasmine and get out through the tunnels in the gym. Layton will only open for the knock."

"Fuck off, I'm not leaving you to deal with this shit on your own!" he argues as I predicted.

"No, you're protecting Jasmine. I won't let her fall into anyone's hands but ours."

Sean looks to Jason, who I know will back me up. Sean stares at him for a moment before nodding and taking a step back.

"Fucking make sure you guys come back. We all know Maximus and I can't keep her under control like you two," Sean curses as I offer him a small smile.

"Trust us, we know," Jason chuckles from beside me. We all share a quick look before Jason, and I place our guns into the back of our trousers.

"Let's get this over and done with, shall we?"

Jason looks at me and nods before letting out a deep sigh. We walk to the doors and nod to the security on either side of us.

"All eyes are on the cars," Terry says before I open the doors.

"Remember the signal?" I ask him; he rolls his eyes.

"Been doing this as long as you, Christian. Just try not to die on my watch; it's not worth the paperwork," Terry smirks next to me. I roll my eyes as I hear Jason's deep laugh.

"Ahh fuck it," I groan as I open the doors and exit into the afternoon sun.

As soon as we walk outside, the driver's door of the first car opens, and the driver gets out with his hands up.

"You do know it's unpolite to arrive unannounced, right?" I call out as we come to a stop at the top of the steps. "Just so you are aware there are six armed men trained on you at this moment. I suggest you tell us who is in the car, or we give the signal."

"Sirs. I have been asked to apologise for the inconvenience, but the people in these cars do not mean any harm to you or anybody in your household. They requested an audience with you and wanted me to assure you they are unarmed."

I turn and look at Jason who's shaking his head; he doesn't like this either.

"Tell them to come out of the cars slowly, one at a time, and we will talk. One fast move, and our guards will shoot!"

Slowly, the driver walks around to the back door and opens it. I anxiously watch before letting out a sigh of exasperation.

"What the fuck, Geralt?" I curse as I cross my arms over my chest.

"You could have just called without all this fucking shit," Jason sighs. But one look at Geralt's face and I realise there's a reason he is being overcautious. I look from the second car back to Geralt.

"Who's in there?"

Geralt holds up his hands. "Just hear me out a second and I'll tell you everything," he starts but the door of the other car opens and Taylor climbs out with his hands up.

"Fucking prick!" Jason yells next to me as we both pull out our guns and aim them at Taylor.

"I'm not here to cause trouble," Taylor yells, his hands still in the air.

"Trouble? Because of you, our Jasmine was attacked with a fucking knife! Give me one reason why I shouldn't put a bullet through your skull!" I yell. I don't need to look, but know Terry has his gun out behind me aimed at Geralt.

"I had nothing to do with your girl's attack. Hudson has

been working for someone else, and I wasn't aware until I was informed about today's events."

"Bullshit!" Jason yells.

"I swear it! I had nothing to do with today. I have no idea who ordered it."

"He's telling the truth; I was with him when Maximus called me. He called Hudson, who told him everything. I heard the whole exchange," Geralt says from his car. He takes a slow step forward. "I've worked with you guys for years; I would have nothing if you hadn't saved me and my family. I owe you our lives, and I would never put yours or the lovely Jasmine's at risk."

I risk a look at Jason, who seems to believe him. I nod at Geralt and lower my gun; Jason quickly does the same. Terry keeps his gun trained on Geralt and will remain that way until I tell him to lower it.

"Why are you here?" I ask as they both stand together.

"Because I want to help, I knew it would be better to come before everyone else descends on you so we could speak alone. I want to tell you everything I know and offer my assistance," Taylor says as he looks at us both.

"How do we know you aren't going to double-cross us?" Jason asks. Taylor shrugs.

"You don't, but at least hear me out, and then you can decide what you want to do with the information."

I turn to Jason, who looks at me and nods. We have no other option but to trust them to an extent.

"Pat each one of them down before they cross the threshold, remove any weapons. I will take them to my study," I order. Terry nods as Jason and I walk back into the house and prepare for our unexpected guests.

Jasmine

If my ankle wasn't screaming at me I'd be pacing the office right now. Layton's positioned by the door with his gun in his hand, looking ready to jump at the slightest sign of danger.

"Do you know what's happening out there?" I ask as I pull at the sleeves of my jumper. Layton looks at me briefly.

"We will find out in a moment," he answers before there's a knock at the door. Three raps, two raps, four raps. Layton reopens the panel, types in a code again, and the door opens. Christian, Sean, and Jason enter the room, and I let out a sigh of relief.

Behind them is Mr Young, whom I met the other week and a man I don't recognise. I jump to my feet, attempting to hide the pain as my ankle nearly gives way, but I'm too on edge to care.

"It's okay, sweetheart. They've come to talk," Christian says as he approaches me and cups my face.

"I'll go to another room?" I reply as I turn to leave, but Christian stops me.

"You will stay with us," he says, offering me his arm for support and leading me to the desk. He sits in his chair and pulls me onto his lap, wrapping his arm around my waist. Jason and Sean stand on either side of us as the people that have entered stand together.

"Sweetheart, you remember Geralt Young?"

"Yes, it's good to see you again, Mr Young. I hope, at least," I say as he offers me a warm smile.

"It's lovely to see you too, Jasmine. I wish it were under better circumstances. I hope you are not in too much pain and heal quickly."

"She had a knife held to her throat, as well as sliced

down her side. She was thrown against a wall so hard that her head needed glueing shut, and you can see the injuries to her face. I think her healing process may take a while. Don't you?" Sean snaps beside us. I look up at him and see him staring at the man next to Mr Young, who is looking at me as if in shock.

"I am so sorry you went through that. It was not deserved," he says softly. I nod not knowing who he is but knowing the guys are not happy with his presence here in our home.

"Sweetheart, this is Joseph Taylor."

I blink at Christian as my heart races. Christian's arm tightens around my waist as I feel Jason place a hand on my shoulder.

"Taylor?"

Christian nods, confirming my suspicions. I turn back to the man who hired Hudson and sent him after me.

"It seems Hudson has changed employers, and it was not Taylor who sent him today," Jason explains as his thumb strokes my shoulder.

"I assure you I have no qualms with any of the O'Reillys or yourself," Taylor says as he looks at me. I place my hand over Jason's on my shoulder and nod. Not trusting myself to say anything at this moment.

"What was it you needed to tell us?" Christian asks as he looks at Taylor.

"We thought you needed to know that your father has been causing trouble with the wrong people."

"That's nothing new," Jason states matter-of-factly. "He's been doing that for years."

"This time, it's different. He owes a lot of money to a lot of dangerous people."

"Tommy's not our problem. What he does is on his own

back. We have cut him off," Christian states as he shakes his head. I can feel his hand resting on my hip as his thumb strokes back and forth. I can't decide if he is doing it to comfort me or reassure himself that I am okay.

"You might want to rethink that because he's telling anyone who threatens him that the quickest way to get any money from you is through Miss Connors."

Christian's thumb stops and his hand grips my hip as Jason's tightens on my shoulder. I place my hand over each of theirs and they both relax a little.

"Who does he owe money to? I've already been told about Flint. He approached us himself and knows we will not pay when it comes to Tommy," Sean asks, as I see his hands ball up into fists. Taylor lets out a sigh.

"Flint is the least of your worries. He owes McIntyre."

Jason and Sean both curse as Christian rubs at his face.

"Why are you telling us all of this? What's in it for you?" Christian asks.

"Because even given our differences in the past, I still respect you all and don't believe you should be punished for your father's wrongdoings." He looks at me and smiles slightly. "Plus, Miss Connors doesn't deserve to be attacked and victimised for your father's dealings."

"We appreciate that. Thank you," Christian says as he looks at Layton, who is standing by the door with Terry. Both still have their guns in their hands. "Can you please ask Mrs Brown to place refreshments in the sitting room? Also, let Maximus know that our guests are not a threat. The last thing we need is for him to come in here with guns blazing."

Layton nods and exits the room quickly.

"I want to know everything you know, including who Tommy owes. Who's a danger to Jasmine, everything,"

Christian says looking at the two people in front of us who both nod. "Terry, please escort our guests to the sitting room, where we will meet in a moment to discuss this further. I just need to confer with my family," Christian adds. I watch as Terry shows the guys out of the office and closes the door behind him.

We all sit watching the door for a moment, listening as Terry tells them to follow him, giving them time to put some distance between them and us.

"I'm going to fucking kill him," Sean curses under his breath as he starts pacing Christian's office. "Who the fuck does he think he is? He would be nothing without us, and this is how he repays us?"

Jason turns and cups my face before kissing me softly.

"No one is getting anywhere near you again, Jazzy. I won't let them," he promises as he looks me in the eye, and I see how worried he is.

"I know," I reply as Christian's arms wrap around my waist. Jason looks at him and nods. "Get Layton to take her to the safe house. Sean, you join them. I want at least one of us at a time to take a little pressure off Layton."

I spin around and stare at Christian.

"You can't send me away!"

"Yes, we can and we will, you need to be safe, princess," Sean states from behind us.

"I'm safe here; I couldn't be safer!" I shout as I try to stand, but Christian stops me. The guys

look at me, and I know there is no point in arguing with them.

"Jazzy, the last thing we want to do is send you away, but no one will know you are there, and it will be harder for them to find you."

"Except it won't."

We all turn and look at Christian, who's staring at us.

"We're talking about Tommy and Hudson here. They know where all our safe houses are and how we defend them. They will still be able to get to her."

"What do you suggest we do?" Jason asks.

"We keep her here, it's the last thing they will expect. Plus, she's right, she is safer here. We'll up the guards and stay in lockdown until we can remove the threat."

"Why don't you just talk to whoever Tommy owes money to and make them see that you have nothing to do with him?" I suggest, but Jason shakes his head.

"We are talking about some of the most powerful people in the country. Why the fuck Tommy got caught up with McIntyre, I'll never know. That family doesn't forgive or forget easily. We have nothing to do with them for a reason."

"But we do."

We all look at Christian as he leans back in his chair.

"What the fuck do you mean we do?" Sean demands as he jumps from the sofa. Christian looks at me and runs his knuckles down my cheek.

"Do you remember what you said at the fight? About keeping friends close."

"And enemies closer," I finish. Christian smiles as he leans forward.

"That's what I've been doing with McIntyre for years. We aren't in any business agreement with him, and he only ever calls in the odd favour, but I've made a point of never going to him for a favour for a reason."

"So that when you do, you could ask for anything and he would feel obligated to give it," I mutter under my breath. Christian nods.

"Exactly." He leans forward and looks into my eyes. "I

could make contact, explain the situation and offer out of respect for him, to honour Tommy's debt. All we ask in return is that he promises to help protect you."

"He would honour it if you show him the right respect," Jason says from beside us.

"I don't like this, Christian. I get what you're saying, but it's a big gamble," Sean says as he leans against the desk.

"Neither do I, but it is worth a try. Either way, we will have to pay McIntyre because if he puts us on his shit list, we are all dead anyway," Jason sighs as he runs his fingers over his head.

"I will start the ball rolling with McIntyre. You three, wait here until Maximus gets back, then go to see Young and Taylor and find out what you can from them. The rest of the guys Maximus called will be here in an hour. We will see what they can tell us and do for us and regroup when they have gone."

Chapter Twenty

SEAN

I walk into the office and am met by my three brothers pressing their fingers to their lips. I frown for a moment until I see Jasmine curled up against Jason's chest asleep. It's been a long and tiring day; I'm not surprised she's fallen asleep. I wish I could join her.

Heading straight to the bar, I hold up our favourite bottle of whiskey; all three nod, and I go about pouring our drinks. After handing them out, I fall onto the sofa next to Maximus. I look over at Jason and wish for a moment that it was my lap on which Jasmine was curled up. She looks so content there in his arms as he strokes her head, making sure to miss where she's injured. Jason looks lost in his own thoughts as he looks down at her and just savours holding her.

"Did she eat anything earlier?" Maximus asks quietly. I turn to him and nod.

"It wasn't a great amount, but after everything she's been through today, I'm just glad it was something."

Maximus nods as he watches our eldest brother pacing around the room.

Christian's been on edge since everyone left two hours ago. It turns out our father has made short work of getting himself into debt with some of the biggest people in our world.

"Any news from you know who?" Jason asks, looking up from Jasmine. Christian nods as he taps the screen on his phone.

"I'm to call him in a few minutes," he answers, glancing down at our girl.

"Want me to put her upstairs?" Jason asks. Christian looks at her for a moment and shakes his head.

"No, she'll just wake up and come looking for us."

Jasmine hasn't wanted to be on her own since the attack, which is fine by us as we don't want her out of our sight. None of us have ever felt fear, like when we realised her panic alarm was activated. Even in the short thirty seconds between me seeing the notification and calling Maximus, I swear my heart stopped, and every worst-case scenario ran through my head at a hundred miles an hour.

Christian stops pacing and takes a deep breath before walking over to his desk and picking up the phone.

"Show time," he mutters under his breath before leaning against the hardwood and listening for the call to connect. It only takes a couple of seconds before a deep voice fills the room.

"O'Reilly."

"Evening McIntire, I hope this isn't a bad time?" Christian asks all business and sounds a lot calmer than any of us are feeling.

"That depends on what you wish to discuss." McIntire

sighs and I know we're going to have to tread carefully as he already sounds irate.

"It has been brought to my attention that our father has been getting into a lot of trouble with owing people favours and money. Your name was brought up. I was wondering if you could tell me if that is true or not?"

I can see from here that Christian is sweating as we hold our breath for McIntire's response.

"Yes, your father owes me a lot of money; he suggested clearing some of his debt by offering me something I have no interest in and also know you would be against."

"What did he offer you as part payment?" Christian asks, standing tall.

"His stepdaughter for my youngest son to marry."

"Cunt!" Christian curses, forgetting himself for a moment.

"I thought that would be your response, which was why I had planned to approach you on the subject."

"So, you know about Jasmine?" Christian asks, looking over at her, still asleep against Jason, who is holding her tighter than he was before.

"He told me she's the daughter of his ex-wife and a virgin. But I've heard a few rumours since."

I have seen my eldest brother look angry, and I have seen him at boiling point as he has killed men, but I have never seen him look like he is about to burn the world to the ground.

Christian has always been a hard book to read, but his feelings are perfectly clear as he hears of the danger our Jasmine is in.

"I can assure you she will *never* be a bargaining chip," Christian growls.

"From what I hear, she's in a relationship with you *and* your brothers?" I can hear the question in his tone.

"That's correct," Christian answers.

"She was also attacked today whilst at her dance school. I hate to ask, but do you know who may have been responsible for that?" Christian asks, still not taking his eyes off the sleeping Jasmine.

"I do not. It isn't something I would have sanctioned, no matter what was owed to me. She's innocent in all of this, and I would come to you first before doing anything out of hand."

We all let out a sigh of relief.

"That being said, your father has assured me that you *will* be clearing his debt."

Christian sighs and grabs a piece of paper.

"Even though my brothers and I have agreed that we will not be paying any of his debts off. We would like to cover it this one time with you. We have always had a good relationship, and I would like to keep it that way," Christian says as he looks at the rest of us. We all nod in confirmation.

"I will email everything over to you, and I'm sure we can come to some sort of agreement. Do you have any idea who was responsible for your Jasmine's attack?"

"All we know is that Hudson attacked her, saying it was for his boss. It turns out he is no longer working for Taylor; we have confirmed that ourselves."

"Then I will keep an ear out and let you know what I hear. If you need any help protecting your little lady, then please shout. You have done things for me in the past, and you are being reasonable in taking on your father's wrongdoings. I appreciate that about you boys. Your father has done you wrong for many years, but you four have stuck together and built what you have from nothing. If I were your father, I would be proud."

"Thank you. I'm not sure what to say to that?" Christian answers honestly as he looks around at us all.

"There is nothing left to say. I will email you about your father's debt, and we will come to an agreement. Usually, my terms are immediate payment, but as this isn't your debt, we will organise something. As for Jasmine, please let me know what you need in terms of protection for her, and I will send over some of my best men. Speak soon."

With that, he hangs up, and we all just stare at the phone in disbelief.

The relief washes through me as I realise we are all safe from the biggest crime family in the country. Maximus lets out a deep breath whilst standing up and walking over to the bar.

"I need another drink," he exclaims as he picks up the bottle and pours himself two fingers of the amber liquid before walking around and refilling all our glasses. I hold up my glass, but I don't take my eye off my eldest brother.

Christian slumps into his chair and runs a hand over his face, letting out an exhausted breath. I can't help wondering if he managed to breathe at all during that call. He looks even more tired now than he did before it. He takes his now refilled glass from Maximus and necks it.

Christian has always carried all our worries on his shoulders. He has tried to protect the three of us as much as possible. Jason has been by his side the longest, but even he doesn't know half the things Christian has done whilst trying to protect us from the world our father forced us into.

Since his first kill at just fifteen, Christian has protected us and would give his life to make sure we can live ours. But looking at him now as he continues to watch Jasmine like she is about to evaporate right in front of his eyes, I realise that he feels the fear of losing her just as much as he feels about losing one of us.

I've never thought that I loved her more than my brothers. Even from the very beginning, I knew we all would die for her. The initial conversation of us sharing her wasn't whether we could handle it; it was more about whether she could. Jasmine is so sweet and innocent that the thought of her wanting to be with us all was something we believed she would struggle with. But as always, just like today, she has surprised us with how quickly she can adapt.

"At least our girl is safe for now; worst case, we can ask McIntire to send extra security," Jason sighs as he kisses the top of Jasmine's head.

"We won't need it. Layton has taken it personally that she was hurt on his watch. He isn't going to let her out of his sight ever again," Christian sighs.

"Are you going to deal with him and the fact that she was hurt?" Jason asks. Christian surprises me by shaking his head.

"No, he's beating himself up enough, as well as Terry giving him hell. We asked them not to be with Jasmine every second, so it's partially on us as well, but things will be changing."

"She will fight you on it," Maximus chuckles from beside me, looking at Jasmine. She stirs slightly in Jason's arms.

"She can try, but she won't win this time. If she wants to be a brat, I'll handle her," Christian answers.

"What have I done now?"

We all chuckle as Jasmine pouts and looks at Christian, who is smiling at her.

"Nothing, *yet*." He emphasises the yet, and I watch Jasmine lean into a smiling Jason.

"How are you feeling, Shorty?" Maximus asks as he watches Jasmine moan as if in pain.

"Like I want some painkillers and my bed," she admits as she looks at Christian through her lashes. Christian looks at her for a moment and lets out a sigh.

"Go to bed, sweetheart. I'm letting you off your punishment,"

Jasmine's face lights up before she winches in pain again.

"But!" Christian continues. "For the next month, you will be spanked ten times for every swear word out of your mouth."

"TEN!" Jasmine yells as she sits up on Jason's lap. "That's not fair! It was his fault I swore!" she adds, pointing at me.

"What did I do?" I ask, trying not to laugh. But when she turns to face me, all the humour from the situation quickly evaporates.

"It wasn't bad enough that I was held at knifepoint, thrown against a wall and threatened to be gang raped. I heard *you* say you wanted to leave me, and *he*," she points to Christian, "said he was considering it too! I had to do something, anything to make you stay!" she yells as she breaks down in tears as the room falls silent. She sobs into Jason's shoulder.

All four of us stare at her, not knowing what to say or do. Jason rubs his hand up and down her back gently as he looks around at us all.

I'm frozen as I think of the conversation she overheard and how, after years of promising her that we would never leave, she heard me suggesting we do just that. I climb off the sofa and walk over to sit on the coffee table in front of her. I make her look at me, wiping away the tears that are making tracks down her cheek as she sobs, all the strength she has shown today crumbling in front of my eyes.

"You're right. I'm so sorry, princess. I didn't mean it, though; I could never walk away from you. I was scared and confused and, to be honest, hated myself for not protecting you. I can promise you I would have never gone through with it, though; I never want to lose you."

"Promise?" she sobs as she looks at me. I lean forward and press my lips to her gently.

"I promise. I'm not going anywhere. None of us are," I reply as she climbs off Jason's lap and moves to mine. I look over her head and see the same expression on all my brothers' faces.

Jasmine has been so strong today that we forgot to check how she was actually doing after everything. We need to do better and take better care of her.

Christian walks over and places a kiss on the top of her head. I know he will feel as guilty as I do. I would give anything for her to have not heard that conversation earlier.

"Sean's right, sweetheart, we aren't going anywhere. But you are going to bed. You have had a rough day, and you need to rest."

Jasmine looks up at him and nods.

"Do you want anyone with you tonight?" I ask as I run my hand down her back. Jasmine nods whilst looking at us all.

"I want you all near," she says softly. I look at my brothers as they all smile.

"Sean will take you up, and Maximus will be there in a minute. Christian and I will be up as soon as we send a few emails, okay, angel?"

Jasmine looks at Jason and nods. This isn't the first night she has wanted us all close to her, and I, for one, don't want it any other way tonight.

I stand up, lifting her into my arms and offering her a small smile.

"Come on, princess, let's get you settled before this lot comes up and takes over the whole bed."

Chapter Twenty-One

CHRISTIAN

I look over at the sofa in my office for the hundredth time today. Jasmine's there fast asleep, wrapped in a blanket. We were all woken by her having a nightmare at three this morning. It had taken all of us to calm her down and get her to settle back to sleep. By four, Jason had snuck out of her bed, and I didn't need to ask where he was going.

Jason has placed a fifty-thousand-pound price on Hudson's head, and when he finds him, I have no doubt Jason's face will be the last thing Hudson ever sees. I've not attempted to call him; there's no point, this is something that should have been done years ago.

Do I hold my brother, my best friend, responsible for Jasmine's attack? Yes. But I don't need to tell him that as he holds himself responsible, too.

I put down my pen and run my fingers through my hair. I've spent the morning trying to get to the bottom of how much Tommy owes people and who we can expect to make a move. So far, nearly everyone I have spoken to has accepted that we are not responsible for Tommy's issues and if they try to use Jasmine to get us to pay, they will be signing their own death warrant. No one uses our girl against us and gets away with it.

I have never felt fear as I did yesterday when I saw the notification that Jasmine had activated her panic alarm. When I saw her injuries, I walked away and lost my shit. I've managed to hide the damage I did in the sitting room; thankfully, Mrs Brown tidied it all away before Jasmine would see anything. By this morning, the broken glasses and decanter from the bar had been replaced, and Jasmine would never be the wiser. Tommy may be my father, but he will pay for sending people after her, I don't care what happens to him anymore after hearing he offered her up as payment for his debts. The fact he would use a person as payment, let alone his stepdaughter, has killed any chance he had of us helping him out. As far as we are concerned, he is dead to us.

A knock at the door pulls me out of my thoughts and, unfortunately, wakes Jasmine.

"Hang on," I call out as I approach Jasmine and run a hand over her head. The bruising on her face has come out over the last twenty-four hours, and her lip still bleeds occasionally. I hate seeing her in pain and her skin marked like this.

"Sorry, sweetheart, I'll take whoever it is to the sitting room."

"It's okay, I'm awake," she replies with a smile. I lean forward and press a kiss on her forehead before walking to the office door. It takes me a moment to realise who is standing there with Sean.

"If you have come to cause trouble for Jasmine…"

"No sir, Danielle just wished to see how Miss Connors is after yesterday. I came to offer any help in finding who assaulted her."

I stare at Peter King in front of me before looking at his daughter, who is standing behind him nervously.

"One word out of your mouth that causes her any upset, and I will remove you myself."

Danielle looks up at me and nods.

"I deserve that," she whispers. I nod and step back to hold the door open. As they walk into the office, I look at Sean.

"Flint messaged; he will be here soon. He says he wants to talk. Can you see him through when he gets here?"

"No problem. How is she?" he asks, looking behind me where Jasmine is talking quietly to Danielle, now sitting beside her.

"I think the tablets are making her sleepy as she's been dozing on and off all morning. I won't let the Kings stay for long."

Sean nods as his hands ball into fists beside him.

"If she gets too tired, shout, and I will take her upstairs and get her settled in her room." He looks behind me as if checking if anyone is listening. "Any news on Jason?"

"Nothing. Maximus still looking for him?"

Sean nods in response.

Maximus had woken up and gone to find Jason, even though I told him not to. Even if Maximus did find him, he would never bring him home. I have a feeling the two of them won't stop until Hudson is six feet under.

"If you hear anything, keep me posted. I'll shout if Jasmine needs anything."

Sean nods again and walks off back into the rest of the

house, where I know he will be trying to keep busy to avoid worrying about his brothers and the situation we have found ourselves in.

I take a deep, calming breath before turning around to see Jasmine and Danielle talking quietly to each other. Even though they don't seem completely at ease, I have a feeling their relationship may have changed after the events of yesterday.

I turn to see Mr King looking at them, obviously thinking the same as me. As I walk into the room, he turns to me and offers a small smile. I nod towards my desk, and we move over to it.

"What do you know about any of this?"

Half an hour later, the Kings have gone home, and I'm sitting on the sofa with Jasmine lying down, her head resting on my lap as she reads on her Kindle. I'm just about to ask if she wants some more painkillers when a commotion sounds from outside the closed door.

"You fucking arsehole!"

Jumping to my feet, I stand ready to protect Jasmine as the office door flies open and Sean and another person barrel through. Jasmine screams behind me as I jump in and grab the person Sean is pinning to the ground. Sean gets out of the way as I lift the guy from the floor and pull my knife from my pocket, holding it against his throat before I even see who I'm pinning to the wall. Two security guards rush into the room, guns drawn but staying a step behind me.

"You think you can come into our home and throw your fucking weight around!" I yell as I look into Flint's red face.

"What the fuck is wrong with you?" I yell, staring at him. I've known Flint for years. I've shared many late-night whiskeys with the guy, and I've never had an issue with him before.

"What the fuck is wrong with *me*? What the fuck is wrong with *you*? What's this about you paying your father's debts off?"

"I told you I wasn't paying you what he owes you!" I yell, getting in his face.

"But you will pay others? I want my fucking money, O'Reilly!"

I growl as I pull him away from the wall, throwing him to the floor. Pressing a knee into his back, I grab a fistful of hair and pull his head, forcing him to look at Jasmine behind Sean, who is standing tall, ready to protect her.

"I want our girl to feel safe in her own goddamn home! What gives you the right to storm in here, attack my brother and scare her? You're lucky I didn't put a bullet through your mother-fucking head!" I look up to Sean as I put more pressure on Flint's back. "What the fuck happened?"

"He turned up, and I was bringing him to you like you said when he tried to jump me as we got to the door," Sean growls whilst staring at Flint. I have no doubt Sean could have taken him. Flint is lucky they fell into the office when they did, as I'm sure Sean would have killed him with his bare hands if I hadn't intervened.

"Give me one reason why I shouldn't slit your throat right here," I demand, looking down at Flint, who's stopped fighting me.

"You think I'm the only one who's pissed off? As soon as word got out, you were paying some people and not others, a target was put on your head."

"They were fucking lying! Who told you that bullshit? I

want names! Now!" There's no way anyone knows we are paying McIntire. When I came to an agreement via email with McIntire last night, he agreed to tell no one. McIntire may be many things, but he's always true to his word.

"I'm telling you fuck all whilst you have a knife to my throat," Flint spits. I look to the security guards and nod. They take over and lift Flint onto his feet, holding him stationary while I stand in front of him.

"Close your eyes, princess," I hear Sean whisper as I lift my knife and slam it into Flint's side, knowing exactly where it will cause the most amount of pain and minimal damage. Flint screams as I leave the knife in him. I pull my hand back and hit him, knocking him out in one punch.

"Get him down to the basement now! I will deal with him there." Security removes Flint from the room quickly. They are trained to do as they are told and never ask questions. I'm a fair man; I may take lives, but I only do so if I have no other choice; they know that and respect me for it.

I turn to see Jasmine holding on to Sean as tears quietly slide down her cheek. I approach her slowly, hoping that she isn't too spooked by what she saw.

All worry is dashed when she throws herself into my arms. I hold her whilst trying to stop the small amount of blood on my hand from touching her.

"Are you okay, sweetheart?"

Jasmine pulls back a little and nods as she wipes at her face. I kiss her forehead and step back to look at Sean behind her.

"I'm going to get Layton to take you upstairs and to stay with you whilst Sean and I deal with Flint."

"Okay, Daddy," she says quietly before offering me a small smile, letting me know that she's okay. I kiss her on the forehead one more time before looking at Sean.

"Stay with her until Layton gets here, then meet me down there."

I don't wait for him to answer; I turn around and storm out of the room, determined to make an example of the prick who thought it was okay to scare my girl in her own home.

Chapter Twenty-Two

JASMINE

I don't know how long I've been upstairs whilst the guys deal with Flint. I try to read, study, take a bath, and do anything to stop myself from thinking about what's happening downstairs in the basement. But nothing works.

I'm surprised how quickly I've come to accept what the guys sometimes have to do. I don't think I have ever really questioned it, but now that I'm seeing the damage they can do with my own eyes, I'm realising how much they are willing to do to keep me safe. That last tiny bit of doubt I had that they don't love me has gone and I know they are here to stay.

I lift my head as I hear a mumbling outside of my door and listen to the sound of Christian talking to Layton. By the time I get to the bedroom door, Christian's nowhere to be seen. I look to Layton, who offers me a small smile.

"He's in his room; you might want to give him a moment."

I shake my head, needing to see him and know that he's okay.

I hobble to his room, my ankle still screaming at me, but seeing Christian is more important than my pain right now.

Pushing open the door I look around his room only to find it empty. The door to his ensuite bathroom is open a little, and I can hear the shower running and see the steam drifting into the quiet room. Looking inside I see Christian leaning over his sink, his head hanging down and his shoulders slumped. Looking at him now, I realise I've never seen him look anything but in control. But right now, he's deflated, and it breaks my heart. I look at his reflection in the mirror and see he has blood splattered over his shirt and face. I follow the blood spray down his arms to find his knuckles are split, his hands have blood on them, and I know it won't all be Flint's.

As I slowly approach, Christian doesn't even acknowledge that I'm there. He's so consumed by his demons that he has no idea what's happening around him. I lift my hand to place it on his shoulder and stop myself, my hand centimetres from his shoulder.

"Daddy?"

I only whisper it, but by the look on Christian's face when his reflection finds mine, I know I've just broken whatever spell he was under. I see a pain in his eyes I have never seen before, and it doesn't just break my heart; my soul shatters knowing how much he hides from us.

I gently place my hand on his shoulder and turn him to face me. For a moment, his eyes fill with worry as I see just how much blood is on him. I reach up and cup his cheek with my hand like he has done to me so many times over the years when all I needed was his touch to calm my racing heart. Christian lets out a deep breath and leans into my hand as his eyes close.

"Let me look after you for a change," I whisper as I run

my thumb over his cheek. Christian doesn't say anything or open his eyes; he just slowly nods once.

I remove my hand from his face and look down at his shirt. Unbuttoning it slowly, one by one. After pulling the cotton from his trousers, I run my hands over his shoulders, pushing the fabric down his back before pulling off each rolled-up sleeve until he is topless in front of me. I look into his deep blue eyes and keep eye contact as I undo his trousers before helping him out of them and his boxers.

I love looking at Christian when he is naked. I usually watch him when he's in the shower just to see the steam rolling around him, making him appear like a god. But today, the steam is like his own shadows wrapping around him, trying to bring some warmth to his cold exterior. I take his hand and lead him to the shower before stripping off and guiding him in with me, being sure to keep my head from the water.

As soon as the water hits his chest, he closes his eyes and allows it to wash over him and soothe him. I reach around and take hold of his shower gel. Slowly, I wash his body, making sure to rid him of any blood and dirt that is a reminder of what he has just done. I don't need to ask if Flint is still alive. I saw the way Christian looked at him, and I knew he would have paid with his life for storming into our home, threatening one of the twins and scaring me. I'm okay with that. Should I be? Probably not, but it is what it is.

Christian leans his hands against the tiles, his head bowed, and his eyes closed. He is lost in his dark thoughts as I continue to wash his body, followed by his hair. Once all the soap studs are washed off, he pulls me into his arms and holds me under the hot water. Even in his lost state, he is cautious of my head wound and the water spray. He doesn't say or do anything; he just holds me like I'm the only thing stopping him from falling apart.

I stay there and let him do whatever he needs to do to calm his heart, which I can feel racing against my cheek as I lean against his damp, smooth chest.

I don't know how long he holds me, and I don't care. All that matters is he's here with me, and for this short time, we are safe.

I'm lost in his arms when I feel Christian's hands thread into the hair at the top of my neck before tightening as he tips my head back and presses a kiss to my lips. He holds me like that whilst kissing me under the warm water as all thoughts clear my mind.

All that exists is him and me.

Christian lets go of my hair and moves his hands down before lifting me, his lips never leaving mine. I instinctively wrap my legs around his waist as his arms tighten around me. Christian shuts off the water with one hand before carrying me out of the shower, not breaking the kiss.

Christian walks us into his room and lowers me onto the bed.

"We'll get everything wet," I point out, breaking the kiss for a moment.

"I don't care," he whispers before his lips are back on mine.

No one can say Christian is a gentle lover. Since that first time, he has taken me wherever and whenever he wants. He loves nothing more than to bite and fuck me hard, and I love it!

But today, there is a gentleness about him that makes me swoon. Even as he kisses my neck and down my body, it's nothing but loving caresses, his lips featherlight, and his fingers trail down until they find the apex of my thighs.

Christian lovingly kisses and licks me until I'm screaming his name as I cum, followed by him slowly making his way back up my body before kissing me on the lips as his hands cup my head. I feel him press his hips forward as he slowly slides into me, and I melt as I stare deep into his eyes.

Even now Christian doesn't go back to his usual strong self, instead, he makes love to me in a way he never has before. Not once does he take his eyes off my face; as he moves in and out of me hitting every single one of my buttons, he lovingly strokes my cheek and presses soft kisses to my lips, cheeks and jaw.

"No one will ever hurt you again, baby," he whispers into my ear as he kisses my neck.

"I know, Daddy," I gasp as he hits that spot within me and grinds against it.

"I will die before anyone hurts you. You are my whole world," he adds through gritted teeth. I want to reply, but I'm overcome by the pleasure his touch is giving me as I grind up into him, needing him more than ever. We move together in perfect harmony and soon are both panting and sweating and climaxing together as Christian holds my hands above my head and kisses every inch of my jaw.

As we come down Christian rolls to the side and pulls me into his arms before looking deep into my eyes and cupping my cheek.

"I love you, baby girl," he whispers as he gently kisses my lips.

"I love you too, Daddy."

"I keep waiting for the moment you realise what being with me means, and you run in the other direction," he says softly before looking away from me. I reach up and cup his face, forcing him to look back at me, but he fights against me. I move so I am on top of him and hold his face in my hands as I straddle his hips.

"Look at me," I whisper firmly. When he finally does, I see nothing but sorrow in his eyes.

"You are the most selfless person I know," I start, but Christian tries to look away from me. "Look at me!" I say firmer this time. Christian does as he's told, and I give him the 'Daddy' look he gives me when I don't listen. Christian's eyes widen a little before a small smirk appears on the corner of his mouth.

"You *are* the most selfless person I know. There is nothing you won't do to protect your brothers and now me. It's one of the reasons I fell in love with you years ago. I know that you carry more guilt over everything you have done than you will ever admit. But you did it all to protect the other three. Do you think we don't know you hurt? Because we do, and it's one of the reasons we all love you so much." I press a kiss to his lips before offering him a smile.

"Plus, why would I run when you are worth keeping around for the sex alone?" I tease with a wink. A smile bursts onto Christian's face before he tucks me against his chest and rolls us back over so he's on top of me again.

"You keep me around for the sex, do you?" he demands, with his brows almost disappearing into his hairline before he starts tickling me, managing to avoid anywhere I'm hurt.

"Amongst other things," I squeal whilst trying to get away from him, and both of us laugh.

He is still tickling me when a commotion sounds from outside, and I hear someone scream in pain.

"What the?" Christian jumps to his feet and grabs a gun from his drawer when Maximus storms into the room covered in blood.

"Jason's been stabbed!"

Chapter Twenty-Three

JASMINE

Everything happened so quickly after Maximus stormed in. Christian grabbed some trousers and rushed out to find out what was going on. I rushed to get my clothes from his bathroom, but when I came back out into the bedroom, Layton was there stopping me from leaving. He was under instructions to keep me in the room until Christian came to get me.

I tried to get past him, but no matter how hard I fought against him, he won. He won't even let me go back to my room for fear I would hear what was happening in Jason's. So now I'm sitting on Christian's windowsill, looking out onto the driveway below.

I hate this. I hate not knowing what's going on. I need to know that Jason's going to be okay. The thought of anything happening to him, or us losing him makes my chest hurt so much that I gasp for air against the pain.

We can't lose him; we wouldn't survive it.

Jason is our voice of reason, the one we all go to as a bounding board. If Christian is being unreasonable, I can almost guarantee Jason will back me up. I can't lose him. I can't lose any of them.

"Sweetheart?"

My head snaps up to the sound of a Christian's voice. I look to the door and see him standing there. My lungs fill with air to the point they hurt when I spot the blood smeared on his bare chest.

When I walked in and saw him covered in Flint's blood, I didn't even think about what that meant. But seeing him now with Jason's blood on him makes my mind race with a hundred different scenarios. How many times has he been stabbed? How deep did the knife go? Were any vital organs damaged?

"Is he…?" I stop mid-sentence. I don't know whether I want to ask if he's okay or …

Christian strides across the room and pulls me to him as I desperately try to get some air into me.

"He's okay, sweetheart. I promise he's going to be all right."

Air is forced from my lungs as I let out a sob against his chest.

"The doctor's still with him. But he's fixed him up and said he is going to make a full recovery."

I pull back from him as I wipe the tears from my face.

"Can I see him?"

Christian nods and holds his hand out for me to take. He grabs a top from his wardrobe before we leave and leads me out of the room and towards Jason's. He stops with his hand on the door.

"Two things before you go in, sweetheart."

I look up at him and hold my breath.

"Jason is sedated and won't wake up for a while. The

doctor had to stitch him up, and it was better for him to be asleep for that."

I nod and watch as Christian takes a deep breath.

"You also need to prepare yourself. Jason suffered a wound to his face. It luckily missed his eye, but he will have a scar down one side."

I bite my lip and nod again, not knowing what to say or do. My jaw clenches as I force myself to swallow back the tears.

"Was Daddy Max with him?" I ask quietly. Christian nods and cups my cheek.

"Maximus is fine and managed to get Jason back here quickly. He needs his Shorty, though," Christian says as he gives me a small smile. I nod and look back at the door as fear nearly has me running in the opposite direction. But Jason and Maximus have been there so many times for me in the past, and I need to be strong and be here for them now.

I take a deep breath and open the door to Jason's room.

Inside, the first thing I see is Sean standing by Jason's bed with his arms crossed over his chest as he looks down at his brother. I feel Christian place a hand on the base of my back and softly guide me into the room. Sean turns and looks at me and offers me a soft smile. His face is pale, and he, too, has blood on his top.

"Come here, princess," he whispers, holding out his arm. I rush to his side as he hugs my shoulders and holds me close. I look down at the bed and see Jason lying there, looking peaceful as he sleeps.

Christian wasn't wrong about his face. I have to hold in a sob as I look down and see the long slash cut from his left eyebrow down to his jaw. It looks red and angry, and there are butterfly strips across it in a couple of areas where the wound is deeper.

"Is he in pain?" I ask as I look up at the doctor, who is on the other side of the bed. He looks at me and smiles at me as he shakes his head.

"Not at the moment; he is heavily sedated and will remain so for a while to give his body time to heal." I can see a bag of blood and fluids on a stand, which are being pumped into Jason.

"Shouldn't he be in a hospital?" I ask, looking at Christian. He lets out a deep sigh before shaking his head.

"In the ideal world, yes. However, the hospital staff would ask too many questions. Dr Evans is perfectly capable of dealing with anything we throw at him and has access to all the equipment and supplies we need. We pay him enough to be the best."

"That almost sounds like a compliment, O'Reilly," Dr Evans says from where he is rummaging in his bag.

"Yeah, well, you just saved my brother's life. I'll be nice for a little while at least."

I see a smirk on Christian's face and wonder how long Dr Evans has worked for them and how many times he has patched them up.

I'm just about to ask when the sound of the bedroom door opening stops me. A very worn-out Maximus walks in. As soon as he sees me, he freezes and stares like he doesn't know what to say or do. I step away from Sean and rush forward, throwing my arms around Maximus's neck. I bury my head in his neck, breathing in his scent as I hold him tight. Thankful that he isn't as injured as Jason. I honestly don't know how any of us would handle them both having been stabbed.

For a second, he freezes before wrapping his arms around me and holding me like he is clinging to life support.

"I'm sorry I couldn't prevent this, Shorty," he whispers into my neck, his whole body shaking as he desperately tries to hold it together. I pull away from him and run my hand down his cheek.

"Don't apologise; he would never have forgiven himself if you had been injured, too."

Maximus looks at me, and for the first time *ever*, I see tears in his eyes.

"But I will never forgive myself for not protecting him."

Two hours later, we are all still sitting in Jason's room, not wanting to leave his side. We have moved three chairs in so the three guys can sit down. I'm sitting either curled up in Maximus's arms or next to Jason on the bed. I can't bring myself to separate myself from either of them, terrified something else will happen to them if I let them out of my sight.

I'm currently curled up on Maximus's lap as he absent-mindedly plays with my hair and watches over his big brother. I'm just about to ask him if he needs anything when a knock sounds on the door.

Christian answers it before stepping back so Terry and Layton can both enter carrying trays of food.

"Mrs Brown asked us to send these up."

I look at Layton, who gives me a small smile and places the trays on the chest of drawers. Terry looks at Christian and points to the food.

"Eat that, or I will send her up to deal with you all!"

I think Terry and Mrs Brown are the only people that

any of the O'Reilly brothers will listen to. They all know Terry matches them in the ring as they work out together regularly. But Mrs Brown is the only person the guys fear. She's like a mother to them, and when she scolds them, they listen.

I attempt to stifle a laugh as I imagine Mrs Brown leaning over them, watching them finish everything on their plate. Christian looks at me with his 'Daddy' look, and I quickly hide my smile in Maximus's chest.

Usually, when I use him to hide from one of my Daddies, Maximus will laugh and hand me over to them. But today, he just tightens his hold on me, not saying or doing anything.

"Sweetheart, come and sit here so Maximus can eat," Christian says as he pushes his chair closer to me. As I stand, I hear Maximus sigh.

"I'm not hungry."

I turn to look at Maximus as Christian and Sean both turn their attention to their brother.

"I don't remember asking if you were. You need to eat as much as the rest of us," Christian points out.

"That shit might work on her, but it doesn't work on me!" Maximus snaps as he glares at Christian, and I wait for the two of them to come to blows for a moment. I let out a deep breath, take Maximus's plate out of Christian's hand and hold it out in front of him. Hoping to avoid any more tension from building. The last thing these two need to do is start arguing with each other.

"Eat your dinner, please, Daddy."

Maximus looks at the food in my hand and shakes his head.

"I'm not hungry, Shorty."

"Well, if you aren't eating, neither am I, and we both

know when Daddy wakes up, he will give us both hell, but he'll only discipline me. So, if I have to deal with a punishment, I hope you know it will be all your fault."

Maximus stares at me for a moment like I've gone mad.

"Please save my ass from a spanking," I add as I stick out my bottom lip. I watch as Maximus's control slips, and there is a tiny lift to one side of his mouth.

"Eat your dinner, brat," he mutters as he takes the plate from me. I lean over and press a kiss on his cheek.

"On behalf of my ass, I thank you," I reply as I stand up and take my plate from Christian and sit in the chair. Christian places a hand on my shoulder and gives it a soft squeeze. I look at him and offer him a small smile.

"You're lucky you are so damn cute," Maximus mutters as he digs into his dinner.

"And you are lucky to have me," I reply, flashing my cheesiest grin. I watch Maximus eat his dinner with a slight smile on his face, and for the first time since he came into the room, he seems to relax a little.

"You have no idea, princess."

I turn to look at Sean, who gives me a quick wink before eating his food.

Chapter Twenty-Four

JASON

I open my eyes and see a sleeping Jasmine next to me. She's curled up on her side, one hand under her face, the other holding mine. She looks so peaceful. I reach to move some hair from her face but hiss as pain radiates down my side.

"Welcome back."

I turn my head to see Christian sitting in a chair by the side of my bed.

"How did I get back here?" I ask as I look around and see all three of my brothers now standing around my bed.

"I brought you back," Maximus says quietly.

It all comes back to me, him trying to defend me and taking down one of Hudson's lackeys before dragging me out of the shithole we found them in.

"You saved my life," I whisper, unable to miss the way his face drops.

"If I had done a better job, you wouldn't be so cut up."

"Don't do that. Don't beat yourself up. Otherwise, I'll do it for you when I get out of this bed."

"Don't make me bang your heads together."

I turn my head to see Jasmine staring at me. I lift her hand and place a kiss on it, wanting nothing more than to pull her into my arms, but I'm not sure if I can handle holding her yet. Just kissing her hand hurts.

I lift my hand to the left side of my face and feel the cut stretching down one side. Jasmine reaches over and takes my hand.

"Don't touch it," she warns.

"How bad is it?" I ask as I look at her.

"Dr Evans thinks it will scar," Christian explains as Jasmine leans in and places a soft kiss on it.

"You are still just as handsome," she whispers, smiling at me. "If anything, it makes you sexier," she adds. I look into her blue eyes and wonder how the hell I got so lucky. I'm lying here cut up, and she still makes me feel like I could take on the world.

I'm not worthy of her love.

"Want to tell us what happened?" Christian asks, dragging me back out of my head.

I tear my eyes away from Jasmine and look at my older brother, who I know is going to be pissed off with me. I broke our golden rule and paid the price.

"After Jazzy had her nightmare, I was too angry to sleep; I needed to do something. So, I left and went hunting for Hudson. It took the best part of the day to find some of his friends and to get out as much information about his known whereabouts as he has been keeping people out of the loop. No one could tell me who he was working for, even after I beat the shit out of them. I had to admit they were as much in the dark as the rest of us.

"It was around lunchtime when Maximus caught up with me. I tried to send him home at first, but after he kept following me, I accepted his help, and we started working together."

"It's a good job you did. If he hadn't been there, we would be organising your funeral right now."

I look to Christian and nod.

"This is why we don't go hunting people down on our own, you know this. It's the one rule we have; we are a team, the four of us," he adds firmly.

"I know, and I won't make that mistake again," I admit as I look at Maximus.

"So, where did you finally find him?" Sean asks.

"He was at a warehouse where someone had spotted him just half an hour beforehand. We raced over and found him there with two of his new lackeys. As soon as I confronted him, he pulled out a knife, and we started fighting. I had a gun, but I wanted him to pay for how he attacked Jazzy. Whilst we fought, Maximus took down one of his guys. He will have to tell you how it went down with the other guy, as I was a little preoccupied.

"Hudson is stronger than he was, plus my exhaustion was kicking in. I know I got in a few good stabs, but he managed to get in a few himself. Nothing compared to the ones I got in, but I know he caught my face as the blood ran into my eye and blinded me; that was when he got two deep ones in.

"I remember getting one to his neck, and then everything started to go black as I struggled with the blood loss. I don't remember anything until waking up here." I let out a sigh as I turn to Jasmine and see a tear rolling from her eye and across her nose as she continues to lie on her side.

"I would do it all again in a heartbeat to make sure you are safe. The only regret I have is not making sure he was dead."

Jasmine reaches over and cups my cheek before pressing a kiss to my lips.

"There is no way he was still alive; he wasn't breathing when I carried you out. When our clean-up guys went to the location, it was already on fire. They heard the fire crew say there were three bodies." I hear Maximus say from where he is standing beside the bed.

"We didn't find out who they were working for, but I don't think we would have managed it anyway as they were determined to take that to the grave," Maximus sighs as he runs his hand over his head.

"So, is it all over?"

I turn and look at Jasmine and shake my head.

"No, it's not Jazzy. Whoever Hudson was working for will have others to do his dirty work, but with him having lost three men, hopefully, he will think twice before sending anyone else after you," I explain. Jasmine looks at me and nods.

"But for now, all we can do is get some rest and regroup in the morning."

I turn to look at Christian, who holds up a bottle of pills.

"Take a couple of these and get some sleep," he orders before looking at Jasmine. "You need to rest as well. Shall I save my breath and just accept you are staying here tonight?"

"I'm not leaving this bed until I know he's okay," she says firmly. I smile as I look at Christian, who is staring at her with raised brows.

"Baby girl, don't start thinking you can top from the bottom. You got away with a little more than usual the last two days, but things will get back to normal soon enough, and you will find yourself over my knee," he warns as Sean laughs. I look at Jasmine and find her chewing on her lip.

"Have you been a brat?"

"No! I made Daddy Max eat when he refused. How is that being a brat? I thought I was being good," she gasps, looking through her lashes at me. I shake my head and look around at my brothers, who are all looking at her with smiles on their faces.

Christian walks over and helps me to take some painkillers and have a little water. As he does, Jasmine crawls under the duvet next to me and says goodnight to the others.

"If you need anything in the night, get Jasmine to come and get one of us. The doctor will be back at nine to check you over and decide how long you are on bed rest," Christian explains as he turns out the lamp and follows the others out of the room.

"I'm glad you are going to be okay, Daddy." I look at Jasmine in the dark and smile as I lift her hand to place a kiss on her knuckles. The discomfort is worth it; no amount of pain will ever stop me from showing this amazing woman how much she means to me.

"It will take more than a psycho headcase to keep me from coming home to you, angel," I whisper as I feel my eyes close and the painkillers quickly start to kick in.

"I love you," I hear her whisper as sleep starts to take me.

"I love you more, Jazzy," I reply before falling asleep with her hand in mine.

Chapter Twenty-Five

MAXIMUS

I find Christian leaning against the entrance to our sparring room. He's watching Sean teach Jasmine self-defence, and I can tell from the way his shoulders are tense that he's not happy about it.

"How's she getting on?" I ask, standing next to him.

"She's a natural. She's picking it all up quickly and has a lot more power in her attack moves than I anticipated."

I watch as Sean holds up some pads, and Jasmine starts punching them. It's standard power training, but as I watch her, I can't help but feel sorry for anyone who ever gets on the receiving end of her fists. I watch her grab a pad and bring it down on her advancing knee, internally cringing and reminding myself not to piss her off anymore.

Jasmine's in some yoga pants and a sports bra. Her hair's pulled back into a ponytail, and she looks like she's putting everything into her training. Sweat glistens down her back as she breathes heavily. She always looks beautiful, even more so when she is on the stage. But watching her in the ring brings out a hot, sexy version of my Shorty. One I knew was hidden behind the innocent persona portrayed most of the time. It's a side of her she only usually shows in the bedroom when she is begging us to choke her, pull on her hair and be as rough with her as we can.

"Stop!" Sean calls pulling me out of my dirty thoughts.

He lowers the pads, and Jasmine leans on her legs, trying to catch her breath. "Get a drink, princess," he adds, pulling the pads off his hands.

Jasmine looks up and sees Christian and me standing in the doorway. She gives us an exhausted smile whilst walking to the side of the ring. She picks up her water bottle and takes a sip before rubbing her face on the towel that's hanging on the ropes.

"How's your ankle?" Christian asks as he approaches her.

"Okay," she answers out of breath. I look down at her ankle, which is bandaged for support. Christian shakes his head and with no warning lifts her good foot from the floor, causing her to grab the ropes to stop her from falling. "Hey!" I don't miss the way her face scrunches up from the pain that must stem from her twisted ankle.

Christian looks up at her with an arched brow.

"That's enough for today," he says as he puts her foot back down. I see her instantly taking the majority of her weight off her bad one.

"But I need to do this. What if-" Jasmine stops arguing when she looks at Christian and sighs. "Fine." I watch as Christian climbs up onto the ropes and cups her face.

"I know you want to learn this stuff, and I promised to let you, but you are still recovering from being attacked only three days ago. If you push yourself too hard, you will take longer to heal."

Jasmine closes her eyes and nods slowly.

"Good girl. Now get your hoodie and come with me; I want to show you something." Christian holds the ropes open, and Jasmine climbs through. I place my hands on her hips and lift her down from the ring so she doesn't hurt herself further.

"How's Daddy?"

"He's sleeping. The doc was happy with his progress, though, and said to give it another twenty-four hours before attempting to get out of bed." I leave out the bit where Jason got out of bed regardless to prove that he could, nearly ripping out one line of stitches in the process. If there is one thing none of us is good at, it's doing as we are told by anyone other than Christian.

I guess that's one of the reasons Jasmine is perfect for us, as she is just as stubborn as she wants to be. She likes to push it with me a little more than the others. I think she just likes it when I call her a brat.

Christian comes to stand next to us and places a hand on Jasmine's back.

"Where are we going?" she asks as he guides her out of the sparring room. Sean and I follow behind, and neither of us knows what Christian has planned.

"There is something I want you to learn to do. Even though I hope you never have to use this particular skill, it could save your life one day."

I turn to Sean and frown. Christian has always been against teaching Jasmine any form of self-defence, but now he wants her to learn this. From the look on Sean's face, he is just as confused by Christians one-eighty as I am.

We follow them out of the gym and down to the sound-proof basement. It is the same place Sean and Christian killed Flint the other day, not that you would know if you saw the place. It's been cleaned up and looks like your regular basement with one added condition.

"A shooting range? You want me to learn to shoot?" From the look on Jasmine's face, it was the last thing she had ever expected. Christian looks at her and nods whilst letting out a deep breath.

"Like I said, I hope you never have to do it, and I never want you to shoot to kill. It's just a precaution. But if you ever find yourself in a situation where there is no other way out but to shoot your opponent, I want you to be able to handle the gun safely and effectively to put them down, so you have time to run."

"I don't want to kill anyone," Jasmine whispers.

"Good, then you never will. You just have to make sure they can't chase after you, to give yourself enough time to get away. We will be the ones to kill them if it has to be done." Christian takes her shoulders and turns her to look at him properly.

"This was the last place I ever wanted to bring you. The thought of you having to yield a gun makes me sick to my stomach." He reaches up and cups her cheek lovingly. "But the last couple of days have proven that you are a target whether we like it or not, and I need to know you are prepared for all situations. Sean will teach you how to disarm a person, and I will teach you to use their own gun against them."

Jasmine looks from him to Sean, and then to the wall of guns we have. She takes a deep breath and looks back to Christian. I can see the determination in her eyes, and my god, if it doesn't make me proud.

She's been helpless before, not only when Hudson attacked her, and she never wants to feel that way again. I know she will do all that she can to make sure that is the case.

"Okay, Daddy."

I sit back and watch Christian correct Jasmine's stance and show her how to hold the gun correctly. He's spent the last hour and a half teaching her about assembling guns and how to reload them. He has shown her three different types of handguns we know our competitors like to use to ensure she would recognise any that could be used against her.

I'm not going to lie; the whole time we have been down here, my heart has been racing, and I feel sick. If Jasmine ever has to use a gun, then I know we have failed her. She should never have to protect herself from anything or anyone. She has two of her own bodyguards as well as the four of us. But if the last few days have taught us anything, it's that she is never going to be one hundred percent safe. It is something that we have to come to terms with quickly.

I lean forward in my chair and watch as Christian steps back from her. She aims at the target sheet on the other side of the room and, for the shortest moment, freezes before letting out a slow and steady breath and pulling the trigger. She jumps as the sound of the shot echoes around the room, and I realise the mistake Christian made. I walk over to the gun cabinet and grab what she needs.

"Hey, Shorty, put these on."

Christian turns to me and nods, taking the sound defenders from my hand. Being inside a soundproof room makes the noise from the gun louder than if we were outside. We have grown accustomed to it, whereas Jasmine hasn't.

Christian places them over her ears and nods before stepping back, letting Jasmine position herself again and steadying her shaking hands. This time, when the gun sounds, she doesn't flinch, and the shot hits the target. I stand up and look at the target sheet.

"Well, that will work," Sean chuckles next to me. There on the sheet is a perfect hole right in the middle of the bullseye.

"Beginners luck, try again, sweetheart," Christian orders as we step back. Jasmine positions herself again and takes another shot.

"Shit, she shoots better than you, Christian," I laugh as Jasmine hits the bullseye again. I turn, expecting to see Jasmine smiling smugly, but instead, she looks pale and close to tears.

I reach down, take the gun from her hand and pass it to Christian before taking off her ear defenders and pulling her shaking body into my arms.

"You okay, Shorty?"

"I hated that," she whispers as she clings to my top. I look at my brothers and see the pain in their eyes. Some people hate everything about guns, from the way they feel in their hands to the way they feel pulling the trigger, knowing that they could be ending someone's life by doing so. We should have known our girl would feel that way.

"You know the basics now; we will call it a day," Christian says softly as he unloads the gun and places it on the table beside us.

"Come on, Shorty, let's get out of here." I keep an arm wrapped around her and start to lead her away from the room. "Do you want a bath?" I ask as we head back towards the gym. She shakes her head and looks up at me.

"I want to see Daddy Jason," she whispers. Placing a kiss on the top of her head, I guide her up to Jason's room.

Since Jason was injured, she's slept in there every night. She's even using his bathroom so as not to be away from him for long. None of us are surprised as we're all checking on him continuously ourselves. Even though he is okay, there is that fear that something could still go wrong, and we could lose him.

As soon as we get to his door, Jasmine walks straight in. Our rooms are her rooms, and a door is never truly closed to her. As I follow her in, I see Jason sitting up in the bed with his TV on. He turns with a smile on his face, which quickly disappears when he sees how distressed she is. Jasmine climbs straight onto the bed and leans against him as if he is the only thing she needs in the world right now.

"What's the matter, Jazzy? What happened?" he asks as he lifts his arm and wraps it around her shoulders.

"Daddy taught me to shoot," she whispers as I hear the slightest break in her voice.

"Oh, Jazzy, I take it you didn't like it?" Jason asks as he looks up at me. I shake my head while sitting down in one of the chairs that is still in the room.

"No, she didn't. She's a natural, though; she even hit the bullseye twice. But I think it scared you, didn't it, Shorty?"

She nods into Jason's chest as he sighs and runs a hand over her head before placing a kiss on her hair.

"I'm glad you didn't like it, Jazzy, as I hope it's a skill you never use. But you need to know how to handle a gun just in case."

"I know," she says quietly as I look from her to Jason, who gives me a one-sided smile.

"Want me to run you a bath, Shorty?" I offer. Jasmine shakes her head.

"I'll do it," she lifts her head so she can look at Jason, who smiles at her, having already guessed what she wants.

"You know you can use my bathroom. You don't need to ask." He leans down and presses a kiss to her lips. "Go and get yourself sorted, then when you are clean and in fresh clothes, we can watch a movie together."

I smile as her face brightens slightly. She climbs off the bed and rushes into the bathroom.

"I'll get you some clean clothes," I call out, hearing the slightest 'thank you' through the closed door.

"So, she can shoot? Thought Christian didn't want her learning how to handle a gun?"

I turn to Jason and shrug.

"I think after the last few days, he wants her to be prepared for every situation. You both frightened us this week, and none of us want to feel like that again."

Jason nods as he rubs at his face, flinching when he accidentally rubs against his facial wound.

"Well, hopefully, with Hudson dead and people learning about what happened to Flint when he tried to demand money from us, we will be left alone, and the worst is over and done with."

I sigh, climbing to my feet to get Jasmine what she needs.

"I hope you are right, Jason. I really do."

Chapter Twenty-Six

JASMINE

One month Later

"So, what do you reckon? Do you think the O'Reillys will let you celebrate with us next weekend?"

I glance at Danielle and shrug.

"I don't know. Things are only just settling down after the whole Hudson thing," I admit, taking a sip of my coffee. We walk through the hordes of students desperately trying to escape school for the weekend. I know how they feel; I want nothing more than to go home and curl up with my Kindle and my daddies.

"That was a month ago, Jaz; there haven't been any issues or threats to you since! You deserve to go out and celebrate. It's not every day you turn twenty-one."

I turn to look at her, shrugging.

"Technically, I'm not twenty-one for twelve more days," I point out, which earns me one of Danielle's dramatic eye rolls.

"Jasmine Connors, are you really going to allow four

men to tell you what you can do the weekend before your twenty-first birthday?" she demands as she places her hands on her hips and glares at me.

"But they are four very hot men who can withhold sex," I point out, causing Danielle to choke on her coffee. I laugh as she shakes her head, grinning before walking off to the studio she has booked, leaving me by the exit.

"Get a backbone, Connors! Sort it out!" she yells as she disappears into the crowd, as I head to the car park.

I never thought Danielle King would be telling me to get a backbone and stand up for myself. Or trying to drag me out for a night of drinking and dancing, but here we are.

A lot has changed in the last month. Jason and I have both healed after our run-ins with Hudson. It has been confirmed that Hudson died from the injuries Jason inflicted on him, and everyone learnt quickly not to come at me or the brothers whilst trying to get payment for Tommy's debts.

Last we heard, Tommy was hiding out somewhere abroad and hadn't attempted to make any contact. Sean went to the villa in Majorca to check if that was where he was hiding. But there was no sign of him. I won't pretend that I'm disappointed. My birthday is coming up, so it's time for our annual trip to the villa.

This will be our first holiday since my relationship with the guys began, and I can't wait. I want to go and ignore all my worries for a week. At the moment, I constantly feel like something is about to come along and cause issues. One possibility is my mother.

Since my attack, I've tried to reach out to her, and she has refused all contact. As far as we are aware, she is still in the house, and the guys pay a cleaner to keep it clean. Apparently, the house stays clean on the days the cleaner isn't there, and we are taking that as a sign that she is having a few good months. Maybe one day she will reach out, and when she does, I will be here. But I also will not let her drag me down again. I'm happy and in a great place with four men who love me, and I have never been happier.

I walk out of the school and head to the car park, where Terry and Layton are waiting for me. This week, they have stopped meeting me outside of classes and following me around the corridors. I have learnt to keep my panic alarm on my person at all times, but I haven't had to use it since Hudson.

"Afternoon Jasmine, have classes finished already?" Terry asks as I climb into the back of the car.

"Yeah, everyone's gone home. Do you know who's at the house?" I ask nervously. Terry shakes his head before pulling out his phone. Being head of security, I have learned he can track us all on our phones. No matter where we are, he can find us using an app he created.

"Looks like everyone is out and about but heading home. Is there anyone you want to speak to?" he asks, but I shake my head.

"No, I was just wondering who will be there when I get back," I reply. I pull my Kindle out of my bag and start reading as Terry drives us back to the house.

As soon as I get home, I rush up to my room and get all my school stuff sorted. I put my phone on charge and freshen up before heading to the sitting room. I know so far, the only one home is Christian, and I'm hoping someone else will be here by the time I join him. If I want to go out next week with a few of the girls, I need someone on my side when I ask Christian. The chances of him agreeing without an argument are slim, to say the least.

As I walk down the stairs, I'm so busy trying to work out how to approach the subject with the guys I don't realise I'm not alone until someone grabs me around the waist and pulls me off my feet.

I scream and throw an elbow backwards, narrowly miss Maximus's face as his deep laugh sounds in my ear.

"Daddy, you arsehole!" I yell before clamping my hand over my mouth and looking around to check if Christian or Jason are close by. Maximus roars, laughing as he throws me over his shoulder and heads to the sitting room. His large hand comes down on my backside, causing me to call out whilst also igniting the inferno between my legs. As he lands the second one, I find myself moaning with pleasure instead of calling out. I hear a growling sound deep in Maximus's chest.

"You're mine tonight. You'll get your other eight as I thrust into you from behind," he growls, lowering me enough to wrap my legs around his waist as he carries me through a door.

"Eight? But it's been over a month since Daddy doubled my punishment. I'm back down to five!" I protest before realising where we are. I see Maximus's smile widen as I turn slowly and see Christian sitting in his usual spot, giving me his disappointed 'Daddy' look. "Uh oh."

"Someone's in trouble," Jason chuckles as he walks over from the bar. I stick my tongue out at him as Christian clears his throat.

"Why would you be questioning your punishment for swearing?" he asks. I try to lean into Maximus for protection, but the traitor carries me over to Christian and puts me on my feet in front of him before walking away.

"It's Daddy Max's fault!" I protest, pointing in his direction. "He made me swear! I think he did it just so he could spank me!" I argue as I cross my arms over my chest. "Tricking me into being punished shouldn't be allowed!"

Christian looks between me and a grinning Maximus.

"You're dealing with this one. I'll leave it for you to decide on the punishment," Christian says as Maximus walks up to me and grabs my ass.

"That's mine later," Maximus growls as I squeal and Jason laughs from his seat; even Christian smiles as I turn and storm away from them to sit on the empty sofa. Even if I am soaking wet at the thought of Maximus and the things he will do to me later.

"Do I even want to know what's put that look on your face, princess?"

I look up to see Sean walking into the sitting room.

"They are all picking on me, and it's not fair!" I huff, crossing my arms over my chest and one leg over the other.

"I am sure you did something to deserve it," Sean replies as he walks over and tries to kiss me. I lean away from him, placing my hand on his chest to keep him from coming any closer.

"Don't come in here being all loving if you aren't willing to back me up."

Sean looks at me for a moment before grabbing my hands and pinning them to my sides before jumping on me to cover my face in little playful kisses.

"Daddy, get off!" I scream as I can hear the others all laughing around me. Sean stops kissing me but pulls me up, wraps his arms around my waist, pinning my arms to my sides and holds me on his lap.

"You are all mean," I pout as Sean kisses my cheek.

"But you still love us all," he laughs.

"I don't know why," I sigh, trying desperately to keep a straight face. I look at Christian and can see how much of a good mood he's in. I open my mouth to ask him about next weekend, but my nerves get the better of me, and I take my lips between my teeth. I can see from his face instantly that he saw my blunder. Shit.

"Cat got your tongue, baby girl?"

I quickly shake my head, but I know he doesn't believe me.

"Spit it out; what do you want to ask me?"

"How do you know I want to ask you anything?" I ask, frowning.

"Because I can read you like a book. What would you like to ask me?"

I take a deep breath and feel Sean's arms loosen around me a little, giving me room to breathe, for which I am internally grateful.

"A couple of girls from school want us to go out for my birthday next weekend," I blurt out and quickly hold my breath as Christian looks at me.

"I know it's a lot to ask, especially with everything that happened last month. But I could have Terry and Layton with me, and I will stick to whatever plan they suggest. I won't drink much and be home at a reasonable time. I just want the chance to go out, let my hair down a little and dance." I risk a glance at the other three guys, and all I can see is them looking at Christian like they are waiting for him to decide for them. I look back at Christian, who is lifting his phone to his ear.

"Can you come to the sitting room?" He hangs up without saying another word. He looks at me for a second before answering.

"And that's how you want to celebrate your birthday?" he asks. I nod my head.

"It won't be my actual birthday. I want to spend that with you all. But I would like to go out to celebrate with friends as well," I answer before there's a knock at the door.

"Come in," Christian calls out, and Terry walks into the room frowning.

"What's up?"

"Jasmine would like to go out next weekend for a few drinks and then to a club. Can you provide a safe way for her to do so?" Christian asks, turning his attention away from Terry and me. Terry looks at me and gives me a soft smile.

"Absolutely. It would be easier if it were one of your clubs, but other than that, I'm sure we could keep her just as safe as when she's in school or here."

Christian looks from Terry to his brothers as I chew on my lip nervously. I know better than to celebrate too early. He might still find a reason for me not to go.

"Will Amber or Sophia be there?" Maximus asks. I quickly shake my head. He never forgave them for leaving me the night I was so drunk I couldn't walk, but he wasn't the only one. I couldn't forget the way they left me that night, either.

"I haven't heard from them for a long time," I admit, looking at my hands. They had been my best friends my whole life, and they dropped me as soon as things got rough. I quickly learnt they liked what I gave to our friendship and weren't willing to give anything in return.

"You promise to follow any rules we or Terry put into place and to not drink excessively?" Jason asks. I nod eagerly. I have no intention of getting as drunk as I used to. I like waking up without a hangover. Plus, I like the idea of coming home from a great night out and jumping into bed with my daddies even more.

Christian and Jason share a look before Jason shrugs whilst sitting back. It takes all my energy to not get overexcited. Christian looks to Terry and nods.

"Work out the pubs and which club would be best, and I will contact the relevant people."

I stare at Christian for a moment, unable to believe my luck.

"So, I can go out?" I ask, wanting confirmation. Christian looks at me as his face softens.

"Baby, you're going to be twenty-one; I would have never said no. I just need to make sure you are going to be safe."

The last of my control snaps, and I squeal excitedly as I launch myself off Sean's lap and throw myself onto Christian. I wrap my arms around his neck and hug him tightly as a deep laugh radiates from his chest.

"There will be rules, and you need to stick to them," he points out as he hugs me back.

"I will. Just like I did at the fight," I promise.

"You better, as there will be consequences if you don't," he warns. I have no doubt there will be. I have no intentions of breaking any rules as I know there will be other times I want to go out. Christian looks into my eyes for a moment, and I watch his soft side come to the front.

"Come on then, baby girl, let's plan your birthday night out."

Chapter Twenty-Seven

JASMINE

"Jaz, you need to turn twenty-one every year because tonight has been epic!"

I laugh as I look at Verity who is sipping her champagne in the back of the limo.

"We haven't even hit the club yet. Wait until you see inside an O'Reilly club, they are amazing!" Danielle declares next to her as she tops up her glass.

For the first time since I met her two years ago, I don't feel like Danielle is better than me. I used to look at her designer clothes and perfect hair, nails and makeup and part of me wanted that. Part of me wanted to be able to afford more than just sale items or even second-hand clothing.

But tonight, I have a short designer dress on that hugs every curve coming to a stop mid-thigh but rides up a little as I walk or dance. My strappy shoes twist around my ankle and are black, just like my dress. My outfit was given to me today by Jason and lord knows this man likes to shop for me. He is forever coming home with new clothes, bags, jewellery, and anything else you can think of.

At first, I struggled with the idea of him spending money on me, and although I still feel uncomfortable about it, I have learnt to accept it as part of being with the O'Reillys. They love to show me how much they care by giving me the best of everything, and I'm realising there is no point in fighting it. That doesn't mean I don't try now and again though.

"Have you been to this club before, Jaz?"

I turn to look at Martine next to Verity and shake my head.

"I've not been to this one, no. I don't think I have been to any of their nightclubs, actually," I admit as Danielle coughs from her seat.

"You have been to one! You went to the one down by the river a few times with those loser friends you used to hang around with! I saw you there!" she declares. I ignore the small flicker of regret I get whenever Amber and Sophia come up in conversation. Part of me wishes they were here tonight, they were at my thirteenth, sixteenth and eighteenth, and they should be here too.

"That isn't theirs!" I argue frowning at Danielle.

"Of course it is! How didn't you know that?" she laughs as I think back to that last night I was there when the twins just happened to be in the VIP sector. I quickly pull out my phone and send a message to Maximus.

Jasmine: You weren't just in the VIP section that night I was wasted! You were there watching over me, weren't you?

Maximus: Have you seriously just realised that? Shorty, I thought you were smarter than this. We always used to watch over you when you went out. Xx

I growl as I shove my phone back into my bag and start wondering how many other times any of them watched over me when I hadn't realised. It also annoys me that Danielle knows more about what the guys own than I do. I did say to them I wanted to know about their business and things like this matter. Well, they do to me anyway.

The feeling of the car coming to a stop pulls me out of my mini sulk as Terry's voice comes over the music we have playing.

"Ladies, we have arrived. Please stay inside the vehicle until one of us opens the door."

The four girls around me all squeal and all the frustration that was taking over a moment ago is lost in the excitement of getting my groove on.

I can't remember the last time I was able to dance the night away and just enjoy time with friends.

In moments, we are piling out of the limo as Layton holds the door open for us and Terry waits on the pavement.

I look up at the tall building in front of us and am taken away by the beautiful black structure. It might be a club, but you can't hear anything from the outside. If it wasn't for the people queuing outside and the sign that reads …

"w]What the hell?" I look up and reread the name of the place. Shorty's Night Club!

I laugh out loud as the girls follow my line of sight and frown.

"Who the hell names a club Shorty's? That's just weird," Martine asks as I laugh again; I hear Layton laugh as he joins us.

"Yeah, Shorty is a weird name," he says with a wink. I look at Terry who is holding his phone up.

"What are you doing?" I ask, placing a hand up blocking his view of me.

"Someone wanted your reaction when you saw it," he shrugs as he taps on his phone then shoves it back in his pocket grinning to himself.

"It's Maximus's club, isn't it?" I laugh. Terry nods before holding his hand to guide us to the front of the queue.

"Who's Maximus? And how did you know that by the name?" Martine asks. I open my mouth to answer, but Layton pipes up next to us.

"Yes, tell us Jaz. Who is Maximus and who is his Shorty?" I spin around and glare at him, putting my hands on my hips.

"Shut your mouth, or I will tell Daddy you watch my bedroom camera when I'm undressing!" I warn cocking one brow and biting the inside of my cheek to stop myself from laughing when his face drops.

"Christ woman, you trying to get me killed?" his eyes almost popping out of his head as Terry roars, laughing behind him.

"You are turning into a true O'Reilly. Your daddies would be so proud!" Terry laughs. I look around and see my friends all staring at me with their mouths hanging open.

"I thought your dad left when you were eight, and your boyfriend's name was Christian, that's who called you earlier," Grace, another dancer from the school asks as I worry my bottom lip between my teeth.

I don't know whether it's the fact I've had a few drinks to give me courage or that I just don't care what people think anymore, but I open my mouth and spill the beans.

"The truth is I'm in relationships with four guys who all know about each other. They are my daddies, like as in daddy doms. One of them is called Maximus, who calls me Shorty." I throw my arm out to point to the sign. "Hence the name." I look around them all and have to stop myself from laughing. Danielle knew all of this as she heard me refer to Christian as Daddy when she came around after the whole Hudson thing. The others had no idea, and I think I may have blown their minds.

"Fuck that's hot!" Verity gasps next to me, and I stare at her wide-eyed. Verity is the type of girl who comes across as innocent and pure, and I have only ever heard her swear once. Never in a million years would I have expected that response from her.

"I think you just unlocked a new kink for Verity," Martine laughs. All five of us burst out laughing as we hear Terry clearing his throat behind us.

"Ladies, can you please follow me so we can get inside and off the street."

We all quickly mutter a sorry and follow him to the front of the queue to a waiting security guard.

"Sorry, the policy is you all need to show ID," Terry says as he looks around. We all nod and pull out our ID cards. Terry takes mine. "Not you. They have you on file."

"Oh, this must be the famous Jasmine. Nice to put a face to the name. Happy birthday, beautiful," the security guard says with a wink as he holds out his hand. I take it, expecting him to shake it, but instead, he lifts it to his mouth and presses a kiss on my knuckles. Terry clears his throat as I take my hand back, feeling a little uncomfortable. The security guard just shrugs his shoulders and smiles at Terry. "It's fine, I know, Maximus." I watch as Terry continues to frown at the guy, and I have a funny feeling he will be checking up on that statement before the night is out.

After everyone has their ID checked, Terry leads us to a lady in a grey pencil skirt, red blouse and long blonde hair, she is stunning.

"Ladies, this is where I will leave you. I will be on the top floor when you get there. If you have any issues, Jasmine knows how to contact me, and I will be close by. Have a great night." Terry and Layton each give us a quick smile and disappear through a door that states 'staff only'. We turn to look at the woman in front of us.

"Jasmine, I'm Laura, it's lovely to meet you. Ladies, you have been put on the VIP list and have the best booth in the house. If you follow me, I'll show you to the VIP area," she explains as she walks a little way ahead of us, presses a card to a pad, and opens the elevator.

"This is the fastest way to the top floor without having to climb all the stairs and fight through the crowds," she explains as the doors close behind us.

"Jasmine, I can't afford VIP prices," Martine whispers behind me. Laura hears and turns around with another dazzling smile.

"I can assure you your money will not be needed here tonight; you have access to an open bar. All drinks and snacks are covered, from champagne to cocktails, shots and, of course, water. When you are ready to leave, your transport home will be provided as well."

"Wait, what?" We all gasp and Laura just keeps smiling as the elevator comes to a stop and opens up onto a large black marble room.

Inside there's a massive dance floor, which has a number of stages and poles. All around the dance floor are several booths, all with a variety of people. I spot several waiters and waitresses walking around with trays of drinks. We follow Laura to the booth at the top of the room, where there are pink and gold balloons and banners, all with the number '21' on them.

"How did you not see this coming?" Danielle says behind me. I can't miss the jealousy in her voice. I turn with a shrug.

"I had no idea they would go to this much trouble."

As the girls all squeeze into the booth I turn to Laura and smile.

"Are any of the O'Reillys in tonight?"

"No, they aren't, but they've told us to ensure you have anything you want. If you want anything delivered, we can organise it. Nothing is too much for you and your friends," she explains to me loud enough for the rest to hear. She then lowers her voice and talks directly to me. "Layton is in the security room watching the cameras. Terry is in the shadows and will remain close all night. All you have to do is get a waiter's attention if there's a problem, and they will get him here in seconds."

"Thank you," I reply with a smile.

"It's no problem at all. Now, there are three bottles of the best champagne on the table, as well as a list of drinks. If there is anything you want that is not on there, then we are more than happy to get it for you. As I said, tonight is paid for, and nothing is too much bother. When you are ready to order anything, please just press that switch on the wall there, and your waitress, Cheryl, will be there to help you."

"Can we not have him? He's hot," Martine asks, pointing to a waiter as he walks past and winks at her.

"I bet they've been told no male waiters are to serve us, am I right?" I ask as Laura nods.

"You know who you are dealing with well," she replies, chuckling.

"And what happens when their instructions get ignored. So please just ignore the horny one in the corner there. She will have to get a man another way," I laugh as Martine flips me off.

"Rude,"

"But true," I point out, laughing as she shrugs.

"Thank you for all your help," I say to Laura, who grins.

"Have a fantastic evening, ladies," she calls as she heads off towards a door at the back of the room. I sit down next to my friends and look at the decorations around us. It is all too beautiful and makes me feel so loved.

I quickly pull out my phone and send a group message to the four of them together.

Jasmine: Best Daddies ever. I love you xx.

It doesn't take long for the replies to start coming through.

Maximus: Have the best time, Shorty, you deserve to celebrate. xxx

Sean: Wish I was there to see you dancing. Will we get a personal show once you get home? xxx

Christian: Glad you are happy. Enjoy your night and be careful. xxx

Jason: Save the last dance for us when you get home, angel. xxx

I smile as I put the phone back into my bag and grab a bottle of champagne.

"Let's get this party started," I call as I pop the cork, and we all start cheering and looking forward to the night ahead.

Chapter Twenty-Eight

JASMINE

When you are out with professional dancers you can guarantee that they will spend ninety percent of the night on the dance floor. Every time we say we're going to take a break, another great song comes on, and we stay exactly where we are.

On occasion, I get the sensation that I'm being watched, but there again, I'm sure I am. I have no doubt that the guys will be accessing the security cameras to check up on me and that I'm behaving myself. Whenever I get the sensation of being watched, I swing my hips a little more and try to look as sexy as possible just to mess with them. I'm hoping all will be home by the time I get in, as I'm considering giving them their own personal dance, which, of course, will end in bed with all five of us sweating and satisfied.

I'm just imagining the hot sex with my four daddies when I feel two hands on my hips. The hands tighten and I'm spun around and into the arms of a guy.

"Hi, beautiful."

I push against his chest as I step out of his arms, being sure to put some space between us. He grins, and I can't help but roll my eyes. He runs his fingers through his blonde hair, it seems he thinks he's God's gift to women, and he's really not.

"Please don't touch me again," I shout over the music as I turn back to my friends, but he grabs me again and pulls me back to face him.

"Oh, come on, you know you want to dance with me."

I lean back as his foul beer breath blows in my face. I push against his chest and step further away from him this time.

"I don't. Now leave me alone."

I turn to see the girls looking at me. I nod my head towards the booth, and we all walk away, leaving the guy on the dance floor. I spot Terry in the shadows frowning as he takes a step towards me, but I shake my head signalling that I don't need his assistance. He nods once and steps back into place.

"You okay?" Martine asks as she squeezes into the booth. I nod, smiling, as I sit on the end of the bench and reach for my cocktail.

"Yeah, just giving him time to find another poor woman to drool over," I giggle as I finish my drink and press the call bell.

Within moments, our waitress Cheryl arrives.

"Hi ladies, what can I get for you all?" she asks.

"Can we have four cocktails, please?" I ask, smiling.

"Of course, I will bring them straight to you," she says with a wink before disappearing. I sit back in the booth and close my eyes for a moment.

"I think I can get used to being waited on in a club. Do

you think you could organise another night in here?" Martine asks as she finishes her drink.

"I can't see why not. I don't think we will get away with free drinks every time, though," I laugh, knowing that's probably a lie. I can't see the guys ever allowing me to pay for drinks in their clubs.

"Isn't your twenty-first coming up?" I ask, looking to Verity, who nods. "Fancy doing this again?" Her face lights up as we start planning her birthday.

We are so deep in conversation that I don't notice the guy from earlier until he slides onto the booth next to me.

"Hey, there you are," he grins as he puts his arm around the back of the seat and places my hand on my shoulder. I reach up and remove it.

"Look, I've done this nicely, now I'm telling you. Leave me alone," I snap at him.

"Oh, come on, beautiful, I saw the way you were dancing; I know you are desperate for some attention," he slurs. God, this man is a prick and drunk, and I'm getting pissed now.

"Just because a woman is dancing a certain way does not mean she wants a guy's attention. Now, last warning, leave me alone." I warn as I pick up my purse, planning to dig out my panic alarm.

"What if I don't want to?" he asks as his hand falls on my shoulder again, this time squeezing a little tighter. I find my alarm but don't have time to press it before a shadow descends on the table. I look up, expecting to find Terry standing over us, but my heart stops when I see an angry Jason.

"Is this guy bothering you, Jazzy?" he asks, staring at the guy beside me. I watch as his jaw clenches and his eyes darken.

"Yes," I answer thankful that it's none of the others standing before us. Jason will defend me, but the others are more likely to make an example of him.

The guy doesn't seem to have a brain cell in that thick head of his as he leaves his hand on my shoulder. I see the moment Jason spots it, something in his eyes shifts, making him look almost primal.

"Get your fucking hands off her now," Jason warns the guy, who just tightens his hold on me as I try to move away from him.

"What are you going to do if I don't?" the guy taunts him. I gasp as I watch the smile spread across Jason's face.

"Carry on touching my woman, and you will find out," he threatens, placing his hands on the table before leaning towards the guy, who's looking a little less cocky. He slowly removes his hand from my shoulder and climbs to his feet with his hands up. I notice Calvin, Jason's personal security guard, and the new guy Gordon next to him, standing behind Jason, who continues to watch every move the drunk makes.

"Good choice, now get this fucking arsehole out of my club." His security nods and takes the guy's arms.

"You are throwing me out over a bit of skirt? I paid good money to be up here," the guy protests, fighting against guys three times his size. Jason stands taller and steps in front of him; all humour has vanished from his expression, and all that's left is the side I haven't seen since he held a gun to that kid's head at Maximus's fight. I have a feeling this would be going down differently if we weren't in the middle of a club.

"That 'piece of skirt' is the most important person in my world. You insult her by ignoring her wishes; you insult me. Do you want to know what happens to people that insult me? Or would you rather leave willingly in one piece? Because I'm happy with either decision," Jason warns. The guy doesn't say a word. "I thought as much." He looks up at the guards behind the guy and nods. "Get this prick out of my club." His security instantly does as they are told, and we can hear the guy arguing as he is dragged out.

Jason turns back to us and smiles, all signs of the anger on his face from moment ago are gone. I slide out of the booth, and as soon as I'm standing before him, he wraps an arm around my waist and tugs me against him. I place my arms over his shoulders as his lips crash into mine, and he kisses me like he hasn't seen me in days. When he pulls away, he has a broad smile on his face.

"Having a good night, angel?"

"The best, thank you. I was told you weren't here."

Jason nods as he signals for me to sit back down. As soon as I'm in the booth, he sits next to me and places his arm where the guys had just been. This time, I lean into the man sitting next to me. I quickly look at the girls, who are all staring at me with their mouths hanging open.

"Sorry, this is Grace, Martine and Verity; Danielle is on the dance floor somewhere. Guys, this is Jason."

Jason says a quick hi to everyone before turning back to me.

"I can't stay. I had to change my shirt, and this place was closer than home," he said before kissing me. "Plus, I heard there was a gorgeous woman in here who was worth checking out," he grins. I shake my head at him and lean my head against his shoulder.

"You couldn't have timed it better, I was just about to press my panic alarm," I admit. Jason's jaw clenches, and he looks to where the guy has just been dragged out. As he turns to say something else, our waitress approaches us with our drinks.

"Mr O'Reilly, I saw you had joined Miss Jasmine, so I brought your usual in case you wanted it," she says, smiling at Jason. I watch as her cheeks flush and her smile widens. I reach up and hold Jason's hand, which is still draped over my shoulder.

"Thanks, Cheryl, just leave them on the table," Jason says as he looks at me and smiles whilst squeezing my hand. He leans in, and I feel his breath tickle over my ear, "Getting possessive, angel?" I turn and let my lips brush against his as I reply.

"Maybe you're not the only one who can lay claim on someone. You are *my* daddy," I warn as I nip his bottom lip. Jason grins as he leans back.

"Angel, you are making it impossible to leave, but I have to go. When are you ladies calling it a night?" he asks as he looks around the table whilst taking a sip of his drink.

"I don't think any of us are in any rush. Plus, not sure we could get Danielle out of here yet." I laugh. Jason looks to the dance floor and then at me, his eyebrows almost in his hair.

"Is that Danielle King?"

I nod, taking a sip of my drink. "Let's just say her attitude did a one-eighty."

Jason starts to reply but notices Calvin walking over to us and curses. "Shit. Sorry, angel, duty calls. See you at home," he says smiling before turning to my friends. "Lovely to meet you all. I'll add your names to the VIP list, so whenever you are here you can come up to this floor," he says with a wink before turning to his security. "Is the car ready?" Calvin nods and stands back to let him pass.

"Happy birthday, Jasmine," Calvin says in his thick

Southern American accent, with a smile before following Jason, who has his phone in his hand.

"Okay, so I need info, and I need it now!"

I turn to look at Verity and smile.

"That was one of the guys you told me was your step-brother," she points out. I smile and nod. "So, the four guys you are dating are your stepbrothers? Damn girl, that's even hotter than I thought!" she says whilst fanning her face. I laugh as I sip my drink.

"You have no idea," I reply, looking back towards the back door. I saw Jason walk through, wishing he could have stayed a little longer.

"Come on, let's get back out there. I plan on making the most of tonight," I announce as I pull my friends to their feet, and we head off for another dance.

Chapter Twenty-Nine

JASMINE

Tonight has been one of the best nights of my life.

We've laughed and danced for hours, and the only reason we are leaving is that the club is closing. I'm sure we could have stayed longer if we wanted to, but Verity is very drunk and needs to go home. She's so drunk we have stopped trying to get her to walk, and Layton's now carrying her as we all gather in the elevator.

"Okay, it's very busy out the front so Layton you concentrate on getting Verity to the car I will get the others. Jasmine, you stay close to me," Terry snaps as he gives me a look, daring me to argue with him, but I know better. If I want a repeat of tonight, I need to show the guys I will follow all orders.

As soon as the elevator opens, I realise there's a problem. There are people everywhere, all in various stages of intoxication. I'm at the front of our group with Terry beside me and Danielle, who is swaying. As soon as we exit to leave, Danielle falls and shouts out in pain.

"Fuck!" Terry yells next to me as he leans down to pick

her up. In the commotion, I get knocked into and nearly fall over but someone catches me at the last moment. I look behind me and see the bouncer who had checked everyone's ID.

"I've got Jasmine. You get the others to the car, and I'll bring her," he yells as his grip on the top of my arms tightens. I can see Terry's about to argue when the noise around us gets louder as a huge brawl breaks out. People are fighting everywhere, and innocent people are getting caught up in the middle of it all.

I watch Terry as he tries to assess the situation, trying to find the safest way for us to all get to the car. I look back at the bouncer and although something is screaming in the back of my head to not trust him, I ignore it and turn back to Terry.

"Get them to the car, and I'll be behind you!" I yell at him.

"Fuck!" Terry curses as a guy knocks into him and Danielle, who is standing on one leg holding her ankle, obviously having hurt it when she fell. Terry turns to Layton, who looks just as conflicted, I know they would both rather look after me, but they have their hands full with my friends, literally.

"Do not let her out of your fucking sight!" Terry screams at the bouncer, who nods behind me as his grip tightens further, to the point it's painful. Terry grabs Danielle and lifts her into his arms and nods to Grace and Martine.

"Hold on to our tops and stay close!" he barks before looking to the bouncer. "Count to ten and carry her to us so she doesn't get knocked about," he yells over the noise before turning away and heading to the car. Layton looks over his shoulder and for a moment, our eyes meet, he's not happy about this. Layton has been extra vigilant since Hudson attacked me. I swear he can be overwhelming at times, but he is great at his job, and I know I'm safe with him.

"Go!" I mouth to him. I watch him let out a deep sigh, turn away from me and rush after Terry to wherever the car is. The second he's out of sight, there is a loud popping noise, which is quickly followed by three more.

"Fuck!" The bouncer yells as everyone starts screaming and running in all directions. The bouncer grabs me and lifts me into his arms. "Fuck!" he screams as the popping sounds again two more times.

"That's gunshots!" I scream as he barges through a door to our right. "Where are we going?" I yell as he runs through another door, which seems to lead us to the back of the club.

"I need to get you away from whoever has the gun; we can get to the car this way," he yells as he places his finger against his earpiece. "I have her come to the back, now!" he barks, and I relax, realising he must be speaking to Terry. I start to wiggle in his arms to be put down, but he just tightens his hold. "Stay still in case we need to run," he barks, and I instantly do as I'm told. Were those shots meant for me? Surely, that's too much of a coincidence, there is no way anyone would know I was here.

The bouncer adjusts his hold on me, and I feel his watch or something scratch against my leg. I yelp from the sharp stabbing pain which eases quickly.

"What was that?" I ask, trying to move to touch my leg, but he tightens his hold on me.

"Just hang on and you can look when you are in the car." He places his finger against his ear again. "Well fucking hurry up!" he growls, and I panic that whoever fired that gun is heading in this direction. I can hear a car in the distance and pray that it's Terry and Layton. I find myself holding my breath as I look up at the bouncer, still refusing to put me down. He's visibly on edge and constantly looking around as if keeping an eye out for danger, which just heightens my awareness of the situation. The guy visibly relaxes when a black car screams to a stop in front of us. I relax a little myself when I recognise the car as Terry's. I can't see inside as the windows are all blacked out, but I know they would have not left without the girls being safely inside it. The back door opens, and I'm thrown into the back before the door is slammed shut. I look around, and no one is there.

Then it dawns on me.

"This is the wrong car! We came in the limo!" I yell as the guy jumps into the front. I grab the door, but it won't open.

"Hit it!" he yells as he throws my purse that he's holding and his earpiece out of the window. The car flies forward, and the force knocks me into the back seat. My head is spinning as I look around and realise, I don't recognise the driver next to the bouncer.

I try the door again but when I try to focus on the handle, I realise I can see two of them. Everything around me starts to spin and move. I don't like this, it's like everything is part of a dream, and it feels strange.

"What the fuck is going on?" I yell as I lash forward and grab at the bouncer, who turns around and pushes me back into the seat.

"Sit down and shut the fuck up!" he yells, glaring at me.

"Let me fucking go!" I scream, but I notice that my words are slurred, and everything is spinning faster. I jump forward again, trying to get to him, but he pushes me backwards.

"How long will the fucking drugs take to kick in?" he yells at the driver.

"Drugs?" I try to scream at them, but I'm overcome with tiredness that wasn't there before. "Fuck!" I curse as I lose the ability to sit up. I slump to the side and hit my head against the door. I blink repeatedly, trying to clear my head, but it isn't working.

"Sit back there and keep quiet, and you'll be fine," the bouncer warns as I look at him and laugh, realising I'm not going to be able to fight the drugs for much longer.

"What's so funny, beautiful?" he asks, grinning. I might not know where they are taking me or to whom, but I do know one thing for absolute certainty as I lose consciousness.

"They are going to fucking kill you."

Chapter Thirty

JASMINE

"Get her in the van now! They are closing in on us!"

I moan as I feel myself being lifted.

"Fuck she's waking up. Give her another dose!"

Dose of what?

Where am I?

I hit something solid and realise I'm lying on something cold and metal. An engine roars to life as something sharp sticks into my leg, and two loud bangs sound out.

"Go! Go! Go!" someone shouts as two more loud bangs sound around me. I try to focus on anything, but I'm too tired; I want to fight and open my eyes, but they just won't open. I hear one last thing before everything descends into darkness again.

"I think we've lost them!"

Chapter Thirty-One

CHRISTIAN

I race from the house out to the car as it screeches to a stop.

"WHERE THE FUCK IS SHE?"

I grab hold of Terry's shirt as he climbs out of the car.

"We lost them."

"You said she would be safe!" I slam him into the closed door. "You were meant to be fucking watching her!" I scream, pulling my arm back to punch him, but Jason grabs me from behind and pulls me back. Sean and Maximus both help Jason as he takes out my legs and pins me to the ground as I fight them to get to Terry.

"Christian stop! There was nothing he could have done," Sean yells above me, but the red mist has descended, and I have lost all control. The only thing I can see is the man who I trusted with the most important person in my life, and now she's gone and is having fuck knows what done to her. I want to kill him. Fuck all the years we've been friends or the times he has kept me and my brothers safe. He didn't protect her, and that is all that matters now.

"Calm the fuck down, this isn't helping anyone, especially Jaz!" Jason shouts as I push up against them. I feel Jason leaning into me further, so his mouth is near my ear. "Jasmine needs you to be level-headed and in control, not charging around beating the crap out of people trying to find her!" he snarls as I feel my body slumping to the ground. Her name is the one thing that pulls me from the darkness.

"Control yourself, if not for the rest of us, then for her. She needs you to be the strong one, the one to take control," I feel Jason leaning back in. "*We* need you to be in control because we can't get her back without you. Sort your shit out for your baby girl, for Jasmine."

Jasmine.

The love of my life.

My sweetheart.

My baby girl.

My world.

I close my eyes and picture her smile, her laugh, and the way her eyes sparkle when she knows she's being a brat. The last thing I see is the way she smiles when it's just the two of us. When she looks into my eyes, she knows how much I love her and how much I will always love her.

I take a deep breath and slowly let it out to focus myself before opening my eyes and looking at Jason.

"Okay."

Jason looks at me for a moment. "You good?"

"Far from it, but I'm in control."

I pull myself to my feet and dust myself off. I turn to my brothers and see everyone's out of the house. All our security is here, having received the notification that Jasmine has been taken.

"I want everyone in the dining room now!" I yell as I look at Terry and the guys behind him. "Get in there and prepare to tell me everything you know," I order. They all nod and head inside, leaving me outside with my brothers.

"We'll get her back, Christian. Jasmine knows how to defend herself and what to do to help us find her."

I turn my attention to Sean and nod before heading into the house. Not trusting myself to speak. Jason's right; I have to keep it together for my younger brothers, who are feeling just as helpless as me.

Waiting inside the doorway, I find Mrs Brown hovering around like she doesn't know what to do. This woman has grown to love Jasmine, and I know she will be worried sick.

"Mrs Brown, you don't have to stay up, go and rest."

"You know I can't do that. Tell me what you need," she says, taking a deep breath as if to centre herself. I nod as I look around, for something, anything to keep her busy.

"Can you get the coffee machine on the go and maybe make up some sandwiches for everyone, please? It's going to be a late night."

"Of course." I watch as she rushes into the kitchen to start; to keep herself active so she doesn't have time to think. I envy her for that. I wish I could pretend none of this was happening and that my girl was safe, but I can't.

I head for the dining room and walk straight to the chair at the head of the table. I look around at the eight security guards, a handful of bouncers from the clubs and my brothers.

They all came running as soon as the call went out. We may be ruthless, but our staff respect us and always come whenever we call. They know what they signed up for and know that we reward a job well done. They also know we have no issues dishing out punishments when they let us down. Most of these men and women have met Jasmine and have come to like and respect her. They understand that as far as we are concerned, she is to be treated and protected the same way we are.

"From this point forward, nothing else matters but finding Jasmine," I snap as I lean on the table, unable to sit still.

Jason's right. I need to keep a level head, and I need to dig deep into my dark side as I know we are going to have a fight on our hands when we go to get our girl back. I shrug off my jacket and place it on the back of my chair. Looking up, I see my brothers standing in front of me: Jason in a shirt and trousers from his meeting, the twins in their signature jeans and t-shirts. All of us have our game faces on. On the outside, we appear in control and ready for anything. But on the inside, we are hanging on by a thread, and we won't feel normal again until Jasmine is home.

I turn to see Terry standing at the side of the desk. "What the fuck happened?" I demand as I undo my cufflinks.

"Jasmine and her friends were leaving the club at the end of the night. Everything had gone according to plan. Jasmine wasn't intoxicated and seemed to be having the time of her life. One of her friends was highly intoxicated, and we believe they may have been spiked as a way of keeping one of us busy.

Another friend was knocked over as we exited the elevator and sprained their ankle. As all this was happening a large brawl broke out, which we now believe to be a diversion. A bouncer grabbed Jasmine and told us he would handle her whilst we got the others to the car. There was so much going on in such a small space it seemed like the safest way to deal with the situation.

"As we got to the car, there were gunshots fired, and when I turned to check Jasmine, she and the bouncer were nowhere to be seen. I rushed back, expecting them to have taken cover, but I couldn't get near the building due to the commotion caused by a second round of shots. Every time I got close, someone would get in my way, or shots were fired. It was absolute mayhem. When I finally reached the building, it was in lockdown. As soon as they realised who I was and that Jasmine was inside I was allowed entry.

"I couldn't find Jasmine or the bouncer anywhere. I went around to the back of the building and outside thinking they may have tried to get to us that way, but they were nowhere to be seen. That was when I found her handbag and his headset. I realised then he had kidnapped her." Terry stops and takes a deep breath before looking me in the eye.

"We found a used EpiPen on the floor not far from the bag. We believe it was used to inject her with drugs. It had some clear fluid left in it that had been sent to a guy I know for testing. He will have the results within the next couple of hours; he knows this is a priority.

"After realising she was gone, I jumped in a staff member's car with Layton. We raced after them as Tim, another bouncer there who used to be part of my team, checked over the CCTV whilst the driver took the girls home. Tim found the registration, and I tracked the car. But I lost it, and by the time I found it again, it had been abandoned. It looks like they transferred into a van, but there was no way to track it. I picked up Tim and came straight here."

I nod at him. "I want to know as soon as you have the results. We can only assume they were knockout drugs to stop Jasmine from fighting." I pinch the bridge of my nose and count to ten in my head, trying desperately to stay in control.

"Who's been called?" I ask, opening my eyes to look at Jason.

"All the guys we trust. They are on the way and offering assistance in finding her," he explains before leaning on the table. "I sent someone to check on Carol as I had this gut feeling I couldn't shake. She wasn't there, and the place was trashed; they sent photos."

"Like it was before?" I ask, assuming she is back on the drugs, but Jason shakes his head.

"Something went down in there. With the amount of blood on the floor, there is a chance she's dead."

"Fuck," I curse, not knowing what to do with that. "How many people know her and what her relation to Jasmine and our father is?"

Jason shrugs.

"Tommy used to flash her about when they were together. He liked to show off in front of her as well," Sean answers as I rub my face. That means people know they could use her to get information about Jasmine.

"The only reason I give a shit about Carol is that Jasmine will. Let's see if we can find out what happened to her, but Jasmine is our priority. If Carol is dead there isn't anything we can do to help her now anyway," I sigh as I look around at my brothers. "Any news on Tommy? There is a chance he is involved in this."

All three shake their heads. I've had a gut feeling about him for a while now, but I haven't shared it with the others. He's been too quiet for too long. The chances are someone he owes caught up with him.

"Keep trying all forms of communication with him." I run a hand through my hair. "Get this room ready for everyone. Also, contact Taylor. He's offered all his men free of charge if anything was to happen. I want Terry to meet with them in an hour. If the rest of the guys are offering help, we will take anything we can get. I have a phone call I need to make, and then I will be back here." I snap before storming out of the room and heading to my office.

I throw the door open and head straight for the desk. As I sit in the chair, I see the photo of Jasmine and me. My heart aches knowing that she is in the hands of someone who could hurt her. She never asked for any of this, yet we dragged her into this world, and now I have to pray all the training Sean has done with her will pay off, and we find her quickly. But I know that to do that, we will need as many pairs of eyes on the ground as possible. Lifting the desk phone, I dial a number and let out a sigh as I slump into my chair. I hear the phone being answered on the other end of the line and sit forward, leaning my arms on the desk.

"McIntire, It's Christian O'Reilly. Is your offer of extra security still on the table? I don't care the cost. I need as many people as you can spare."

"What's happened, O'Reilly?"

I swallow as I say the three words that I hoped I would never say.

"Jasmine's been taken."

Chapter Thirty-Two

JASMINE

The first thing I notice as I start to wake up is the pain in my head and how strange my mouth feels; it's then I realise I've been gagged. My eyes fly open, but everything stays black. I start to panic when I realise I'm blindfolded, *fuck*. I move my hands, intending to pull the gag out of my mouth when I notice that my hands are tied together behind my back, and when I try to move my legs, they are also tied.

Fuck. Shit. Bollocks.

It all comes back to me, then. The night out, trying to get to the car, but there was a fight and a gun fired over and over again; getting separated from Terry and Layton, and the bouncer shoved me into the wrong car.

My heart starts racing as I try to think what to do first, but so many things are running around in my head that I just can't think straight; it's like my brain refuses to cooperate. I need to breathe and calm the fuck down.

Sean has spent weeks preparing me for every scenario. I take a deep breath and count to ten before slowly releasing it. I do this a few more times, reminding myself that panicking isn't going to get me anywhere. I make myself think about how helpless I felt against Hudson and how I never wanted to feel like that again. By the time I have counted to ten, four more times, I am more level-headed and in control of my mind at least.

With my head a little calmer, I know the first thing I need to do is see where the hell I am. I remember when I was fifteen, a friend showed me a video of a woman who was tied up the same way as I am now. Her arms were behind her back, and her ankles were tied together. She somehow got her arms in front of her by moving them under her legs. I'm very flexible, and I wonder if I could do it.

Luckily, I'm already lying on my side, so I start to manoeuvre my hands down my legs until I feel my ankles and feet; it's certainly not easy, and I feel like I'm going to pull a muscle but with a little bit of wiggling I manage to get my arms under my feet and bring them to the front of me. I take a second to catch my breath before lifting my hands and pulling the fabric that is over my eyes. If I can just see where I am, it might help me to work out a plan. This way, I can also check if there is anyone else around. I've tried to listen out for someone else breathing, but so far, I've heard nothing.

The fabric around my head is tied tight. But I manage to wiggle it from over my eyes, and the brightness coming from the window blinds me. I have to close them again and shield them from the light.

Taking my time, I open my eyes a little until they adjust, and I can see again.

I find myself in a very basic and small bedroom. The bed I'm lying on is uncomfortable, and the bedding itself is minimal. I manage to wiggle my legs around and sit up on the edge of the bed. Now I'm in a better position; I start pulling at the gag tied around my mouth. If I can get my mouth free, I can use my teeth to untie the knots around my wrists.

Eventually, I have my gag off and my hands untied. I quickly reach down and untie my legs before standing up and looking around the room properly.

There isn't much in here, a chair, a bed and one decent-sized window. I rush to it and look out to see that I'm at least three floors up, and it's just a sheer drop to the ground. No trees or drainpipes, nothing I can use to climb down to safety. But even if I was to escape out of the window, where would I go? I have no idea where I am. I'd have to pray that I could get away before they realised I was gone and tracked me down. I look down at my outfit and bare feet and sigh. I'm not going to get very far without shoes or in a tight mini dress, either.

I walk away from the window and tiptoe to the door, hoping there's no one nearby who will hear that I'm up and about. There is no peephole, and I know that if I open the door and someone sees it, I'll be tied back up before I can say *The Nutcracker*. I settle for pressing my ear against the door and waiting to see if I can hear anything. I strain and hold my breath but hear nothing. I take a deep breath to calm my racing heart and nerves and reach for the handle.

"I wouldn't bother if I was you."

I jump as the deep voice fills the room. I look around but can't see anyone; that's when I notice the speaker in one corner of the ceiling; next to it is a surveillance camera.

Crap, why didn't I think to check for cameras. What an idiot! Let's see if they can hear as well as see.

"Why am I here?" I call out as I look up at the camera.

"Because your boyfriends owe me something, and I wanted to make sure I got it," the voice calls back.

So they can hear me then. At least I can communicate with someone. The voice from the speaker sounds familiar, but I can't place it.

"You do realise they will kill you when they find me," I call as I walk over to the chair and sit down, hoping to stay as far away from the bed as possible.

I can hear murmuring from the speaker before the sound of heavy footsteps outside the door. I jump to my feet and put the chair between me and the door as I hear the lock turning before it opens. I quickly look for a weapon, but the chair is the only thing I can see. I look up at the person who walks into the room and feel my jaw drop.

"You're meant to be dead!"

I stare at Hudson, who walks into the room, grinning at me. I feel bile burning up my throat but quickly swallow it. There's something about this guy that absolutely terrifies me. The way he looks at me makes my skin crawl.

"As you can see, I'm very much alive," he announces in that cockney accent that has haunted my nightmares.

"You might be alive, but you look even uglier than before." I chuckle as I look at him and realise one of his eyes doesn't look right. His nose is to one side, and his cheek is scarred. Unlike Jason's, Hudson's doesn't make him look sexy. "You need to fire your plastic surgeon, or did Jason give you the new look?"

"I hear Jason has some scars from our little encounter himself. Apparently, I got his face real good." I look at Hudson's smug face and shrug.

"Unlike you, he pulls off the new scar. It makes him look even more badass than before." I watch as his lip curls up. I'm getting to him, and it makes me feel a little better about the whole thing. He steps forward and glances at the ropes on the floor by the bed.

"You're a flexible little thing, aren't you?"

"Means I can kick higher," I point out as I hold on to the top of the chair, ready to swing it if he comes towards me.

"Oh, I know how high those legs go. I enjoyed watching you from the shadows as you practised that day. It was quite a turn-on. I couldn't help wondering what it would be like if I fucked you against one of those mirrors."

"Fuck you," I growl out through gritted teeth.

"Oh, I think you'll find it will be me fucking you," Hudson says with a grin before walking over to me. I pick up the chair and swing it at him, but it's heavy, and I'm too slow. He blocks it with ease and pulls the chair out of my hands before launching it across the room so hard that it shatters against a wall.

"Nice try, bitch," he growls as he reaches up and grabs my hair. I scream as he pushes me towards the bed. I throw my arm back as Sean taught me and hit him in the face. As soon as his grip loosens on my hair, I spin around and knee him between the legs. Unfortunately, he sees the move coming, and I don't get the impact I was hoping for. I pull my arm back and throw a punch, but he blocks me and hits me in the stomach, knocking the wind out of me. Even as I gasp for breath, I try to fight against him, but he manages to push me backwards hard, and I land on the bed. He grabs the rope from the floor and straddles me, being sure to pin my arms to my sides against my body. No matter how much I buck my hips and try to push him off me, he's just too heavy and strong. He reaches up and wipes the blood from the corner of his mouth, from where I managed to make contact. If I can make him bleed once, I can do it again, so continue to fight against him.

"Darling, you can keep bucking like that. All it's achieving is you turning me on. But by all means, continue."

I stop instantly, and a laugh slips from his disgusting mouth.

"That's what I thought. Now, are you going to be a good girl and let me tie you up?" As soon as he moves to pull an arm up, I try to fight him again, but he anticipates it this time, and I can't get the upper hand. He manages to grab one wrist and ties it to the bedpost with such speed I have a feeling he likes to tie up defenceless women. I try and fight as he moves to tie my other wrist but stop when his cock starts bulging through his trousers, and I realise all I'm achieving is I'm turning him on further, which makes me sick to my stomach.

"See, you can be a good girl when you want to be."

I think it's safe to say, him calling me a good girl does not have the same effect as when my daddies do. When he says it, I want to crawl out of my skin and get as far away from him as humanly possible.

"Is this the only way you can get it? By having the woman tied up so she can't fight you?"

"It's better when they fight, and I can see the realisation in their eyes that they are powerless against me." He smiles as he ties my other hand to the opposite bedpost. He looks down at me, and his smile widens. "You are going to look amazing as I fuck you. I know you will hate every second of it and will never be able to hide it in those beautiful eyes of yours."

"They are going to kill you," I growl as Hudson just shrugs.

"Probably, but I'm going to have fun with you before they do. I'm going to record it as I fuck every hole in your body. Then I'm going to send the videos to Jason and wait for him to lose his shit."

I quickly swallow bile back down. This man makes me sick, and the fact I believe every word he is saying is not helping. There is no way he will not take the opportunity to get one over Jason and the others.

Hudson moves off my legs and I start kicking out towards him, catching him once in the stomach.

"Bitch!" He backhands me across the face so hard I see stars. I'm trying to refocus when I feel him grabbing hold of my ankles and quickly wrapping the rope around them before tying them to the bed. I'm still blinking against the pain in my face and head as he takes advantage and straddles me again. I feel something cold and sharp against my face, possibly a knife, and stop moving instantly.

"Now, are you going to listen to what I have to say? Or do I need to shove something in that mouth of yours?"

I watch as he leans forward with a hand on his belt.

"I'll be good," I reply with gritted teeth as I try to ignore the panic that races through me. But he sees that fear in my eyes, and I see just how much it turns him on. He grins down at me and taps my cheek before climbing off my hips. Even when I see him walking across the room towards a large chest of drawers, I can still feel his weight on me, and I hate it.

I watch as he positions his phone on the top of the drawers.

"I think I might enjoy my time with you. I'm sure your *Daddies* would like to know that all your needs are being met whilst you are under my care." Hudson turns around and walks back over to me, picking up the gag and blindfold from the floor as he approaches. He forces the gag into my mouth before tying the blindfold in place. No matter how much I fight against the restraints, I'm powerless, and he knows it. I'm glad when the blindfold is in place because he can't see the tears that flood my eyes as the fear consumes me.

Hudson leans close to my ear, causing my body to freeze as he whispers.

"Time to send Jason a little preview of what's to come."

Chapter Thirty-Three

JASON

"Please! You must believe me! I have no idea who he's working for, I swear!"

I look up from the knife I am playing with as I lean against the ropes. Our only lead is tied to a chair in the middle of our ring. Maximus has already beaten the crap out of his left-hand man, who's unconscious on the ground next to him.

"Here's the thing, Michaelson. I've been told differently, and I trust the other person a hell of a lot more than I trust you." I push myself off the ropes and take a few steps towards him. I can see the sweat on his brow as he watches the sharp blade in my hand before turning back to Maximus.

"They are lying to you! I told you, Max, I have n-" he gets cut off as Maximus punches him.

"Shorten my name again, arsehole, and I will kill you myself."

"But I've heard her call you ... that!" Michaelson sobs

229

as blood trickles from his nose and mouth. Maximus grabs the hair at the back of his head and yanks it hard.

"That's because Daddy Maximus is hard to call out. Plus, she sucks my cock real good. You going to suck my cock, Michaelson?" I have to turn around to hide the smirk on my face as Michaelson's eyes bulge from his head, and he shakes it vigorously. "That's what I thought, prick!" Maximus growls as I hear Michaelson groan. I turn just in time to see Maximus standing next to him with his arms back across his bare chest as Michaelson shakes his head as if to clear it.

"Let's try this again, shall we?" I sigh, walking behind him and press my knife to his shoulder. "Hudson and you were seen talking the day before I killed him. What was it about?" I ask as Michaelson's shoulders shudder.

"I told you. I asked him to pass on a message to Taylor, and he told me he didn't work for him anymore and had left the area." He turns to look at me. "That's all he told me. He wouldn't say who he was working for or where he was now based. All he told me was his new employer let him have more fun than Taylor would, and we all know what kind of fun he was into."

I look at Maximus as he curses under his breath.

Hudson was known for his particular sexual preferences. Most people like to have sex with someone awake and participating. Hudson likes to rape women who are tied up, unconscious or both. Consent means nothing to him. Taylor had warned us about it and told us he did all he could to stop him; he at least kept a tight rein on that leash. But, if Hudson is working for someone who allows him to fulfil those particular fantasies, then Jasmine has a real chance of being sexually assaulted or raped by whoever has her now.

Sexual predators like to stick together; they are less likely to be caught that way.

"Who do you know who also enjoys that kind of shit?" I demand as I push against the knife, and it sinks a little into Michaelson's skin, who screams like the fucking pig that he is.

"I don't know! Why would I know?" he yells as I push the blade a little deeper.

"Because you're a perverted little fucker who likes to drug women before fucking them," I growl in his ear. "Now, who else would also enjoy that kind of perverted shit? I want a list of all your sick friends that visit that dirty little club of yours and whose clubs you visit," I add as I twist the knife a little.

"Okay, okay! I will tell you everything I know."

We leave a couple of our guys to clean up the mess. Michaelson will be patched up and locked in one of the rooms we have under the club. The last thing we need is him running off and giving his perverted little friends a heads-up that we are coming for them.

I haven't decided if I will allow him to live after we get Jasmine back. I did point out that if she has been assaulted, I will make sure he knows *exactly* how she feels.

I open the car door and freeze as I think of the names on the list Michaelson has given me.

"Fuck!" I scream as I slam my door closed and pace beside the car with my hands on my head.

"Fuck!" I yell again as I feel the need to punch or kill something. My control is close to snapping right now. The thought of her being hurt or abused makes my blood burn as if it were acid.

"Jason."

I turn to see Maximus looking at me. Now it's just me and him; his pain is there on the surface, fuck if I don't feel it too. I hate how helpless we all are to protect our girl. I walk up to him and pull him into a hug.

"We are getting her back," I tell him for the hundredth time since she was taken.

"If they've hurt her," he starts, but I pull back and shake my head.

"They won't; she wouldn't let them," I answer. I'm not sure who I'm trying to convince more, him or me. I quickly pat him on the shoulder, giving it what I hope is a reassuring squeeze, before walking to the driver's door as my phone vibrates. I pull it out of my pocket to see a text message from an unknown number. I open it and nearly drop my phone when I see Jasmine tied to a bed, blindfolded and gagged, still in the dress I got her for her night out.

Everything around me stops when Hudson comes into view as he sits on the edge of her bed. The fucker has been alive this whole goddamn time! She instantly tries to move away from him, but he places a hand on her stomach and holds her in place as she yells, no doubt profanities through the gag. I can hear the anger in her voice, even if I can't make out the words.

"It's okay, darling. I'll be untying you real soon, and then the fun can really begin," he turns to the camera and smirks, "Surprise fucker!" he struts up to the screen and switches off the camera.

I stare at the phone for a second, and it takes every ounce of strength not to throw it to the floor. Instead, I get the keypad up and dial the number I need.

"Can you get a location from a phone number if they send a message?" I ask as my hands shake. I'm clenching my jaw so tight I swear I can feel my teeth starting to crack.

"More than likely, who's been in touch?" Terry asks as I hear him tapping on a keyboard. I know he will be hacking into my phone.

"Who's with you?" I ask.

"Christian," Terry answers.

"What's been sent?" I hear Christian ask. I swallow, knowing this is going to kill him.

"Terry, there is a video in my messages. Hudson's alive and sent it. Prepare yourself, Christian," I say as I hear them both cursing, and I know they've found the message. There is silence on the other end of the phone for a few seconds before I hear the unmistakable sound of Christian exploding.

Chapter Thirty-Four

JASMINE

I hear the door open, and my stomach drops.

I'm still blindfolded and tied to the bed, so there's no way for me to know who has walked in and what the hell is going to happen next. I hold my breath and try to listen to see what I can hear.

"Are you asleep, darling?"

That fucking voice goes through me. I feel the prick pull the gag out of my mouth, and I quickly move my jaw to ease the ache.

"Why don't you untie me and find out," I reply through gritted teeth. Hudson chuckles before I feel his hand on my leg. I instantly try to pull away from him, but being tied up means there's only so far I can move, and it's nowhere near enough. I need to think of a way to get out of these restraints. I have to be able to move, to protect myself. I know the guys will be trying to find me, but I have no idea how far away from them I am or how long it will take, so until then, I'm on my own.

I feel Hudson's callused fingers drift up my leg and I

squeeze my eyes closed under the fabric that covers most of my face. The further up his fingers drift, the harder it is not to move. He likes it when I fight against his touch, he's told me how much it turns him on. It makes me feel sick to my stomach. So far, he hasn't touched me other than on my stomach, but the further his hand drifts, the realisation hits that I may not be lucky for much longer.

"Did you know, when touched in a certain way, I could make you orgasm even when it is the last thing in the world you want? I can force one from you." I feel his hand sliding up to the bottom of my dress and start moving it further up my leg.

"What do you think your boyfriends would think if they saw you wiggling under my touch as you cum all over my hand?" his hand cups me between the legs, and I have to stop myself from crying.

"They would think of all the ways they are going to make you suffer before they kill you," I growl. I force a smile, "Fuck that. Before *I* kill you," I add.

Hudson slaps me hard across the face. Because of the blindfold, I hadn't seen it coming. The shock and pain cause me to cry out. I instantly hate myself for it. I hate that he gets any reaction out of me. I feel him tug off the blindfold, causing me to blink against the bright lights. When I finally focus, I see his phone in his hand and a smirk on his face.

"Smile for the camera, darling."

I look into the lens and tune into my inner O'Reilly.

"Untie me and I'll smile as I watch the life drain out of your fucking eyes you piece of shit."

This time, I see his hand coming towards me, and I manage to stop myself from crying out as it makes contact with my face. Instead, I turn my head to look at him and spit out the blood that's in my mouth from where I bit my inner cheek.

"Fucking bitch!" he screams as he throws his phone onto the bed before tightening his hands around my throat. I try not to fight against him; it's what he will want, but panic starts to kick in as I try desperately to get some air into my burning lungs, but his hold is too tight, and nothing is getting in or out.

I instantly start to thrash against his grip but to no avail. Things are starting to darken around the edge of my vision and I know I'm close to losing consciousness.

As I let my eyes close and stop fighting against him, I think of my daddies, of how they smiled at me the last time I saw them, and of how Jason's lips felt as he kissed me. How Maximus probably smiled when I texted him, calling him out on stalking me. Sean laughing when I promised to come and see him when I got back from the club. And Christian, god what I would give to see that smile he only ever shows me, the soft side of him that is my happy place. The four of them smiling is the last thing I remember as I slip into darkness.

Chapter Thirty-Five

MAXIMUS

"SON OF A BITCH!"

I jump up from the chair as Jason storms into the dining room, his phone in his hand.

"I'm going to enjoy killing him!" he yells as he thrusts the phone at Terry. "Use that to track that fucking prick!" Terry looks at the phone in his hand and heads around to the computer he has set up here.

"What did he send?" I ask, approaching Jason. I go to place a hand on his shoulder, but he shrugs me off.

"I haven't watched it all! I want it tracked quickly!" he yells as he starts pacing around the room. I look to the door as Christian rushes in. He takes one look at Jason and then at Terry, who is tapping on the computer.

"Another video?" he asks as he walks to stand by Terry. I quickly follow suit, and we both lean over his shoulder as he pulls up the video from Jason's messages. We watch as Hudson touches her, he films as his fingers slide up her leg, push her dress out of the way and cup her, touching her lace black underwear I know she would have worn for us to find when she got home.

I listen as he taunts her about forcing her orgasm and Jasmine answers him back threatening to kill him, more than once. My heart swells with pride as she doesn't back down and doesn't let him see she is scared because as brave as she is acting, I can see the fear in her eyes. Only those who know her will see it, but it's there and I hate him for it.

We watch helplessly as he hits her a second time, and then the phone gets thrown out of the way but keeps recording. A noise fills the silence, and for a second, I can't figure out what it is.

"He's choking her," Terry stutters as we listen to Jasmine fighting to get her breath, her arms and legs thrashing against the restraints as she tries to fight him and just as quickly, everything goes silent. My heart stops as I strain to listen for any sign that she is still breathing, that she has managed to get free.

"Fucking breathe," Terry whispers as we all stare at the screen, Jason now beside us as we all wait for something to happen.

Suddenly, the sound of Jasmine gasping and coughing comes through the speaker, and we all let out the breath we were holding with her. I can hear my own heartbeat pounding in my ears as the phone gets picked up, and we see Jasmine out cold on the bed, her face bright red, having passed out from being strangled. The red marks are already showing on her neck, and I can see a trickle of blood running from her mouth. Hudson's face comes onto the screen.

"You've been too soft on her, she doesn't know how to behave herself. I think it's time I taught her a lesson or two." The screen goes blank as the video ends. We all stay looking at the computer screen for a moment, all too shell-shocked as speak.

Christian is the first one to move, he doesn't say a thing. He just gets up and storms out of the room. Terry, Jason and I all share a look, and we know someone has to go after him to make sure he doesn't do something stupid. I watch as Jason turns and heads out of the door.

"I'll try and track the signal again. Hopefully, with the video being longer, we can find out at least what area they are in." I turn to Terry and nod before he starts typing away on the computer again.

"If you get a location, call me."

Terry looks at me and nods. I turn on my heels and head out of the sitting room, heading straight for the garage. I can hear voices coming from Christian's office, but I can't face them, not right now.

Sean will be back in a minute. He was planning on asking around at the school to see if anyone had spotted Hudson hanging around. He also wanted to check on her friends, as it's what Shorty would want us to do.

I don't want to be here when he gets back; I need space to think and clear my head. I jump into my car and pull out of the garage, heading away from the house as quickly as possible.

Everyone seems to have their jobs to keep them busy so they can say they have done something useful.

What am I doing? Nothing. That's what I'm doing. As usual, I'm just the one that follows Jason and Christian around, I'm the fists, the one to beat the information out of people. The problem is no matter how hard I beat them, they can't tell us shit. We're no closer to finding Jasmine than we were when she was first taken.

I drive out of the property and head for the open road. I

turn the music on, and fucking Nickelback instantly starts blazing. The last time I was in the car Shorty had picked the music and of course, it was her favourite band. The song "Because of You" blasts out, and I listen to the lyrics as they sing, *"I won't stand around and I won't watch you die."*

I swerve the car off the road and come to a screeching stop.

"Fuck!" I scream as I hit the steering wheel.

"Fuck! Fuck! Fuck!" I clutch my head in my hands and yell into the air. I'm fucking drowning here, and I don't see a way out.

My whole life, I have known that if I don't know how to deal with a situation, then my older brothers will be there to help me. But this; this is out of all our hands, and none of us knows what the fuck to do next. I try to think, clear my head and work out what I can do that might help. For some reason, a conversation I had with Shorty comes to mind.

I'm watching Jasmine work through a new dance, and she keeps stopping and going back to the start.

"Why don't you just dance the whole thing and then practice it all together?" I asked after she stopped for the fifth time. Jasmine looked at my reflection in the mirror as she got into her starting position.

"To climb a flight of stairs, you have to take each step one at a time."

"What the hell does that even mean?" I ask, frowning. She placed her hands on her hips and turned to face me.

"It means that you take everything one step at a time. For example, I learn dances one section at a time. Once I know it to that point, I start again and let myself go a step further. Eventually, I will get to the last step, and I will have climbed the stairs successfully, achieving the best outcome I could."

"And when you get stuck, you go to the first step and start again," I add, finally understanding her process.

"Exactly."

Before I start to have any doubts, I wipe my face and turn the car around, the wheels spinning as I head to the place where it all started.

If I start from the beginning with a fresh mind, I may be able to pick up on something we missed.

Chapter Thirty-Six

JASMINE

If my calculations are correct, then this is my third day here.

I'm still tied to the bed, but I'm allowed off now and again to use the toilet. The first day I was here, I screamed bloody murder until two guys came in and took me. I'm still in the clothes I wore for my night out, and to be honest, I stink.

As much as I want nothing more than to have a shower or even a wash, I'm hoping the fact that I stink is enough to put Hudson off touching me.

I still have no idea who Hudson's working for. I don't believe that he is doing all of this just to get one over on Jason. As much as he loves making his little videos and sending them to him, he hasn't done much more than grope me for now, and I can't help thinking whoever he's working for is the reason he hasn't taken it further.

I look around the room as the morning light starts to fill it, and I can't stop the pang in my heart as I ache for my guys. Before the last few days, I could count on one hand

and still have fingers left over, the times I have woken up alone. I miss the sound of Maximus's soft snoring or the way Sean moans as he turns over in his sleep. I want to feel Jason's arms around me or Christian's touch as he kisses the top of my head. More than anything, I want to go home.

Everything is quiet until I hear the sound of boots outside of my room, getting closer. I take a deep breath to try and calm my racing heart. I refuse to show any sign of weakness to the prick, especially after he tried to fucking kill me. That wasn't an experience I wish to relive.

I hear the bolt being slid open before the door opens, and Hudson and one of his lackeys walk in.

"Good morning," I call out, adding a smile for good measure.

"What the fuck are you smiling about?" Hudson walks over to the bed and starts undoing my ankle restraints. "Remember what I said?"

I roll my eyes as I look at the dickhead behind him.

"I have to do as he says. I can't escape as there's nowhere to run to. I'm not to fight him as he will strangle me again, and if I start to misbehave, he will take me over his knee and spank me like a naughty little girl."

He never actually said the last bit, but I'm hungry, tired, and getting ratty.

"Are you always such a brat?" Hudson asks as he starts to untie my hands.

"I don't know. Why don't you phone Jason and ask him? I'm sure he would love to hear from you."

I know I've pushed my luck when Hudson grabs hold of my hair and pulls me from the bed. I try to keep up with him to stop the hair from being ripped from my head. Hudson drags me from the room and throws me into the bathroom, which is next door. I slide across the floor and hit the bathtub, luckily managing to stop myself from getting injured. As I look up, Hudson throws a bag and a towel at me.

"Get showered and put them on. Don't try and do anything stupid," he barks before storming from the bathroom, leaving his friend in here with me.

"Someone's in a mood this morning," I sigh as I stand up and open the bag.

Inside is shower gel, shampoo and deodorant, as well as a pair of leggings and a baggy t-shirt. "What? No conditioner or underwear?"

"Just get showered and dressed. We haven't got all fucking day," the guy snaps.

"Rude." I roll my eyes before looking back at him. "Any chance of some privacy?"

"Don't push your luck," is all I get back in response. Great.

I turn to the bathtub and see a shower head attached to the wall and a shower curtain. It won't give me a massive amount of privacy, but some things better than nothing.

Standing in the bath, I draw the curtain before pulling my dirty clothes off. I have a feeling this guy won't do anything because if Hudson hasn't yet, I'm sure his lackeys won't either. I still shower as quickly as I can, washing my long hair twice and scrubbing every inch of my stinky body.

Standing at the back of the bath, I dry myself the best I can with one towel and pull on my new clothes. They are all too big, but anything is better than nothing.

"Will you hurry the fuck up!" the guy standing guard calls.

"All right, keep your hair on!" I pull back the shower curtain and look up to see that the guy is bald, "Or not," I add, which earns me an eye roll. He bangs on the door once, and it unlocks from the outside.

Hudson opens the door and looks at me as I run my fingers through my wet hair.

"Any chance of a brush?" I ask as I walk past him and start heading towards my room. If I'm forced to stay in one room, then I will walk there on my own terms.

I walk over to the window and look out at the garden below me, looking for any sign of where we are. I was knocked out for the whole journey here, so we could be anywhere.

"Looking for a way out?" Hudson laughs behind me. I shrug as I turn to face him.

"So, what's the overall plan here? You've kidnapped me and recorded your little videos. What's next?" I ask as I lean against the windowsill with my arms across my chest. The move instantly makes me think of Christian, and I have to stop myself from smiling.

"You will find out soon enough. The boss wants to see you."

I cock one brow as I look at Hudson's friends.

"Is he not the boss?" I ask, nodding towards Hudson.

"Will you shut your mouth for once in your sorry life!" Hudson snaps as he heads to the door. "Come on in."

I watch the door, my anger getting the best of me when I see the two men who walk in.

"You son of a bitch!" I cry out as I fly towards him, Hudson manages to catch me around the waist before slamming me to the floor. His knee instantly digs into my back as he holds my arms behind me.

"Now, Jasmine, there is no need to be like that," Taylor smirks as he looks down at me.

"You sat there and lied to our faces over and over

again!" I yell at him. "I think I have every right to be pissed off right now! And you!" I turn and look at Tommy O'Reilly. "You are the lowest of the fucking low. Your sons have done plenty for you!" Tommy's face turns red with anger.

"They cut me off because of you, you little bitch. This is all your own doing!"

"I suppose you have the right to be pissed off. But you see, the O'Reilly brothers think they are bigger than they are. It's time they were brought down a peg or two. Who better to do it than their father and an old friend? It seems they really will do anything for you, which will make their demise even sweeter when they lose everything, including you," Taylor grins.

"Let me guess, you're going to let ugly here rape me on camera so you can send it to the guys before killing me in the hope it will destroy them. Then Daddy dearest goes to comfort the guys and gets his hands on the money again," I reply.

Taylor smiles as he shakes his head. "No, I don't think I'll kill you. I think it will be more fun watching you break their tiny, pathetic hearts first. I do love it when someone gets their souls crushed; in this case, it will be four of them."

"There is nothing you could do that would make me hurt them," I point out, glaring at him. But Taylor just looks at me and smirks as he watches me fighting against Hudson, who applies enough pressure to my back that I cry out in pain.

"I think I know just the thing."

"You can try, but they have hidden nothing from me. There is nothing that would surprise me."

"Oh, I think there is, and the fun part is they don't even

realise it involves you," he chuckles before turning to Tommy, who looks a little confused.

"Although I'm not sure if I included you in this part of the plan. Did I ever tell you there is a third party involved?" judging by the look on Tommy's face, I guess not.

"What the fuck are you on about? Third-party? You mean that moron?" Tommy asks, pointing to Hudson. Taylor laughs, shaking his head.

"God, no. I think it will be easier if I introduce you properly." Taylor looks over his shoulder and calls out, "Come and say hello, dear."

I watch the woman who walks into the room and stands beside Taylor, and my heart sinks before the anger takes its place. Judging by Tommy's face, this was the last person he expected to walk through the door.

"What the fuck are you doing here?"

"Is that any way to speak to me?" she smirks, standing beside Taylor, who puts his arm around her waist. She looks down at me and smiles. "Hello, Jasmine." Her smile is as fake as her hair and eyelashes. She looks nothing like the last time I saw her, and I don't know whether that's a blessing or a shame. I want nothing more than to get off this floor and beat the living shit out of her, but instead, I clench my teeth as I growl a reply.

"Hello, Mother."

Chapter Thirty-Seven

SEAN

"And you have no idea where he's gone?"

I turn to look at my two older brothers.

"If I did, I'd be going after him!" I snap as I lean against the breakfast bar. I run my fingers through my hair and take a deep breath. "He isn't handling this well. I know none of us are, but Maximus has taken it personally since he hired that bouncer, Trent, himself."

I walk over to the coffee machine and pour myself a cup. God bless Mrs Brown for keeping this machine going. I don't know how many cups I've drank in the last three days. I always tell Jasmine that coffee isn't food, but it's the only thing keeping me going right now.

I take a sip of my drink and look around at my brothers. Both stare into space, lost in their pain. It's only a matter of time before someone snaps, and then all hell will really break loose. My fucking twin isn't helping matters either.

Twenty - four hours have passed since Jason received the video of what we believe is Hudson strangling Jasmine. I wasn't here at the time, but when I finally saw it, I had to walk away and spend half an hour in the sparring room. Every time I punched or kicked the punching bag, I pictured Hudson. It was there that Jason found me and told me Maximus was missing. It seems he took off after seeing the video and has yet to return.

As if we don't have enough to worry about, now it seems he's gone off on his own to look for her. We had confirmation that he was at his club, where Jasmine was taken two hours after he drove out of here. He went through the staff records on the system, watched the CCTV, and then ran to his car, but now we have no idea where he is.

"If he got an idea of where she was, would he go off to rescue her alone?" Christian asks. I shake my head.

"He might be many things, but reckless when it comes to Jasmine's life is not one of them. He would let us know where she was and would take as much backup as possible, that I'm sure of. Especially after what happened with Jason."

Christian sits on one of the kitchen stools and rubs the bridge of his nose. He looks exhausted; we all are. None of us are getting much sleep. How can we when Jasmine is out there somewhere?

I pull my phone out of my pocket and am just about to try Maximus again when I hear his car pulling into the garage.

"I'm going to kick his ass," Christian growls jumping to his feet and rushing towards the garage door, Jason and I quick on his tail. Christian reaches him in seconds and has him against the car.

"Where the fuck have you been?"

"I got the fucker who took her!" Maximus yells, pushing Christian away from him and walking to the trunk. When he opens it, a laugh sounds from Jason because there, tied up and gagged, is the bouncer, Trent. Maximus looks up at me, and I see a level of determination on his face that even scares me.

"Help me get him to the basement."

———

It's been three hours since Maximus arrived with our new guest, but other than beating him nearly to death, we are no closer to finding out who Hudson is working for. Trent has told us everything he knows. It may have taken quite a bit of persuading, but he doesn't know anything else.

Turns out Trent was paid to get friendly with Maximus. He was to get a job as a bouncer and wait to see if Jasmine had her birthday at one of our venues. Apparently, Hudson knows a lot about Jasmine, such as how she goes out every year for her birthday and would always end up in a club. Trent had been keeping an eye on the VIP lists on the system after hacking into them and waited for her name or ours to show up. Once he knew where she was going to be, he managed to swap with another bouncer to make sure he was there that night.

We already had confirmation that the other bouncer was unaware of the real reason Trent wanted a swap. He had told the guy it was due to his sister being in town and wanting to keep an eye on her and her abusive boyfriend. Our guy fell for it, but who can blame him? Everyone who has had any dealings with Trent has told us what a down-to-earth and great guy he is. None of them could believe he had been involved in the kidnapping of our girl.

Trent informed us that another guy drove the car to a woodland area and put Jasmine in the van before getting away from Terry. They drove the van to a farm an hour away and met with Hudson, who took it with Jasmine still unconscious in the back and gave them a car. They got a hefty payout for it, all in cash, so there is no way to track it.

We asked Trent about the guy who drove the vehicles, and all he could tell us was that he had dropped the guy off at the airport and had no idea what his name was or where he was going. Seems he had the common sense to run, knowing we would kill him.

It had taken Maximus a whole day to track down where Trent had been hiding out. He had been at a friend's house three hours away. I don't know how Maximus managed to find him. It just shows how clever he can be when he puts his mind to it. My twin always hides behind his physical strength. It's an act he's played for as long as I can remember. But for his Shorty, he will happily use his brain and do everything in his power to try and find her.

"So, it was all for fucking nothing!" Maximus shouts as he punches Trent one more time before storming out of the room.

"It wasn't for nothing. At least we know he leads to a dead end," Christian calls after him. But we all know he wasn't listening. Jason and Christian both turn and look at me. I sigh as I push myself away from the wall I'm leaning against. They know times like this, other than Jasmine, I'm the only one who may be able to make him see sense.

"Let me speak to him." I walk out of the basement and follow Maximus. I'm just reaching the main staircase when I hear his bedroom door slam shut. I jog up to his room and take a deep breath before entering, not bothering to knock.

"I'm not in the mood, Sean!" he calls from his bathroom as I hear the shower being turned on.

"Well, tough. You are going to listen," I reply, walking in after him.

"What?" he yells, turning to look at me. He's naked, and there's still blood on his chest and arms from beating Trent and others whilst looking for him, no doubt.

"Today wasn't a waste of time. You did more than the rest of us have been able to. Not only did you find out where Trent had been hiding, but you also managed to rule out that he knew anything else. Sometimes a dead end is good as it lets us focus on the shit that might help."

"Why did you just sound like Shorty when she's trying to get away with something?" he asks, frowning. I can't help but laugh.

"I think she may have said something along those lines once after failing a test a couple of years ago."

Maximus rubs his face as he looks at the floor.

"I miss her, Sean. I hate knowing that he's hurting her, and there's nothing we can do."

"I know. But Jaz is a hell of a fighter, and I know if she gets a chance, she will cause some serious damage."

"I hope so," he sighs before looking at the still-running shower. "What time is everyone getting here for this meeting Christian's called?"

"You have an hour to get cleaned up. Mrs Brown is making dinner for us all, and you know she'll watch over us until we eat it."

"How's she doing?" Maximus asks, looking at me.

"She's as can be expected. She and Jaz have grown close. I think they have the mother/daughter relationship they both always wanted."

Mrs Brown has been with us for years. I can't remember her husband, who used to be the gardener and maintenance man for our family home and various fight clubs. They never had any children of their own; I don't think they could.

Mr Brown died when Maximus and I were two, and Mrs Brown has never truly gotten over his death. She threw herself into looking after us, especially after our mother died when we were twelve. Watching the interactions between Mrs Brown and Jasmine, it's evident that they care greatly for each other. It also gives Jasmine a female to talk to about certain things. Having four men around can't be easy for her, but Mrs Brown is more than happy to be that female confidant that she needs sometimes.

I let out a sigh and walk out of the bathroom, leaving my twin to have his shower.

"Get sorted. I'll meet you in the kitchen for coffee," I call as I walk out of his room. I try not to look in the direction of Jasmine's room for fear of the pain consuming me. But as I walk away with my back to it, I silently make a promise to her.

"I don't know where you are, princess. But we will not rest until we find you and bring you home."

Chapter Thirty-Eight

JASMINE

To say I'm done with surprises would be a fucking understatement after today.

Of all the people to have paired up with Taylor I never in a million years would have imagined my own fucking mother!

We are now all standing or sitting in various places around the room, having a cosy conversation with Mum, and what? My new stepdad? As well as my old stepfather, who could also become my future father-in-law.

I couldn't make this shit up; I need to start my own brand of greeting cards for fucked up families.

"Does someone want to tell me what the fuck is going on?" Tommy demands as he stands against the wall. He looks furious, and I can't help but feel some satisfaction from that.

"Isn't it obvious? We've been using you to get the intel on your sons so that when we bring them down, there will be no way back for them," Taylor admits casually as he leans back in a chair with his arm across the back of my mother's.

"So, what is it, Mum? You realised you couldn't sell my virginity anymore, so you just sold *me*?"

"Don't be so dramatic Jasmine, not everything is about you."

I throw my hands up in the air emphasising our surroundings.

"I'm sorry I forgot me being kidnapped was hard on you," I sigh, sarcastically. She looks at Taylor and points to me.

"You see what I've had to put up with. People wonder why I turn to drink and drugs; well look no further than the daughter I was forced to bring up." The woman has the audacity to make out like I'm to blame for all her bullshit!

Five months ago, I would have probably accepted that and felt guilty. But if my daddies have shown me anything, it's that I'm not to blame for anything my mother has done. She was turning to drugs before my father left; how can that possibly be my fault? I was eight! No, I refuse to let her blame me for any of it.

"Don't make me laugh. You didn't bring me up; you were too off your face to do anything but sleep and run off with whoever you were fucking at the time," I laugh. "Seriously Mother, you are one of a kind."

Mum's face turns beetroot red as she looks ready to explode. She looks to Taylor, lets out a deep breath and sits back in her seat. I take it he doesn't like her outbursts. It's amazing how quickly her personality changes based on who she is sleeping with at the time. It was one of the reasons I liked her with Tommy; she seemed laid back and content with her life. There again, both ripped me off and tried to sell me to the highest bidder, so no wonder they got along so well. Two people that are looking for ways to make money from others.

"I think we all need to take a deep breath and calm down, don't you? You are in no position to disrespect those caring for you," Taylor warns before his phone starts ringing. He looks down at the screen and points to me, "Gag her."

Before I can blink, Hudson has a gag wrapped around my face and forced into my mouth. I start to moan against it as I try to pull the fabric from my face. He pulls it tighter with one hand as his other hand tightens around my throat.

"Shut your mouth and don't move, or I will cut off your air supply until you pass out again."

I know better than to test him after last time.

"Christian, any news?"

I glare up at Taylor as he answers his phone. It kills me to know that Christian is just on the other end of the phone, talking to someone he thinks he can trust. I find myself straining just in the hope of hearing his voice, but Taylor is too far away from me.

Out of the corner of my eye, I spot movement. I look to see Tommy messing with the cuffs of his trousers. As he looks up, he seems to take note of the fabric around my mouth, and for a split second, he looks almost angry. As our eyes met, he looked at me for a split second before looking at the chest of drawers beside him. I look away from him in time to see Taylor's eyes snap to Hudson.

"You found the guy who took her?" he repeats, and Hudson shrugs his shoulders, not looking worried in the slightest. "He couldn't tell you anything at all? I'm sorry to hear that … No, I've tried a few different contacts of Hudson's, and no one has seen hide nor hair of him. He hasn't been in touch since the last video?... Okay, what time do you want me there? ... I'll see you then." Taylor ends the call and looks furious when he turns to Hudson.

"Maximus was able to track down Trent! If that moron can track down one of your mates, it won't be long until the others find someone!" Taylor roars. Hudson loosens his hold of my throat and lets go of the gag, removing the disgusting piece of fabric from my face.

"No one knows where we are or that I'm still working for you. The only people who know aren't allowed to leave this estate. It's fine. I've covered all bases." Hudson looks at me with that arrogant grin; I roll my eyes as I look towards Tommy, who's staring at Taylor.

"Do you want to tell me where the fuck I fit into this little plan of yours? We had a deal; you help me get access to their money again, and I back all your new ventures. You better not be double-crossing me, Taylor."

Taylor laughs as he shakes his head. "Why do you think I'm keeping her alive? I don't plan on you having access to their money. I plan on killing all four of them and taking everything they have," Taylor smiles as he looks at me. My blood runs cold, and I feel physically sick. "You're the only thing that will distract all four of them enough for me to take them out. One. By. One."

I start to rise from my seat, but Hudson places a hand on my shoulder and pushes me back into the chair whilst growling a warning for me to listen.

"Once they are all dead, do you know who gets everything? The money, clubs, houses, right down to the clothes on their backs?" I shake my head as Taylor smirks before looking back at Tommy. "Her. Jasmine is to inherit everything they have; you are to get nothing; the paperwork has already been filed."

"This was never part of the deal, Taylor. You will not

kill my boys!" Tommy yells. I've never seen Tommy act like a father before. But now I see a side of him I always secretly hoped existed. Those boys mean something to him. It might not be the love they deserve, but it's something, nevertheless.

"Do you really think you will be able to stop me? You are nothing without me, and you know it." Taylor growls before his back straightens. "Actually, I've got all I need from you." A gunshot rings through the room, causing my mother and I to scream. I look at Tommy as he slides down the wall to the floor, his eyes staring at my mum, unblinking with a hole in his chest. I'm struck dumb; my eyes fill with tears as I stare at the guys' father, dead. All I can think is how much this is going to kill them. They've said they are done with him, but he is still their father.

"I've got to go and show face to these morons. Need to keep them sweet until we are ready to make our next move," Taylor announces as if nothing just happened. I thought Tommy and him had been friends for years. Yet he just watched his friend die and didn't even blink.

He places a hand on my mother's shoulder. "Do you want to have this chat with her now or later?" Mum looks at me and shrugs. Apart from the initial shock of the gunfire, Mum seems unfazed by Tommy's death. She was married to the man for just short of three years! What the hell is wrong with these people?

"I'll come back later; it's not like we won't have time." She stands up and takes the arm Taylor holds out for her. He looks over his shoulder to Hudson.

"Leave her untied; she isn't going anywhere. Get him moved, though. I don't want him stinking the place up."

With that, Taylor turns and walks out of the room with my mother.

"Get in here and help me move this prick!" Hudson

shouts as he moves away from me and towards Tommy's body. The guy who watched me shower before comes in carrying a plastic sheet. The realisation hits me then. They planned on killing him today; they had everything in place.

I can't stop the sob that leaves my body as they pick him up and throw him on the sheet before rolling it up and taping it to ensure no blood leaks out. Wrapping him like a piece of shit their dog has left behind. It's wrong. He was a human being, a father. He may not have been a decent one, but he must have loved his boys deep down. I'm sure of it.

As Hudson and the other guy move the body, a third comes in with a bucket, towels and brush. Hudson turns to me.

"Clean that blood up if you want to eat for the next week!" he snarls. I stand up and shake my head.

"You killed him, you fucking clean it, you piece of shit!" I yell, my temper getting the best of me. Hudson and the guy lower Tommy's body, and he launches himself at me. I fall backwards and hit my head on the edge of the bed. I bring my knees up to push him away from me as I throw my arms up, wanting to punch him, scratch him, do anything just to get him off me. But one of his friends grabs my arms and pins them down above my head. Hudson pins me to the floor and hits me hard; I feel my nose break as my eyes burn. His other friend grabs my flailing legs and pins them to the floor.

"Do as you are fucking told! I've had enough of your talking back! You carry on with this shit and I will fuck you up; do you understand?" he roars as he shoves his hand down my leggings and thrusts two fingers into me, making me scream as I feel pain like I have never felt before.

"This is mine now, I will fucking take it whenever I fucking want! The more you talk back, the harder I will be on you. Do you understand me?" he growls as he thrusts his fingers deeper into me, and I cry out again.

"Next time, it will be my cock, and you will take it like the good little slut you are!" he leans his head down. "You can forget all about the O'Reillys. From now on, I own you. I say who fucks you and when. I don't care how fucking much they hurt you." He thrusts his fingers into me again before pulling them out. He holds them up for me to see a small amount of blood on them. The smile that spreads across his face is something that will haunt my nightmares for years to come. Hudson turns to the other guy.

"I love it when they bleed," he growls before sticking the fingers into his mouth and sucking off the blood. He climbs off me as his friends let my arms and legs go. I instantly curl into the fetal position as I cry. "Get that blood cleaned up before I get back. Or your blood will be joining it." He throws the towels on me before heading back to Tommy's body.

"Fucking move it!" he screams, and I scramble to my knees and crawl over to the blood. There's so much of it; I grab a towel and place it over the blood as I hear them carrying out Tommy's body.

"See, women are just like dogs. All you need to do is show the bitch who's boss, and she'll do as she's told," I hear him laugh before the door closes.

As soon as it clicks closed, I break down. I cry harder than I have in ages. My crotch is throbbing, and I feel dirtier than I've ever felt before. I grab a clean towel and hold it to my face before I scream into it. Unable to hold back the tears as I cry out over and over again. I'm still gasping for air, unable to stop the tears, when I spot something just hidden behind the chest of drawers beside me. I look around to check if I'm alone and take a closer look. I pull the object out and realise it's Tommy's mobile.

Did he leave it here on purpose? Was this what he was doing when I saw him messing with his trousers? Did he know he was going to die and wanted me to have a way to warn his sons? I look around and quickly shove the phone back behind the chest of drawers, which is out of sight but within reach. I wipe at my face and quickly get about cleaning up the blood whilst plotting how I can get word to the guys. I need to make sure to do it right. Otherwise, Hudson and Taylor may realise and move me. Then the guys will never find me, and Taylor will kill them quicker.

Knowing I have that phone hidden away gives me a new lease of strength, one I don't plan on letting Hudson break. I just have to bide my time, but there is light at the end of this very long, dark tunnel.

Chapter Thirty-Nine

JASON

What the hell did Christian think this meeting was going to achieve? We are no closer to finding Jasmine, and no one has any new leads. Taylor has offered more help, but the way he's acting seems off. I can't put my finger on it, but he seems too eager to help us find her.

I sit back in my chair and rub the bridge of my nose. I'm exhausted. Actually, I'm past exhausted, but there's no way I could sleep whilst my Jazzy is out there, having God only knows what done to her.

"I think it's time to call it a night, gentlemen."

I look up at Christian, who looks even more tired than I am. I don't think he has had an ounce of sleep since she was taken and it's showing. I don't know who blames themselves more; all of us feel like we are to blame. Maximus because he hired Trent. Christian because he feels he failed her. Me for letting Hudson live when I should have killed him years ago, and Sean, who fears he hasn't trained her enough. Either way, we all let her down the moment she was taken.

I stand up with the others as they start to leave.

"Jason, can I have a quick word?" I turn to see Geralt Young looking up at me. I nod and lean back against the wall whilst he puts his coat on and checks his phone. I notice he keeps looking up as if to see who is still in the room. Christian looks at me and frowns as he sees the last two guys out of the door. I nod towards Geralt, and Christian lifts his head in acknowledgement before leaving the room. Geralt looks around as if to make sure no one else is left here before turning his back to the table and leaning against it.

"How are you doing, Jason?"

I close my eyes for a moment and let out a deep sigh before looking back at him.

"As can be expected," I admit, running a hand over my face. I decide to take this opportunity to speak to him without the fear of being overheard.

"Are you sure there is no way Taylor is involved? For someone who couldn't stand us a month ago, he is being very helpful. Maybe a little too helpful."

Geralt tugs on his ear as he looks down at the carpet. It's his tell; he always does this when he has a bad hand of cards when we play poker or if he is uncomfortable with a situation. I push myself away from the wall as I pay attention.

"What do you know?" I demand.

"Nothing concrete, but I've been wondering the same myself. Don't get me wrong, I've known Taylor for many years and always found him to be trustworthy. But recently, something has felt off, like the fact Hudson just left, and he had no idea. He sees Hudson like the son he never had, and for Hudson to just leave him makes me think there is more to the story than he's letting on."

I nod in agreement; it just all seems a little too convenient for my liking. I need to speak to my brothers and see what they think on the matter. I know Sean and Maximus have always been dubious about Taylor's intentions and have voiced their concerns more than once, but Christian seems to have been reaching out to him a lot since Jasmine was attacked.

"You keep your friends close and your enemies closer."

I look at Geralt, place my hand on his shoulder, and squeeze as things start to click into place.

"Thanks. I think I might keep an eye on him and see what he's up to." I look into his eyes as I add, "This conversation stays between the two of us until I have a chance to speak to my brothers."

Geralt nods and offers me a warm smile.

This man has always been more of a father figure to us than Tommy ever was. He has stayed close, but more so since Jaz's attack. He has even brought his family around for dinner a couple of times, and I know his daughter, Abigail, has become good friends with Jasmine, as they are around the same age.

"Of course, Jason. Anything you need, you just shout. Know we are here for you all. Abigail is beside herself with worry. I know she is hoping her friend will be back soon; we all are."

I nod as we head out of the dining room, and I lead him to the front door. As we stand on the front steps, I watch as the last few cars drive away, Geralt's driver being the last one on the large drive.

"Thank you, Geralt. I will keep you posted." I squeeze his shoulder one more time and force myself to go back into the house before it becomes harder to hide my pain.

I close the front door behind me and head to the sitting

room in the hope of finding my brothers, but it's empty. We don't seem to come in here now; it's become this room we spend time in as a family, but our family isn't complete without Jazzy. I try Christian's office next and again find it empty. There are only two other rooms that he will be in at this time, and I have a feeling I know which one it will be.

I make my way through the house to the stairs and listen out to see if I hear anyone, but the house is too quiet. We've become accustomed to the sound of Jaz laughing or singing to herself as she walks around. I miss the tell-tale squeal she does when she has pushed Maximus's buttons or the way she lets out a high-pitched laugh when Sean catches her off guard and sweeps her off her feet. Before Jasmine, we hardly ever heard Christian laugh, mainly because he was hardly ever here, and when he was, he worked. But now we can hear the two of them laughing together daily, and he seems to have become the old Christian we haven't seen in many years.

I'm just about to head upstairs when I hear the sound of someone crying quietly in the kitchen. I reach the door and see Mrs Brown dabbing her eyes as she cleans the sides, crying quietly to herself. I walk in without saying a word, pull her into my arms, and hold her. For a moment, she freezes before wrapping her arms around me and crying into my chest.

After a few minutes, she pulls away from me and wipes her face on the tea towel she has in her hand.

"I'm sorry," she whispers before turning away from me.

"Don't apologise, we all miss her. We will get her back."

Mrs Brown reaches up and pats my cheek.

"I know you will. I don't doubt it," she replies before turning around and walking into the small annex she has at the back of the house. I let out a sigh as I turn around and head back to the stairs to find Christian.

As expected, I find him in Jasmine's room, just looking at her bed. I can still smell her perfume in the air and the sweet scent coming from the roses that Mrs Brown keeps fresh in here.

I lean against the door and cross my arms over my chest. I don't think Christian sees me to start with. He's just sitting back in the chair, drinking a glass of whiskey and staring at the bed. I think back to the time I sat just like that, watching her sleep before tying her to the bed and punishing her by withholding her orgasms. I swear I will never withhold them again if we can just get her home.

"This isn't how I expected to spend tonight."

I let out a sigh and look from the bed to Christian.

"This isn't how any of us expected to spend tonight," I sigh. "We should be making love to our girl before whisking her away to the villa to celebrate."

Tomorrow is Jasmine's birthday, and we had so many surprises planned. We had booked a flight to Majorca and planned on spending a week treating her to anything she wanted. Instead, she is tied to a bed somewhere, possibly having unspeakable things done to her, and we are powerless to stop any of it.

"Everything I have built and all the things I've had to do over the years to get us into the position we are in, was for nothing."

I look at Christian and shake my head.

"It wasn't for nothing, Christian; none of it was for nothing." But when Christian's eyes meet mine, I see no life in them. It's like he has switched off all emotions. They are like two voids; I can't even see his pain. He looks like he has died inside.

"If it wasn't, then why can't I find her? Even after everything I've done to make sure we are feared and people know not to fuck with us, it wasn't enough to stop her from being taken or hurt. I thought we were feared, but we are being laughed at. They have the nerve to taunt us, fuck with us, and there is nothing we can do to stop them-"

"Yet," I point out, interrupting him. "There is nothing we can do to stop them *yet*. But we will burn this fucking world to the ground if we must, to make sure we get her back. Someone has become cocky, and they will pay for it; they will die as an example of what happens if anyone tries to take her from us again." I push myself away from the doorframe and walk further into the room, heading for my brother, not stopping until I am right in front of him.

"No one will go unpunished for what's happening. No one will dare put our family through this again. Hudson and whoever he is working for will pay with their life for taking her from us, and I, for one, will not lose a wink of sleep over it. If we are not feared now, we will be by the time we have avenged Jasmine's suffering and pain."

Christian looks up at me and nods once.

"You suspect Taylor, don't you?" I ask. Christian looks at me and nods.

"I wasn't sure until this evening. But the more he offers to help, the more I doubt they are honest intentions," he admits before leaning his arms on his thighs as he cups his glass with both hands. "I think he is trying to point us away from wherever Jasmine is being kept. I didn't want to believe it to start with; it seemed too simple. But the more I sit here and consider everything that has happened, it seems to be the only explanation." Christian looks at me and sighs. "I am trying to work up the courage to start looking into the possibility, but I'm terrified I will be wasting my time on another dead end. It's all we seem to find."

I take a deep breath and place my hand on his shoulder.

"Then let's all tackle it together. We get Terry, Calvin, and Layton to help, and between the seven of us, we are sure to find something." I give his shoulder a squeeze and head out of the room. "We will all be in the sitting room in ten minutes. Bring you're A-game, as I'm not stopping until we bring her home."

We have been at it for three hours and can't seem to find any solid leads.

"What time is it?" Sean asks as he stands up from the sofa and stretches.

"Just gone midnight," Maximus answers without looking up from his laptop.

Both twins look ready to drop. I have seen their heads dipping now and again as they fall asleep where they sit.

"I'll get a fresh pot of coffee on," Sean announces as he goes to walk out of the room. I'm just about to suggest some food when Terry jumps up and pulls a phone out of his pocket.

"Fucking superstar!" he curses as he rushes to the laptop Christian's working on at his desk, pushing him out of the way.

"What's that?" Christian asks as he stands from the chair, pushing it to Terry, who takes it and sits immediately. He holds up a finger to silence everyone as he types on the keyboard. His fingers moving so fast that they are almost a blur!

"Got her!" he yells excitedly.

"What?" All four of us jump up together and rush to stand around Terry.

"She's shown us how to find her, and I swear if you don't marry her, I will!" Terry turns the screen around, and we see a text to his untraceable burner phone.

Tommy: Don't reply. Hudson is working for Taylor. Jaz

Chapter Forty

JASMINE

I'm lying on the bed, hungry and covered in Tommy's dried blood. I'm hurting after being violated by Hudson, which has left me feeling sick and dirty. All I can do is wait for the time to be right so I can retrieve Tommy's phone and send a message to the number Terry made me memorise. It's a phone he always carries with him, and we are to make contact with it if we are trying to hide who we are messaging.

I hear footsteps coming closer to the door and jump to my feet and away from the bed, ready to fight Hudson. I have no doubt he will make good on his threat now. The thought of him touching me again is enough to drive me mad. I need to make sure the guys get here quickly, as I don't know if I will ever recover if he rapes me. Physically or mentally.

The footsteps come to a stop, and the bedroom door opens. I know what I need to do to protect myself, but it's not Hudson who walks in. It's Taylor, followed closely by my mother.

"Evening, Jasmine." He looks at me like I should be glad to see them, there is something very wrong with his man.

"Taylor," I bark back. "Take it the meeting went well?" I ask as I move so my back is against the window and cross my arms over my chest.

"Very. They still have no idea I'm playing them. You would think they'd have some kind of doubts by now, but they are so distracted by your disappearance they aren't paying attention to anything else."

"That must make you happy," I reply rolling my eyes. I look at my mother and her ridiculous fake blonde hair. Naturally, her hair was as dark as mine, but as soon as it started to turn grey, she dyed it blonde. "Is there something I can do for you? Or have you just come to check on your leverage?"

Mum stares at me for a moment and shakes her head.

"Really, Jasmine, sometimes you are so uncouth."

I have no idea who she's trying to impress. I once thought she could change, I even believed she had when she met Tommy. But I was wrong. No normal person could sit there and watch her ex-husband being shot and not show the slightest ounce of remorse. Tommy was a lot of things, but he was good to her most of their time together. She can't say he didn't make her happy because he did.

"Why are you both here? I'm tired and want to sleep." I move towards the bed and sit on the edge of it.

"See, this is your problem, Jasmine. Everything has always been about what you wanted or what your father wanted. None of you has ever thought about what I wanted. Did I want kids? No! But your father refused to let me get rid of you, and then he was gone, and I was stuck with you."

I stare at her, and for a moment, I'm speechless. She was stuck with me? I was stuck with her!

"If you hated me that much, why didn't you leave me with my grandparents? Or put me into care?" I ask, thinking there is no way she could get any lower, but boy, was I wrong.

"I did leave you with your grandparents, and if you'd just been there when you were supposed to have been rather than staying at Amber's, you would be dead with them too!"

My face and stomach drop as I stare at my mother, the one who gave birth to me, as the realisation dawns on me.

"The gas explosion wasn't an accident, was it?"

"Of course, it wasn't! It took weeks to get it set up, allowing a small leak here or there so the authorities knew there was an issue, so it didn't look suspicious. Then, the night of the explosion, I thought you were in your bed, but no, you had snuck out!"

"Why the fuck did you kill them? After everything they did to try and help you, you murdered your own parents. For what?" I scream as my eyes and throat burn. I feel like I can't catch my breath.

"The money, of course! If you had died with them, I'd have got it all. But no! You had to sneak out and live! I couldn't kill you after that; it would look suspicious, so instead, I had to get it if and when you gave it to me. Why do you think Tommy charged you rent? It was me who put the idea in his head! I wanted what was rightfully mine! It should have gone to me, not you!"

I stare at her, unable to process it all. This woman is evil. She is the definition of a psychopath. She killed her parents and attempted to kill her daughter, all for money. All so she could keep living the life she wanted, full of expensive clothes, holidays in the sun and an endless amount of drugs.

She could have done so much with her life. But this is how she turned out.

When Mum was in school, she was smart. She went to university to become a lawyer. Even when my father was still around, she worked hard and kept herself in the life she had become accustomed to. But the problem was she wanted more; she always wanted more. Even from an early age, I remember her complaining that the nice handbag she wanted was too expensive, and Dad had to work extra shifts to get it for her. The house wasn't big enough, and she wanted a separate dining room, not a kitchen diner. He worked so hard to keep up with her spending and her drug habit I never blamed him for leaving.

This is why I will never take the money the guys splash on me for granted. I know if they lost everything tomorrow, I would still be happy as long as we have each other. Their love is all I want from them, but my love was never enough for my mother. She never loved me, and even though I spent years trying to gain it, I have now finally concluded that she will never love me the way I wished she would.

But to hear that she killed her parents and the only reason I'm still here is that I snuck out, and again, she doesn't show one ounce of remorse for what she's done. I look back at things she has done in her life, the way she stood there when I was ten and let a man touch me inappropriately just so she could get some drugs. She never cared about me, and her new revelation proves that.

I look across the room at her and see her smiling smugly; she reminds me of the Joker from the Batman films. I realise then that she does feel something for what she's done. She feels pride in knowing that she killed her parents. She must know that she has just broken that last thread of hope I held on to that she was a decent person deep down. There is no hope for her, not now, not ever.

"You are sick," I growl at her. That smug smile instantly being removed from her face.

"I'm sick?"

"Yes, Mother, you are sick!" I declare through gritted teeth as I grip the mattress so hard I feel my nails breaking.

"If I'm sick, what the fuck does that make you?" she snarls, with so much hate in her eyes.

"Me?" I yell jumping to my feet. "In what world am I anything like you?"

Mum jumps to her own feet, and Taylor holds her back as she tries to launch herself at me.

"You, my darling slut of a daughter, are fucking four men at the same time. Not only are they your stepbrothers, you call them all Daddy! What the fuck is that about? You are a grown-ass woman who still has daddy issues after how long? Get a grip of yourself, for God's sake!"

"At least they give a shit about me and look after me! They have done more for me than you ever have! They love me for me!"

"They love you? Please! The O'Reillys know nothing about love; they are using you like they use everyone else!"

Taylor lets go of her, and she storms forward and slaps me across the face. As I jump forward to punch her, Taylor grabs me and pushes me back down on the bed. He keeps me in place by holding my shoulder as she leans over me.

"You think they love you? Well, maybe it's time you learnt some hard facts about the O'Reillys and why they could never love anyone."

It's late into the night, and I can't sleep. Mum and Taylor left long ago, and what Mum revealed to me is still swimming around in my head. Does it change the way I look at my daddies? I hate to say it, but yes. Do I still want to save them and get the hell out of here? Also, yes.

Earlier tonight, I managed to sneak the phone into the bathroom with me and sent a message to Terry. Now I just need to wait and hope they have received the message and will come for me before Hudson gets to me again or before my mum decides to finish what she started when she tried to kill me with my grandparents. Please, Daddies, please don't leave me here alone anymore; I want to come home.

Chapter Forty-One

JASMINE

I have no idea what time it is or how long it's been since I sent the message. It feels like time is slowing down as I wait for something, anything, to happen.

Did they receive the message? Do they know where I am so they can come and get me? I've been on edge waiting for either the O'Reillys to turn up or for Taylor to find out what I've done and come in to kill me. When Hudson stormed in here this morning and threw my breakfast of two slices of toast on the table, I thought he knew, but he turned around and stormed back out, not saying a word. I'm guessing he and Taylor are still at each other's throats. I hope it stays that way.

It must be around lunchtime when what sounds like the fire alarm sounds. I jump to my feet and look out of the window. There is smoke coming from downstairs and I can see some sort of commotion, but the smoke is too thick to work out what's going on.

The door's thrown open, and Hudson charges in.

"Have you been burning the toast again?" I ask,

laughing as I look at him. He looks furious, and it suddenly dawns on me why when I hear the **pop pop pop** of gunfire.

"They finally found me then?" I laugh. Hudson grabs my arm and pulls me towards him as Taylor and my mother rush into the room.

"Got her. Let's get out of here," Hudson shouts over the noise of the fire alarm.

"You think I'm going to leave with you? Fuck no!" I yell as I pull my arm out of Hudson's grasp. He turns around and backhands me across the face, hard. I lose my balance and fall into one of the chairs. My ribs hit it hard as I land, causing me to cry out in pain. That doesn't stop Hudson from grabbing me by the hair and pulling me onto my feet.

"You are fucking leaving with us if I have to carry you out," he growls as he grabs me again. But now I know I'm almost free, I fight back. I elbow him in the stomach before punching him in the face.

"Fuck you, arsehole," I yell as I turn around and come face to face with Taylor. Who grabs me around the throat, with both hands and pushes me back against the wall.

"Do as you are fucking told!" he growls as he lets go with one hand and pulls out a gun with the other. He turns to Hudson and nods to me. "Get her under control for fuck's sake and let's get out of here."

Hudson grabs me as an explosion sounds in the house.

"They are going to bring the place down around us!" My mum screams as she grabs hold of Taylor. Please, someone shut her up.

"I have a way out," Taylor says as he places a hand on her back and starts pushing her towards the door but stops when I hear Maximus shout.

"I found the floor!"

"I'M HERE!" I scream as loud as I can before Hudson slams a hand over my mouth and pulls me back against him, quickly holding a knife to my throat. Taylor rushes forward and slams the door shut before turning a key in the lock. Does he really believe that will stop the O'Reillys from getting to me? I can hear the commotion outside, which sounds like a load of people filling the hallway.

"Open this fucking door now, Taylor!" I hear Christian shout, and my heart races.

They're really here.

No one answers, and I try to shout out, but Hudson's hand is still over my mouth.

"Three. Two. One."

With one loud bang, the door flies open, and I see six figures, all in black, charge into the room. Each is armed with a gun, protective body gear and masks. Even with their faces partially covered, I can make out my four daddies, Terry and Layton, who are also here in front of me with at least three guys behind them.

"Carol?"

I hear the surprise in Sean's voice, quickly followed by Maximus cursing. Taylor jumps at them, but Layton takes him down quickly, disarming him and pulling him to his feet.

"Keep that fucker alive, I want to kill him myself!" Christian snaps before his eyes find mine, and my heart races.

"Hudson lower that fucking knife, arsehole," Jason yells, his eyes trained on the knife by my throat.

"Get the fuck out before I slit her throat, you son of a bitch!" Hudson growls from behind me, and I realise he is using me as a shield. I feel his other hand slide across my stomach and down towards my leggings.

"You touch her, and I won't need this fucking gun!" Jason yells out.

"But she tastes amazing and is so fucking tight," Hudson taunts him. I feel his hand cupping between my legs, and a small sob leaves my chest. I'm still sore from what he did to me yesterday.

"Did he rape you, baby?"

My eyes move from an angry Jason back to Christian, who has his eyes set on my face. I know he will be taking note of each bruise left by Hudson and Taylor.

"No," I answer, as I feel the knife press a little harder.

"But he touched you?" Christian asks.

"Yes," I confirm as Hudson sniggers.

"She bleeds so easily, doesn't she?" Hudson taunts from the safety behind me, and I close my eyes. My bottom lip starts to tremble. He's trying to get a reaction out of them, he knows he will never leave this room alive.

"Princess, look at me."

I open my eyes and look at Sean who's looking nowhere but at me. "We don't care what he did; you are still our girl. *Remember* what I told you."

I look at him for a moment, confused. He nods once, and it comes back to me. I nod slightly and take a calming breath. I let my body go limp and for the briefest second, Hudson grabs me to stop me from falling, but as he does the knife moves from my throat, and I'm ready for it. I grab his hand with the knife and spin myself underneath it, twisting his arm and causing the hand to open. The knife starts to fall, but I catch it with my free hand and stab it into his side as he goes down screaming. I move out of the way quickly as a shot rings out, and I see Hudson's eyes still trained on me, and a bullet hole in his head. Sean is beside me in seconds, as I turn around and see all guns now trained on my mum, who has a gun in her hand, pointed straight at Christian.

Christian

"Lower your weapons," I order. I risk a glance at Jasmine and see her looking terrified in Sean's arms, her sight set on her mother. She's safe, and that's all that matters. I lower my gun to the floor and put my hands up whilst looking at Carol, and the gun trained on me. I don't care if she shoots me now. I won't take her from Jasmine. I pull the mask from my face and put my hand back up.

"I don't know what your role is in this, Carol, but I won't shoot you. You are family."

If Jasmine marries one of us, Carol will become our mother-in-law. That's why I've been filling her home with food and sending cleaners in. I want her to survive and realise her daughter needs her more than she's willing to admit.

I watch as Carol's face changes, and she bursts out laughing.

"You are no family of mine. You destroyed my family. You took from me and I can't wait to see how your *family* reacts when I take you from them."

"You don't want to shoot me, Carol. You don't want another person's death on your conscience," I point out as I take a step away from my brothers. If she does shoot me, I don't want to risk them getting hit if the bullet passes through me. Carol cocks her head, and I notice her eyes are dead of all emotion.

"You think I give a shit about any of your lives?" her

gun flies to the side where Layton has Taylor and a shot rings out, but before I can even take a step forward the gun is trained on me again. I hear Jasmine scream, but I can't risk taking my eyes off the gun.

"Fuck, Taylor's dead and Layton's down," Terry calls behind me.

"Nobody moves, or he's next!" Carol shouts.

"Don't do this, Mum. I know you are mad, but please stop," Jasmine yells. I can hear the pain in her voice. There's so much I want to say to her. If only I had more time.

"Baby, it's okay. Whatever happens, know I love you," I say calmly as I take a step forward. I want to put more distance between my brothers and me.

"You fucking bastard," Carol snarls as I see her finger twitch on the trigger. I close my eyes as the shot sounds, and I wait for the pain, for anything, but I feel nothing.

I can hear my brothers cursing and Jasmine screaming. My baby girl sounds like she is in so much pain.

"Get her out of here!" Jason yells as someone grabs me.

I open my eyes and realise I'm still standing. I look at Carol, who's on the floor, staring up at the ceiling.

What the fuck?

I can hear Jasmine screaming hysterically as she's carried away.

"Christian, come on, we need to burn the place and get her out of here. She's hysterical." I turn to look at Jason and frown confused. I was so sure I was about to die.

"What happened?" I ask, looking down at myself and seeing no signs of bullet holes. Jason grabs my shoulder and looks at me.

"Jasmine took Sean's gun and shot her."

Chapter Forty-Two

JASON

I look around at the four of us sitting or standing in various locations outside of Jasmine's room. All feeling helpless to do anything to help our woman inside. We have no idea what's going on in there, as Jasmine asked us to leave. Mrs Brown offered to stay with her, and she thankfully agreed.

Sean had gotten Jasmine out of the house as we sent the clean-up crew in. We still have no clue what happened in that place. There are so many questions left unanswered. Like how did Jasmine get hold of Tommy's phone? Why Carol was there? Why did Taylor take her? The only thing we know for sure is Jasmine shot her mum to save Christian, and for that, I'll be forever in her debt.

Watching my brother look down the barrel of a gun will be something I will never forget. He was ready to die to protect us all. I noticed the way he kept moving to put some distance between himself and us. The idiot was still trying to protect us even when staring death in the face.

Everything had happened so fast after we received Jasmine's message. We knew we only had a small window of time to get to her as we didn't know what she had done to get hold of Tommy's phone. If anyone realised she had contacted us, they could move or kill her. It wasn't a risk we were willing to take.

Luckily, the phone stayed on, and we were able to track it thanks to an old tracking device we had installed years ago. Tommy has never been very good at keeping up to date with technology, but he finds a phone he likes and sticks with it. There had been no sign of him at the house. The area was searched after we left, and nobody else was discovered.

As soon as we tracked the phone and found the location, we bundled into the cars and vans with as many guys as we could get on short notice. We couldn't risk calling other people in as we weren't sure who we could trust. Christian took the risk of calling McIntire, who sent ten men. I have no idea how much or what his assistance is going to cost us, but I know it was worth it as we got Jasmine back.

One good thing about us being in the weapons trade is that we have some of the best equipment on the market. We were able to get to the site and use drones to look around the premises and through windows to locate Jasmine. We knew where she was and worked out the quickest route to her using the blueprints of the house Terry found online. The rest was straightforward. Distract and kill as many people as possible to get to where our girl was being held. They had no idea we had found them until we stormed the place.

Seeing her held there at knifepoint, with Hudson's hands on her, knowing that he'd hurt her, touched her, I'd never felt rage like it. But she was so brave and strong. She managed to get herself free and even stab him before I put a bullet through his head. I'm in awe of this woman. I would have loved to cause him endless pain, to have dragged out his suffering, but I couldn't risk him hurting her again. Jasmine has been through enough, and the main objective was achieved, and she is free from him.

I look around at my brothers, all of us still in our black gear and exhausted. Maximus is sitting outside her room, leaning back against the wall. Sean is next to him with his head in his hands. He held her all the way home as she cried into his chest. As much as we all wanted to be the ones she clung to, we left Sean to comfort her. The last thing we needed was for us to crowd her when she was so overwhelmed, as can be expected after everything she has been through

I watch Christian pacing back and forth outside her bedroom door, looking up at the slightest sound that comes from within. The doctor had been here when we got back and went into the bedroom with Mrs Brown. Jasmine had let Sean carry her into her room and then asked us all quietly to leave. We wanted to tell her no, that we weren't letting her out of our sight, but we also understood. We've all taken a life before, and we know the first is tough to come back from.

All our heads snap up to the sound of Jasmine's door opening. The three of us sitting on the floor jump to our feet as the doctor walks out and closes the door behind him.

"How is she?" Christian asks, standing in front of the doctor.

"Physically, she has a possible bruised rib, broken nose, and bruising and rope burns on her ankles, wrists, face and neck. She also has a nasty bump on the back of her head, as well as being dehydrated and in need of a few good meals. She is sleep-deprived, and he caused some minor damage below. She says she wasn't raped and that he used his hand,

and I believe her. I successfully reset her nose, so it should heal, no problem.

"She is coping with the physical pain better than the emotional. She went through a lot, and her mother didn't help. She's struggling to get her head around everything and is rightfully a little emotional. I've left some pain relief as well as sedatives if she needs them."

"Thanks, doc. I appreciate it," Christian says, holding his hand out. The doctor shakes it before taking mine.

"If you need anything else, please shout. She's a sweetheart, so strong and brave; she's been through a lot. I hope she can rest now knowing she is safe," he says before turning to the twins and shaking their hands.

"Thank you," I add as he turns and sees himself out.

I look at Christian and find him staring at the bedroom door. He still blames himself, and I know part of him wants to let her go, but he won't be the one to walk away. Because, like the rest of us, we don't want to lose her.

The bedroom door opens again, and Mrs Brown walks out. We all look at her and can see her eyes are bloodshot from crying.

"She's okay," she reassures us, holding her hands up before any of us can ask. "She's had a bath, and the painkillers the doctor gave her have helped her to calm down enough to start working through a few things. She's ready to see you all, but take it slow. She has been through Hell, and I'm glad that mother of hers is dead because otherwise, I would kill her myself."

I never thought I would hear Mrs Brown mutter a bad word about anyone other than our father. Whatever Jasmine has told her about Carol must be bad. It's a subject we are going to have to approach carefully for the time being, if at all.

She walks up to Christian and cups his cheek,

"I know you want to go barrelling in there demanding answers and to know what happened, and she's ready to tell you. But let her do it in her own time. She needs her loving Daddy right now, not the one who disciplines her." Mrs Brown looks at the rest of us with one arched brow.

"That goes for all of you. Be gentle. Let her deal with this in her own time, let her adjust, and if she swears, let it go," she shoots Christian another look, and we all nod.

"Yes, ma'am," the four of us reply together. Mrs Brown is like a mother to us, and we have so much respect for her and love how much she cares for Jasmine.

Mrs Brown gives us all a soft smile and walks away, no doubt heading back down to the kitchen to make Jasmine her favourite food. I look at my brothers, and we all have the same looks on our faces. We are all terrified of what we are going to find behind that door. We have been the ones in control for so long, that to have no control of a situation has been a harsh lesson. We want to do the best for Jasmine, and that means being here for her and doing whatever she needs.

Christian lets out a deep sigh and heads to the door. He places his hand on the door handle and stops with his head bowed.

"No matter what she says, we need to control our anger. If you feel like you are losing it, walk out and come back once you are calmer," he says quietly.

"And if she wants us to let her go?" Sean asks quietly, voicing our greatest fear.

"We do as she asks," Christian replies before opening the door.

Christian

I can't handle this. I don't know if I can be the strong Daddy she needs. I'm dying inside, and I'm terrified. I swallow deeply, trying to clear the lump that's formed in my throat before opening the door and walking into Jasmine's room.

I look up and find her sitting on her bay windowsill, looking out over the garden. She has a cushion on her lap, which she is fiddling with and looks lost and broken, and I hate it.

"Hey, sweetheart," I say softly as I walk into the room and head towards her, too scared to get close in case I upset her further. She turns to look at us and gives us a soft smile that doesn't reach her red, swollen eyes.

I hadn't noticed how bruised her face was before; I was just so glad to see her breathing. But now I look at her face, I can see the bruises and swelling around her broken nose, eyes and neck. I'm about to turn and walk out, unsure if I can control my temper yet. I want to find every single person who has ever caused her harm and kill them over and over again. I want to beat them until there is nothing left. As I decide to leave, I hear her soft, broken voice.

"Hey, Daddy."

Those two words are a reminder of the promise I made to look after her. She needs me to live up to that today more than ever. It doesn't matter how I feel right now; it's about her. It has been since the day she walked into our lives, and it will remain that way until I take my last breath.

"Do you need anything, Jazzy?" Jason asks next to me. Jasmine shakes her head and turns back to the window.

"No, thank you." Her reply is so quiet that we only just hear it. For a moment, we all just stand looking at her, not knowing what to do or say. I don't like this; I don't like seeing her look so small and lost. It's Sean who steps up and sits down next to her, taking her hand. She looks down at their hands entwined before looking up at him.

"Do you need more time, princess? You tell us what you need, and we will give it to you, no questions asked. But for us to help, you need to talk to us."

Jasmine nods and looks at us all. "I don't want to be alone, but I don't know where to start. There's so much to say." I see a small tear slip out of her eye and slide down her cheek. Jason sits in the chair next to the window and takes her other hand between his.

"How about we all sit in here, and you tell us in your own time? If you need a break, we can stop," he suggests, and she nods. I walk over to the bed and move an old shoe box out of the way so I can sit down. I catch Jasmine looking at it before letting go of the guys' hands and holding the cushion to her chest.

"Are the girls all okay? I heard gunshots," she whispers. I nod, offering her a small smile.

"They were already in the car when the gun was fired. No one was hurt," I explain. "Miss King has been on the phone every day demanding to know what was happening. She has been giving Layton a hard time." A small smile appears on Jasmine's face.

"Yeah, he has my sympathy. Is he okay? He said he was ok in the van, but there was so much blood."

"Layton is fine, Jazzy. The bullet was removed easily, and he's had stitches. The blood wasn't all his," Jason explains. Jasmine nods again before looking at Maximus, who is leaning against the bedpost.

"I heard you found the bouncer. Taylor was furious."

"Didn't do us any good; he couldn't tell us anything," Maximus shrugs. Jasmine shakes her head.

"It gave me a giggle. As I said, Taylor was furious at Hudson," she adds before the smile slips from her face and she looks at the floor. "Do you know whose phone I used to get the message to you?" she asks.

"Tommy's," Sean replies. She lets out a sigh and looks at us all.

"He had been working with Taylor. They planned on getting Tommy back in with you somehow, and then he was going to use your money to fund some venture Taylor was coming up with. But Taylor had other plans, and Tommy swore to stop him, so Hudson shot him."

My heart stops, and a heavy feeling in my chest takes hold.

"Tommy's dead?" Jason asks quietly. Jasmine nods as she holds the pillow tighter to her chest as if she is feeling my pain.

I never expected to feel anything if he was killed, but I'm surprised to find I do. It hurts almost as much as when Mum died.

"He was shot when Taylor announced he planned on killing you all. Tommy wasn't going to allow him to physically hurt you. He might not have shown it like a normal father, but there was no way on this Earth he was going to let anyone kill his sons."

"He gave you his phone?" Maximus asks. Jasmine looks back to the window before she answers.

"I don't know if he meant for me to find it or not." I watch as she takes a deep breath but doesn't look away from the garden. "Tommy was killed in the room they were keeping me in. Taylor had just hung up from hearing about the bouncer being found, and Hudson had held a gag in my mouth so I couldn't shout out. Once the call ended, Tommy told Taylor he wouldn't let him kill you, and Hudson shot him. Taylor and my m-"

For a second, I can hear her throat contract with the thought of Carol, but she swallows and continues.

"Mum left, leaving me with Hudson and Tommy's body. Hudson called in one of the guards, and as they were carrying Tommy's body out wrapped in a plastic sheet, he demanded that I clean up the mess." Her body becomes tighter as she pulls her knees to her chest, and I know what she's going to say before the words leave her mouth. "I refused, so he gave me a taster of what he would do from then onwards when I didn't do as I was told."

"He sexually assaulted you?" Sean asks quietly. Jasmine nods and wipes her face.

"After that, I had no choice but to do what I was told. I was hurting and scared. So, I started cleaning the blood from the floor. But as I did, I noticed Tommy's phone behind the chest of drawers he had been standing by. Then I remember him messing about with the cuffs on his trousers when Taylor had been on the phone with you. He must have dropped it behind there on purpose," she explains.

"Knowing that you might find it and contact us," Jason adds. Jasmine looks at him and nods.

"He was a lousy father, but he was determined to protect you in the end," Jasmine says as she looks around at us all. "He cared. I saw it in his eyes before he died," she whispers before looking back out of the window.

The room is silent for a few minutes whilst we all try to process what she's just told us.

Tommy's dead.

It doesn't hit the way I thought it would. I'm not a fool.

Jasmine was right; he was a lousy father. But if she's correct, then he died trying to protect us and finally acted like the father he should have been all along.

I look around at my brothers and see the pain on all their faces. This is going to take time to process. It's something we need time to deal with together.

"How did you get the message out to us?" Jason asks. Jasmine turns back to face him, and the hold of the pillow softens slightly.

"I had to be careful as there were cameras in the room. I hid the phone deeper behind the chest of drawers, hoping that if they had realised it wasn't with Tommy, they wouldn't have found it. Later that night, I made a show of my hair getting on my nerves. I used an elastic band I was given and put it up and down before throwing it at the chest of drawers in a mood. I made sure it went behind it so I had an excuse to pull the furniture away from the wall, and when I got back in view, they would see me tying my hair back up in a top knot. What they didn't see was the phone that was hidden in my hair."

"Genius," Maximus chuckles, and I must agree that it took some quick thinking.

"I was quite proud of that one," she replies, a small smile playing on her lips.

"Once the phone was safely in my hair, I made a fuss about my stomach hurting and needing the toilet. One of the guards took me, and when he tried to come in with me like they usually did, I made a point of saying I thought it was my period. He near enough ran from the room and slammed the door closed. Tommy didn't have a lock on his phone, thankfully, so I was able to send the message in seconds thanks to the number Terry made me memorise."

"I'm so proud of you, baby. You thought on your feet

and did amazing." I don't think I could be prouder of her right now. To be that creative when under so much pressure.

"I just wanted to come home and get away from that evil bitch." I see the hatred in her eyes, and I have to bite my tongue from asking about Carol. Maximus, however, doesn't even try to stop himself.

"Why was Carol there, Shorty? Was she taken too?" he asks. We all stare at him, but he isn't looking at us; his eyes are trained on Jasmine. Who looks back out of the window.

"She was with Taylor; they were dating. But I think it was more about what he could do to help her get what she wanted: to see you all lose everything." Jasmine takes a deep breath and looks back at us.

"Taylor told me and Tommy about you all leaving everything to me in your wills. Tommy wasn't impressed, but I also don't think he was surprised. I think my mother figured once you were dead and I had your money, she could kill me and take everything."

"She would kill you for the money? Her own daughter?" Sean asks, amazed. I expect Jasmine to struggle to answer, but instead, she laughs.

"She already tried once when I was younger. She admitted the gas leak at my grandparents' was her fault. She thought I was there the night she did it, but she didn't know I had snuck out last minute to stay at Amber's. She thought she had killed the three of us. When she realised I was alive and I had all the money, she couldn't kill me without raising suspicion. She settled for taking as much of my money as possible."

"Fuck, Jazzy, that's messed up."

I look at Jason and nod.

"So, it was all about money? All of it?" Sean asks. But Jasmine shakes her head before looking directly at me.

"No, it was revenge. She wanted you to suffer and to lose someone you love as she did." I'm staring at her, confused. She looks from me to the shoe box. "Do you recognise that?"

I turn to look at it, and for a second, I don't, but then it hits me.

"It was the shoe box I got from under the floorboards in the house when we went to get your stuff."

Jasmine nods. "Open it."

I look at her before picking up the box and opening it. It's only small, maybe for children's shoes. Inside is a small teddy sitting on a bundle of letters and a picture. I look at the photograph and freeze.

"Those letters were from my father when he left, or I thought they were. I never told you this before, but when my father disappeared my grandparents changed our names. I wasn't born Jasmine Rose Connors. I was Rose Jasmine Grant, my father was-"

"Connor Grant," I finish for her as I look at the letters and the picture in my hand.

"Yes," I hear her sigh as my hands shake, and the realisation hits me.

"I killed your father," I whisper as I look up to see Jasmine nodding. Tears slide down her face. "I didn't know." I barely got the words out.

"Me neither. Mum told me last night. Apparently, Tommy got drunk one night and let it slip. That's why the marriage ended," she whispers through the tears.

"Who was Connor Grant?" Maximus asks next to me.

"My first kill," I answer, unable to tear my eyes away from Jasmine.

"When you were fifteen?" Sean asks. I nod before it

becomes too much, and I fall on my knees in front of Jasmine.

"I'm so sorry. I didn't know. I didn't want to. Hardy made me. It was him or Jason. Please forgive me, sweetheart!" I beg as I clutch her hand as I kneel in front of her.

"I'm so sorry." I can't stop the tears that breakthrough, and I cry harder than I have since that night. I feel Jasmine move and expect her to run from me, but she doesn't.

Jasmine throws her arms around my neck, holding me, straddling my lap. I freeze for a second before wrapping my arms around her waist and burying my face in her neck as I continue to cry.

"I don't blame you," she whispers into my ear as she runs a hand over my head.

"Jason had a gun to his head; I had to do it. Grant even told me to do it to save my brother," I gasp and hear Jasmine shushing me. "Please forgive me. Don't hate me. I can't handle you hating me as much as I hate myself," I beg.

Jasmine leans back and holds my face in her hands.

"There is nothing to forgive. You were only fifteen. I know how much that death has haunted you. I don't hate you. I could never hate you. You are my daddy, and I love you. You were willing to save my mum because you know it would have hurt me to see her die." A small part of her lip lifts in a smile.

"It was a waste of time, though, as I ended up killing her anyway," she chuckles nervously before crying again.

I hold her to me, unable to let her go as we both come to terms with the fact we each killed one of her parents, both of us doing it to protect someone we love.

Chapter Forty-Three

JASMINE

It's been three weeks since I was rescued.

Two days later the guys and I boarded a private plane and flew to Majorca, and we've been in their villa since.

The guys had initially planned on cancelling the trip, but I told them I wanted to come. I needed to get away from everything and everyone. It was the right move, as I don't think I could have healed quite so quickly at home.

I love it here; it's always felt like my second home. The guys have brought me back every year around my birthday, and this year was no different.

Except, I'm different now.

Not only because I have four Daddies who I love more than anything in the world. But because of my few days being held by Hudson and Taylor. I wish I could say I haven't been plagued by nightmares, but I have. I've also watched as Christian has been tormented by them, too, and it breaks my heart.

A big part of me wanted to hide the truth from him, to do all I could to protect him from the pain I knew it would bring him. But I know that what I have with Christian and the guys is forever, and I don't want to hide anything from them, especially something this big.

Jason asked me a few days after we got here if I feel differently about Christian now, and I admitted that I do, but not in the way he expected.

Christian may have taken my father from me, but if he hadn't, someone else would have. Maybe they would have killed me and my mother, too. I've always respected him, but seeing what he did from such a young age to protect his brothers just made me respect him even more.

Christian told me the hit was put out for my father due to him selling drugs for Hardy to make money. From what we know now, we think the problem was Mum kept getting into his drug stash and using it. One day, he couldn't cover the cost of how much she had used, so Hardy accused him of using it himself. Rather than let Mum take the bullet, my dad stepped up and took the blame. Tommy was also in trouble with Hardy, and to make amends Hardy wanted to teach Tommy a lesson by dragging his kids into it. The result was Tommy and Mum got away with everything scot-free, my dad lost his life, and Christian's life was altered forever. Christian may not look at it in the same way, but I know what he did took a lot of courage for a fifteen-year-old, and I will never forget that.

I'm sitting on our personal beach, looking out at the sea as the sun sets. As the cold air starts to stir around me, I stand and dust myself off before turning back towards the villa. I look up at it in the fading sunlight and sigh.

We are going home in two days, and part of me wants to stay here forever. I don't want to go back to face the girls, and I don't want to be asked a hundred questions about where I've been. But more importantly, I don't want to go back and for Christian to find every excuse to be away from me.

Since we arrived, Christian has been distant. I know we both have a lot to get our heads around, and I know he feels guilty about what happened, but there is more to it. He doesn't give me the 'Daddy' look any more or discipline me. It's like he thinks I will break if he tries, but I won't. What Hudson did to me was horrible, it hurt, but it could have been so much worse, and I know that. It will haunt me for the rest of my life.

I don't want it to take what I have with the guys away from me. But Christian seems to think that if he dominates me, I will become this fragile shell of a woman. I need it, I want him to be my daddy again. More than anything, I need him to show me that although we know the truth now, it doesn't change us.

I reach the villa and wipe my sandy feet on the mat before walking into the lounge area. As I close the patio door, Christian and Maximus walk in.

"Hey sweetheart, you been on the beach?"

I look up to Christian and nod, just to see what he says. He gives me a smile before turning back to Maximus, who's frowning at me.

"You okay, Shorty?"

"Yeah," I reply, walking from the room, but Christian grabs my arm to stop me.

"What's the matter? Are you okay?" he asks, that worried look back in his eyes that I'm starting to hate.

"I'm fine," I snap.

"You're lying to me, what's happened?" Christian asks softly. I pull my arm from his hand with ease and throw it up in the air.

"Why has everything changed? Do you not want to be

my daddy anymore?" As soon as the words leave my mouth, I see the shock and upset in Christian's eyes.

"Of course I do. Where is this coming from?"

"Oh, I don't know. Maybe it's because you have been going soft on me."

"Sweetheart, I've been a little softer on you but not that soft. You went through a lot, and I didn't want to push you."

"Really? Not that soft? What did you do when I stubbed my toe yesterday?" I ask, placing my hands on my hips.

"You were hurt; we all swear when we hurt ourselves," he sighs shaking his head. I stand in front of him and cross my arms over my chest.

"I'm not hurt now," I point out. "And I didn't use my words, and you made no comment. Maybe I need to stop using my words altogether to get a reaction out of you?" I suggest as I turn on the spot and storm through the hallway towards the dining room with my head held high stubbornly. The guys love accusing me of being a brat, so let's see what they do when I am one.

"We haven't finished this conversation," Christian calls behind me, my inner brat comes out further as I turn around and stick my tongue out at him and carry on walking away. I'm just getting into the dining room when I see Jason and Sean playing cards at the table.

"Hey Jazzy. Are you okay?" Jason asks as I walk past him and glare at him. He frowns at me before looking to the door as Christian and Maximus walk in.

"Okay, sweetheart, you proved your point," I hear Christian say as Maximus chuckles. I turn to look at him knowing the table is safely between us. I cup my ear as if I can't hear him. I can see Sean and Jason looking between Christian and me.

"Have I missed something?" Sean asks as Maximus laughs again.

"Somebody just accused Daddy of going soft."

"Well, she has got a point," Jason chuckles as Christian glares at him. I throw my arms out dramatically. Christian turns his attention back to me and for the first time in weeks, I see the corner of his mouth lift slightly as if daring me to carry on.

"Fine, you are right. I've been soft on you. You went through a lot, and I was being cautious. But now I'm telling you to use your words, baby girl." The warning tone is back in his voice, and when he calls me baby girl, I swear my panties flood. But I'm in full brat mode now, and I just cup my ear and lean forward. Maximus and Sean both burst out laughing as Jason chokes on the drink he's sipping.

"Oh, baby girl, I hope you know what you are starting here. Because if I catch you, you are mine, and I will not hold back again. Last chance, are you going to use your words?" Christian asks his arms crossing over his broad chest and his ''Daddy' look making its first appearance in so long, I almost moan with pleasure just from the look alone. I slowly shake my head as I grin back at him. I watch as his eyes darken and he takes a step forward, and I take one step back, already having a route through the house planned out in my head.

"Get her!"

I squeal as I run from the room, leaving the sound of the chairs scraping behind me as Sean and Jason jump to their feet. I rush through the kitchen, past a confused Mrs Brown as I squeal a 'sorry'. I can hear the guys laughing as they follow and Mrs Brown calling for them not to run in her kitchen. I rush back towards the lounge through the entrance hall, planning on getting up the stairs and leading the guys towards the bedrooms. They haven't touched me in so long that I need this.

I rush into the lounge, almost being caught by Maximus as he jumps out at me from the hallway.

"Too slow, Daddy," I call as I bolt up the stairs, lifting my long maxi dress as I go, with Maximus and Sean right on my heels. I glance back and see Christian and Jason catching up with them. The four of them grin as they race up the stairs, and I run for my room and only just slam the door shut in time as they reach it. I close the sliding lock and try to catch my breath as one of them knocks on the door.

"You think you are safe in there, princess?" Sean calls out.

"Yep, the doors are locked, so you can't come in!" I reply.

"I think you are forgetting who you are dealing with, Shorty. You just challenged the big guns. Who do you think is going to win? You or him?" Maximus adds as I laugh, stepping away from the door.

"None of you can get in here though can you," I call out as I continue to walk backwards until I feel something large, solid and warm behind me.

"Wanna bet?"

I scream and spin around as Christian grabs me and throws me on the bed. I look to my right just in time to see Jason jumping onto the balcony from his room next door and walking through the patio doors.

"The balcony, shit!" I curse as I throw my hands over my mouth and look up as Christian climbs over me, grinning.

"Oh, baby girl, you are just clocking up the punishments

here," he growls as I hear the bedroom door being unlocked, and the twins burst into the room laughing.

"Not looking so cocky now, Jazzy," Jason laughs as he stands between the twins with his arms crossed.

"Fuck," I curse, again slamming my hand over my mouth. Christian looks at me like all his birthdays and Christmases have come at once.

"I think we need to do something about that potty mouth of yours, baby girl." He jumps off the bed and pulls me to my feet before thrusting his fingers into the hair at the base of my head and pulling me forward. His lips crash into mine, kissing me until I think my legs might give out from underneath me. He steps back and grins at me before looking at his brothers.

"I hope you are ready to assist, as this is a lesson she needs to learn from all of us."

"I'm sure we can all participate in one way or another," Maximus growls as he steps forward. He looks down at my maxi dress and smiles. "Remove the dress, Shorty, and put your hair up."

I step back, grinning as all four of my daddies stand together. Their eyes darken with desire as I gather my hair and secure it with my scrunchy. I lift my hand to my shoulder and slowly pull down the spaghetti strap from one shoulder and then the next before letting the fabric fall to the floor. I'm only wearing bikini bottoms underneath, and when they realise, they all give me looks that vary from I'm a goddess to Christian's 'Ddaddy' look.

"I don't see any tan lines on your chest, baby girl," he points out as I shrug.

"There's none on my bottom either, Daddy." Turning around to prove it and look over my shoulder at the four men standing together. Maximus and Jason both roar, laughing as Sean whistles.

"You've been taking advantage of me not paying attention, I see," Christian growls, walking up to me. I look up at him through my lashes.

"Maybe you need to keep a closer eye on me, Daddy."

Christian growls deeper, before turning me back around as he wraps my hair around his hand and pulls my head back a little.

"Obviously, I do. Are you going to remember to use your words now? Or do I need to remind you?" he asks, as his lips brush my neck.

"I'll remember," I gasp as he continues to kiss just below my earlobe.

"And when you can't use your words?" he asks as he strokes my bottom lip with his thumb.

"Slap your thigh three times."

Christian stands up and looks down at me with a smile. "There's our good girl." Just as my stomach knots with his praise, he tugs on my hair and forces me to my knees.

"Sean," he calls as he grins down at me. "I know you like nothing more than teaching her dirty little mouth a lesson," Christian says as he lets go of my hair and steps back. Sean steps forward, smiling.

He leans down and takes my chin in his hand.

"You going to remind me how good that mouth of yours can be?"

"Yes, Daddy," I reply, looking up at him through my lashes. Sean kisses me, and like Christian, there is nothing loving about it; his mouth dominates me like I know his body will at any moment.

"Free me from my jeans, princess," he groans against my lips. I quickly do as he says and sigh when I see him rock hard and right in my face. I look up at him again. "Open that dirty mouth of yours and stick your tongue out." I do as I'm told, and he places his cock straight onto it and drags it off.

"I'm going to fuck your mouth until the tears stream down your face. Then one of your other daddies is going to decide on your next punishment." Sean looks down at me. "Remember what you need to do to stop this?"

"Yes, Daddy," I reply, smiling.

"Good girl, open wide." I instantly do as I'm told, and Sean takes control of my head by using my hair. He starts off slow before becoming harder and faster as he hits the back of my throat, and I gag. The more I gag, the harder Sean pushes into me, which just turns me on more.

I don't know how long he continues to fuck my face. But the longer it goes on, the more turned on I become. I start to move my hand between my legs when I see Christian moving in the edge of my vision.

"Oh no, baby girl. You don't get to touch yourself," he warns, but I don't move my hand. I feel Sean getting closer to finding his release as his cock pulsates against my cheeks.

"Fuck, princess," he growls as he gets closer. My finger rubs against my aching pussy. I see Christian pulling his belt off, and my hand quickly moves away from me.

I feel the first squirt from Sean's cock and instantly start swallowing as he explodes, stream after stream, into my mouth.

Fuck I love the way he tastes. It's been so long since we last did anything, and I need them all so much.

"Fuck I love your pussy, but your mouth is something else!" Sean hisses as he pulls his softening cock from my mouth. I purposely continue to suck until it pops out and smile up at him.

"Put your hands out in front of you, baby girl," Christian growls from beside Sean. I instantly do as I'm told, frowning. Christian starts to wrap the belt around my wrists and pulls it until it tightens slightly. He looks at me, and for a moment, I see the worry in his eyes.

"Tighter," I whisper. Christian leans forward and kisses me on the lips as he tightens the belt further.

"If you want it off …"

"I won't. But if I change my mind, I'll say."

Christian seems to accept that as he kisses me again and pulls me up with him. I look behind him to see Jason and Maximus both sipping a drink and grinning at me.

"Get on the bed, Shorty," Maximus growls as he walks forward, necking the last of his drink and handing the glass to Christian. I walk backwards until my legs hit the bed. Maximus stops in front of me and pulls off his t-shirt before placing his hands on my bent elbows and placing me on the soft mattress.

"Lie down and lift your hips." I quickly do as he says so he can pull my bikini bottoms off. "Fuck I've missed this," he whispers as he buries his face between my legs and licks my core.

"Yes," I cry as he licks me again. He lifts his head and shakes it at me whilst grinning.

"Oh no, Shorty; you're not allowed to cum. You are still receiving your punishment. Do not cum until I tell you to," he smirks before he goes back to licking me as I groan.

"That's not fair!" I protest. "Please, Daddy!" I call out as he slides one finger into me, and I almost cum from that sensation alone. "Please, I need to cum," I call out again. Maximus stops and looks up at me.

"Are you going to be quiet, or do you need something to keep your mouth busy?" he asks, grinning. I clamp my mouth shut but look up at Christian, who has refilled Maximus' glass and is sipping from it. I look down at his body to see his enlarged dick pressing against his jeans. I lick my lips as Maximus licks me again, and I moan loudly.

"Someone want to keep her quiet?" Maximus asks as he winks at me.

"Fuck."

I turn to the sound of Christian as he strips and quickly straddles my chest. "Open up, baby girl. Daddy needs to be in you."

I open my mouth as my eyes roll back with the pleasure Maximus is giving me with his fingers and tongue. I feel Christian enter my mouth and nearly choke as I cry out with pleasure.

"Don't cum baby, not yet," Christian growls as he leans forward until his hands are on the mattress and he starts fucking my throat hard. Between him and Maximus, I'm soon on the edge of losing my shit.

Every time I get close to coming, they know and change how they give me pleasure, leaving me on the edge. I want to cry out and beg for release, but Christian's cock in my mouth is preventing me, which is turning me on even more.

"Fuck, I can't hold out," Christian calls before I feel him spilling into my mouth just as Sean did. I quickly swallow everything he gives me until I feel him softening in my mouth.

"Please let me cum, Daddy!" I call as Christian pulls out. I'm too far gone to open my eyes. I know Christian and Maximus have both moved away from me, and I'm panting as I cling to the edge, so close to finding that orgasm, but, at the same time, so far.

"Please," I beg as my overstimulated body aches. It feels like every muscle is wound tight, desperate to be let loose. I feel someone take my tied hands and lift them until they are over my head, and I flash back to being tied to the bed. My eyes fly open, expecting to see Hudson leaning over me, but it's Jason. I can see on his face he instantly sees my panic. He lets go of my hands and cups my face.

"It's me, angel. I'm right here." His lips brush against mine as I realise, he's naked and between my legs, his hard cock right by my entrance.

"Hold them," I whisper as the panic eases. I loved to be restrained before I was taken. I want that back.

"Are you sure?" he asks.

"Yes, please, I need it," I reply, and Jason kisses me again.

"Just say the word, and I'll let go," he whispers against my lips before I feel him holding my hands down on the bed above my head. I lift my lips towards him and feel his dick brush against my entrance.

"Daddy, please!" I beg as I lift against him again.

"I need to be in you," he growls as he slides into me, stretching me for the first time in weeks. "I've missed this. You belong to us; you are ours," he growls as he thrusts into me harder this time, and my eyes roll back as I listen to him declaring himself to me. "No matter what you do, you can't push us away or make us leave," he continues whilst grinding into me.

"Daddy, please, I need to cum," I beg as he changes his thrusts, and I lose the orgasm that was brewing. Jason lets go of my hands and loops them around his neck before rolling onto his back and pulling me with him so I am on top with my ass in the air. In seconds, I feel something wet against my back passage, and I moan.

"Yes. Please." I beg, knowing what's coming next. One

finger pushes into my ass quickly, followed by a second and then a third as Jason continues to move underneath me.

"You ready for me, Shorty?" Maximus whispers as his breath tickles my ear, and I feel the head of his cock at my back entrance.

"YES!" I call seconds before he slowly enters me, and I moan loudly. Maximus reaches around to hold my throat, and the panic consumes me.

"NO!" I scream, causing Maximus and Jason to both freeze whilst still in me. Maximus's hand instantly drops from my throat as he starts to pull out of me. "Don't stop, just not that," I beg as I calm the anxiety it brought out of me. Jason looks at me for a second before looking over my shoulder and nodding. The two of them start moving in me again, and I start chasing the orgasm that was right there.

"Please," I beg as the three of us get into the perfect rhythm. "Please, I need," I beg as a sob leaves my throat; my whole body is alive and overstimulated.

"Cum for us, gorgeous," Maximus growls as he thrusts into me hard, and I cry out as I fall over the edge.

I swear I'm not even finished with one orgasm as the second hits, my body responding all over from how sensitive I've become. I feel Jason finding his release as he shouts my name and buries himself deep within me, mere seconds before Maximus does the same. The three of us stay still for a moment, catching our breath as we stay in a sweaty heap.

Maximus starts placing soft kisses over my shoulder and down my back before pulling out of me and helping me to climb off Jason. Christian steps forward to undo the belt still wrapped around my hands.

"You okay, baby girl?" he asks softly. He rubs at my wrists, and I lean back against Maximus's bare chest.

"Better than okay, Daddy," I smile up at him through

half-closed lids. I stay there in Maximus's arms as Sean cleans me up with a warm flannel. Maximus lifts me as someone pulls back the covers on my bed, and the five of us get comfortable and curl up on the bed together as the night draws in outside.

"How you feeling, Shorty?" Maximus ask as his finger skims over my collarbone.

"Good," I reply, smiling to myself. Christian, whose chest I'm leaning my head against, runs a knuckle over my cheek.

"Thank you," he whispers, kissing the top of my head.

"What for?"

"Showing us you were ready. Showing me that I was going soft on you. Just for being my baby girl." He places another kiss on the top of my head, "For being ours," he adds.

"You are all stuck with me. I'll always need my daddies," I reply with a smile.

"We are more than happy to be stuck with you, Shorty," Maximus chuckles as his fingers run up and down my arm.

"I love you, all of you," I whisper. "I wouldn't change what we have for anything," I add as a smile slips onto my lips. "Well, maybe one thing."

"What's that, princess?"

I turn onto my stomach so I can look at all four of my men at the same time.

"Well, everyone tells me I act like an O'Reilly. I would like to make it official," I admit nervously.

All four men stare at me for a moment, no one saying or doing anything. I start to worry that I've said the wrong thing. But Christian grabs the back of my head and kisses me hard. Pulling away from me, I notice all four have a smile on their face.

"Whatever you want, you got it. Whether you marry one of us, have a ceremony with all four of us or just change your name. You name it, angel," Jason says from next to us as he leans over and kisses me softly before pulling away.

"I just know I want to be yours forever," I reply as I close my eyes and lean my head back on Christian's chest, feeling content and loved

"You already are," I hear Maximus whisper as he strokes my head, and I fall asleep surrounded by my men.

Epilogue

JASON

It's our last night here before we head back to reality tomorrow, and it couldn't have ended more perfectly.

I'm sitting on the patio overlooking the beach that I sat on three years ago when an amazing woman came into my life. Jasmine may not legally be my wife, but as far as I'm concerned, she is in every sense of the word.

Tonight, the four of us presented Jasmine with a ring we had commissioned for her birthday. After everything she had been through, we decided not to give it to her at the time so as not to overwhelm her. We wanted her to heal first, and last night, she showed us she was ready.

The ring looks like it is made of four different ropes made of white gold which knot together at the front. We all have matching bands, ones we wear on our left ring finger. All of us married in our own unique way.

When we get back we are going to hold an official wedding where Jasmine and Christian will be legally wed. But the three of us will stand beside him, knowing she is also ours. It seems only fitting that Christian is the one to marry her after everything they have both been through, from Christian's role in her father's death to her killing her mother to save him.

Following straight after the official wedding our family will have a blessing of our relationship, nothing or no one will break what the five of us have built together.

Christian is already planning on taking Jasmine off her birth control in a little over a year, eager to watch her stomach swell with our child. We don't care who fathers them; as far as we are concerned, they will have four fathers who love them unconditionally. I've never been one to look to the future because, before Jasmine, I never thought there was anything to look forward to. But now I have this amazing woman in my life, and I can't wait to see what the future brings.

"Daddy, save me!" Jasmine yells, jumping on my lap and grabbing me around the neck. I look up, startled and see her grinning at Maximus.

"What did you do?" I sigh as I wrap my arms around her waist.

"Nothing! He's picking on me!"

I laugh as Sean appears behind his twin.

"She took his last brownie," Sean chuckles.

"Prove it!" Jasmine demands, but when I look at her face, I notice a small chocolate crumb on the corner of her mouth. I reach up and swipe it with my thumb.

"What's this then, angel?" I ask as I show her the crumb.

"Shit," she curses before her eyes widen and she jumps off my lap, backing herself slowly away from us. "Sorry, I didn't mean to swear!" she protests. She looks amazing in the light of the full moon with the sea blowing her long silk dress around her legs and her hair to the side. She looks like a goddess. The goddess of the brats, maybe, but a goddess, nonetheless.

"Come here brat," Maximus declares as he and Sean rush for her and she runs away squealing. I can't stop the laugh bursting from my lips as I watch the three of them running around on the sand.

"I was gone for five minutes, and she managed to get herself into trouble."

I turn to look at Christian, who is leaning against the open door with his hands shoved into his pockets. He watches the three of them. Maximus manages to get hold of Jasmine and throws her over his shoulder before marching into the sea, and she screams for him to let her go.

"You know we have our work cut out with that one," I laugh.

"Don't! I'm getting grey hairs just thinking about it." Christian bursts out laughing as Maximus and Jasmine disappear under the water. Jasmine comes up screaming and spluttering. "She's worth it though," he adds chuckling.

"She sure is. Let's just hope she doesn't push her luck too much."

Christian looks at me with an arched brow.

"Something tells me the fun has only just begun. Maybe we should change her middle name to Trouble as it follows her wherever she goes."

We continue to watch as Maximus and Jasmine kiss in the water, the moon shining over them.

"All we can do is pray we can do enough to keep our wife safe."

As I watch Jasmine and Maximus, I realise he's right, but one thing I'm sure of is that the four of us are ready to defend our wife no matter what comes her way.

Bonus Scene

"Thanks for the sparring match. I needed a challenge," Sean gasps as he grabs his towel from the floor and wipes away the sweat pouring from him.

"You finally admitting I can take you?" I tease whilst unwrapping my hands.

"You can't take me; we are evenly matched. We just have different styles," he answers with a smirk.

"Yeah, your punches are weak, so you have to make it by using your feet."

Sean punches my arm as I roar, laughing. I always know how to push his buttons; he makes it easy.

"Fuck you, prick," he mutters, rolling his eyes as I slap him across the back, ignoring the ache his punch has left on my arm.

"Well, if we are evenly matched just over a week from my last fight, I say that makes me stronger," I point out, grinning, drying my face with my top, wishing I had grabbed a towel.

My body has started repairing itself from the fight, my

wounds are all nearly completely healed, and my ribs are just a persistent ache now rather than constant pain.

I grab my things and head towards the main part of the house, and Sean does the same beside me. Glancing over to the dance studio we built for Jasmine, I consider going in and fucking her against one of the mirrors. I haven't had her to myself in five days, and I'm desperate for some alone time with my brat. But I know she is working on an exam, so I need to leave her to practice. I make a mental note to try and get to her when she finishes to ensure we get the alone time I need.

"Has Christian set you up for any fights?" I ask my twin as we climb up the stairs away from the basement where our gym and Shorty's dance studio are.

"We are in talks with a couple of guys. Young reckons his latest fighter would be a good match for me. I don't know anything about him, though. Christian is going to watch him train and decide. Young seems really sure of this one."

I find myself nodding in agreement; I've heard Young talking about this guy, Jessops. He had initially entered him as one of the warm-up fights before mine, but his opponent had pulled out due to injury, so Young was forced to pull his fighter, too. He hadn't been happy about it, but that's the life of a fighter and their manager.

I stop in the hallway and look towards the sitting room, knowing that's where my brothers will be. I can't decide if I want a shower first or to wait for Jasmine so I can steal her away. I lift my bottle to my mouth and curse when nothing comes out.

"For fuck sake," I mutter, lowering it. "Give us your bottle." I reach out to grab Sean's, but he snatches it out of my way.

"Fuck off and get your own. I don't want you drinking out of mine!"

"Why not? We share everything else, including our girl," I point out. "Let me have a sip. I'm boiling!" I reach for the bottle, but he jumps out of the way, laughing.

"No!"

As I reach for it again, laughing as I consider punching the pain in my ass, I hear a voice behind me.

"Here, Daddy!"

I turn to the sound of my girl smiling. Only to be sprayed in the face with water.

"AHHH! What the?" Lunging forward, I reach for Jasmine, but she jumps out of the way, screaming and rushing out of view, laughing at the top of her lungs. Pulling my now wet top off, I wipe at my face as the cold water runs down my bare chest.

"Little brat!" I mutter under my breath as my brother laughs. We approach the sitting room, where I know she has run for protection. I'm not even surprised when I find her hiding behind Christian.

"Come here now, brat!"

Jasmine stays behind Christian, shaking her head.

"Daddy, save me," she begs as I step forward, leaving Sean behind me as he laughs at the two of us.

"What did you do?" Christian sighs, looking at Jasmine, who stares at him with those huge puppy dog eyes.

"Daddy Max said he was hot, so I cooled him down," she answers innocently.

"By spraying a bottle of water in my face!" I point out.

"But it cooled you down!" Jasmine answers dramatically as all three of my brothers burst out laughing. Christian turns and looks at her, shaking his head.

"You really expect me to save you when you bring it on yourself?" he asks her with arched brows.

"Yes! You always save me!" she protests.

"Not this time. Maximus, she's all yours," he smiles, moving out of the way. Jasmine screams as she tries to run, but I manage to grab her and throw her over my shoulder before marching out of the room, already planning all the ways I'm going to discipline her.

"Daddy, you traitor!" Jasmine shouts, pointing at Christian, who I catch smiling at her. I hear Jason laugh, and her focus snaps at him.

"You are just as bad!" she yells.

"Don't do the crime if you can't do the time, Jazzy!" Jason calls as I carry her away.

"Daddy put me down!" she laughs, wiggling on my shoulder. Lifting my spare hand, I bring it down on her backside, causing her to cry out. "What was that for?"

"You know exactly what that was for you, brat," I smirk, taking the stairs two at a time, being sure not to drop her.

"I was only trying to help you!"

I spank her again as I reach the landing and head straight to our room. Since Jasmine moved in, I haven't been able to think of it as my room, as everything I have is also hers.

Walking into the bedroom, I kick the door closed before turning and placing her in front of it so I can cage her in. Jasmine looks up at me with her big, beautiful eyes and flutters her eyelashes at me, showing me the softest smile.

With my hands against the door on either side of her, I arch one brow and give her my best Daddy look. She instantly smiles before placing a hand on my chest.

"Why are you always such a brat for me?" I ask as she

lifts onto her toes and leans in close so she can put her arms around my neck.

"Because I'm your brat, and you love it when you get to discipline me." She's not wrong. I love teaching her a lesson. She loves it just as much, which means she loves to be a brat. Wrapping an arm around her waist, I tug her close so her body is pressed against mine.

"I'm going to enjoy disciplining you tonight," I growl through gritted teeth as I stare deep into her eyes. I can feel her heart racing as she tightens her arms around my neck.

"Not tonight, Daddy," she whispers, grinning smugly.

"And why's that, Shorty?"

Jasmine grins as she loosens her arms around my neck to place her hand on my chest.

"Because I'm bleeding."

I step back, releasing her from my grasp and stare at her momentarily. The little brat thinks a little bit of blood will save her from punishment, and she can think again.

Walking over to the bed, I grab the duvet, pull it off and throw it on the ground. Grabbing a towel from the chair where I luckily left it earlier for my shower. I throw it onto the bed and hold out a hand for her to see.

"There, problem solved."

"You can't be serious!" she laughs. Crossing my arms over my chest, I arch one brow to prove a point.

"I'm deadly serious. Now strip."

Jasmine looks at me for a moment, her mouth hanging open.

"I am not stripping," she laughs, crossing her arms over her chest.

"You are unless you want me to do it." I walk over to the cabinet below the mounted TV, knowing there is a pair of scissors I was using earlier. I pick them up and make a show of cutting the air with them. "I am more than happy to cut you out of them, Shorty."

Jasmine stares at me for a moment before a huge smile spreads across her face. She darts for the bathroom, squealing with laughter as she goes. Dropping the scissors, I chase after her, knowing she will try to lock herself in, but I get there with seconds to spare and shove my foot in the way as she tries to slam the door. I hear her scream again as she tries to put some distance between me and her.

Walking into our large bathroom, I close and lock the door behind me. This door has an old lock, which requires a key. I changed it when Jasmine started to show me her bratty side so that if I ever found myself in this situation, I could keep control.

Pocketing the key, I look across the bathroom to where Jasmine is smiling from ear to ear and knows deep down she has lost.

"Are you going to be a good girl and strip? Or am I going to have to do it for you?"

"What if I don't want to?"

I watch her for a moment, gauging the situation. It doesn't take long before I know it's part of the play for her.

"Then you know what you need to say," I point out, giving her a chance to say her safe word.

Shorty stands there momentarily, chewing on her lip, with her hands behind her back, looking all cute and inno-cent. I can't help smiling, knowing this girl is anything but. She just stares at me, and I know she's giving me the go-ahead.

"One."

Her face lights up as I hold up one finger, knowing she has until I reach five.

"Two."

Jasmine starts looking around, trying to devise a plan that may save her.

"Three."

Her eyes start moving quicker as she searches for any escape.

"Four."

I string the word out as she starts to giggle and bounces on the balls of her feet, ready to run when I say …

"Five!"

I jump to the left as Jasmine screams and runs the same way, the little brat aiming for the door, but I anticipate it and switch directions. She mirrors me, and we are both rocking from side to side for a moment. But she doesn't realise that I'm closing the distance between us until I'm in the right spot.

"Shit!" she realises at the last second that there's nowhere to run. "Daddy, no!" she screams as I grab her around the waist, lifting her into the air and carrying her over to our shower cubicle. "No! No! No!" she screams as I hold her tight with one arm and open the door with the other, turning the shower on. Shoving her into the cubicle under the water, she starts laughing, screaming, and banging on the door as I close her inside.

"Daddy! Let me out!" she screams with a huge smile on her face as she tries to push the water off her face.

"Clothes off, brat." I want to come across as dominating and superior, but watching my brat soaking wet and laughing whilst trying to keep dry makes my cheeks hurt from smiling so much.

"No!" she squeaks as I reach into the cubicle, blocking her only way out and place my hand on the temperature dial.

"Strip or I will turn it to cold."

"You wouldn't!"

I arch one brow at her as I turn the dial a little.

"Daddy, stop you win!" she tries to grab my hand, but I wrap an arm around her, holding her close.

"Are you going to stop being a brat and do as you're told now?" I ask, looking deep into her eyes. She blinks up at me with a big smile on her face. Slowly, she nods her head, and I remove my hand from the dial.

Taking a step back, I signal for her to proceed, and she grabs the bottom of her wet top and pulls it quickly over her head.

"Slowly, Shorty." Jasmine looks at me seductively before slowing down. As she reaches behind her back to unfasten her bra, I take in the way the white cotton is going see-through with the water. I can just make out her nipples through the material, and it takes everything in me not to reach out and cup her sweet breasts.

Jasmine drops her bra onto the floor and unwraps the skirt she has been practising in. The material is clinging to her and emphasising each of her perfect curves. I need to get her wet whilst dressed more often because fuck, she's so sexy. As her skirt joins the rest of her clothes on the floor, I grab my cock, which is rock hard and restricted by my shorts. I can't stop myself from stroking it slowly whilst my cock hardens further as she starts to slide down her thong and tights. I know I should tell her to lower one at a time; I even open my mouth to say the words, but one glimpse of that sweet heaven between her legs and I lose the ability to speak.

Jasmine knows exactly what she does to me because, without any prompting, she turns and bends over, wiggling her ass seductively, showing me just how I want to take her. I reach forward and spank her once, knowing the water will add to the sensation. The moan that leaves her has me grasping my cock harder.

"Fuck, that sound," I moan, rubbing my cock again. I have to keep reminding myself that my brat wants to play. Otherwise, I would forget the whole thing, get her to place her hands on the tiles and fuck her until we are both coming apart at the scenes. "Get the shower gel, Shorty."

Jasmine reaches for the shelves and grabs my bottle of shower gel next to hers. When she turns to look at me, I can see her arousal in her eyes. I swear they change colour slightly the more turned on she becomes.

"You know what to do." It's all the instruction she needs. This isn't our first shower together, nor will it be the last. Like everything in our relationship, I can't help but fantasise that it's just the two of us, not just for tonight but every night, and that there are no brothers who she wants as well. But I know that will never be the case, and I have learnt to accept that now.

Jasmine squeezes some gel into her hand and lathers it up before reaching up to wash my neck and shoulders before travelling down to my chest.

"Turn around, Daddy." Her voice is deeper and filled with need. I know she's turned on. She once said that when I make her do things like this, she has to keep her hands busy; otherwise, she would have to touch herself. We have a strict no-touching-yourself rule with Jasmine for a reason. The four of us love being the ones to give her any pleasure she needs. If she has four men and still feels the need to touch herself, then we are failing her.

Jasmine continues to lather up my back, giving me a light massage at the same time. I love the feel of her hands on my body. I am so hard now that it's getting uncomfortable, and I know I will need to fill her soon; otherwise, I may blow my load in my shorts.

"Daddy, your shorts are in the way." Her voice pulls me from my depraved thoughts, reminding me she still needs to be punished for what she did.

Turning around, I look down at her with an arched brow.

"Then you better take them off, hadn't you," I reply, smirking at her. A smile spreads across her face as she slowly lowers to her knees and places her hands on the waistband of my shorts before lowering them until my cock is freed from the restraints. I don't miss the way she licks her lips, not taking her eyes off my manhood as she continues to lower my shorts.

Taking it in my hand, I stroke it once, twice, and by the third, there is a collection of precum sitting on the head. I run a hand over her head, moving her wet hair from her face.

"Stick your tongue out." She does as she's told, looking up at me through her lashes. "Good girl," I whisper before wiping the tip of my hard cock across her tongue, leaving my small release on the tip of her tongue. She doesn't look away as she takes it into her mouth and swallows it.

"Can I wash your cock, Daddy?" She looks up, and my insides turn to mush. In reality, she could do anything she wanted to me, but I won't tell her that.

"Yes, Shorty." Before I can say any more, she takes me in her hand and strokes me before licking from my balls all the way to the tip of my dick. My head falls back, so I lean against the cubicle door. I curse through gritted teeth as she takes me in her mouth for the first time. For someone who had never given head until a few months ago, she is the master of cock sucking. I can never last long in her mouth, so I know I will be forced to stop her soon.

After only a few minutes, I can't take anymore without blowing my load down her throat. Pulling my hips back, I release my cock from her mouth. Jasmine looks up at me, smirking, knowing full well what she does to me.

"Stand up, Shorty." Jasmine does as she's told, all the while grinning like she has won. "Don't look so confident. I'm still going to punish you," I warn, unable to hide my own smile. "Turn around and put your hands on the tiles." When she's in position, I run a hand down her back, over her ass, until I grasp her warm pussy. I can feel the string of her tampon, reminding me she is bleeding and probably more sensitive.

I lean over her so my lips are against her ear.

"Have any of your other Daddies fucked you whilst you are bleeding?" Jasmine shakes her head and moans as I circle her clit with my finger and grind my dick against her ass. "Are you going to let me be the first to do it?" I ask.

"Yes," the word barely a whisper from her lips as she arches into my crotch, desperate for my touch.

Smiling to myself, I take hold of the string between her legs and tug out the tampon. It doesn't come out as smoothly as I thought I would, and for a brief second, I worry I'm hurting her. But when she doesn't complain or tell me to stop, I remove it completely. Dropping the tampon onto the shower floor, I reach back between her legs and test how much she can take by first circling her clit with my finger and then slowly pushing one inside of her.

Jasmine moans as her head falls back. I scrape my teeth across her shoulder before biting her. She moans louder and grinds against my hand, trying to keep pace, forgetting that this is meant to be a punishment.

Smiling, I remove my hand and start rubbing a finger over her back entrance. My girl loves anal play, and it's something the two of us do often. I know each of her limits, what she finds pleasure in and what has her screaming my name as she orgasms.

The second she realises what I'm doing, she tries to push her ass backwards, searching for the penetration she wants, but I'm not going to give her that yet.

"Have you forgotten that this is a punishment, Shorty?" I whisper in her ear as I grind my cock against her again.

"No, Daddy," she grasps, pushing back against me. "But I want to please you and give you pleasure."

Shaking my head, I find myself smiling at her attempt to get what she wants.

"And what would give me pleasure?" I ask already knowing how she will reply.

"By fucking me, hard," she moans as the edge of my cock presses against her back entrance, to the point it nearly enters her, but I don't allow it to. I slide my hard dick down so it's rubbing against the entrance to her pussy and don't miss the way her legs shake. She's even more sensitive than I thought, and I may need to rethink how I plan to tease her. I had planned on withholding her orgasms until she was begging for me to let her cum. But seeing how she's reacting to the slightest touch, I don't think that will be possible.

"I think that's more of a pleasure thing for you, isn't it?" I ask as I enter her warm pussy, ever so slightly. Instantly she starts to contract about the head of my penis, and the feel of her alone is enough for me to thrust into her needing to feel it around my whole cock.

"Daddy," she cries out as I grab her hips and hold her tight so she can't move. Fuck she feels so amazing like this. I will never get tired of the feeling of her around me. "Daddy, please," she begs as she attempts to move again, but I stop her. Holding her tight, not allowing the friction she so desperately needs.

"Tell me what you are pleading for, Shorty."

Jasmine leans her head back, and I can see the desperation in her face as she begs.

"Please move, I need you. It's too much. Please, Daddy." The sound of her begging turns me nearly feral. I'm all for disciplining her, but hearing her beg me for her pleasure is always going to be the thing that turns it from discipline to me worshipping her.

"Fuck." The word is growled through gritted teeth as all restraint is lost, and I start working in and out of her. In seconds, I can feel her tightening around me as she builds towards her first orgasm.

"Daddy, Please," she begs as I reach round and rub her clit with my finger.

"Cum for me, Shorty."

In seconds, I can feel her whole body shuddering as it comes alive from her orgasm.

"Daddy!" I love that sound. Her screaming my name as she falls apart around my cock. I stay still inside of her as her body comes alive, with the aftershock of her falling drastically over the edge. Removing my hand from between her legs, I grab her face and turn it to face me so I can kiss her. Our mouths clash together as we meet in the middle, but I can't get the angle I want so I can kiss her properly.

Reluctantly I remove myself from her pussy so I can turn her around to face me. forcing her back so she is pressed between the cold, wet tiles and me, and I can kiss her hard. It's not a loving kiss; it's messy and feral. Our tongues are at war, desperate to invade each other's mouths.

Grabbing her ass, I lift her so I can thrust back into her

pussy. I don't need to tell her to wrap her legs around me; she does it anyway, whilst thrusting her fingers into the hair at the back of my head, ensuring I can't pull away from her, not that I would ever want to.

For a few short seconds, I pound into her, as her back is against the tiles, but no matter what I do, I can't seem to get the right angle. Turning her away from the shower, I walk out, still buried deep inside of her, whilst refusing to let my mouth leave hers.

Walking through the bathroom, being careful not to slip on the water I reach for the door, only to find it locked.

"Fuck!" I curse, remembering the key is in my shorts, which are still in the shower.

"Don't stop, please!" Jasmine begs against my lips. I turn and place her on the counter between the two sinks and push back into her.

"What do you need, Shorty?" I ask, pushing my hips forward, making sure she can feel me deep within her.

"Fuck me, Daddy, please!"

Those four words send me feral as I start to pound into her hard, just the way she loves it. Her body is on fire, and she's so sensitive I lose count of how many times she clamps around me as she cums. One orgasm follows another, and her whole body comes alive, shaking as she screams my name.

"Maximus, please!"

Hearing my actual name on her lips sends me over the edge as I thrust into her three more times before filling her with my release.

"Fuck, Shorty." Her name is a loud yell through gritted teeth as every nerve ending in my body seems to fuse with hers, and we become one.

My arms around her, which have been holding her to

me, tighten as I bury my face into her neck, breathing in her sweet scent.

"I love you." Those three words I have whispered every day since my fight flow from my lips. I always knew Jasmine was the love of my life. From that first moment, I saw her standing next to her mother, nervously smiling at me. Something clicked inside me, and I knew I couldn't rest until I made her mine.

But those feelings have grown tenfold since we brought her home and made her ours. Nothing or no one will ever take her from me.

"I love you too, Daddy." Lifting my head, I look into her eyes with a smile. "But I think we may need another shower." I look down between us and see blood all over our thighs and my cock. I laugh as I lift her from the counter and carry her back towards the shower, which is still running.

"I'm more than happy for an excuse to shower with you again," I laugh as we get back under the stream of water, and I place her on her feet.

"Am I still a brat?" she asks, looking at me with her wet eyelashes. Taking her face in my hand, I press my lips to hers lightly before running my fingers into her hair at the back of her head, tightening them, pulling her head back and holding it in place as I look into her eyes.

"You are the biggest brat I know," I point out before smiling. "But you are my brat, and I never want you to change."

Next in the O'Reilly Fight Club Series

vinci-books.com/Fakingit

She wanted one good date. She got three alpha SEALs.

Chelsea's not looking for love—but when a dating app matches her
with three sexy security contractors, she might just find exactly
what she never knew she needed.

Turn the page for a free preview…

Faking It With The SEALs:
Chapter One

CALVIN

"Alright, traitor!"

I turn to see Terry and Layton walking towards me, smiling and laughing.

"Less of the traitor shit. Remember, I can still kick your ass, pipsqueak," I jest, flipping Layton off before shaking Terry's hand.

"He's just sour because he's got to escort Jaz to get her nails done, and he couldn't get an appointment himself," Terry laughs as Layton glares at him. "So, today's your last official day as a member of the team?" Terry asks, ignoring the rookie. I nod, smiling.

"Yep. I'm officially no longer working for the O'Reillys."

"How does it feel?" Layton asks.

"A little daunting, to be honest. It's been a good five years. They've looked after me as much as I've looked after them. Being my own boss will be strange, but I know it's the right time."

Terry claps me on the shoulder before gripping it.

"I'm proud of you. You struggled returning to civilian

life after leaving the SEALs, but you worked hard and achieved a lot in the time you were with us. I know you will make a great boss and achieve big things with your own business." He squeezes my shoulder one last time before removing his hand. "How are your mates handling the change?"

"Yeah, they've settled into English life as well as can be expected. Everything's been snowballing, and it feels like we haven't stopped," I laugh, rubbing the back of my neck. I check my watch and curse. "I gotta go. Christian wants to see me before I leave."

I shake hands with Terry and Layton as they wish me good luck, and I head towards the main office, where I know Christian O'Reilly's waiting for me.

Seven years ago, I was injured in the line of duty and medically discharged from the SEALs. I moved to the UK with only the clothes and belongings I could fit into a suitcase and holdall. Did I know what I was going to do when I got here? No. I only knew I would stay with an old friend I met when serving. Terry helped me get back on my feet and adapt to life outside the SEALs. He knew I wanted a new way of life and helped me find it here.

Terry got me a job working as security in one of the O'Reilly clubs. He helped me gain my security license, as well as many other work-related courses. He gave me everything I needed, and I will be forever grateful. I wanted a fresh start, and I got it, but I always felt like I was destined for more. I pushed myself to prove my worth, and after defusing a dangerous situation in a club, which involved me nearly taking a bullet for Jason O'Reilly, he promoted me to be his personal guard.

It was a step up from bouncing and a role that often tested my loyalty to the O'Reillys. But I'm proud of what

I've achieved in the five years I've been guarding Jason, and I've kept him alive and relatively unharmed. I don't take any blame for the facial injury he received five months ago. He went off without telling me. It's his own stupid fault. He took a knife to the face and has a scar down the left side. The idiot learnt his lesson and now doesn't go anywhere without backup.

Now the duty of protecting his stubborn ass falls on to the guy I've spent the last two months training. It will take a little time to get used to not seeing him daily, but I've already promised to pop in now and again for a drink. Let's face it: why would I give up the chance to taste the fantastic yet highly priced bourbons these guys drink?

I stop outside Christian's office and knock three times. I hear him talking to someone inside before calling for me to enter.

Inside, I see two O'Reilly brothers and Jasmine, their fiancée. All four brothers are in a reverse harem with Jasmine Connors, who they met when their father married her mother six years ago. Even though they've only been in the poly relationship for approximately eight months, there's no mistaking the soul-bound connection between them all. There's nothing they wouldn't do for each other, which they've shown time and time again.

"Hey, Cal! How does it feel to be a free man?" Jasmine asks, grinning at me from Jason's lap. Jason and Christian laugh as I smile at her.

"You have no idea. At least I don't have to take you to the hairdresser or clothes shopping anymore."

"Hey! You only took me once!" she protests, pouting.

"I was talking to Jason."

Christian and Jasmine both roar, laughing as Jason flips

me off. Jasmine climbs to her feet, still laughing and kisses Jason.

"He's not wrong; you do shop a lot," she teases. Jason threads his fingers into the hair at the back of her head and holds her in place.

"But who do I shop for the most, angel?" he asks, looking deep into her eyes as she grins.

"Me, and I thank you for it in my own way," she teases, kissing him again before standing up and walking away. She stops in front of Christian, who wraps an arm around her waist and kisses her hard on the mouth.

"Be good and try not to get into trouble whilst you are out," he smiles as Jasmine steps out of his arms.

"I'll be on my best behaviour, I promise," she smirks at him as he arches one brow at her. We all know she could get into trouble in her sleep.

Jasmine takes me by surprise by throwing her arms around my neck and giving me a big hug. I chuckle as I hug her back.

"Keep safe, and don't be a stranger."

I give her one last squeeze before kissing her cheek and taking a step back.

"I wouldn't dare. I have a very important wedding to attend in six months," I reply with a wink. She pats me on the chest before walking towards the door, no doubt to find Layton, her personal guard.

"See you all later," she calls, leaving the office. I turn back to catch the O'Reillys watching the door, even after it's closed firmly in place. They worry about her every time she leaves their sight, which isn't surprising after all she has been through.

"So that's it? You're done protecting my ass?"

I look to Jason and smile whilst Christian pulls a seat

around for me. I thank him before sitting down as he walks over to the bar.

"Yeah, I guess so. You've got Gordon now; he will do you well."

"If he doesn't, I will hunt you down," he smirks as he takes a glass from Christian, who also passes me one with a measure of bourbon in it. I thank him before taking a sip.

"So, you all set to focus purely on your company?" Christian asks as he sits beside his brother.

"I think so. We have a large workforce, and our client list is growing daily. We also have two big events lined up where we are providing security. It's all looking good," I explain as I take another sip of the liquor, the flavour exploding on my tongue. The O'Reillys really do have the best taste in drinks.

"I have put the word out about you guys and given you glowing references," Jason says, leaning back and placing his ankle on his opposite knee. "If you need anything else, don't hesitate to ask. We are happy to help where we can."

"Thank you. I appreciate that." I don't know why I'm shocked. The O'Reillys are fair employers; if you show them the respect they deserve, they give it back tenfold.

"I would like to give you a little advice if you will hear me out," Christian says as he leans his elbows on his knees.

"I'll take any advice you have." I mean it because what this man doesn't know about business isn't worth knowing.

Christian sits back next to his brother and takes a sip of his drink.

"You need to start networking. I know you already have when you worked a few of our events and fights, but you need to do more. I will put your name down as a guest at a few charity and social events. Use them to get in people's faces and make them want your company. But don't take your mates to these events; take a date. It will look better, and people won't assume you are only there to talk business. If they think that, they will avoid you."

"You got anyone you can take?" Jason asks, and I quickly shake my head. "Thought as much, you haven't done anything but work for the last five years. Have you ever taken a holiday?"

I shrug whilst chuckling.

"What can I say? Keeping your ass alive was a full-time job."

"Well, that's another thing. You want to show people you are serious about your work, but they need to see that you are also human. Don't work as security unless you have no other choice. The three of you must prove that you can manage the company, not work it. Always have people on standby, so you are covered if you need them for an event."

That shouldn't be too hard. So far, we have about twenty-two people, all trained and situated in various locations and roles. We also have fourteen more down to be called in when needed. After seeing how well it worked for this team, I thought ahead with that one.

"The most important thing is to enjoy your work. If you don't enjoy it, there is no point as you won't put your heart and soul into it like you otherwise would."

That's no problem either, as I have always loved protecting others. It's why I joined the SEALs and would still be enrolled if the accident hadn't happened. That's why when Terry said he knew of a security position that would be perfect for me, I jumped on the next plane out of the States and haven't looked back since.

"Whatever happens, if you need a job, you know we are just a phone call away. There are no hard feelings about you leaving; we are all sorry to see you go. Not just Jason, but all of us."

I look to Christian and smile whilst nodding.

"I'm sorry to be leaving if I'm honest. But this will be good for me and the guys. It's been a long time in the making, but I know it will be worth it."

I down the rest of my drink and place my empty glass on the table. The three of us stand up together, and the O'Reillys walk around the coffee table to stand in front of me. Christian takes my hand and grasps it between his own.

"Thank you for everything; you will be missed."

"Thanks, Christian. I wouldn't be where I am now if you hadn't trusted Terry and given me a chance."

He nods once before letting go of my hand, and I turn to Jason. He takes my hand and pulls me into a hug.

"Thanks for everything, brother. You have saved my ass more times than I care to admit, and I will never forget it."

"Your ass was worth saving," I reply, slapping him on the back before stepping back. "Anyway, like I said to Jaz, I will see you all at the wedding and no doubt before," I add with a smile. The two guys look at each other, and I can see how much they are looking forward to making Jasmine an O'Reilly. Even though it's only Christian who is marrying her legally, the five of them are having their relationship blessed afterwards.

I step back from the two brothers and give them one last nod before leaving the office and heading off to my next big adventure.

Faking It With The SEALs:
Chapter Two

CHELSEA

"Oh, come on, Chels, surely even you are sick of sitting in your pyjamas every weekend now?"

I look at my friend Penny and smile.

"I'm perfectly happy to spend my free time in my PJs and slippers, thank you very much. Why would I do anything else when I can get cosy on the sofa with Luna and relax?" I ask as we reach our cars in the work car park. I open the back door and throw my bag onto the footwell before opening the driver side door and grabbing the scrunchie from between the seats.

"I don't know, maybe because you are forty-two and haven't had a date in years! *Years*, Chels!" she throws her hands up dramatically to emphasise the fact. I roll my eyes whilst pulling my blonde hair into a high ponytail, glad to finally get it off my neck.

"I tried dating, even got married; look how that ended," I point out with an arched brow.

"Not all men are like that nut job!"

"I don't want another man in my life, Penny. I have

337

Luna, that's all I need." I turn to look at my friend, who is leaning on the roof of her car and looking over at me. I know she means well, but I can't date.

"I'm not going to argue with you; I get it, I do. But you have every right to enjoy your life and don't give me that crap that you are, because I know you're lying. A part of you is lonely, and you know it." Penny climbs into her car as her passenger window opens, and she leans towards it from the driver's seat.

"I will see you Monday, and we'll make plans for next weekend. Luna can have a sleepover at mine with Ayva watching them. No arguing." Before I can say anything else, she backs out of her parking space and yells. "I'll call you tomorrow!" before driving out of sight as I wave.

I laugh to myself as I climb into my car and connect my phone to the console. I quickly check my surroundings, back out of my parking spot and start the short journey to my daughter's school.

I know Penny means well, but I've worked hard and endured a lot to be as at peace as I am now. I don't want to risk anything changing that. So what if I wish now and again I could come home to someone else having done the housework or cooked dinner? That doesn't mean I'm lonely; I'm just a little sick of doing everything myself.

I pull up outside Luna's school and let out a deep sigh. I hate it when people assume I need a man in my life just because of my age. I worked hard to get us where we are today. I will never put myself in a position where I have to answer to anyone but myself again. No one, and I mean *no one*, means as much to me as my little girl. She is my every-thing, and there's nothing I'm not willing to do to keep her happy and safe, even if that means accepting that it's just me, myself and I.

Who am I trying to kid? Of course, there are nights I find myself sitting on the sofa with nothing but a blanket to comfort me, wishing someone would hug me. Maybe now and again, it would be nice to have an adult conversation in the evening or someone to hold me when nightmares plague me. I certainly wouldn't say no to the occasional meal out, but the fear of history repeating itself is enough to stop me from ever dating again.

I sigh as I climb out of my car and head up the path towards where I need to collect Luna from the after school club. Maybe one day, a knight in shining armour will sweep in and rescue me from this lonely life and make me his everything. I stop myself from laughing out loud at the sheer thought of it.

Knight in shining armour? Please, knowing my luck, I'd get a twat in tin foil with a toy horse's head on a stick.

No, I'm better off on my own. I know that everything else would be a fantasy, and I know it will never happen. Dreams don't come true for single mums in their forties; they don't for this one, anyway.

Faking It With The SEALs: Chapter Three

DREW

I look around the bar, and it all still seems so unreal.

If you had asked me three years ago where I saw myself now, I would have said in the SEALs, fighting for my country and doing all I could for the America I love. I never thought I would move to England to start my own security company because I was medically discharged from the only job I have ever known.

All my life, I knew I wanted to join the SEALs, and nothing was going to get in my way. From the age of fifteen, I worked out every day to make sure my body was in peak condition. I studied my ass off to ensure I got the grades and constantly checked in with recruitment to see if I was on the right track.

The day of my passing out parade was the proudest moment of my life. I had sacrificed everything to get to where I was, and it was worth every single drop of tears, blood and sweat that went into it. Even my old man was proud of me that day, and that's saying something as he has had no problem telling me I was wasting my time and would never make it; I soon proved him wrong.

"Earth to Bambi, you in there, buddy?"

"What?" I turn to see my friend and fellow ex-SEAL Logan standing beside me. He pushes a bottle of beer towards me, which I pick up and take a swig of as he sits on the other side of the table. At least it's not the warm piss they serve in other bars.

"You were a million miles away then. Everything okay?" he asks before taking a sip of his drink. I nod, looking down at the bottle in my hand.

"Just thinking how this still feels so unreal. We have been in the country for five months, and I still expect to wake up back home." I turn to look at Logan and find him looking at me. "Do you know what I mean?"

Logan nods as he takes another sip of his beer.

"Yeah, I do. This is the last place I ever thought I would be at thirty-nine. But here we are, and we might as well get used to it. England's been good to Cal; otherwise, he wouldn't have suggested us joining him. We need to trust the process, or whatever they say these days."

I know he's right, and I'm sure everything will click into place. We've worked hard for what we've accomplished so far. It wasn't easy, mainly when we still lived in the States, but we made it work. We conducted interviews via apps like Zoom when we couldn't come over and do them in person. It's been tough, but now everything has finally fallen into place.

"Hey, there you are. I was starting to think you weren't turning up," Logan calls next to me.

I look up to see Calvin walking into view, his hands shoved in his trouser pockets and a grin on his face.

"Yeah, sorry. I got held up talking to the O'Reillys,"

Calvin explains as he sits at the table and takes the beer bottle Logan pushes towards him.

"How did your last day go?" I ask. I know he's been apprehensive about today. As excited as he is to run our company full-time, he has enjoyed working with his old team and will leave some good friends behind.

"It was good, they were all giving me the typical shit, so I know there's no hard feelings about me leaving. But as much as I'm going to miss them, I'm looking forward to being able to concentrate on our growing team. I certainly won't miss working two jobs. I'm past exhausted." He looks at the two of us and smiles. "So this is it. No going back now. I can now concentrate purely on expanding our company." He holds his beer out, and we both tap ours against it.

"Cheers, guys. Let the fun times roll," Logan chimes in next to me before grabbing the menu. "But first food, I'm starving."

"So, who's this guy you're meeting with tomorrow?" I ask Calvin as I sit back in the booth and stretch out a little after our meal. I'll give the English one thing: they can cook some fantastic grub.

"His name is Geralt Young; I met him through the O'Reillys. He recently had to change all his security after a trusted friend was anything but. Taylor had supplied all of Young's security, and when he showed his true colours, Young fired them all. But that left him open to attack, which means he's been hiring off other people. He needs some of his own guys, and I dropped a hint or two, as did Jason when he saw him."

"What's he into? Everything legit?" I ask, picking up my bottle of beer and finishing it.

"Mostly. He has a side hustle with illegal fighters and some legit ones. Other than that, it's all real estate and land ownership. He's just made his money's worth, and there are always vultures ready to take what they can." Calvin finishes his beer and places it on the table before running his fingers through his hair.

"What time are you going? Want either of us with you?" Logan asks from his seat. Calvin looks at him and nods.

"I've got to be there for ten. I was thinking you could come with me," he turns his attention to me, and I nod, glad to have something productive to do. "Afterwards, we could go and meet with the team and let them know what they will be doing there." He turns back to Logan and smiles. "You okay to go and open up the office and check the emails first thing? We should be done by eleven, so we can meet you for lunch before the meeting with the team at one."

Logan nods as he is more than happy to sit behind the scenes and keep the paperwork up to date and the contracts typed up. Logan may be comfortable around the two of us and those who are expected to follow his orders. But he isn't great with people he's just met. He's more likely to come off as unapproachable, which is why it's better if Calvin and I do the talking.

"There was one thing Christian said to me that we may need to think about seriously," Calvin says from his seat as he leans forward and rests his arms on the table. Both Logan and I sit up and pay attention.

"He's put our names down for various events and fundraisers. He has suggested that when we attend, we take a date. Apparently, it's a way to make it easier for people to approach us or some shit. But the first one's in just over a week, and I have no idea who I'm going to take," he admits, running a hand over his face.

"Are you telling me you don't have any women around here just waiting for your call?" Logan teases as I laugh out loud. Calvin never had a problem finding a girl whenever he was on leave. He would have a list as long as his arm of ladies waiting for him to return from deployment. But now I think about it, I don't remember him mentioning a woman once since he moved here. Maybe there isn't the usual line of them waiting for him.

"I don't. I have thrown all my time into work and building our contacts. Women just weren't a priority. I've had a couple of one-night stands, and that's it."

"There has to be a way to meet women around here. Singles night? Speed dating?" Logan asks, looking around.

"There's always Tinder? It seemed to work okay in the States. I'm sure the English also use it," I point out.

"It's worth a try. Have either of you used it in the past couple of years?" Calvin asks, looking from Logan to me. Logan shakes his head, which doesn't surprise me in the slightest. I roll my eyes and pull my phone out of my pocket.

"Do I have to do everything around here? Give me your phones, and I'll set up your profiles. I'm sure I can make you seem at least a little appealing to the ladies." Both guys roll their eyes at me as they push their phones across the table, and I start uploading the app before helping them to fill out their profiles. I have no idea how this is going to work, but anything is worth a try. It's not like we have time to go out there and find a girl the old-fashioned way. We don't have months on our hands. We have a matter of a week.

I turn to Logan, knowing he will be the most reluctant

of us. He doesn't date; he hasn't for years, and I'm not sure how he'll feel about this. I know he will be willing to do it for the sake of the business, but how far is he ready to go to help us get the word out about what services we offer? Surely, we can find a woman who can help with that and even pretend to like one of us as we do it.

Faking It With The SEALs: Chapter Four

CHELSEA

It's Monday morning, and I feel relaxed and refreshed after a lazy weekend with my little girl. We baked cookies, watched her favourite film every day whilst eating popcorn and just enjoyed not having to get up for work or school.

"Chelsea, can you come in here for a moment please?"

I look up from my desk to see Mr Young retreating into his office. Not giving me a chance to gauge what mood he's in.

"Of course, sir," I call back, grabbing a notepad, pen, and the tablet his schedule's on and hurrying after him.

"Close the door, please, Chelsea. Then take a seat."

"Yes, sir," I reply anxiously. I'm not usually his personal assistant; I'm only his PA's assistant. But Harper's been off for the last three weeks, and I've been filling in for her. I thought I'd done well, but looking at Mr Young now, I can see he looks stressed as he rubs his face and leans his elbows on the desk in front of him. I quickly rack my brains for anything I might have missed, but nothing comes to mind.

"I have just gotten off the phone with Harper. As you know, her mother had a fall and broke her hip, which is why she's been off. Unfortunately, her mother will need around-the-clock care for the foreseeable future, which Harper has decided to do herself. This means she has resigned with immediate notice."

"I'm sorry to hear that, sir. She has always enjoyed working for you, and you rely heavily on her."

Mr Young nods as he sits back in his desk chair and lets out a deep sigh.

"She has been my PA for many years and is part of the family. She speaks to my wife and children, Abigail and Gethin, more than I do most days. Many will miss her, but I understand why she is leaving. Family is important, and we must always look after our own."

I nod in agreement whilst opening my notepad and clicking my pen.

"Would you like me to start advertising for a new PA for you, sir? I can get the notice out in the next couple of hours." I start scribbling the role details and expected working hours on the paper.

"No, I want you to start advertising for my PA's assistant role."

My heart and pen stop abruptly.

Am I being fired? Did I do that bad a job whilst in charge?

"Did I do something wrong, sir?" I ask quietly whilst blinking back the tears. I can't lose this job. How can I afford the bills without an income? My hands start to shake, and I can't bring myself to look at Mr Young for fear of bursting into tears.

"Quite the contrary, you have done an amazing job filling in for Harper. I've been very impressed."

I slowly look up to see Mr Young watching me with a smile.

"Then I don't understand. Why am I being let go?" my voice starts to break as the smile on Mr Young's face drops.

"You're not being let go, Chelsea. You're being promoted."

"What?" My heart restarts only to race at a million miles per hour. Did he say what I think he said?

"Chelsea, you have done a fantastic job whilst Harper has been away. She's just sung your praises on the phone. She told me several times she called to ask you to do something, but it had already been done. You haven't let me miss a single appointment and have exceeded my expectations of you. My life has never been so organised; I don't think you realise how good you are at your job or how much I have relied on you the last few weeks."

"I don't know what to say; I thought you were getting rid of me."

I watch Mr Young laugh as I try to process it all.

"I think Harper would hunt me down if I got rid of you. No, Chelsea, I think you have proven time and time again that you are more than capable of fulfilling the role." Mr Young stands from his chair and heads over to the pot of coffee I brought up half an hour ago. I watch him pour two black coffees, adding two sugars into one and none into the other.

Walking back over, he stands before me and hands over a mug before leaning back against his desk.

"Now, how about we discuss pay and what I will expect of you before you go about your day." He takes a sip of his coffee as I take the time to sip on my own, trying to hide how excited I am for things to be heading in the right direction.

"So let me get this straight. Not only do you get the promotion, but a huge pay rise, and your own assistant, too?" Penny asks as we sit in the break room on her floor. I finish making my coffee and turn to her, nodding.

"Yeah. I still can't believe it. I'm half expecting him to tell me it's all a joke," I admit as I sip my drink.

"Why would he? You deserve this, Chels. You work harder than anyone I know and are bloody good at your job."

I know she's right; I always go above and beyond, but that doesn't mean I deserve to have everything handed to me like this. I thought I'd have to at least interview for the job, but apparently not. Mr Young has said that today is my first day in the role and that I'm to list anything I may need. He also explained that Harper would be coming to see me in the next few days to go over a few things and collect her belongings. I really hope I'm doing the right thing here and that I won't find myself in over my head or that Mr Young will start regretting his decision to promote me.

"Earth to Chelsea. Are you in there?"

I look at Penny, surprised that I've completely blocked her out.

"Did you say something?"

"When do you start advertising for someone to fill your role?" Penny asks, rolling her eyes at me.

"This afternoon. I have already started putting together the job description. I'll finish it after a meeting. Mr Young wants me to sit in with the new security firm."

"Oh, hot security men, can I sit too?" She wiggles her eyebrows as I roll my eyes.

"It's the owners of the company. They are probably old

men who hire people to do the work they used to do thirty years ago." I look at the clock on the wall and curse under my breath. "I need to go. I'll see you at lunch." Turning on my heels, I head for the door, needing to return to my desk in five minutes.

"You better, as we need to work out a way to celebrate! I'm thinking of a pizza party at yours tonight!" Penny calls behind me as I close the door and rush towards the elevator. Luckily, as I reach it, the doors open for someone to exit. I go to step inside but almost trip over my feet when I see the two hot guys standing inside. I quickly remember myself and step into the elevator before the doors close.

Lifting my hand to press the button for my floor I notice it has already been pressed. I glance at the mirror beside me and see the two men looking straight ahead at the doors. No other buttons on the panel are lit up, and it dawns on me that these are probably the guys from the security company. Penny would have a field day if she saw them. I think every woman in a five-mile radius would kill for a moment with these two, especially if they were to detain and cuff them. I quickly push that thought out of my mind as the last thing I need right now is to have inappropriate thoughts whilst in the meeting.

Both men are over six feet tall, with brown hair, and look younger than me. Are they old enough to have any real experience of providing security? One of them looks like he's just left school. Okay, he doesn't look quite that young, but he has a definite baby face.

I force myself to look away from the mirror and back to the panel showing our slow journey to the top floor. The elevator stops abruptly, and the doors open, revealing a large filing cabinet. The maintenance guy, Grant, doesn't look before pushing the filing cabinet into the cramped space, and I only just manage to jump out of the way in time. I start to lose my balance on my high heels and would have fallen if two hands hadn't grabbed my arms from behind, steadying me.

"Hey! Watch where you're pushing that thing, buddy!" a thick American accent calls from behind me. I stand back up and look to my right, where the older looking of the two is watching me, his hands still on my arms from where he caught me.

"Are you okay, ma'am?" he asks, his voice a little deeper than the one who shouted at Grant, but his American accent is just as thick.

"Yes. Thanks," I stutter before stepping away from him. His grip on my arms loosens, but he seems to take a step with me as if to check I'm truly stable on my feet. "Thanks for catching me," I add, not knowing what else to say. He smiles, his head tipped slightly to the side.

"You're welcome."

Our eyes met, and I can't tear myself away from them. They are a gorgeous shade of brown that reminds me of the hazel desk my father used to have in his office. They may be the most beautiful eyes I've ever seen.

"You alright, Chels?"

I look at Grant and give him a reassuring smile.

"I'm fine. But be more careful next time, please."

"I will. I'm so sorry, Chels."

I place a hand on his arm before giving it a reassuring squeeze.

"No harm done, so don't worry about it."

The doors close, and we continue our journey. I try not to notice how much closer I am to the American who caught me, but I can feel his presence behind me like a solid wall. The smell of his cologne overpowers my senses and leaves me wanting to smell it up close and personal.

What the hell?

Thankfully, the elevator opens, and Grant leaves with the filing cabinet. I quickly follow behind him, desperate to distance myself from the hot Americans. I hear Grant asking where I want the cabinet, and I remember I'd asked him to bring it up before I went on my coffee break. What the hell has gotten into me in the last few minutes? It's like my mind stopped working when I saw those hot men.

Needing to clear my head before I'm forced to endure being near those two hot Americans, I show Grant into the office at the far end of the floor. After showing him where to place the cabinet, I thank him again before returning to my desk. As soon as it comes into view, I see the two Americans standing, talking to Mr Young, who turns his attention to me and smiles.

"Ah, here she is. Chelsea, come and meet the owners of the new security company who will be taking over the contract."

I stand beside Mr Young and smile at the two gentlemen before me, reminding myself to be as professional as possible.

"Chelsea, this is Calvin Anderson. Calvin, this is my PA, Chelsea Hughes," Mr Young announces as Calvin holds out a hand, which I give a quick shake. He's the one who caught me in the elevator.

"It's a pleasure," I say, trying to keep my tone as professional as possible, but my heart is racing a hundred miles an hour. He doesn't reply; he just smiles and nods as Mr Young draws my attention to the younger guy beside him.

"And this is one of his business partners, Drew Cambell."

"It's lovely to meet you, Mr Cambell," I smile. He has a dazzling smile that lights up his baby face. God, how young is this guy?

"You too, Mrs Hughes. But please call me Drew," he says, shaking my hand. I nod once, returning the smile as I look between the two men.

"It's Miss, and please call me Chelsea." Why did I feel the need to point out I'm not married? *Get a grip, woman.*

"Why don't we all go into the office and discuss a few things before I give you a tour of the premises," Mr Young announces beside me, and I quickly make my way to his office door and hold it open for the three men to walk through. Calvin comes to a stop beside me first and takes the door.

"After you, Chelsea," he says in a voice that I bet sounds amazing if he were to whisper in my ear. *Oh my god, sort it out, Chels!*

"Thank you," I reply quickly before walking into the office, hoping to get some control of my body and inappropriate thoughts before I make a complete fool of myself.

Grab your copy...
vinci-books.com/Fakingit

About the Author

D.E. Bartley lives in Wales, UK, with her husband, three feral boys, four cats, and a budgie.

To say her home is a madhouse would be an understatement, but she wouldn't have it any other way.

When she isn't running around after her tribe or driving her husband up the wall, she can be found reading and hoarding books like a dragon.

Nothing is as important to her as time with her family, and she loves her trips home to Cornwall with them more than anything in the world. What could possibly compare to sitting on a Cornish beach, with a glass of Cornish gin in one hand and an authentic Cornish pasty in the other, while the monsters, I mean children, play and bodyboard in the sea?

Absolutely nothing.